I0955367

B/T

THE GIRL

IS MURDER

THE GIRL IS MURDER

KATHRYN MILLER HAINES

ROARING BROOK PRESS
New York

Published by Roaring Brook Press
Roaring Brook Press is a division of Holtzbrinck Publishing Holdings Limited
Partnership
175 Fifth Avenue, New York, New York 10010
macteenbooks.com

Library of Congress Cataloging-in-Publication Data
Haines, Kathryn Miller.
    The girl is murder / Kathryn Miller Haines. — 1st ed.
        p.   cm.
    Summary: In 1942 New York City, fifteen-year-old Iris grieves for her
mother who committed suicide and for the loss of her life of privilege, and
secretly helps her father with his detective business since he, having lost
a leg at Pearl Harbor, struggles to make ends meet.
    ISBN: 978-1-59643-609-1
    [1. Interpersonal relations—Fiction.   2. Fathers and daughters—Fiction.
3. Private investigators—Fiction.   4. Missing persons—Fiction.   5. Social
classes—Fiction.   6. New York (N.Y.)—History—20th century—Fiction.]
I. Title.

PZ7.H128123Gir 2011
[Fic]—dc22

                                                            2010032935

Roaring Brook Press books are available for special promotions and premiums.
For details contact: Director of Special Markets, Holtzbrinck Publishers.

First edition 2011
Book design by Alexander Garkusha
Printed in the United States of America

10 9 8 7 6 5 4 3 2 1

For G & G and all the fathers

THE GIRL

IS MURDER

CHAPTER

1

*September
1942*

POP'S LEG WAS ACROSS THE ROOM when I came
downstairs. I didn't ask him how it got there. Its location
made it clear that the prosthetic had been hurled at some
point, with enough force to bring down the photo of Mama
that used to sit on the Philco radio.

"Morning, Pop," I said as I came into the room just off
the parlor that he used as an office. He flashed me an index
finger and pointed at the telephone receiver cradled against
his ear. I got it; he was busy. He was always busy. This was
how it was with him and me; he tried to be a private detective, I tried to pretend like I no longer existed. So far, I was
the more successful of the two of us.

The minute passed and it was clear he wasn't going to be
getting off the phone anytime soon. He covered the mouthpiece with his hand. "If you're going out, you might want to
see if Mrs. Mrozenski needs anything at the grocer's."

1

He returned to his call before I could correct him. I wasn't going *out*, I was going to school, my first day of public school, which he would've known if he ever listened to anything I said. I trudged across the parlor and out the front door. Mrs. Mrozenski was sitting on the stoop drinking coffee from a dented tin cup. Beside her head hung a small sign that read AA INVESTIGATIONS.

"Good morning, Mrs. Mrozenski," I said.

"Good morning, Iris. Don't you look nice today?"

I smiled halfheartedly. I'd worried half the night about what to wear to school. Gone was my private school uniform. In its place was a uniform of my own making: my mother's pearls, a Peter Pan blouse, a plaid skirt, bobby socks, and saddle shoes.

"You have breakfast?" she asked. Mrs. Mrozenski was technically our landlady. She owned the whole house, but usually limited herself to two rooms: the kitchen and her bedroom. The rest she had given over to Pop and me, only interfering when one of us committed the unforgivable sin of moving one of her knickknacks from a table to a bookshelf or entering the house from the kitchen door.

"Not exactly."

"You cannot start school on an empty stomach." She got up like she was going back into the house. I could see what was coming: pots and pans, eggs and toast, a feast that on any other day I might've welcomed. But this was my first day at a new school. I would be lucky if I could stomach water.

2

"I'm all right," I told her.

She gave me a look that told me she knew what I was going through even if she was kind enough not to say it aloud. "What about lunch? You pack food?"

It hadn't occurred to me to do so. I never carried a lunch at Chapin. "I'll get something there."

"With what money?" She didn't wait for me to answer. She dug into her pocket and produced a handful of change. "You get something at the cafeteria. Promise?"

I slipped the money into my pocketbook. "I promise."

"Your father, he is good?"

I shrugged in response. Who knew how Pop was?

"He's trying to do the right thing by you, Iris. It is hard." Again, I didn't respond. What was the point? "I make pierogi tonight. Maybe some pork, too."

"Thank you. That sounds delicious."

Mrs. Mrozenski cooked dinner for us every night, asking nothing in return except for clean plates and our ration tickets. Pop was always reminding me to say thank you to her, as though Mama hadn't drilled common decency into me. But then how was he to know what I did and didn't learn in those years he was gone?

"Maybe I invite my daughter," she said.

"I don't know if Pop's going to be home tonight," I said. She was always trying to pair her daughter, Betty, with Pop. In her mind, my mother was nine months dead and it was time for Pop to move on. It was funny how nine months could seem like an eternity to one person and the blink of an eye to another. I don't need to tell you which one was my experience.

"Another time maybe. Have a good day, Iris," she said.

"You, too." As I started down the walk, I turned and waved at her. Mrs. Mrozenski waved back, and from the front window a flag with a single star waved along with her. It commemorated her son, a marine who'd been at sea since February.

It was drizzling as I trudged down the street from our house to Public School 110. The scenery matched the dull gray sky: garbage cans awaiting pickup lined the road, filling the air with the sweet scent of rotting vegetables. A pile of steaming manure lay in the cobblestone street where one of the horse-drawn delivery trucks that still operated in this area had paused in its mission.

Pop had tried to sell our move to Orchard Street as an adventure. With everything else that had happened, a fresh start would be good for us. At first I tried to be cheerful about the whole thing, but as weeks turned to months, I could no longer see the move as a change for the better. To my eyes the Lower East Side wasn't just a different neighborhood from the one we'd come from. Its name and its surroundings made it clear that we had experienced a downfall, slipping from the good end of town to the bad, descending from the top of the mountain to somewhere near its bottom. Not *the* bottom. After all, we were on the Lower East

4

Side, not the *last* of the East Side. That, I thought, was yet to come.

FROM THE MOMENT I entered the doors of P.S. 110, I was dodging, ducking, and holding my breath, hoping that whatever I just saw would pass by without doing me harm. The kids were rough in the way that feral cats were rough; it was like they were fighting to survive and didn't give a damn what it took to make that happen. Public school was exactly what I imagined trench warfare was like. More than once one of them locked eyes with me and I got the feeling that if I didn't move NOW they would pounce on me and eat me for lunch. I stayed close to the tan-colored walls, my hand always on the plaster, like a mouse looking for a hole I could disappear into.

"Outta the way, meat." A girl in a too-tight cardigan cut across my path, sending me toward a row of lockers. Two boys holding each other in a headlock forced me in the other direction, until I bumped into a box set aside to collect tin cans. I pictured myself tumbling headfirst into the metal scraps, but I was lucky. Not only did I stay on my feet, but the box was empty. Apparently, nobody here had time to collect aluminum and tin for the war.

I backed away from the box and checked to see who had witnessed my stumble. Only the poster above the empty collection bin acknowledged my presence. WANTED FOR VICTORY, it announced in bold type. WASTE PAPER, OLD RAGS,

SCRAP METAL, OLD RUBBER. GET IN THE SCRAP! Only someone had altered the last line with a pencil, so that the wanted items now included bloody rags. Conveniently, they'd also drawn a picture indicating what part of the female anatomy those rags might come from, just in case you were confused.

I tried to hide my shock and ducked into the girls' bathroom, hoping to catch my breath in the privacy of a stall. The doors were missing, though. A blonde in a sloppy joe sweater sat on the radiator by the window, smoking a cigarette. She didn't even shift her position when I came in. If anything, she seemed annoyed that I had interrupted her.

"What?" she said as I stared dumbly at the sight of someone smoking—*smoking*—on school property.

"Nothing," I said. "I have to . . . use the facilities."

"The *facilities*? You in the wrong place, meat?"

At first I misunderstood her—was she saying that the bathroom was not in fact the place where one relieved herself? But then I realized that her question had a different purpose: why was I in this school to begin with?

"No," I said. "I'm new."

Her eyes tracked me from the top of my pin-curled head to the toes of my scuffed saddle shoes. They lingered at my gored plaid skirt, the one I'd made after seeing the pattern in *McCall's* (years of wearing uniforms and a sudden summertime growth spurt hadn't left me with much of a wardrobe). She condemned my homemade sense of fashion with a shake of her head.

"Why did you call me *meat*?" I asked.

She crossed her legs and pointed a spectator pump toward the ceiling. "It's meat as in *fresh*. Fresh meat."

Oh. "But I'm a sophomore."

"Doesn't matter. Fresh is fresh."

"I'm Iris, by the way."

"And I'm busy. You're here to pee? So pee," she said.

Her gaze didn't leave me. I wanted to turn around and go, but those brown eyes issued a challenge that I knew in my heart I had to take. So I entered a stall, hiked up my skirt, and sat on the toilet even though it was the last thing I wanted to do.

She kept watching me. I offered the toilet a trickle and then continued sitting there, hoping to die.

"I'm Suze," she said.

"Nice to meet you," I said from my perch.

"You want a gasper?"

It must've been clear that I didn't know what she was offering me, because she produced a pack of Lucky Strikes and wiggled them my way.

"No, thanks."

Her Indian bracelets rattled as she returned the pack to her purse. "Why you want to leave the Upper East Side and come here?"

"How do you know where I'm from?"

"You got your glasses on." What was she talking about? I didn't wear glasses. "Those pearls real?"

7

They were, but I wasn't sure I'd win any favors by telling her so. "I don't know."

She huffed at my answer. "So what's your story, morning glory?"

"Excuse me?"

"Why you want to come here?"

I almost laughed at the question. Did she honestly think I was here by choice?

She seemed to recognize that she'd made an error. "Your pop overseas?"

"Something like that." I wiped, flushed, reassembled myself. I was going to be late for my first class. Not that I knew where it was.

"What branch?"

"Navy," I said.

"Bet he's an officer."

"He was."

"My man's in the Air Corps."

Did she mean her father? I didn't think so. With the paint and the clothes, Suze could pass for eighteen easy. It wasn't hard to imagine that she had a boyfriend who'd joined up.

I went to the sink and washed my hands. What should I say now? Usually, I had a gift for gab, but in this new place, with all these new people, my former self didn't have enough air to breathe.

"You think he's going to make it home safe?" she asked.

"Sure." And he had. Pop, who had never expected to fight in a war but got caught in the beginnings of one anyway, had made it home safe and sound. Except for the leg.

"Your mama must be scared."

"She's dead," I said.

"Ouch, baby," said Suze. "How?"

I answered without thinking. "She killed herself." I'd never said the words out loud before. You didn't talk about suicide. Not in a normal voice, anyway. You whispered euphemisms for it, trying to pretty-up an awful thing by calling it something else. *She took her own life. She died by her own hand. She couldn't bear to carry on.* Even the newspaper obituary had taken the stark awfulness out of what she'd done by reducing the act to a single adverb: *suddenly.*

Ingrid Anderson, *suddenly*, December 31, 1941.

And now here I was talking about it like it was no big deal. All my fear about P.S. 110 suddenly disappeared. A new school was nothing compared to what I'd already been through.

Suze stared at me for a long, silent moment. It wasn't the kind of story that she thought a girl like me was going to tell. "They shouldn't take a man with kids when there's no woman at home," she said.

That was funny. She thought I was an orphan, or just about one. "He'll be back soon," I said.

"And so will my Bill. He's young. He's strong." Suze tipped her head back and exhaled a stream of smoke that seemed to draw her name in cursive letters. As quickly as it appeared, it was gone.

Now that I was standing close to her, I could make out the sweetheart wings pinned to her sweater.

"Roosevelt says it will be over soon," I said.

In just three months the war would celebrate its first anniversary. None of us wanted to believe it would linger long enough to mark a second.

She leaned her head against the window, her cheek against the pane. Her breath fogged up the glass. "That's good," she said. "I don't think I can take much more. I'm beat to the socks." She tossed her butt into the sink, fluffed her hair in the mirror, and made sure the victory rolls in her hair were pinned firmly in place. Once she was sure her appearance was up to snuff, she turned back to me. "You better make tracks, baby girl. You don't want to be tardy on your first day."

"Thanks."

"Want a tip?" she said.

"Sure," I said, trying to be casual.

She pointed at the lower half of my body. "Burn the skirt."

I assured her I would.

FIVE MINUTES LATER it was me I wanted to destroy, not the skirt.

A bell rang its warning that we had two minutes to get

into our seats. I stashed my pocketbook in my locker and tried to read the room numbers on the schedule card I'd been given in the front office. Unfortunately, the ink had smeared after I washed my hands—pretty ironic, given that my first class of the day was something called Personal Hygiene. I searched the halls for someone to help me, but in an instant the bustling crowd had vanished.

Or so I thought. At the end of the hall stood a cluster of five boys and girls, chatting like all they had was time. Like Suze, the girls were tall and broad-shouldered, their busts jutting out in a way that showed they enhanced their bosoms with handkerchiefs. They wore heavy makeup and such elaborate hairstyles that I had to imagine they'd been up since the crack of dawn rolling and pinning them in place. As teacher after teacher closed their doors and implored their classes to stand for the Pledge of Allegiance, they said their farewells and started toward their destinations. At least most of them did. One of the boys remained behind.

"You lost?" he said. I looked over my shoulder for whoever it was he was talking to. There was no one in the hallway but us.

"Yes," I said. "I'm supposed to be in a class called Personal Hygiene, but I don't know where the room is."

"Who's the teacher?"

I looked at the card but found my eyes unwilling to focus on the print that hadn't been smeared. I'd talked to boys before—friends' brothers and fathers—but to be around them in school was just . . . weird. Especially a boy like this one. His hair was greased back with pomade, and he had a smell about him that seemed to be a combination of his morning shower, a cigarette he'd smoked before entering the building, and something else I couldn't identify. His eyes were sleepy and at half-mast, as though there was nothing on this earth that could ruffle him. Not girls. Not teachers barking for everyone to sit down and be quiet. Not even the war. How on earth were we supposed to be able to learn with people like him around?

"Hello?" he said. Plenty of time had passed for me to read the name off my schedule card, but I still stood there, silent.

"It's smeared," I finally said. "But I think it says Mr. Pinsky."

"Right. Pinsky's down that way." He pointed toward one of the hallways that branched off to the left of us. "Last door on the left. Don't sit up front if you can avoid it. He's a spitter."

"Thanks." So that was two people who'd been kind to me, and first period had barely begun. Maybe public school wouldn't be so awful after all. "I'm Iris Anderson. I'm new."

"So I guessed. Pleasure to meet you, Iris Anderson." He had a slow smile, the kind that took so long to appear that you knew that when he offered it to you, he meant it. "I'm Tom Barney."

"Shouldn't you be in class?" I said.

"Shouldn't you?"

I blushed. I couldn't help myself. There was something about the way he talked that made me think I was doing something forbidden. Or maybe he just made me wish I was.

One of the girls who'd been with him earlier reappeared at the top of the hall. She frowned when she saw me, and then cleared her throat to get Tom's attention. "Look who got a hall pass," she said when he turned and acknowledged her.

"Lucky you," he replied.

"Want a smoke?"

"Absolutely. I'll meet you out back in five," he said. "I'm helping Iris here find her class."

"I'm sure she can find it herself," said the girl.

"Cool it, Rhona. I said I'll see you in five ticks."

"I'm giving you four." She turned tail and disappeared.

"I can find it on my own," I said. "Really. It's just down that hall, right?"

"Right," he said.

"Thanks again for your help."

"Any time, Iris Anderson."

WHEN I ARRIVED in Mr. Pinsky's class, one of his students was reading the morning announcements off of a mimeographed page. Rather than letting me take my seat, Mr. Pinsky gestured for me to remain near the door until the recitation ended, putting me on display for the entire room. I spent an eternity staring at my shoes while the pug-nosed girl ended her morning spiel by reminding the students that the principal wished them to "remain vigilant about their personal possessions until such time as the person or persons responsible for the locker thefts has been apprehended."

So public school not only welcomed fights in the hallway and smoking in the girls' room, it attracted thieves, too. I made a note to retrieve my purse from my locker as soon as possible.

By the time the announcements concluded, every eye in the class was watching me. Somebody faked a cough and muttered "Fresh meat" under their breath. I took a seat as the class buzzed with two topics: the new girl and who was behind the locker robberies.

I tuned out the comments about my clothes and focused on the more interesting topic.

"I heard they actually cut the padlocks open," said one girl.

"It's one of the guys in the Rainbows," said a girl with a pinched face and a husky voice.

"Sure, but which one?" asked her red-faced friend.

"Probably one of the Eye-talians."

My eavesdropping wasn't as subtle as I hoped. The girl with the pinched face turned my way and offered me a sneer. "What are you staring at?"

"Nothing," I said. I could feel color bleed into my face. I

looked away, hoping they wouldn't see my embarrassment. It was too late.

"Hold your tongue, Myrtle," the pinch-faced girl said to her friend. "You don't want to make the square from Delaware clutch her pearls."

Sadly, that was the kindest welcome I got for the rest of the morning.

Every class I went to I was stared at. I was asked to introduce myself before the students assembled in Home Economics by announcing my favorite meal to cook. When I told them toast, I was laughed at. I didn't know how to cook. There'd never been a need for me to do it before.

My walk was mimicked, my voice was aped, and I was reminded at every turn that I didn't belong. What had Pop been thinking, sending me into the jaws of public school without any kind of warning? He hadn't been thinking: that was the point. How could he know who I was when he hadn't known who I'd been?

Finally, lunchtime arrived. I went to my locker to retrieve my lunch money, anxious the whole time that the combination I thought I remembered was incorrect. I needn't have worried; the lock was gone and the locker was empty. My purse and everything in it was missing.

That did it. For the first time that day, I let myself cry. I was beyond caring who saw me.

I didn't have the heart to report the crime—aside from my house key and the money Mrs. Mrozenski had given

15

me, there wasn't much of value in my purse. And I certainly didn't have the strength to go to the cafeteria with nothing to eat and no one to sit with. Instead, I retreated to a girls' bathroom stall and waited out the hour.

THE AFTERNOON was more of the same, just one embarrassment after another. I longed for a friendly face to make it all go away, but Suze never reappeared. Tom did, though. Just as I left my last class of the day, I saw him in handcuffs, being led out of school by two police officers.

What on earth was going on?

A boy with a camera dangling around his neck stopped to watch the action. As Tom was guided into a squad car, the boy took a photo. That task complete, he produced a notepad and pencil and jotted something down.

"What's happening?" I asked him.

"They arrested Tom Barney for the locker thefts."

"Why?"

He half snorted, half laughed. "Because he confessed. I knew it had to be one of the Rainbows, I just didn't know which one."

My heart broke: not only had I been robbed, but one of the only two people who'd been nice to me that day was the thief.

2

WHEN I RETURNED HOME to the Orchard Street house, Pop had a client. There was an unspoken rule that I was to remain scarce when he was in the middle of business. In fact, I think he preferred it if I was scarce even if he wasn't. But I wanted to plop down near the radio and listen to *Kitty Foyle* to take my mind off the day. So I took a risk and stayed in the parlor, keeping the Philco's volume down low so I wouldn't clue Pop to my presence. Mama's picture had been returned to its usual place, but the glass was broken out of it and a scratch had pierced the photograph, stabbing the still image somewhere near her heart.

I closed my eyes and let the tales of scrappy Kitty trying to move up in the world soothe me. For fifteen minutes I was somewhere else, caught between Kitty's world and my own the year prior. When I came home from a bad day back then—and let's face it, they had been few and far between—Mama would sit beside me and run her fingers through my hair, telling me that everything was going to be all right, peppering her English with German. *"Alles hat ein Ende, nur die Wurst hat zwei,"* she would say, trying to make me smile. "Everything has an end, except sausages, which have two." Sometimes it annoyed me, but more often than not I was lulled by her calm reassurance. It would be all right. Everything did have an end, even my minor calamities. I would be fine, just like she was. Anything I was going through she had already endured.

In fact, she'd survived much more than me. Mama was a German immigrant. She'd already made it through one war.

Maybe that was why she had killed herself—perhaps she couldn't stand the thought of going through a second one.

I closed my eyes and tried to picture her there beside me. What would she say if she was here? *It will get better, Iris. You mustn't be afraid to stand on your own.* She wasn't. There was nothing Mama wasn't willing to do by herself. I'm sure part of that came from Pop being absent for months at a time, but some of it must've been because she was German. When everyone is looking at you with suspicion because of where you came from, you couldn't depend on them to help you.

It was working. I was calming down . . . until snippets of conversation taking place in Pop's office forced their way into the room.

"I would like my money back," said a voice I didn't recognize.

"All I need is another week. You have to understand, you can't force things. The opportunity has to be right," said Pop.

"You've had plenty of time. She's going somewhere every night. For all your dillydallying, I could've taken my own pictures by now and been done with it."

"You're right," said Pop. "Of course you're right." I left my spot by the radio and approached the door. It was closed, but there was a vent near the bottom to help the radiator heat circulate from one room to another during the winter. I kneeled near the opening and watched the agitated client as he paced in front of the desk. Usually, Pop just dealt with missing persons—it was his specialty, or so he claimed in the advertisement he took out in the phone directory. But this didn't sound like a missing person case to me.

I heard Pop open his desk drawer and riffle through it. "Here's the entire retainer."

"I'm disappointed in you, Arthur. You said you could help and I believed you."

"I still can. I just need more time."

"I should've gone to your brother's agency, but I wanted to give you a chance."

Even with the door between us, I could imagine Pop's expression at the mention of Uncle Adam. Detecting is in my family's blood. My uncle's in the business, too, only he has his own agency, uptown, under the family's original

19

name, Ackerman. At the beginning of summer, after those first rough weeks in our new home, a home they'd begged us not to take, Uncle Adam and Aunt Miriam had stopped by with a pot roast, a plant, and a plan. Pop could work with Uncle Adam at *his* agency, strictly desk work, mind you, but Adam would give him a fifty-fifty split. Pop had refused the plant and the plan. He wasn't crazy enough to turn down one of Aunt Miriam's pot roasts, though. Especially with rumors of a meat ration already on the horizon.

"I don't want your help," he'd told Uncle Adam. A rift had grown between them in the months since Pop's return. When I asked about it, Aunt Miriam dismissed it as a momentary difference of opinion.

"Come on now—it's not charity," said Uncle Adam. "I've seen you do amazing things with nothing more than a phone at your disposal."

"I'm doing this on my own, Adam."

"Art—this is foolish. You can't do this on your own. Your leg—"

"Is the least of my problems."

"I've got a name and a reputation. It will take you years to build that up."

"Your name isn't my name anymore, remember?" Pop had changed our surname years before, when he'd first joined the military and didn't want to stand out.

"You know that doesn't matter."

"God damn it—I said no!"

Everything in the room stopped. I thought Aunt Miriam's bulging brown eyes were going to launch right out of her head. Instead, she turned her gaze toward me as though focusing on the child was the balm she needed to survive this moment.

"Go to your room, Iris," she said. She wasn't a woman you said no to even if there wasn't pot roast involved. I slinked away, up the stairs and presumably out of earshot, though really I lingered just beyond the turn of the hallway wall, unseen to anyone downstairs. To increase the realism of my exit, I stomped my feet on the wooden floor, then stretched a leg across the hall and kicked a door closed to further simulate that I was safely shut in my room.

"Think of Iris," said Aunt Miriam after she was sure I was gone. "She was so happy at her school. There's no reason to uproot her now."

I fought a grin. Thank God for Aunt Miriam, I thought. There was still hope. There was no reason I had to stay with Pop. I could live with Adam and Miriam, attending classes at Chapin as though nothing had changed.

"I *am* thinking of her. She's not your child; she's mine." Pop had paused, the breath in his chest rattling. Even though he'd been in New York since January, his injury still seemed fresh in those days, the pain warranting a series of pills he kept stashed on his bedside table. He hadn't yet given in to the prosthetic leg. His pants leg hung empty and he hobbled around the house on crutches, only moving

21

when he absolutely had to. "I want you both out of this house."

"You must be reasonable, Arthur," said Aunt Miriam. "You can't rely on Ingrid's inheritance to last forever."

Pop laughed. It wasn't a joyful sound. Like a burned marshmallow, it was so charred around the edges that you couldn't enjoy the part of it that should've been sweet. "You think there's money, Miriam? There's nothing left. But don't you worry—Iris and I will be fine on our own. We don't need your *husband's* help."

"Let's go, Miriam," said Adam. From my hiding place I could see him open the front door. Aunt Miriam didn't join him.

"Let us make this right."

"And how are you going to do that? By going back in time?"

A sob escaped me, but I don't think anyone heard me. First Mama, then Uncle Adam and Aunt Miriam. Was I going to lose everyone who mattered to me?

They left after that. For a long time I stayed in the upstairs hallway, wondering if anything would be gained by going to Pop and telling him that I wanted to stay with Adam and Miriam. I'm not sure what stopped me; maybe it was the fear that I would lose him, too. Eventually, I fell asleep on the hard wooden floor. In the morning I awoke in my own bed in my new room with no memory of how I got there. Pop never said a word about it.

Now, in his office, Pop cleared his throat until it sounded like a growl building in his chest. "If you want to hire my brother, hire my brother, Mr. Wilson. That's up to you. He might work faster, but you know as well as I do that he won't be as discreet and he'll charge you twice as much."

Someone thumped his fingers on the desktop, playing a tune of indecision. Was it Mr. Wilson, or Pop regretting his words? "Tell you what," said Mr. Wilson. "If you can get me something in two days, I'll return the money to you. Otherwise, I'm taking my business elsewhere."

Pop exhaled heavily, his lips momentarily knocking together and making the *pfft* noise that horses pulling carriages in Central Park made by way of greeting. "That's very generous of you, Mr. Wilson. Very generous. I'll be in touch."

Mr. Wilson turned and started toward the door. I leaped to my feet and jumped across the parlor, landing on the sofa with a thud. By the time he opened the door and joined me, I had a copy of *Calling All Girls* on my lap and the dull air of a fifteen-year-old who couldn't care less what the adults were up to.

Mr. Wilson saw me, tipped his hat, and left the house.

Pop joined me a few minutes later. His tie hung loose about his neck, and the furrows in his face, the ones that he'd had since he returned from Pearl Harbor, seemed deeper. His limp was exaggerated, as it often was when he'd worn the prosthetic for too long. It didn't fit him right, but he didn't want to spend the money to get it fixed. The military would've done it for him, or so Mrs. Mrozenski claimed, but Pop acted like he would rather die than ask them for anything.

He picked up my magazine and looked at the cover, shaking his head at the picture of Joan Leslie holding up a U.S. flag.

"Who's that?" he asked.

"She was in *High Sierra* with Humphrey Bogart," I said. *She played a cripple*, I almost added. I'm not sure what stopped me.

"What's a sub-deb?" he asked. He was referring to the subtitle of the magazine, *The Modern Magazine for Girls and Sub-Debs*.

"Kind of like a debutante."

That didn't seem to clarify things for him.

Pop had been only eighteen when he married Mama, nineteen when they had me. Responsibility had aged him—at least that's what Mama always claimed—but he was a handsome man. Back in our old apartment there'd been a picture of him in uniform on the fireplace mantel, and more than one of my friends had feigned a swoon at the sight of his broad shoulders and delicate features.

Where was that photo now? I hadn't seen it since we moved.

"How long have you been home?" asked Pop.

"Not long." He was wondering how much I'd heard. I turned the page of the magazine and focused on an advertisement for a powder that would take the sheen off my nose.

"What did you do today?"

"I started public school, remember?" It came out snottier than I'd intended. I tried to soften it with a smile.

"That's right. And how was it?"

Awful, I wanted to say. *I was robbed and ridiculed. I don't belong there. Don't come crying to me when I start wearing tight sweaters and smoking.* But Pop looked so defeated by what had transpired with Mr. Wilson that I couldn't bear to bring him down even further. My complaints could wait. "It was all right." I turned another page of *Calling All Girls*, trying to appear nonchalant, and landed on the beginning of "Mystery at the Lookout," a new serial by the author of Nancy Drew. "What did that guy want?"

"His money back. He wanted me to prove that his wife was cheating on him." Pop became an officer in the Navy when I was ten years old and visited us only a handful of times each year for the next five. Each time he came home, it was like I was meeting him for the very first time. If there was anything positive to come from not knowing my father for so long, it was that he never really learned to be a father. He lacked the filter that most adults possessed, the one that told them to clam up in front of the kids.

"And you couldn't prove it?" I asked.

He smiled, deepening the creases on his face. "I tried. But I'm starting to think I'm too slow for the detective business." He thumped his thigh, just above where his leg ended and the wood began.

"He's giving you a second chance, though, right?"

"You were listening."

I froze. Boy, howdy—I hadn't wanted to let him know that. "He's a loud talker."

He raised the knot on his tie. "It doesn't matter. He's right. If I can't get what he needs in two weeks, I certainly won't accomplish it in two days. He should just call Uncle Adam and be done with it."

This was the most Pop had spoken to me in weeks. Like I said, he didn't know how to be a father, and while that meant he sometimes told me things he shouldn't, it also meant he often avoided me so he wouldn't give away that he didn't know *what* to say to me. "I thought you were only doing missing persons," I said.

"Unfortunately, not enough of them are missing." His eyes twinkled at the joke. Mama used to say he had a wicked sense of humor, but I rarely saw signs of it. I just assumed it was something he'd lost along with his leg. "We need money, Iris." Just as soon as he said it, he seemed to recognize that it wasn't an appropriate thing to tell me. He approached me, put his hand on my head, and ruffled my hair. I had a feeling that it was something he used to do when I was very small, but the memory was too far away for me to be sure. I stiffened at his touch. "But don't you worry about it. Your pop's taking care of things. I've got to go out for a while tonight."

"Dinner's going to be ready soon."

"You'll have it without me. Tell Mrs. Mrozenski I'm sorry I can't join you."

Tell her yourself, I wanted to say, but my heart wasn't in being disobedient. "All right."

He tweaked my nose with his finger. "Don't forget to do your homework. You don't want to rot your brain reading romance magazines."

I waited until Pop was out the door and out of sight to break the news to Mrs. Mrozenski. She was hunched over a large pan of sizzling cabbage, alternating between stirring the food and mopping her brow with a dishcloth. As she worked she danced to a tune only she could hear. Her feet were surprisingly nimble for a woman who had to be twice Pop's size.

"You hungry, Iris?" she asked as I ducked into the kitchen.

"I'm getting there." I was still getting used to her kitchen. Gone was the electric refrigerator we'd had on the Upper East Side. In its place was an icebox that leaked so often it had warped the floor beneath it. And the stove used coal— *coal*—to make its heat, burping a thick black fog that coated the porcelain surface and turned everything white to gray, including underwear we'd hung to dry on the line behind her house. Bins of coal sat outside the back door, where Pop retrieved it each morning to make sure Mrs. Mrozenski had everything she needed to run the cooker.

"Pop can't join us tonight," I said.

"Oh." She frowned at the pan. "He leave something for me maybe?"

It was my turn to scowl. "Like what?"

"Like an envelope?"

Money. He was late on the rent. That was why he was skipping dinner.

"He must've forgot," I said.

Her face relaxed. "Of course. Is no problem. I call you when it's ready?"

"Sure."

For a while I lazed by the radio, listening to *Captain Midnight* and trying not to think about the rent. Pop had lost jobs before; I knew that. It had happened twice that I knew of right after he had started up his company that summer. He couldn't follow people quickly. He was never going to be able to chase someone down. His busted pin meant that he did his best work behind a desk and on a phone, only that wasn't the kind of work that paid well. And well-paying jobs were what we needed.

It was funny how aware I'd become of money in the past few months. We were never rich before, at least not compared to my friends, but I'd never wanted for anything, either. There was always cash for comics and candy, new dresses and new movies. I didn't wonder how tuition was paid, food bought, rent kept up to date. It just was. It was shocking to go from a world where everything was provided without effort to this constant awareness that everything I did—even the air I breathed—felt like it came at a cost. At first I resented it because I believed Pop had caused it. If he hadn't been injured, if he hadn't left the military, if he hadn't come home, things wouldn't have had to change.

And maybe Mama wouldn't have killed herself.

I shook the thought out of my head. Mrs. Mrozenski turned on her phonograph and a polka platter began to compete with the noise of the radio. The smell of frying onions signaled that dinner was minutes from being ready. I had homework to do—an essay on what it meant to be a citizen that would take me a half hour at most—and then the whole evening stretched before me with nothing to fill it. I don't know what made me do it—the boredom, the loneliness, the forced cheer of the polka music—but I got up and went into Pop's office.

It was rare that I went in there. Pop never told me I couldn't, probably because it never occurred to him that he should, but the space was so much his that merely crossing the threshold felt like a violation. He had only two rules: don't disturb the paperwork on his desk and stay out of the locked cabinet that sat to the left of his chair.

The first one was easy to disobey, provided I memorized the exact order things had been in when I'd found them. The second one I had no choice but to respect. After all, the cabinet was locked. How could I do anything but stay out of it? Besides, I was pretty sure I knew what he kept inside it: his gun. He had to have one, right? All the detectives in the movies did. It seemed like precisely the sort of thing you hid in a locked cabinet.

Mr. Wilson's file was still sitting on top of the desk. I sat in Pop's chair and opened the folder. In his chicken scratch he outlined Mr. Wilson's first visit to him and described, in detail, why the man was concerned that his wife was being unfaithful. Pop had tried to follow her on three different occasions, and while he didn't write down the results of that work, it wasn't hard to read the outcome in the description of the places he visited: Upper East Side hotels one entered by climbing long flights of stairs. Pop didn't stand a chance catching Mrs. Wilson red-handed. He probably hadn't been able to catch his breath.

The job looked pretty easy to my eyes. All the man wanted was evidence of what he was already certain was going on: a photograph, confirmation from a witness, a description of the man his wife was keeping time with. No wonder Pop had failed. Even if he had been able to follow Mr. Wilson's wife, he would've drawn attention to himself. A man with an obvious limp could expect two responses:

pity or a rude attempt to ignore him. Either way, Mrs. Wilson had to have noticed him the first time he appeared on the scene.

What Pop needed was someone who could blend in, whose age and appearance meant they were easily ignored. Someone who could sit in a hotel lobby looking like a bored little rich girl waiting for her parents, and nobody would think twice about her.

Uncle Adam was right when he told Pop he couldn't go it alone. But maybe it wasn't *his* help Pop needed—maybe it was mine.

By the time Mrs. Mrozenski called me into dinner I had a plan: I was going to help Pop.

3

TWENTY-FOUR HOURS LATER I was on my first stake-out, outside the Wilsons' Upper East Side apartment building. I'd passed it a thousand times in my former life, had even been inside it once while visiting a friend after school. Now I took up space on a bench across the street. Just as I took on the posture of a bored, privileged young woman, familiar voices rang out: Bev and Bea, or—as they were usually referred to in the halls of Chapin—the twins. Blondes with blue eyes and perfect ski-jump noses, they were identically clad in Chapin's plaid skirts and white blouses. As they headed for home they were exchanging the day's gossip, their voices rising and falling with amusement as they relayed who said what to whom. I slouched down on the bench, hoping they wouldn't notice me.

"Iris?" said Bea.

I straightened up as though it wasn't them that had

caused me to slouch, but exhaustion they'd just shaken me out of. "Bea? Bev? It's so great to see you."

If they found it strange to find me loitering on a bench at twilight, they didn't admit it out loud. Instead, they surveyed me for a moment as though they weren't certain what to say next. Compliment my clothes? Nope, no hope of that. Tell me they missed my witty comments during English Lit? Doubtful.

I decided to help them out of the tight spot. "I'm waiting for my aunt," I said. "We're having dinner."

"How lovely," said Bev. "Isn't this funny—we were just talking about you today."

"Oh, really?" I stood up. For some reason I wanted to be on the same level as the two of them. Even though we were all the same height, I felt smaller. Maybe it was their school uniforms. Strange as it seemed, I missed the brief skirt and scratchy blouse and how they magically made me one of them rather than the outsider I felt like now. Wasn't it funny how a uniform, which was designed to create conformity, could make me feel so special? I bet Pop must have felt the same way when he shed his military duds and rejoined life as a civilian.

"Yes," said Bea. "We were just asking Grace if she'd heard from you."

In the weeks after we'd moved to the Lower East Side, some of the Chapin girls had attempted to stay in contact with me, chief among them Grace Dunwitty, my former best friend. She called me every other day and invited me to spend my weekends at her apartment, where I could forget the Orchard Street house while we passed our time pasting pictures of Deanna Durbin into our scrapbooks and slept beneath Grace's pink canopy.

The visits meant I had to endure Grace's endless questions about our new life. She must have thought years of sharing lunches and sleepovers meant I owed her something: *Do you miss having money?* (I guess.) *What's it like to have a father with only one leg?* (I'm not sure I know what it's like to have a father, period.) *Do you miss your mother?* (What do you think?) They were logical questions, ones I might've asked myself if I had the courage, but—boy, howdy—I resented how easily Grace asked them, how she made no attempt to hide her curiosity, how different she made me feel from everyone else. And so eventually I stopped making an effort to ride the subway uptown, stopped responding to her invitations, rejected offers to meet me halfway between her world and mine. On the Upper East Side I was the girl whose life forever changed when her mother had killed herself. But in our new home, I could just be Iris Anderson, daughter of an injured vet, a man who'd bravely endured Pearl Harbor.

"She said she's tried calling you," said Bev.

"I've been awfully busy," I said. "New school and all that."

"You have to tell us all about the Lower East Side." She

34

made it sound like some exotic destination she was thinking of visiting if she ever got her passport in order.

"There's not really much to tell," I said.

"Oh, come now," said Bev. "What are the people like?"

Just like you, I almost replied. *Only without the money.* "I've kind of kept to myself," I said.

"It's probably safer that way," said Bev.

"And how is public school?" asked Bea.

"Swell." I could see they weren't buying it. And why should they? We'd spent years mocking the kids who went to public school. "It's so strange being around boys," I added. I could tell that piqued their interest.

"What's it like?" asked Bea.

"More nerve-racking, I guess."

"Could you imagine getting to eat lunch with boys every day?" Bea said to her sister.

"I don't think I'd like it," said Bev. "I like going to an all-girls school."

"Don't be such a prude," said Bea.

"I'm not. Besides, it's not just boys Iris is around, it's colored boys, right?" She lowered her voice when she said it, as though admitting I went to school with kids of other races might cause me to contaminate their neighborhood.

"There are Puerto Ricans and Italians, sure."

"Well, be careful," said Bev.

I wanted them to go on their way, but it was clear I was going to have to be the one to end the conversation.

35

I looked off into the distance, where a woman wearing a hat festooned with a peacock feather was stepping out of a cab. "There's my aunt," I said. "I better go. Tell Grace I said hello."

"We will," said Bea, and then she took her sister by the arm and left. I waited until I could no longer see them before reclaiming my seat on the bench.

A breeze ruffled the pages of the *Archie* comic I'd brought along to occupy myself. With the wind came the aroma of early fall and something else—Mama's perfume. I turned, half expecting to find her behind me, but the air was empty. In our new house there was never any fear of stumbling upon her—after all, she'd never been there in life. But here on these streets, where she used to shop and visit with her friends, my mother's voice carried on the wind, her heels click-clacked down the sidewalk, her apartment keys jingled at their peculiar frequency. Was this why Pop had moved us? Not because of money, but to escape her memory?

Stop it, I told myself. *Focus on the task at hand.*

According to Pop's notes, Louise Wilson left the house every Tuesday night at seven for a Veterans of Foreign Wars Ladies Auxiliary meeting, or so she said. Lately she'd returned late in the evening with some new excuse about organizing clothes for Bundles for Britain or losing track of the time while knitting socks for soldiers and exchanging gossip. Once Mr. Wilson had gone to the church where the group was allegedly meeting, only to find its lights turned off and no sign of the dozen or so women Mrs. Wilson claimed came to every meeting. On another occasion, he followed her all the way to the Waldorf, where she disappeared inside before he was able to determine which direction she'd turned.

He had provided a photo of her that I'd struggled to memorize in the hours when Pop wasn't home. In it she stood beside her husband, her hands meekly folded in her lap, her smile tight and toothless. Her side was glued to Mr. Wilson's, as though she only represented half of the whole the two of them formed. She could've been attractive, but the years had softened her figure in a way my own mother had constantly fought against.

I continued to feign boredom on my bench, flipping through the *Archie* comic book but not reading what was on the page. My attention was riveted to the apartment building, where the uniform-clad doorman was tipping his hat as a woman exited the revolving door.

Was it her?

She asked him something, and he replied in a strong, clear voice, "Six-forty-five, Mrs. Wilson." She paused in the light leaking from the front windows and wound her watch. Then, with a smile at the man, she continued on her way up the street.

Bingo! I followed twenty paces behind, splitting my attention between her and the shop windows. If she turned to look back, I'd pause at the nearest display and pretend to examine what it had to offer.

My ploy wasn't necessary. She seemed to be in her own little world, moving forward with single-minded purpose to get to her destination. I used the time to examine her. It was a game Mama and I used to play—she would pick a random stranger as we waited for a cab or walked in the park and make me list three things I could tell just by looking at them. *Appearances are everything*, she would tell me when we stopped playing. *Remember that*. Mrs. Wilson's nails were freshly painted. There was cat hair on her coat. Her heels were expensive, but worn. They didn't strike me as the kind of pumps you donned to see a secret lover.

But then if she had a lover, she probably wasn't planning on keeping them on for very long.

I blushed at the thought. What made me such an expert on s-e-x? I couldn't even say the word out loud without spelling it.

Mrs. Wilson turned the corner, then another one. No Waldorf this night. We were headed toward the Plaza Hotel. I held back long enough for her to enter the building. I pretended to chew a wad of gum and swung my arms with the sort of entitled boredom most visitors to this address regularly demonstrated. As I walked into the lobby, I offered the doorman a sneer for his trouble.

I surveyed the room for Mrs. Wilson. She was already gone.

How was that possible? I'd only been seconds behind her. Hardly enough time for her to make it into the Palm Court, or one of the other restaurants that fanned off from the main lobby. My gaze landed on the closed powder room door. That's where she had to be. If she was meeting someone, she would want to freshen up beforehand.

I sauntered through the door and found her standing before the long row of mirrors, a tube of bright red lip cream in her hand. We both ignored each other as I disappeared into a stall and pretended to do my business.

When enough time had passed, I flushed the toilet, left the stall, and washed my hands. She had switched from makeup to hair care. She removed her hatpin, peeled off her straw hat, and used her fingers to fluff the slightly matted mess it had left behind. My own reflection danced in the glass. There was a time when I thought I might be pretty—perhaps even on my way to beautiful. Mama had been. With her blond hair and pale eyes, she cut a striking figure no matter what she wore or whom she accompanied. I hadn't been blessed with her coloring, but I was fortunate enough to not, in the words of Grace's mother, look too Jewish. I had asked my mother what she meant and she'd laughed it off as the insensitive words of an insensitive woman. But now in the flattering lighting of the Plaza's powder room, I could see hints of ethnicity. I was growing darker with age, my features slightly coarse, as though all of Mama's delicacy had vanished when she died.

Mrs. Wilson's reflection smiled at me. I tucked my hair behind my ears and smiled back.

I left her to her work and returned to the lobby, selecting a seat that would give me a good view of her when she finally returned. Instead of reading the comic, I pulled a camera from my purse and pretended to fidget with it. This wasn't Pop's preferred instrument of surveillance, a 1930s Leica he used because he claimed there was no better camera on the market. Instead, I had the small Brownie camera I'd gotten for my fourteenth birthday, a gift from Uncle Adam that took serviceable pictures, provided you were no more than ten feet from your subject. I stared through the viewfinder and pretended I was interested in capturing the ornate ceiling, then an impressionistic landscape in a gilded frame, then the pattern in the thick Oriental rug. Just as I came up from my study of the fleur-de-lis pattern, Mrs. Wilson entered the lobby and took her seat opposite me.

I continued to click away, then frowned at the camera as though I were uncertain how to operate it. She busied herself with a copy of the newspaper that had been discarded in the lobby, dividing her attention between the headlines and the elevator bank across the room from us.

"Togo Resigns as Japanese Foreign Minister," screamed her newspaper. "Fuel Rations May Be Widened to Cover Midwest."

I decided to shift positions. If whomever she was

waiting for was coming from the elevators, I needed to be closer to them if I was going to catch them on film. I tucked the comic under my arm and shouldered my pocketbook. Then I continued clicking the camera, capturing a poodle being herded across the lobby by the concierge and a floral display that prominently featured small American flags among its more fragrant offerings. The elevators dinged open and an assortment of people exited into the lobby.

I glanced toward Mrs. Wilson, waiting to see which of the men—if any—might catch her fancy. My money was on a fellow in a blue pinstriped suit. He was about her age and looked a little like Robert Young, if Robert Young had jowls. I got ready to take his picture. Her hand dashed into the air and she waved at the exiting crowd. Instead of Robert separating from the pack and heading her way, a young serviceman did, greeting her with a wide grin while he bisected the lobby in three easy strides.

They embraced and I captured their union three times, making certain to get the man's face in every shot. After their chaste meeting, they disappeared into the Oak Room, presumably to get a drink. Would this be enough to satisfy Mr. Wilson? So far all I had was proof that his wife wasn't where she claimed to be and that she was keeping company with a member of the opposite sex, neither of which seemed like evidence that she was having an affair. After all, this could just be a friend in town on leave whom she decided to get together with. Without telling her husband. In a hotel.

On second thought, maybe this *was* bad.

I decided to stay in the lobby to see what they'd do next. An hour passed, during which I read *Archie* cover to cover, and then the two left the bar and headed toward the elevators. I watched the dial indicating which floor the car was bound for, then stepped into another car and asked the operator to take me up. I arrived too late. The hallway was empty. That meant either they had run to their room or the man was staying in one of the ones closest to the elevator. I surveyed each door in turn. On one a DO NOT DISTURB sign gently swayed to and fro.

Bingo.

I put my hand on the knob and tried to turn it. It was locked. From behind the door came a deep, feminine giggle. Surely a married woman didn't come up to a hotel room with a man who was not her husband for innocent reasons. Was this enough evidence for Mr. Wilson?

Was it enough evidence for me?

I had Pop to think about. If he was going to get paid, if he was going to keep Mr. Wilson from going to Uncle Adam, he needed a photo, something more than the chaste pictures I'd captured in the lobby. Just as I was starting to think that the situation was hopeless, a maid came down the hallway, pushing a cart filled with towels, soap, and other amenities. I frowned and widened my eyes.

"Excuse me?" I said.

She looked up at me and grinned. "Can I help you, young lady?"

Boy, howdy, could she. "Gosh, I hope so. I thought my parents would be back in our room by now, but they haven't arrived yet and I don't have a key. Could you let me in?"

Her smile widened. "Of course." She produced a ring of keys and inserted one into the door. With a click, she turned the lock and gestured me in. "Now make sure you lock it behind you," she said.

"I will. Thanks. That was awfully swell of you." I kept up the little-girl act until I was inside. Fortunately, the bedroom area wasn't immediately visible to the door—there was a sitting area that one had to pass through. I quietly shut the door and armed myself with my Brownie. Then, after taking a deep breath and begging my arms to stop their shaking, I rounded the corner and captured the couple just as Mrs. Wilson was removing her brassiere.

I was out the door before she screamed.

CHAPTER

4

I DIDN'T WANT TO TELL POP what I'd done until I had the pictures in hand. The only problem was, I was broke. The year before, I never left the house without a little walking-around money in my pocket or purse, always placed there by Mama in case I needed anything. It wasn't essentials she was thinking of, but a trip to the subway arcade, a picture show at the Rialto, or a new 78-rpm disc or comic book I just had to have that afternoon. Pop was either unaware of the financial needs of fifteen-year-old girls or simply didn't have the money to share. Either way, it was too uncomfortable a subject to broach. I would find a way to get what I needed without bothering him.

The next morning, my Brownie in hand, I sought out the school newspaper office.

At Chapin, the newspaper had been run by everyone in rotation, the bulk of the work falling to the seniors.

The paper was a privilege we all looked forward to, the information it contained a handy way to spread gossip and anoint who was worth talking about and who wasn't. I expected something similar at P.S. 110, a sort of blind worship of the printed word, but as I neared the office, I noticed the teetering stack of untouched newspapers that remained outside the cafeteria and auditorium.

It was a shame, because what I saw as I leafed through the pages on my way to the newspaper room was a wealth of information. This wasn't insider scoop about an exclusive school and its airy alumni. The stories were commentary on the media's claims that ours was a generation of layabouts who would never contribute anything worthwhile. There were opinion pieces written for and against lowering the minimum age for the draft to eighteen, and profiles on the students who'd already signed up and shipped out.

I knocked on the newspaper door and waited for someone to invite me to enter. Through the small pane of glass set in the door I could see several desks with typewriters and a chalkboard covered with story ideas that someone had already marked up with lines and check marks to indicate which they'd keep and which they'd toss. Two people were at work in the room. A girl hunched over a typewriter, hunting and pecking her way through an assignment. And a boy stared down at a folder with such intensity you would've thought it contained Axis war plans.

The boy was familiar. He'd been the kid with the camera who'd caught me up to speed when Tom Barney was arrested.

Neither responded to my knock. I turned the knob and walked inside.

The girl continued to ignore me. Her task was so strenuous that her Coke-bottle glasses practically met the page she was trying to type. The boy looked up at my entrance and then returned to the folder he had been looking through. From my new vantage I could see that it was full of glossy photographs. He wore a hat on his head, a fedora similar to one Pop owned. The band across it held a piece of paper in place that read PRESS.

"Hi," I said to the room in general. Still nothing from the girl, though the boy removed his hat at the sound of my voice, as though he was embarrassed to be caught wearing it. I approached him and decided that he was my best bet. "Remember me?"

If he did, his face didn't show it.

"I saw you taking pictures of Tom Barney the other day. When he was being arrested." Still nothing. Was I really that unmemorable? "That's a great camera you've got." I held up the Brownie and wiggled it. "As you can see, I'm not so well outfitted."

"You new?"

"I just moved here this summer."

He nodded, then focused on cleaning his lens with a

46

handkerchief that had been burrowed in his pocket. Initials were embroidered in one corner: P. L. "The editor already left for class. You looking to shoot for us?"

I couldn't tell if he thought that would be a good thing or not, though I suspected, given the hint of desperation in his voice, that anyone being interested in what he and the girl with the thick glasses did would be welcome.

"Oh, I'm not good enough for that." What was the best way to get someone to do something for you? Mama believed false modesty and flattery were the keys that opened every door. Whenever someone acted like she was nothing more than a dumb immigrant, she played it up, batting her eyes and musing that if she were as smart as they were, she would be so much better off. "I want to learn," I said. "I've read the paper and it's . . . amazing. The photos are really good. Like Dorothea Lange good." Okay, so I exaggerated.

"Really?" He wasn't unattractive, but there was a paleness to his skin and a scrawniness to his body that implied he either spent every hour of the day indoors or had been a sickly child who had never quite grown out of it.

"Our paper was a joke at my old school. Nobody took it seriously. I'd love to be able to do what you do, but I can't even develop film."

"I could teach you."

"Seriously?"

"You got anything in the camera now?"

I nodded and passed him the Brownie. "I'm Iris," I said.

"Paul," he countered, and shook my hand. He tipped his head toward the girl in the Coke-bottle glasses. "That's Pearl."

I said hi and got a nod in response. Paul led me to a small room connected to the one we were in. Inside sat several trays of chemicals that combined to make the air virtually unbreathable. He flipped a switch, turned on a fan, and warned me that the room would be completely black when he turned out the lights.

He wasn't kidding. I couldn't see my hand in front of my face.

"I'm starting by taking the film out and putting it on a reel. Then I'm going to put it in the developing tank."

I made a noise that I hoped sounded like "That's fascinating."

"What's your last name?" asked Paul.

"Anderson."

He moved something in the dark. "You Jewish?"

"No," I said before the question had left the air.

"Oh. Sorry," said Paul. "I thought you might be."

And what? I wanted to say. *You were going to blame the war on me? Tell me that I wasn't allowed in the newspaper office? Ask me if it was true our kind made love through a hole in a sheet?*

"There's a club that meets after school for Jewish students. I belong and so does Pearl. She's my sister."

"Oh." I forgot that the Lower East Side wasn't quite so homogeneous when it came to religious beliefs. At Chapin,

I was one of the only Jews in my class. I quickly learned not to talk about my religion, an easy task since neither Pop nor Mama was particularly observant. But when I stayed with Adam and Miriam, that changed. I was expected to cover my head and attend synagogue, even if it meant drawing attention to myself.

When Pop and I moved, I went back to my old ways. After all, I was the daughter of Arthur Anderson, not Arthur Ackerman. It was so much easier to pretend not to be Jewish. That way I could fool myself into believing that what was happening overseas had nothing to do with me or my family.

The lights came back on. "I just thought, if you were Jewish, you might want to come, too," said Paul.

I felt like a creep. He was trying to help me out. And now it was too late to do anything but either admit my lie or keep pretending it was the truth. "Well, I'm not, but thanks."

He poured developer into the tank and looked at his watch. As an eternity passed, I struggled to find something to say, but nothing seemed appropriate. Paul drained the developer and poured in the stop bath. Another look at his watch. Was he timing how long the developing took, or how long he was going to be stuck with me? "You know about the Jive Hive?" he asked.

I shook my head.

"It's a club just for teens that they run out of the fire hall on East Broadway. It's open every Saturday night. You should come."

Was he asking me on a date? Is that how it happened— some boy you'd just met invited you out before you knew his last name? "What do people do there?"

He drained the stop bath and poured in the fixer. "Dance. Play cards. Just bust loose, really. A bunch of kids run it. It's a good time."

"Thanks. Maybe I'll come by sometime. If I'm not busy."

The bell rang, warning us that we had ten minutes until first period began.

Paul glanced at his watch as though he didn't believe what the bell was telling him. "Nuts. This needs at least another five minutes and then the film needs to be rinsed."

"I could do it," I said. "I'd hate for you to be late for your first class."

He looked at his watch again. "I'm responsible for making sure the room is secure."

"The doors lock from the inside, right? I can make sure they're locked before I leave."

He looked at me skeptically for a moment. "All right. Just make sure the doors are locked. After you rinse the film, it's going to need to dry for a couple of hours. If you want, we can make prints after school. I'll be back here right after last bell." He exited the tiny room and in the split second the door was open I could see Pearl watching me.

Once I was safely behind the closed door, I rinsed the negative of a naked Mrs. Wilson scrambling to hide herself behind a hotel sheet, and mused over my inability to share my own secrets.

I DIDN'T LOCK THE PHOTO LAB DOOR or the newspaper room door. Instead, I hung the film to dry and wedged enough newspaper into both doors' jambs to keep them from closing properly. There was no chance I was going to risk having Paul make prints of my photos. I'd stop by after lunch to get my film. Then I'd figure out another way to get prints made.

My hope of going back to the lab was thwarted by a schedule change. Instead of letting us out for lunch at the normal time, we were kept in our classroom while the president's Appeal to Youth was broadcast over the PA system. As President Roosevelt warned the youth of the world that the Nazis, Fascists, and Japanese had nothing to offer them but death, I pictured Paul examining my film with a shocked look on his face. As soon as the speech was over and we were released to the cafeteria, I took a detour to the newspaper office and went to retrieve the roll. Unfortunately, someone had gotten there before me. The wad of newspaper had been removed from the door jamb and once again the knob was fixed and locked.

I felt sick at the discovery. How was I going to explain having pictures like that in my possession? Paul was going to think I was weird, for sure. And what if he told someone else? Or worse—what if they wrote about it in the school paper?

I was useless in my afternoon classes. Every time someone looked my way, I was certain they knew about the photos I'd taken. I headed out of P.S. 110 with a heavy heart. I'd almost cleared the property line when Paul's sister Pearl caught my eye. With a gesture I might've missed if I hadn't been looking for it, she waved. I checked behind me to make sure I was the person she was signaling to, then crossed the distance to her, terrified that I was going to have to endure some humiliating news from this odd, silent girl.

She put a finger to her lips, passed me a folder, and then spun on her heel.

She hadn't just returned my film; she'd made prints. Each image was carefully covered with a sheet of paper to keep it from sticking to the next one on the pile.

Pearl was gone before I could thank her.

Pop wasn't home when I returned from school. I left the photos beside the typewriter on his desk and focused on my homework. At six-thirty he arrived, his tired gait making it clear he'd spent the afternoon walking the streets in pursuit of something for a case. He landed so heavily in his desk chair that I could hear him make contact with the wood. With a sigh he removed the prosthetic and tossed it aside. It landed in the doorway, spanning the distance between him and me.

"Iris?" he said after a minute had passed.

I approached his door slowly, unable to read if it was anger or pleasure coloring my name. "Yes, Pop?"

"What's this?" He limply held the stack of 8×10s, so fresh they still smelled of their chemical bath.

"It's Mrs. Wilson and the man she's been seeing. I caught them at the Plaza last night."

"You followed them there?"

I didn't respond. It still wasn't clear if he wanted to praise Caesar or bury him.

"How did you get into the hotel room?"

This was good. We'd bypassed *Why were you out so late?* and *What possessed you to go uptown alone?* "I told the maid I was staying there and got her to unlock the door for me."

He stared down at the photos. "They must've seen you."

"I got out of there pretty fast." It hadn't occurred to me that I shouldn't be seen. The goal was to take a picture, not preserve my anonymity, right? And besides, what did it matter if Mrs. Wilson saw me? She was the one doing something wrong. "I was surprised by how young he was. Do you think that was the draw—that he was younger than Mr. Wilson?"

"Maybe. Or it could be . . ." Whatever he was about to say vanished and he turned his attention back to me. "They probably called the hotel detective and reported you. Did you talk to anyone? Give them your name?"

"No, of course not." My hands danced in and out of my pockets. This wasn't going the way I'd hoped. I'd done well, hadn't I?

"It's not right, Iris."

"The pictures are clear. There's no question what's going on in them."

"That's not what I mean and you know it. This isn't your business."

"I was trying to help."

"You help by going to school. By making good grades and keeping your nose clean. This isn't a business for women."

Since when was I a woman?

He waved the photos at me. "Don't do this again."

"All right."

"I mean it, Iris. If the wrong person saw you, if this man in the photo decided to come after you to get the film, what would you have done?"

I shrugged. I saw no point in hypothetical questions. Those things hadn't happened, so what did it matter? "Run, I guess."

"And if he had a gun?"

Ducked, I thought about saying, but even I knew that was too snotty. "I don't know."

"Exactly. You're a child. Be a child." And with that he tossed the photos into the garbage can.

I was heartsick that night. I understood his point: it

could've been dangerous. If something had gone wrong, I wouldn't have known how to react. But was it really fair to ask me to sit around and do nothing when the rent was late and Uncle Adam had been invoked and I was capable of helping?

As I lay in bed, staring at the few pieces of furniture that had been moved from our uptown address, my anger grew. My old Shirley Temple doll grinned at me from the dresser, her bold blue eyes staring blankly at a space just beyond me. The framed photo I'd gotten from my Deanna Durbin fan club membership smiled from the nightstand, her upper body bisected by her signature. Why had I kept these things when we moved? They didn't belong here any more than I did. Didn't Pop see how miserable I was? Didn't he understand that for one brief twenty-four-hour period I'd felt like I had a purpose?

Didn't he know how much I missed Mama?

I pinched a blanket and rubbed the satiny edge between my fingers. It was my baby blanket, a pink knitted thing much too small to do anything more than get lost in my sheets. But ever since I was born, or so Mama claimed, it was the talisman I turned to when I needed something to help soothe me to sleep. One rub of the fraying satin edge and whatever worries I had would melt away.

It wasn't working. I was too tense for sleep. If I didn't say something to him, the hours would pass and I'd find myself too exhausted to function the next day. And—boy, howdy—the last thing I needed to do was battle P.S. 110 on too little sleep.

I stuffed the blanket under my pillow, put on my robe, and pattered down the stairs. Pop was still in his office, typing up case notes. I cleared my throat to get his attention.

The typewriter ceased its noise. "What are you still doing up, Iris?"

"I can't sleep."

He cocked his head toward the kitchen. "Why don't you make yourself some warm milk?"

I took a step backward, but my feet refused to do anything more. The time for speaking up was now. "I didn't do anything wrong. I was trying to help."

He addressed the handwritten notes he'd been transcribing. "I know that."

"No, you don't. There are all these signs around school about how we can help with the war effort by collecting clothes and cans. If the government wants my help, how come you won't accept it?"

He lifted his head, finally meeting my eyes. "This isn't a business for little girls."

Before I was a woman; now I was a little girl? What had changed in the last few hours, other than my clothes? "Pop, I know I made mistakes. But I can learn. I can be good at this. I want to be good at this."

"In four years, if you feel the same way, we'll talk. Now go back to bed."

He was being a father for the first time since he had returned home, and rather than relishing it, I resented it. He missed five years of my life, the five years when he could've sent me to my room and I'd have had to accept it. But those days were past. Who we were now didn't allow for that relationship. I couldn't go back to being Iris Anderson, privileged girl on the Upper East Side, and he couldn't be a father who sent me to my room without giving me a good reason for it.

"No," I said.

He was shocked. That much was clear.

I marched over to the wastebasket and fished out the 8 × 10s. I put them on the desk in front of him. "I know we need money. I know you can't do everything anymore. I made mistakes. I admit it. But I worked hard to get these. I studied the file. I memorized Mrs. Wilson's face. I figured out how to get the photos developed without anyone being wise." Sort of. "And I'm going to keep working at it. You can throw out the pictures. You can criticize my efforts. Or you can accept my help and teach me to do a better job the next time. It's your choice, Pop, but I'm not going away."

He sighed heavily. In the movies, if Deanna Durbin had stood up for herself like this, she would've gotten exactly what she wanted, followed by an emotional embrace that cemented the fact that, even if she was standing up for herself, she would always be Daddy's little girl.

There would be no hugs and tears for me. That's not who we were.

He picked up the photos and examined them more closely. "What camera did you use?"

"My Brownie." It felt like a betrayal. After all, Uncle Adam had given it to me.

He held a photo up to the lampshade. "These shots are grainy. The light quality isn't very good."

"It was night. There wasn't a lot of light in the room."

"They saw you. Detectives have to be invisible. No one's going to forget a child with a camera."

Child? Seriously? "I can be discreet."

"I can't use these." He dumped them back into the trash can.

I stared at him, willing the tears I knew wanted to come to wait until I left the room so I could retain a little dignity. But then why not let him see me cry? He deserved to know how much his decision had stung.

"You're making a mistake," I said between trembling lips.

He shook his head at me, and the ripples on his forehead grew four feet deep. "That's the way you see it. From where I sit, I'm finally doing the right thing."

* * *

58

THE NEXT AFTERNOON I arrived home early from school and discovered Pop's office door closed. From inside came the familiar sound of Mr. Wilson. He had come by to retrieve the photos—*my* photos—and return the money he'd taken from Pop. I waited for him to ask how Pop had finally gotten the shot after all those failed attempts, but he never did. He didn't care how Pop had done it; all he cared was that the job was done.

I could barely contain my excitement. Surely Pop had changed his mind and was ready to give me a chance to show him what I could do.

Mr. Wilson tipped his hat at me as he exited the office. I feigned interest in *Ten Cent Love Story Magazine*, a romance slick that Mrs. Mrozenski had brought home with the groceries.

When Pop returned from walking Mr. Wilson out, I was waiting for him with my arms crossed, shoulders squared. "I thought you threw the photos away."

"I didn't think you'd be home yet."

"We had early dismissal today."

Pop unfurled a ten-dollar bill from his pocket and passed it my way. "Here."

"So does this mean you've changed your mind?"

"No." He put the money on the coffee table in front of me. "Take the money. I don't want you to think I'm taking advantage of you. Buy yourself something for school." He turned to head back into the office. In another thirty seconds his door would be closed, and then who knew how many hours would pass before he'd talk to me again.

"He said the photos were good, right?"

He froze and his back turned rigid. His left shoulder was higher than his right one. "That's not the point, Iris."

"Then what is?"

He sighed heavily—had he always relied on sighs to convey emotion?—and spun back toward me. "Do you know why that man wanted me to follow his wife?"

"Because she was having an affair."

"No. Because he wants out of his marriage. His mistress wants him to get a divorce and he doesn't want to lose her, but he doesn't want to lose his money, either. So he's held out until he has something on his wife that will make the separation go a little more smoothly. Those photos you took just guaranteed that his wife won't get one red cent in the divorce settlement."

I was having a hard time connecting the dots. "So he was cheating on her first? That doesn't seem fair."

Pop suddenly looked uncomfortable, and not just because his leg was bothering him. "It's the way the law works, Iris. They don't care who behaved badly first. All they care about is who can prove it. These people I work for, they aren't all good people. They aren't always asking me to help them do good things. A lot of them are like

Mr. Wilson; they want proof that someone else is doing something wrong so that they can justify their own bad actions. I don't want you around that."

Poor Mrs. Wilson, with her under-eye bags and her desperate smile, was going to have her goose cooked because of me. A knot tightened in my stomach. "If you knew that was what he was up to, why did you take his money?"

"Because there are bills to pay and no one but me to pay them." He looked tired. I wasn't the only one who'd spent half the night awake. "It can be ugly, the things I'm asked to do. But I'm not being paid to make judgments, understand? And it's a good thing, too, because sometimes who's right and who's wrong isn't always so cut-and-dried. When I'm hired by a client, I'm only privy to a small part of the story."

So that's how he justified dealing with the Mr. Wilsons of the world.

"Many of the people I'm hired to look into don't want me to find out what I'm trying to find out. Often there's money at stake for them—sometimes something that's even more valuable. This job can be dangerous. That's what I was trying to explain to you last night. If you're seen, if they know where to find you, some of them will do whatever they can to make sure you don't do your job. Understand?"

I wasn't the only one at risk; he was in danger, too. That had never occurred to me before. I may not have known Pop very well, but I certainly wasn't prepared to lose him. Ever since he'd come home, I'd just assumed he was safe.

But he was more vulnerable than ever. He might've had the experience to know what to do when, but I was the only one of us with two good legs.

"So what are you going to do the next time someone hires you to follow his wife?" I asked.

"Do what I did this time, I imagine."

"But you couldn't do it this time." *I had to do it for you*, I almost said. *And I can run. At least I stand a chance at getting away.* "What happens if they take the job to Uncle Adam instead? Mrs. Mrozenski isn't always going to be willing to take the rent late, you know."

He looked at me like he was seeing me for the first time. Had I said too much? Would he disappear into his office and never come out again? "How do you know all that?"

"I just do."

He rubbed at his upper thigh, just above the prosthetic. His face took on an ashen hue and his features momentarily pinched. He was late taking his pills.

The pain he felt wasn't just the chafing and discomfort from the prosthetic. When he first came home, Aunt Miriam had warned me about something called phantom pain. *It only happens to amputees*, she'd said. *The severed nerves go haywire and sometimes the person missing a limb swears they can feel pain in the arm or leg that's not there anymore.* I'd

62

seen it with my own eyes, how Pop would move to scratch the calf that wasn't, his hand brushing the air beneath his knee the way Roland Young's hand passed through Cary Grant's ghostly body in *Topper*.

But Aunt Miriam was wrong about one thing: phantom pain didn't just happen to amputees. Anyone who'd experienced a sudden loss could fall victim to it. I felt it every time I entered a room and expected to see Mama, only instead of clusters of severed nerves going haywire, it was my heart that seized in agony.

"Do you want me to get your pills?" I asked Pop.

"No. Not yet." He continued rubbing. "Not every job is going to be like this one. I'm still a good detective."

"I'm not saying you're not."

He held up his finger to signal that he wasn't done talking. "I can't do what I need to do if I'm worrying about your safety. I appreciate that you want to help, but you can do a lot more good staying at home where I know where you are and where Mrs. Mrozenski can keep an eye on you."

Tears crested at the corners of my eyes. I was supposed to be the dutiful daughter who did her homework, ate her vegetables, and went to bed with a smile on her face. Why did I have to be a girl? Maybe if he'd had a son, he would've been more willing to trust me.

I sniffled, more loudly than I'd intended. "Maybe I could—"

His face hardened into a slab of granite. "This isn't open for discussion, Iris. Hate me if you want, but this is my decision to make, not a fifteen-year-old girl's. Now go to your room."

I threw the ten-dollar bill beside his good leg and did as he said.

5

I DIDN'T LEAVE MY ROOM again that day. Instead, I lay on the bed, trying to figure out how things had gone so wrong. Didn't he see how much I could help? I couldn't fathom that it wasn't obvious to him.

I didn't sleep at all that night. Not even my baby blanket helped.

What did I think would happen? That he'd embrace me and thank me for helping him. Then he'd school me in the detecting business and we'd become close—better than close—not just sharing everything with each other, but comfortable enough in each other's presence that when there were silences they wouldn't cause my stomach to churn with anxiety.

I would tell him everything. Stories about the boys I was interested in. How mad I was at Mama. And he'd do the same, opening up about that awful day at Pearl Harbor and his own grief when he found out Mama was dead.

Everything would change between us because of this one little photograph.

And maybe it still could.

I wasn't going to go away without a fight. I knew he needed me, and if he was too stubborn to see it because of whatever danger he thought I was at risk for, that was his choice. I'd become the best detective I could be on my own, and then I'd show him exactly what he was missing out on.

"Do you want to go see a movie tonight?" Pop asked two days after he'd sold my photos and ended my detecting career.

"No, thank you."

"It's the new Ginger Rogers film."

"I have homework."

"I thought you already did it."

"Then I guess you thought wrong."

I could see the hurt in his eyes. And the truth was, I did want to go to the movies. But I thought my rejection of him would get me what I wanted, so I was determined to stand firm.

In the meantime I spent every waking moment learning to be a detective. When I wasn't at school, I read detective comics, listened to the spy serials, and made sure I was always in earshot of Pop's door during those times when clients came to meet with him. When he wasn't home, I sneaked into the office and studied his notes from earlier cases, not just the ones he'd taken since coming home from

Hawaii, but those he'd worked on with Uncle Adam years before, when they used to have an agency together. He filled folders with carefully typed descriptions of his environment and the people he observed. Like Mama, he found volumes of useful information in the clothes people wore, their behavior, and the places they chose to go. He could read guilt and suspicion in the choice of a hat or a misplaced verb. It was amazing stuff.

I went through his collection of props and tools: hats that hid his face in shadows, street and phone directories, city maps, picklocks, counterfeit IDs, and uniforms used by utility workers. Other things were more unusual and, I suspected, had come from his time in the Navy. For his camera, he had dozens of different parts that could improve an image under the worst of circumstances. He had tiny recorders that he could leave anywhere to capture a conversation. And there were other gadgets that I couldn't even guess at the purpose of.

But you could only learn so much by observing fictional detectives and Pop's collection of props. The best education would only come from watching Pop at work. The catch was, I had to do it without him knowing.

I'd already mastered the art of eavesdropping on him. Instead of just doing it when clients came by, I began to do it when he was the only one in the office. Much of his job was done by telephone. I had no idea what a good actor he was, how he seamlessly donned a new identity, complete with a new voice, and confidently asked for information that should've been denied him. He could be shockingly personable when he needed something.

"Good afternoon," he began one call as I huddled on the other side of the door vent. "Is this Gloria Armour? I'm so glad I reached you. I know you probably don't remember me, but this is Jack Gaviston. I met you through Bill." There was a pause. "I'm flattered that I made such an impression on you. I ran into Bill the other day and he was telling me that you knew the best way to get in touch with Randall Smythe."

There was a lot to learn from this brief exchange, even if I didn't know the details of the Smythe case. Pop knew that by implying that Gloria wouldn't remember his fictional alter ego, she would insist that she did just to get out of a potentially embarrassing situation. Hoping to cover up her own lie, she was then eager to tell Pop whatever she knew. After all, if she didn't, he might suspect she was bluffing.

It was a brilliant scheme, and from what I could tell, it worked almost every time.

There were real connections that Pop relied on, too. He had friends at the phone company, the Department of Motor Vehicles, and the utility offices who could call up phone extensions, addresses, and other information in a matter of hours. He always opened his requests with questions about how their families were doing, displaying a remarkable skill for remembering spouses' names and the pursuits of various children he'd probably never met. He seemed to understand that the best way to get people to want to help you was to show them that you were interested in them.

I tried to put what I had learned from Pop to practical use during my time at school. I trained myself to sit in a classroom and take in every detail about the students around me: what did they wear, who was sitting where, what could I tell about them from the choices they made? I studied those who seemed to be looked up to by everyone else, those who could get away with things, and those who could not. I began to know the people around me intimately. It almost made up for the fact that I had no real friends.

The person I watched the most was Tom Barney. He'd returned to school a week after his arrest, appearing no worse for wear. When he came back, so did his bounty, or at least part of it. The purses and wallets he'd stolen, including my own, were turned over to the front office, where those of us who'd been victimized were invited to retrieve them. I did so, though, like everyone else, I found my purse empty and my money long gone.

From the little I was able to pick up in the halls, Tom had been sent to a juvenile detention center for the duration of his absence and was let back into P.S. 110 on a probationary basis. I was fascinated by someone who could rob his peers and so easily slip back into the school without showing a hint of remorse for what he'd done. Maybe everyone else was willing to let bygones be bygones, but I wanted him to know how much he'd upset me. I didn't have the courage to just go up to him and confront him, though. Instead, I watched him from afar, biding my time in the same way I was biding it with Pop. Someday Tom might talk to me again, and when he did I'd give him a piece of my mind.

In the middle of September, as I sat in the lunchroom longing for the clock to move faster, I was greeted by Suze. "Hey, baby girl. Long time no see." I hadn't seen her since that first day in the girls' bathroom, and I responded to her reappearance with a mixture of relief and fear. Here, after weeks of being ignored, was a somewhat friendly face. At least I hoped she was friendly.

"Hi," I said.

She peeked under the table and took in my skirt. It was pencil cut, conforming closely to the curve of my hips. Pop had bought it for me as a peace offering. "Nice rags."

"Thanks."

"So what's tickin', chicken?"

In front of me was the notebook I was using to write down all the details I was trying to recall after giving myself one minute to look around the room. It was a way of testing my memory, and I believed that after two weeks of doing it, I was already becoming much better at analyzing my environment.

But it wasn't the kind of thing that you could share with someone. Even I knew it was kind of weird.

"Just homework," I said.

"You do a lot of homework, don't you, baby?"

I nodded, uncertain if I'd just damned myself by agreeing with her.

"How come you were staring at my friends?"

Had I been? I followed her gaze to a table near the back wall, where a group of girls in tight sweaters and heavy makeup were conversing with dark-skinned Italian boys with slick ducktails and chains that joined their pocket watches to their waists. How had I missed that Suze was there? What kind of detective doesn't make note of the one person she knows by name?

"I wasn't staring at anyone," I said.

"You sure about that? Rhona said you've been watching Tom since he sat down." She cocked her head toward the table, where Tom Barney sat with the blonde.

"I didn't mean to stare," I said. "I was just thinking and that's where my eyes landed."

"It's okay, baby. No harm. You were just making Rhona nervous, you dig? I told her you were copacetic."

I thought about telling her what Tom had done to me, but it occurred to me that telling her he'd robbed me wasn't going to help me stay in her good graces. I mean, she knew he was a thief, right?

"Heard from your pop?" she asked.

That's right—I'd led her to believe he was off being a soldier. "Not a word. What about you? You heard from Bill?"

She beamed, my earlier infraction completely forgotten. "Got a letter yesterday. Course most of it's blacked out." She pulled a note from her cleavage and unfurled it. Thick black lines crossed out much of what Bill had written to her. Either he was too free with his information or the war censor was still trying to get a handle on what should be considered sensitive information. "He couldn't even tell me where he is."

"It's to protect them," I said. "Just in case the wrong person gets ahold of the mail."

"Who's going to be reading my mail?"

"You never know," I said.

She looked back toward her friends. Despite their tough exteriors, they looked like they were having fun.

She knocked on the table with a closed fist, bidding me farewell. "I better evaporate, baby. Be good. Remember: no staring."

"I will," I said.

DESPITE MY PROMISE, I couldn't give up watching Tom. Now that I knew he was part of Suze's crew, I found myself watching all of them whenever the chance arose. There was no one at P.S. 110 more alive than them, no one more fascinating. The boys were strangely feminine, almost not boys at all. They paid attention to what they wore and moved liked cats, their long graceful limbs working at a pace that seemed slower than everyone else around them. And the girls seemed so old and wise, as though they'd lived a hundred lives before this one and somehow managed to retain the knowledge from those previous lifetimes.

They were a different species than the kids I'd known at the Chapin School. But they were also a different species than most of the students at P.S. 110. In fact, the rest of the school seemed to view them as outsiders, but they didn't seem to care. They were outsiders by choice, not because someone else had put them in that position. I envied that they didn't need to belong. I suppose that's how it was when you had a group. You didn't need to be accepted by anyone else; you had already found your people.

I had to face it: there would be no group for me. The groups I might've been welcomed in—like the one for Jewish students—I didn't want to join, and the ones I used to belong to were no longer available.

"You had another phone call," said Mrs. Mrozenski one afternoon just after I'd arrived home from school. "Grace wants you to telephone her."

It was the third time Grace had called since I'd run into the twins uptown the night I'd followed Mrs. Wilson. Each time I took the message and pretended like I was going to do it right away.

"She say you no call her back before."

"I have, she's just never home."

"She just called, so she must be home now." Mrs. Mrozenski glanced toward the party-line phone that sat on a table just outside the kitchen. There was a second phone in Pop's office—a private line intended for business only.

"I'll call her from Pop's office," I told Mrs. M. She raised an eyebrow. "It's about a boy, so I think she wants a little privacy. Pop won't mind."

I shut myself into the room and sat at Pop's desk, but I never lifted the receiver. What would I say to her? *I go to a school I hate filled with people who only ever talk to me to tell me to stop staring at them. Pop and I barely speak because he thinks my wanting to be a detective is some childish fantasy. Oh, and we're so broke he frequently ducks our landlady so she won't ask him for the rent money. How are you?*

No, there'd be no telephoning Grace.

I couldn't deny how lonely I was, though. I needed friends before I permanently became that strange girl whose name no one remembered.

The next day I decided to do something about it. I arrived at school early and went straight to the newspaper office. Just like the first time I visited there, Paul and Pearl were working alone. They didn't seem surprised to see me. At least Paul didn't. Pearl was so wrapped up in her work that I couldn't tell if she was even aware of my presence.

She was the one I wanted to talk to, but it was clear that

as long as her brother was there, that wasn't going to happen. So instead I directed what I'd come to say to him.

"Remember me?" I asked him as I entered the room.

"Sure. I was wondering if I'd ever see you again. What happened? I thought I was going to show you how to make prints."

"Something came up." I looked toward Pearl. She licked the end of her pencil and pushed up her glasses. "Is the Jive Hive still around?"

"Every Saturday," said Paul. "Has your schedule opened up?" His tone didn't escape me.

"I'm sorry if I seemed rude that day. It's just when you're new . . ."

"You're not sure who's shrewd and who's square. It's all right." He tossed a look Pearl's way. She was still looking at everything but us. "If you do want to go, you're welcome to join us. There are some potent people I could introduce you to." Us? Did that mean Pearl would be there? "How 'bout you join us this weekend?"

"That would be swell," I said. "I'll see you on Saturday."

BY THE TIME SATURDAY rolled around, I was having second thoughts. What if Paul thought this was a date? What if Pearl wasn't part of the "we" he was talking about? I considered not showing up, but the rudeness of the act outweighed my discomfort. If private school had taught me nothing else, it had made it clear that it was better to be uncomfortable than impolite.

Pop was thrilled that I had plans with people from school. "I'm glad you're keeping busy tonight," he said.

What did that mean? "It's no big deal," I said, not even willing to let him feel joy at my burgeoning social life. "It'll probably be boring." No, it definitely would be. Pearl had taken a vow of silence from what I'd seen, and Paul was clearly flat.

But at least I'd be out of the house for a while and not forced to continue my stalemate with Pop.

Paul had asked me to meet him at their house at eight. Pop wasn't thrilled that a young man would expect me to escort him rather than the other way around. He insisted on walking me to the address, two blocks over, and waiting on the sidewalk while I rang the bell and waited for some-one to answer. As I stood on the porch, smelling the rem-nants of their family dinner, I noticed a flag with a single gold star winking from the window. This was a gold star house, meaning someone in the family had been killed in the war. Before I could contemplate its significance, the front door opened and Paul greeted me with a lopsided grin.

"You made it."

"I told you I would."

I waved at Pop to let him know I was at the right place

and wasn't about to be mugged or murdered. He waved back and strolled away.

"Was that your father?"

"Yes."

He stared after him. I wondered if we had violated some code of behavior. Should Pop have come onto the porch? Met Paul's parents? But then if we were going to be strict about it, shouldn't Paul have met me at my house? "What's with the limp?" asked Paul.

So that was what drew his attention. Boy, howdy—and to think I was the one who was worried about being thought rude. "He lost his leg at Pearl Harbor."

I expected an "I'm sorry" or "Gee, that's rough," but Paul wasn't the kind of person to descend into sentimentality. Or manners. "That must've been something, being right there at the start of the war."

I was feeling disagreeable. Pop being hurt was hardly something to brag about. "The war had already been going on for years before then."

"You know what I mean." He pointed his thumb toward the window. "We lost my brother four months in."

Now it was my turn to be trite. "I'm sorry."

He shrugged. "On the bright side, I can't go." He pointed at his chest. "Asthma." He turned his head and hollered into the house at a volume that made me question how bad his lungs really were, "Pearl! Let's make tracks!"

We walked side by side, Paul in the middle, to the fire hall that the Jive Hive operated out of. Pearl was silent, her attention focused more on her feet than on the air in front of her. Paul rattled on about the Princeton-Navy game that afternoon, wrongly assuming that I cared about football. I tried to feign interest, but my mind was already counting down the minutes until I could fake a headache and go home.

We arrived at the fire hall and went down to the basement, where the Jive Hive was in full swing. Frank Sinatra, fronting the Tommy Dorsey Orchestra, sang from the phonograph as we entered the large, low-ceilinged room. To the right was a table loaded with refreshments: cookies, cupcakes, punch, and Royal Crown Cola. To the left, card tables were set up with checker and chess sets and decks of cards. In the center of the room was an impromptu dance floor, where two couples clutched each other and swayed to Frank's request to "be careful, that's my heart."

I recognized some of the faces from P.S. 110, though it was hardly a fair sampling of the crowd I encountered every day. Everyone here was white and clean-cut. Either Suze and Tom Barney and the rest of their crew hadn't arrived yet or they weren't welcome.

Before we were allowed to enter, we had to sign in. A stern girl in cat's-eye specs scrutinized my information after offering Paul a much warmer welcome. She ignored Pearl entirely. In fact, she made such a point of not looking at her that I was embarrassed at her rudeness.

And then something interesting happened: Pearl spoke.

"Iris is new. This is her first time here."

The stern girl offered me a tight smile and passed me a sheet of paper. "Welcome, Iris. These are the rules. Make sure you follow them."

I scanned the sheet. No pickups was the first rule. No gambling the second. Dates must be registered in advance. The rest were a litany of dos and don'ts related to behavior. Most everything on the list seemed designed to keep the room clean and adults at bay.

Paul was greeted by a blonde who wore her hair in tight pin curls. Without looking my way, he took her by the hand and joined her on the dance floor. I was prepared to disappear into a corner to wait out my time when Pearl spoke again.

"That's Denise Halloway. Paul's girlfriend."

"Oh."

"You didn't think you were his date, did you?"

"No," I said, too quickly.

"That's good. You could do so much better than my brother." She paused and examined her thumbnail. "So why did you come out with us? Are you hoping to use him again?"

"What?"

"Like for the photographs."

My back went rigid. "I wasn't—"

She cut me off. "Sure you weren't. Want to play checkers?"

It felt strangely like a threat: play checkers with me or I'll let everyone know what you were up to in the newspaper office. Was I reading her right? I couldn't be sure, so I said yes and followed her to one of the tables.

She disappeared long enough to claim two sodas and a plate of cookies for us. As she sat across from me, I noticed for the first time how pudgy she was. The top button on her skirt was left open to accommodate a roll of fat that hung over the waistband. Her blouse strained at the buttons. Either Pearl shopped for the figure she one day hoped to have or her weight gain was recent.

We started the game in silence. I couldn't tell if Pearl was terrified of people or simply preferred silence to conversation. I wondered how Grace would've dealt with her, assuming she had no choice but to spend time in Pearl's presence. She probably would've chattered away, insisting on creating conversation where there was none. Chapin girls weren't known for loving silence. It was, they believed, rude.

"Paul told me about your brother. I'm really sorry."

She tilted her head to the left, like she had water in her ear. "Thanks." She picked up a cookie and put the whole thing in her mouth. Frosting oozed out of the corner of her lips. She pressed it back inside with a practiced gesture and studied the checkerboard.

I wanted to ask more, like what was his name and where had he died and did they know how, but common sense prevailed and I kept my yap shut. What made me think this quiet girl wanted to talk about a tragedy that was so raw that the mere mention of it made her shove an entire cookie (no, make that two—she'd moved on to the second one) into her mouth?

I felt like I owed her something, a wound of my own for her to pick at. I didn't want to tell her about Mama, so I offered her the next best thing. "My pop lost his leg at Pearl Harbor."

She shook her head. What did that mean? Was it a quiet acknowledgment of Pop's loss or a way of silently saying that what I'd experienced wasn't even close to what she'd experienced, and how dare I think otherwise?

"Is he still in the military?" she said when she'd swallowed the cookie.

"No. He's a private detective now."

She nodded with more enthusiasm. While her tragedy may have trumped mine, I'd at least offered her an interesting tidbit. "Does he let you work on cases?"

"Sort of." I wasn't in the mood to explain about the disagreement between Pop and me. And I had a feeling that her thinking I worked for him made me a lot more interesting than if she thought I didn't.

She jumped one of my black checkers with one of her red and claimed the captured piece. "I've seen you watching people at school. I guess that's why you do it, huh?"

I nodded, embarrassed that I'd been caught. Hadn't I learned anything from tailing Mrs. Wilson?

"Is that what the photos were for? A case?"

Another nod.

"Thanks for that, by the way," I said. "You know—getting me the pictures."

"Paul would've flipped his lid."

"So he didn't see them?"

"Oh, no. You didn't want him to, right?"

"Right."

"So I figured." She studied the checkerboard. "Was it an affair?"

"Yeah. The husband paid us to follow the wife." *Us.* So it wasn't the complete truth, so what?

"I figured that was the case from the look on her face. What did he want?"

"A divorce."

She nodded again. The record was changed and Sammy Kaye begged us to "remember Pearl Harbor." I squirmed in the uncomfortable metal folding chair. Did they really need a song to convince us not to forget something like that?

"They call me that, you know," said Pearl.

Had I missed part of the conversation? "What?"

"Pearl Harbor. It started last year, right after."

"Why do they call you that?"

"They don't like me. They think I'm a cold cut." She cocked her head again and met my eyes, obviously daring me to disagree with their diagnosis.

"That's a terrible thing to call someone." I knew it

probably wasn't what she wanted to hear, but I also wasn't sure I was ready to tell her people were wrong about her. My eyes unconsciously circled the room, looking to see who, if anyone, was watching us talk. Weird was contagious. I knew how it worked. Just sitting next to Pearl would set me up in people's minds as someone just like her.

And yet she'd gotten me the photos.

She picked up another cookie and shoved it into her mouth. There was only one left on the plate, and I realized that she hadn't gotten them to share with me; her intention, all along, had been to eat them herself. Maybe she assumed I wouldn't stick around long enough to enjoy them. "Paul says it's my own fault," she said.

"That doesn't seem very fair."

"It's probably why he invited you out with us that first day. He thinks I need friends."

"You don't agree?"

"I had them. They're the ones who couldn't cope."

I'm not sure how I knew what had happened—maybe it was intuition, or maybe my weeks of observation were paying off—but I suddenly realized that when Pearl said they started calling her Pearl Harbor "after," she wasn't referring to December 7, 1941. Her brother's death had started all this. Her friends couldn't stand the doom and gloom that descended on her when she'd lost someone she'd loved. And she wasn't strong enough to fight the changes the grief had made in her.

I knew that change. Last year I'd been a completely different person. What did I worry about back then? A new pimple that blazed on my cheek the day class photos were taken. The way last year's waistbands strained against this year's waist. Whether or not my breasts would ever fill my brassiere.

I didn't worry about war. I didn't think about my father, serving in someplace called Pearl Harbor. In fact, I rarely thought about Pop at all. As for Mama, she flitted around the edges, always smiling, and convincing me that I would be all right as long as there was the two of us. It had been just the two of us for so long.

And then it was all gone. Mama dead. Pop returned, but different. And the house, the school, the friends—all traded for a dingy brownstone on Orchard Street that smelled of Mrs. Mrozenski's cabbage rolls. And why the change? The war, of course. It ruined everything. Including me.

We were alike, Pearl and I. And she knew it, which was why she was telling me all this.

I looked back toward the front door of the club, where the girl with cat's-eye specs had been joined by another girl, this one in pearls and a plaid blazer. They caught me looking at them and quickly turned away. Former friends of Pearl's, I'd bet, wondering how it was that she'd found a new friend to spend the evening with.

"You're interesting, though," said Pearl. "I kept hoping you'd come back to the newspaper office." She lifted the last cookie. Instead of sending it to her mouth, she extended it my way. "Want one?"

"No, thanks." I looked at the checkerboard. I was being slaughtered. It was a matter of minutes before the game was over and she was declared the victor.

"So what do you think of P.S. 110?" she asked.

"It's different."

"I always wanted to go to a private all-girls school." She knew that about me, too. How? She must've seen the question in my eyes. "I work in the office during study hall, helping with attendance. Anyhow, that's how I know you went to Chapin."

I nodded, not feeling as reassured as she thought that news might make me. "So you work for the newspaper and the office?"

"I don't really work for the paper. I just hang out there with Paul in the morning so I don't have to talk to anyone. He hates it, but he hates typing more, so he lets me stay if I agree to help type up the articles. Do you miss Chapin?"

Slowly, I nodded. Whatever I said to Pearl would be safe. She wouldn't repeat it to Paul, who clearly didn't think much of his sister. And there was no one else for her to confide in.

In some ways, it made her the perfect friend. At Chapin, I never knew what Grace might repeat to someone. This girl, on the other hand, was a locked box.

"I feel like such a square here," I said. She nodded,

encouraging me to go on. "And going to school with boys is . . . strange."

"They're better than most of the girls. Believe me. It was so much easier here before they started to enlist, and if the draft passes, it's going to be even worse. The girls gang up on you around here."

"That happened at Chapin, too."

She didn't seem convinced. But I'd witnessed it often enough to know it was true, even if I hadn't been on the receiving end of those attacks. "Have you made any friends?"

She had to know the answer was no, but I hated to admit it out loud. "There's one girl I've talked to a few times who seemed nice. Suze?" I realized I didn't know her last name. Claiming her as a friend when I didn't know that one simple fact made it seem like even more of a lie.

Her eyes grew wide. "Suze Armstrong? Really?"

I nodded. So there was only one Suze. "Why are you so surprised?"

"She's a Rainbow."

"A what?"

She leaned toward me and lowered her voice. "A Rainbow. It's what they call that gang she's in."

"You mean the people she hangs out with?"

She nodded.

"So what do the Rainbows do?"

"According to them, nothing. According to the school,

steal anything that's not nailed down. You heard about Tom Barney, right?"

"Heard about him? I was one of his victims. He robbed my locker my first day at school," I said.

Pearl's eyes grew as wide as the checkers. "Seriously? What did he take?"

"My purse. I got it back but not the cash. And the worst part is, I actually talked to Tom that morning. He seemed so nice—he even helped me find my first class. I guess I must be an idiot, huh?"

"You're not an idiot. Tom is nice. In fact, up until his freshman year Tom was tight with Paul. Worked on the newspaper, played basketball—he was a real Abercrombie. But then he fell in with the Rainbows and started doing whatever they were doing, including wearing the zoot."

"The what?"

She seemed to take pleasure in educating me.

"The zoot suit. Surely you've seen them? A lot of the colored boys wear them out on the town, and the Italians and Puerto Ricans have started, too."

I might've read something in the newspaper about them a time or two, but it's not like I'd encountered a lot of boys of different races during my time at Chapin. If you were colored and on the Upper East Side, you were either lost or somebody's chauffeur.

"What do they look like?" I asked.

"Fancy suits. Bright colors. The jackets have shoulder pads, like women's clothes, and the pants are cut close to the ankle. You've seriously never seen them?"

"Not at school."

"Ah, they don't wear them at school. The zoot's strictly after-hours attire. For jitterbugging, mostly. The zoot and dancing go hand in hand." She got a strange look on her face, almost like longing. "I think they look dapper, but my father says they make whoever's wearing them look like a gangster. Or a cream puff."

I took in the group assembled at the Jive Hive. Every boy there was wearing crisp, pressed shirts and slacks with precise pleats ironed down their centers. A sweater vest broke up the monotony here and there, but otherwise their clothes were clearly chosen to make them fit in, not stand out.

"So why do you think Tom became a Rainbow?"

"Rhona, of course. She's the blonde in the tight sweater who's always with him."

"Is she bad news, too?"

"Rumor has it she can't go into the five-and-dime without the manager patting her down. And she went away for a long time last year."

"She was sent to juvie?"

"Nothing like that. The story was she'd been sent away after *getting in trouble*. Came back when it was all taken care of."

What did she mean? My question must've shown on my

face. Pearl raised both of her eyebrows multiple times. Sex. She was talking about sex. Rhona had been pregnant.

"Was it Tom's?"

"Who knows? And I don't even know if it was true. Anytime a girl leaves school, people talk."

"How long have they been a couple?" I don't know why I was so curious about them. I think I was still trying to figure out what made someone like Tom—who could help you and rob you in one day—tick.

"At least a year. That's why everyone was so shocked that they broke up." She hesitated before continuing. "She's awful. He deserved so much better. He's actually quite smart, though you wouldn't know it from the way he ditches classes now."

Why did Pearl know so much about them? Was she this observant about everyone, or was Tom someone she kept closer tabs on? "They broke up?"

"Yeah, right after he was arrested. I mean, they're friendly to each other still, but they're no longer a couple."

By eleven o'clock I'd played four games of checkers, consumed three Royal Crown Colas, and learned everything there was to know about the student body at P.S. 110. Pearl may have been an outcast, but she was an observant one. I wasn't the only one she'd scrutinized, just the only one who bothered to talk to her.

"I probably should go home," I told her. "It's getting late."

"I'll get Paul to walk you. You shouldn't be out alone."

She returned the checkers to the board and started to go in search of her brother. Something stopped her, though, and she turned back toward me. "You don't have to talk to me at school if you don't want to. I'll understand."

What had brought this on? "Will you talk to me?" I asked.

"Sure."

"Then why wouldn't I talk to you?"

Her mouth fluttered, but she didn't have an answer for me.

Paul, Denise, and Pearl walked with me to Orchard Street and waited until I was safely in the house. Pop's office door was closed, so I figured he was working. As I crossed the parlor and headed toward the stairs, the newspaper on the table caught my attention. As I moved closer for a better look, it wasn't the headlines that drew into focus, but the date.

It was Mama's birthday.

So that was what Pop meant when he said it was good that I had plans. And what about him? What had he done to mark the occasion?

I approached the office door and knocked.

"Pop?"

"Yeah?" His voice sounded strange. I opened the door and found him seated at his desk. His face was a blotchy mess. Had he been crying? Pop never cried—not even when his leg was at its worst—and yet all the signs were there.

"I just wanted to let you know I was home."

He forced a smile on his face. "Have fun?"

"It was better than I thought it would be."

"Good, good."

"What did you do?"

He cocked his head toward his typewriter. "Just typed up some case notes. You better get to bed. It's getting late."

"All right." I felt like I should say more, but I was uncomfortable seeing him in his grief and embarrassed that I'd almost let the day pass without feeling any of my own. "Good night, Pop," I finally said when nothing else came. And then I went upstairs and cried myself to sleep.

6

I SLEPT IN THE NEXT MORNING. When I came downstairs Pop was sitting in the office writing notes in long-
hand.

"I was wondering how long you were going to sleep," he
said.

"Sorry. I was pretty beat. Where's the typewriter?"

"Repair shop." He pushed an envelope my way. "Give
this to Mrs. Mrozenski for me."

"Aren't you joining us for breakfast?"

His head tipped toward the tablet in front of him. He
was looking at a row of numbers. It wasn't hard to imagine
what these figures represented. Nor was it difficult to put
together what the pawn ticket he'd tried to hide under the
pad of paper meant. "Too much work, I'm afraid. I'll make
it up at lunch."

I gave Mrs. Mrozenski the envelope just like he asked.

Now that I had a friend and found school slightly more

tolerable, money became my new obsession. Not only did I worry over what we owed, I was constantly thinking about money I used to have and how wasteful I'd been with it. Maybe if Mama hadn't been so indulgent, Pop wouldn't be struggling now.

As sore as I was at Pop, I couldn't stand the thought that he would be selling his office, little by little, to make ends meet. I wanted to help and that meant hocking the only thing I had of value: Mama's pearls.

I took them to a pawnshop I'd seen on the way to and from school, a small storefront that always sparkled with jewelry that told the sad tale of life since the war: a wedding ring had less value if the person who'd given it to you had gone away.

I lingered on the sidewalk for a long time as I tried to get up the courage to go inside. What would Mama think if she knew I'd sold her jewelry? Would she be proud of me for helping Pop out, or mad that I'd gotten rid of the one thing I had left of her?

What did it matter what she thought? If she wanted to dictate what I could and couldn't do, maybe she shouldn't have killed herself.

"How's Personal Hygiene?" said a voice just past my shoulder.

I turned to find Tom behind me. What was he doing there? Was he hoping to pawn something, or steal it? "It's fine," I said.

"You okay?"

I was crushing Mama's pearls in my hand. I eased my hold and dropped them in my pocket.

"What do you want?"

He put his hand on the display window and leaned against it. "I hear you used to go to Chapin."

My already sour mood gave me the strength to say what was on my mind for once. "Is that why you robbed me? Because you thought that if I used to go to private school it meant I had money?"

"Come again?"

"You heard me."

Before he could respond, the pawnbroker banged on the glass and gestured for us to move away. It was Tom that was the problem. He didn't want some thug scaring away his customers. "I better blow," he said.

"Yeah, you better."

He tossed a look my way but didn't say another word. If I hadn't known any better, I would've sworn he looked embarrassed.

I never got up the courage to go inside.

I told Pearl about the conversation over lunch. We sat together every day now, and walked home from school most afternoons.

"Why were you at a pawnshop?" she asked.

"I was just walking past," I said. "He didn't even have the

guts to apologize to me. I guess now I know why he talked to me on my first day of school. He was probably casing me. Did he seriously think that if I was rich I'd be going to this school?"

She mulled this over a mouthful of sandwich. "He just found out you went to Chapin."

"Huh?" I said.

"He didn't know that when he robbed you. He came into the office a few days ago and said he'd heard that someone who used to go to Chapin went here now. I told him it was you."

This was new. "Why did he want to know?"

She shrugged. "Beats me."

For the next three days I tried to linger in places where I knew Tom hung out, hoping he would appear and explain why he was so interested in Chapin, but it never happened. On the fourth day I arrived at school only to find Tom wasn't there. There was nothing new about that, of course, but his absence continued for five consecutive days.

"Have you noticed Tom Barney is missing again?" said Pearl during lunch about a week after I'd realized Tom was gone. We were in our usual spot at a table near the front of the cafeteria. She always brought her lunch, a strange concoction of sandwich, fruit, and some sort of dessert it was obvious her mother or grandmother had slaved over. I longed to try these confections—after all, sugar was becoming a scarcity—but I could tell that they were one of the only things Pearl could depend on to help her get through the day. She ate them so quickly, with such a ferocious hunger, that I had to wonder what would happen if one day she opened her plain brown bag and found they weren't there.

"What was he arrested for this time?" I asked.

"Nothing. He's actually missing. His mother met with Principal Deluca this morning."

"How do you know?"

"I saw her." Pearl studied me until her frown matched mine. "What's the matter? Are you worried about him?"

"Hardly." If anything I was irritated—I wanted to know why he'd been asking about Chapin and why he'd had the gall to rob me. "Why? Are you?"

She shifted her focus to what remained of her lunch. "No. Why would I be?"

The school that day was abuzz about the disappearance. Wild theories were tossed about wherever I went. Tom Barney had joined the Mob. He'd robbed the wrong person and paid for it with his life. He'd gone off to Hollywood. He was riding the rails. He was holed up somewhere drowning his sorrow in cheap booze over the breakup with Rhona. The only people who didn't seem to be talking about Tom were the Rainbows.

At least not in public.

The next day while I was in the cafeteria restroom doing my business, Rhona and Suze came in to touch up their makeup.

"I'll bet he went to the Jersey Shore again," said Suze. "He'll come back when he's ready. Just like last time."

At the sound of her voice, I stopped what I was doing. Unlike the restroom in the main hallway, these stalls mercifully had doors. Slowly, I pulled my feet off the floor.

"I don't know. I've got a bad feeling," said Rhona. Her voice was surprisingly gentle. I couldn't see her, but I was pretty sure I could hear tears weighing down her words. "I can't believe he hasn't called to let me know he's okay."

"Sorry, baby doll, but you aren't his to call anymore."

"Still . . ." Rhona was definitely crying. I shifted, hoping to catch a glimpse of her face through the crack in the door. The toilet seat groaned when I moved and all activity in the bathroom stopped. "Who's there?" asked Rhona. I didn't respond though I was certain they could hear my heartbeat.

"Let's make tracks," whispered Suze.

I waited ten minutes before following them out the door.

A week passed and Tom didn't reappear. Then another week, and another, until I was certain Tom Barney was gone for good.

I was just getting used to the idea that he wasn't coming back when one afternoon, a dour-faced freshman interrupted my typing class with one of the dreaded notes that directed a student to go to the office immediately.

"Iris Anderson," announced Miss Wisnieski, our instructor. She didn't need to finish her sentence, though she did anyway. "You're wanted in the front office."

There were two reasons you were called to the office: for discipline and for bad news. I wasn't the kind of girl who got into trouble. That meant, as everyone in the room probably knew, that bad news was waiting for me.

But what? Had something happened to Pop? "Should I take my things?"

She studied the note more closely, but apparently all the information it had to offer had already been communicated. "No. You may come back for them."

As thirty faces watched, I left the room with the slip clasped in my hand.

"Psst . . . Iris. Over here."

I followed the sound and found Pearl near the girls' bathroom. She waved me in and, once I was safely inside, blocked the door with her body.

"I'm supposed to go to the office," I said.

"You're kidding, right? I sent the note."

That's right. It was her study hall, when she worked in the attendance office. "You can do that?"

"Apparently so. It's my first time abusing my power." She beamed with the jolt of having done something forbidden. I would've been happy for her if I hadn't convinced myself the note meant something horrible had happened.

"So what's going on?" I asked.

"Your pop was here."

"At school?" She nodded. "How do you know?"

"Paul told me. He saw him right before lunch. He said he was trying to talk to the Rainbows."

How come I hadn't seen him? Probably because he didn't want to be seen by me.

"Do you think it has something to do with Tom Barney?" asked Pearl.

"I don't know." I was so dumbstruck that Pop had been at the school that I didn't know how to respond. Was he checking up on me? It wasn't possible. The only friends I'd mentioned to him were Paul and Pearl.

"Anyway, I thought you should know."

"How'd Paul know it was him?"

"Paul remembered seeing him the night we went to the Jive Hive." It was the prosthetic that had given him away. Try as he might to hide it, Pop's limp was the first thing you noticed about him. "Paul asked me if he was a cop, because I guess the Rainbows thought that was the case. And I told him, no, he's a private detective, and that you sometimes help him out. He was pretty impressed by that."

"What would my pop want with the Rainbows?"

"Your guess is as good as mine."

We waited out the period in the restroom, testing out theories of why Pop was there. When the bell rang, I grabbed my things and headed home. I was dying to find out what he was up to, but it looked like any fact-finding was going to have to wait. Pop was in the office with the door closed when I arrived home. And he wasn't alone.

Through the vent I eyeballed a man and woman. The woman's face was long and horselike, her eyes underscored by bags so dark I would've thought they were makeup if it wasn't clear she avoided the stuff on the rest of her face. Her husband was round, his face ruddy. They didn't look like the kind of people who could afford a detective.

"Here's the photo you asked for," said the woman. From her pocketbook she produced a small, framed picture.

Pop took it, gave it the once-over, and set it on the desk. "And this is how he looked at the time he disappeared?"

The man and woman exchanged an indecipherable look. "Not exactly," said the woman. "The photographer made him put on that getup. He was fit to be tied, I'll tell you. He wanted to wear that awful zoot suit of his, but the school was having none of it."

Zoot suit? So Pop *had* been to school because of Tom. And these must be his parents.

The man I believed to be Mr. Barney looked at Pop through lowered lids; now that I knew who he was, I saw the resemblance between him and his son. "Did you have any luck today?"

"I talked to a few of his friends and got access to his locker. Does the address 240 Houston Street mean anything to you?"

"No," said the woman. "Why?"

"Someone left a note in his locker with that address. *If you're serious, meet me at 240 Houston Street #7D at 4:00.* It's something to follow up on, anyway," said Pop.

"And how much is that going to cost me?" asked Mr. Barney.

"Frank!" said his wife.

"This is ridiculous, Louise. You know it and I know it. The no-good kid has run off."

"But he wouldn't do that. Not our Tom."

Mr. Barney shook his head. "He hasn't been our Tom for a while."

"He was always such a good boy. Never gave us trouble. And then two years ago he got these new friends and suddenly he was talking back, breaking curfew, and going to those . . . places."

Mr. Barney leaned toward Pop. "Negro clubs."

"He said they went there to dance. They liked the music. In any case, we didn't approve," said Mrs. Barney. "Those are dangerous places. We've heard stories."

"Drugs. Drinking," said Mr. Barney.

"You didn't tell me he'd been arrested for stealing," said Pop.

Mr. and Mrs. Barney exchanged another look. "It wasn't his fault. He was forced into it."

"Louise—" said Mr. Barney.

"You know it's true. Tom's not a thief."

"According to the school secretary, he admitted it," said

Pop. "And spent a week at a detention center. I'm surprised he wasn't expelled."

The Barneys exchanged a look. Even from my vantage I could read it: they'd begged the school to take him back.

"How were things at home after that?" asked Pop.

"How do you think?" said Mr. Barney. "I let him know that that was the last straw. I wasn't fixing things for him anymore. One more mistake and he was out of our house for good."

Pop's chair squeaked as he leaned back in it. "Then isn't it possible that's what happened here? He made a mistake and took off, knowing he wouldn't be welcomed home?"

"That's what I've been saying since the beginning," said Mr. Barney. "The kid screwed up and didn't want to pay the piper."

"He wouldn't run away. He wouldn't do that to me," said Mrs. Barney.

But he had run away before, if what I'd overheard Suze say was accurate.

"I think we're done here," said Mr. Barney. His chair creaked as he started to stand.

Mrs. Barney grabbed onto him and pulled him down. "Please, Frank—we need to find him. I can't take another month of this. If something's happened to him, if some-one's hurt him, we need to know that."

"Okay, okay—stop with the tears already." Mr. Barney

passed his wife his handkerchief. "What did those kids he hangs out with tell you?"

"Not much," said Pop. "They're scared. They're terrified they're going to get into trouble."

"This isn't about them!" Mrs. Barney's voice rose into a shriek. I jumped at the sound, accidentally rattling the door vent. They all looked my way. Slowly, so as not to make any other noise, I backed away from the door and prepared to bolt. "I'm sorry," said Mrs. Barney. "I forgot myself. It just seems to me that if they're his friends, they'd want to help."

"Don't give up hope," said Pop. "They have to know that Tom's disappearance is going to bring them under close scrutiny. And they'll eventually realize how much more suspicious their silence makes them seem."

Would they? It seemed to me that they'd never talk to Pop unless they trusted him, and that wasn't going to happen. He was an adult, after all.

Which was precisely why he needed my help. There was nothing dangerous about roaming the school halls and trying to find out what the scoop on Tom was. And I was bound to be loads more successful at it than Pop. I was innocuous and supposed to be there. He stood out like a lion in a den of cubs.

"I've only been on the job a week. Time has a way of working in our favor in cases like these," said Pop. "Eventually, one of them is going to make a mistake and lead us to your son. You can count on it."

"And what do we do until then?" asked Mrs. Barney.

"We wait," said Pop.

THE BARNEYS LEFT TEN MINUTES LATER. By then I'd planted myself on the sofa and was humming with so much excitement that my legs were vibrating.

Pop walked them to the door and then turned to face me. "You're home."

"Only for a few minutes." I could tell he was trying to analyze what sort of mood I was in. I decided to play it cool. Not cold, but clearly not interested in anything he might've been up to, either. If he was going to let me work on Tom's case, it needed to be his idea.

"How was your day?"

"A little strange. A boy's gone missing and it's all anyone's talking about." I picked up the radio guide and flipped through it like I was looking for something more interesting to entertain myself with. "I heard you were at school today," I said.

"How'd you hear that?"

"Paul saw you. He remembered you from the night you walked me to his house." I deliberated how to play the next part. I could mention Tom by name, or I could let Pop introduce the topic. The latter made more sense to me. "Am I in trouble or something?"

He seemed surprised at the question. And a little re-lieved. "No. There was some paperwork they needed. Records from Chapin. I thought it would be easier to bring it over in person."

"Oh." To say I was disappointed was like saying Frank Sinatra was okay-looking. Seriously? He expected me to be-lieve that lie? "New clients?"

"Old clients come for a follow-up."

I ground my teeth. My previous attempt to thaw failed and I could feel the ice returning to my spine and shoul-ders.

He thumped his fingers on the fireplace mantel. "Are you all right?"

I offered him a tight, false smile. "Of course. Why wouldn't I be?"

He didn't join us for dinner that night.

I WAS SO STEAMED I was willing to let Pop flounder on the case. Let him hit a dead end and tell the Barneys they had to take their business elsewhere. But as the evening wore on and reality set in, I knew he couldn't afford another failure. My pride wasn't worth us missing another month's rent. He wasn't going to ask me for my help—I had to accept that. After telling me to stay out of the business before, he couldn't go back and tell me he'd changed his mind. After all, it had to have hurt his pride to need his fifteen-year-old daughter's assistance. But what if I were to do a little work on my own, just to see if there was anything worthwhile to be found?

Things looked slightly more fraught in the light of the next day. It was all well and good to say I was going to investigate Tom's disappearance, but how did I expect to pull it off? A normal girl would've just put her ear to the ground and asked her friends for the scoop, but I was an outsider. How on earth could I expect a bunch of cool cats who'd barely looked my way to confide in me? Sure, there was Suze, who'd at least talked to me, but even she was bound to get suspicious if I went up to her and started quizzing her about Tom.

Especially if she put two and two together and realized that the private eye who'd been interrogating the Rainbows was the father I claimed was still at war.

7

I SPENT MOST OF THAT first morning trying to come up with a plan of attack. By lunch I had . . . nothing. I was desperately unprepared.

"What's eating you?" asked Pearl.

"Tom Barney's parents came to see my pop yesterday."

Her eyes grew enormous behind her Coke-bottle lenses. She set down the cookie she was about to devour and gave me her complete attention. I let it all out then—well, most of it. I didn't tell her that I was looking into things without Pop's blessing. Or how worried I was about money. Instead, I focused on how ill-equipped Pop was to find out anything from the Rainbows. She waited until I was done before responding.

"So that's why he was here yesterday. You are so lucky."

"Lucky or not, I don't know how to find out any more than what we already know."

"Your sources are right there." She jerked her head toward where the Rainbows were sitting.

"Sure, I'll just go up to them and ask where Tom is."

"You said Suze talked to you once before, right?" I nodded. It was twice, actually, but who was counting? "So see if you can't get her to do it again."

I thought about it for a minute. Pop said that one of the reasons I screwed up the Wilson case was I didn't stay invisible. Pop knew how to charm information out of people—he did it all the time. It was all about ingratiating yourself to them. You had to make them want to tell you stuff.

Asking about Tom straight out would definitely tip my hand, but that didn't mean that Suze couldn't be a way to get information. She'd been nice to me because of our connection—both of us were suffering the agonizing uncertainty of having loved ones off to war, or so she thought. I could ask her about Bill again, but coming out of the blue that might seem strange. No, if I was going to get her to talk to me, it had to be because *I* had received some news.

It was, in many ways, the perfect setup. After all, I'd been pulled out of typing class the day before. As far as anyone knew, the news could've been delivered then.

I didn't tell Pearl my scheme. I didn't want to admit that the tenuous connection I had with Suze was built on a big fat lie. And I certainly didn't want my one friend to know that I was about to play on Suze's sympathy by claiming that I had bad news about Pop.

Fortunately, Pearl had to leave before the lunch period ended.

"I'll find out if there's any other talk in the attendance office," she told me as she packed up the cookie she still hadn't eaten. "Meet me after school on the steps."

"Sure."

As Pearl exited, Suze, Rhona, and a third girl headed for the girls' restroom. The hot lunch that day was liver and onions—the liver was cold in the middle, and the onions hadn't been cooked at all. I'd pushed the onions to the side when I ate, having no desire to eat them raw and reek of them all afternoon. When the girls made their exit, I shoved the onions into my napkin and gently blotted the gravy from them. Once they were more white than brown, I squeezed them until their juice oozed through my fingers. Just in case anyone was watching, I feigned dropping something under the table, and when I bent down to pick it up, I pressed my onion-soaked fingers against the corners of my eyes.

I hadn't been prepared for the stinging. Or for the smell.

The onions worked their magic, though. Instantly, I had a face full of tears. I picked up my things, clutched a napkin to my cheek, and entered the girls' bathroom.

All three girls were smoking. The cigarette smoke combined with the onion fumes was pure agony.

"Oh, sorry," I said between tears that had progressed from pretend to real. "Is it all right if I . . . ?"

Rhona shrugged. The girl I didn't know exhaled a plume of smoke. Suze said, "Go on, baby."

I eased myself into a stall and tried to figure out what to do next. Hadn't they noticed my tears? Or had I miscalculated and smeared liver gravy down my face?

I wiped my cheek with a tissue to check for signs of food. My face was clean. I put my fingers against my eyes again and reignited the water. I sniffed, I sighed, and when that failed to stir any reaction, I blew my nose as loudly as possible.

The warning bell rang. We had ten minutes to get back to class. "You coming, Suze?" asked the nameless girl.

"I'm right behind you," she said.

The door groaned opened and closed. My eyes longed to be flushed with water. I eased out of the stall and found Suze waiting for me.

"Everything copacetic?"

"I . . ." I squeezed my eyes tight and willed more tears. They didn't come, and so I forced my mind to wander to the saddest thought it held: Mama. That did the trick. No longer did I need onions and cigarette smoke. The emotion was real now. "No. Not really."

"Did something happen to your pop?"

I nodded to let her know that yes, that's exactly what was upsetting me. "He's been wounded."

"Oh, no."

"We got a telegram yesterday. They pulled me out of

typing class to tell me. I can't stop thinking about him." I was a terrible person. At least part of it was true. I *had* been pulled out of class and Pop *had* been injured. It had just happened ten months before.

"Are they sending him home?"

"They didn't say. I don't know how bad it is. I don't know if he can come home. I don't know if he might . . ." My voice trailed off.

"Oh, baby, you must be sick inside." She put her arm around me and I breathed in the scent of My Sin perfume and baby powder. Sick inside? She didn't know the half of it. Someone knocked on the bathroom door and with the authoritarian tone of a teacher told us to clear out and head back to class.

"You better go," I said. The onion was getting more potent, turning my waterworks into a waterfall. I tried to stop the flow, but without some water and alone time, that wasn't going to happen anytime soon.

Suze got a wad of toilet paper from the stall and passed it my way. "I can't leave you like this. You got someone you can talk to?"

I hesitated before shaking my head.

"Well, now you do. Meet me on the front steps after school. And try not to think too much between now and then. Seriously, baby—it won't help anyone." She wrinkled her nose and took in a whiff of air. "Do you smell onions?"

I mopped my eyes and shook my head.

"Must be this whole damn place. I can't stand it when they serve liver and onions. Even when I don't eat it, it follows me wherever I go."

THE CLOCK COULDN'T MOVE fast enough. I had no idea how I was going to get Suze to talk about Tom, but that didn't matter at the moment. Maybe I couldn't get everything I needed in one day. This afternoon might be about building trust. Once she and I were true friends, I could figure out how to find out everything Pop might need to know.

I worried she might've forgotten about me at the end of the day—after all, it had been four hours since we last spoke—but after school she was waiting for me just where she said she would be. And she wasn't alone—Rhona and the nameless girl who'd been with them in the restroom were with her.

"Hi," I said, feeling uncomfortable that my audience of one had grown to three. The two girls gave me the once-over, their eyes at half-mast. The idea of spending time with me was clearly not high on their list of things they wanted to do. *Don't worry*, I wanted to tell them, *I'm not looking forward to this, either.*

From the corner of my eye I saw Pearl exit the school. She had a book with her and settled down on a bench to wait for me.

"Hope you don't mind, but Rhona and Maria wanted to join us," said Suze. So that was the girl's name—Maria. I wasn't aware there was a destination for this meeting, but the group started walking and I trailed along, wondering how on earth I could ask the three of them about Tom without appearing like I was digging for information.

It was obvious I couldn't. At the very least Rhona wouldn't appreciate my interest in her ex-boyfriend.

Rhona poked a thumb over her shoulder. "Aren't you friends with that girl over there? Pearl Harbor?"

She and Maria shared a giggle.

"Not really."

"I always see you two eating lunch together."

"She's tutoring me," I said.

"In what?" asked Rhona. "How to gain fifty pounds?"

I wanted to defend Pearl, but I had a feeling that would do little to endear me to them.

"Why do you call her that?" I asked.

"Because she's gotten big enough to be a target from the air," said Rhona. "And she's the worst disaster to ever strike the U.S. on its own soil."

"Rhona's just sore because Pearl was going around telling everyone she was knocked up last year," said Maria.

Rhona shot her a look that should have struck her dead.

"Are you sure it was her?" I asked. "She doesn't strike me as a gossip."

"Trust me—your little friend is more than happy to go around talking about me and anyone else who catches her eye." Rhona stepped toward me until I could smell the cigarette still on her breath. She put her index finger into the center of my chest and pushed with so much force that I had to fight to stay upright. "You tell her that the next time she opens her mouth to say my name, she's going to find my fist in it."

"Shush," said Suze. Rhona lifted her finger and looked ready to deliver another blow to my sternum when Suze shot her a look that made her instantly step away from me.

Was Suze defending Pearl? Or me?

My chest burned where Rhona had poked it. I rubbed the spot, certain I was going to find a hole that went all the way through me. "I'm sorry she said stuff about you. Her brother was killed in the spring," I said. "I think that's why she eats so much." As soon as the words came out of my mouth, I wished I could take them back. I shouldn't be talking about Pearl, not even if I thought I was defending her. I certainly wouldn't have been happy if Pearl was going around telling everyone her theories about why I acted the way I did.

Maria rolled her eyes. "What a bringdown."

"Grief does weird things to people," said Suze.

Rhona's scowl remained fixed. Nobody in high school wanted to be talked about. Nobody.

"I'm sorry about your pops," said Maria. "What branch is he?"

"Navy," I said.

She lit a cigarette, discarding the match on the pavement beneath her.

"Rhona's got a Navy boyfriend," said Suze.

I saw my opportunity and leaped at it. "I thought you went with that boy Tom Barney."

"Not anymore. He took off and I took up with someone new." Rhona threw her head back and laughed. The other girls echoed the sound. "It's about time I found someone more mature."

"Rhona's Jim is twenty-three," said Maria.

"Wow," I said, unable to hide my surprise. Could this really be the same girl who'd been crying about Tom just a few weeks before?

I realized they were all staring at me. How long had I been musing on this in silence? "How old is Bill?" I asked Suze.

"Nineteen," she said. "He graduated last year."

"And what about you?" I asked Maria. "Do you have a boyfriend who's joined up?"

"Maria likes a little chocolate in her milk," said Rhona. "She goes with a boy from a colored school."

"But he's talking about enlisting when he graduates," said Maria. It was funny how defensive she sounded. What was so great about dating someone who had joined up? It wasn't like you could step out with them once they were overseas. Wouldn't you rather they were here, safe with you?

As though she'd heard my thoughts, Suze told Maria, "Don't wish for it. Staying home doesn't make him less of a man."

"And it won't turn him pale, either," said Rhona. "You stuck on someone?" It took me a minute to realize the question was directed at me, and even longer to figure out what she meant.

"No," I said. "I mean, I don't really know anyone."

"That'll change," said Suze.

The group turned and entered Normandie's Pharmacy on Catherine Street. Suze snagged a booth in the back and we each slid across the red leather upholstery, Maria and Rhona on one side, Suze and me on the other. "You like egg creams?" Suze asked me.

"Sure." I didn't have any money on me, and even if I did, I could hardly afford to spend it on soda. "I think I'll just have a glass of water," I said.

"Don't worry—it's my treat," said Suze. She held up four fingers and the man behind the counter caught her signal and nodded his acknowledgment. Across from him, the pharmacist worked with a mortar and pestle to crush pills into a powder.

Rhona killed her cigarette and lit a fresh one. Maria

followed suit. They both looked my way like I was a circus animal they were hoping would entertain them. Why had they come? Had Suze suggested they join her just in case spending time with me bored her to death?

Maria leaned over and whispered something to Rhona. The two women slid out of the booth, telling Suze they'd be right back.

"They don't like me," I said.

"Rhona's just sore about Pearl. And Maria doesn't like anyone Rhona doesn't like."

"So was it true?"

Suze shrugged. "About Pearl being behind the rumor? Who knows? Rhona wants to blame someone, so she blames your friend. And if Pearl gets the blame, so does anyone who knows her."

I thought about once again claiming that Pearl wasn't my friend, but I didn't want to feed Suze another lie, not when I was hoping she'd be honest with me.

"Maybe I should go." I slid toward the edge of the booth and dragged my purse after me.

Suze snagged my bag and gently pulled me back. "They don't know you, baby. That's all. When you're a senior, fresh meat seems like a thousand years ago."

"So why did they come?"

"Rhona wants to talk to me and didn't want to wait. Where Rhona goes, Maria goes." Her eyes drifted toward the ladies', where the two girls had disappeared. How many hours did they spend in public restrooms? "Don't worry about them. Let's talk about you. You feeling better?"

I shrugged, uncertain of how far to take this charade. "Just scared, I guess. I don't know whether to hope there's another telegram at home or to be terrified of the same thing. I almost didn't come to school today."

It was a telegram that had told us Pop's fate right after Pearl Harbor. I had come home from Chapin to find Mama in tears, the brief scrap of paper clenched in her hands. She never let me read it. Instead, she told me what it said, trying to frame it as potentially good news since it meant Pop finally got to come home for good.

I remember wanting to share her tears, but I couldn't find it in me to cry. Instead, I buried my head in her shoulder and pretended to sob until Mama's own tears dried up. It was the last time she ever held me.

"I was that way when all Bill was giving me was radio silence," said Suze. "But you can't sit home and suffer. It doesn't change the way things are going to turn out, you dig? Besides, they got you out of class once for news. If there was more, they would've done it again." Suze was so mature. I always assumed public school girls grew at a different rate, lacking access to knowledge those of us of privilege were exposed to. But while it was clear that I might have been more book smart than the average girl at P.S. 110, they possessed a world-weariness that made me seem like a baby in comparison.

"Right," I said. "But it's not like I have much choice. All I have is home and school." *And Pearl*, I should've said.

"Not anymore, baby—you've got me."

I raised an eyebrow. "Come on now, Suze. It's swell of you to take care of me like this, but you have to admit, you don't want to spend every afternoon babysitting someone like me."

She cocked her head to the right. "How old do you think I am?"

"Eighteen?"

"Try sixteen."

"How come—?"

"I'm hanging with the big fish? You don't choose your friends, they choose you."

Suze was sixteen, only a year older than me. And yet with all our differences, she might as well have had a hundred years on me.

"You're still thinking like a private school girl, where everyone stays in their neat little rows, wearing their pressed plaid skirts. You've got to get out and live a little, baby. It'll take your mind off your pops and it will make the day go a heck of a lot faster."

"You're right," I said. "I'd like that."

The dark-skinned soda jerk came over with a tray of glasses. He set the four egg creams on the table and offered Suze a wink. "You off today, Suze?"

"Yeah, Reggie."

"You work here?" I asked after Reggie had disappeared.

"Only three days a week." She played with one of her wooden bracelets. "It's mainly coffee and doughnuts, but it's enough to keep me in clothes and out of trouble. You got a job?"

I shook my head no.

"Must be nice," she said in a way that made me wish I'd invented something.

"I guess most everyone at P.S. 110 works, right?" I said. How could I turn the conversation around to Tom?

"Some do, some don't—just like anywhere else. You know what—you should come out with us Friday night," said Suze.

My heart skipped a beat. What did they do on Friday nights? Prowl the streets? Rob the elderly? Shoplift? "Are you sure Rhona and Maria want me to?"

"I'm asking, not them."

I tried to squelch the excitement building inside me. "What about the others? Won't they mind?"

"What others?"

"Those boys I always see you with. Tom Barney and those two Italians?"

"Tommy's AWOL. As for the other cats, they do what they want to do, just like us."

"What do you mean Tom's AWOL?"

"Absent without leave. He's been missing for weeks now."

"Missing? Is he all right?"

"Knowing Tommy, he's fine. School's not his game. He'll come back when he's ready."

The questions I wanted to ask fought for supremacy. Before I could decide which one to voice first, Rhona and Maria returned.

"When who's ready?" asked Rhona. She claimed an egg cream for herself and downed the first sip, smearing a crescent moon of bright red lip cream on the edge of the glass.

"Tommy," said Suze.

Rhona's eyes narrowed. "What are you talking about him for?"

"Iris was asking why he hasn't been around."

"Why?" asked Rhona. "You interested?"

I blushed. "I was just curious. I hadn't seen him for a while."

"Tommy goes where Tommy goes," said Rhona. "Don't hold your breath waiting for him to reappear. Pity, though; you are his type."

What did that mean?

"Thank God that crippled private eye didn't reappear," said Maria. "I thought for sure he'd be waiting for us outside the cafeteria again."

"I told you I'd take care of it," said Rhona.

I concentrated on my drink, hoping that by doing so they wouldn't notice that I'd turned as red as Rhona's lip cream.

"Tell Suze what you did," said Maria.

"I picked up the horn, made a call." Maria gave her a look that made it clear that this explanation was insufficient. Rhona rolled her eyes and pantomimed lifting a phone receiver. "Hello, Principal Deluca? This is Mrs. Randall Hyatt, Rhona Hyatt's mother. I understand that you've permitted male strangers to harass young women on campus. This is unacceptable, and if it doesn't stop immediately I will go to the school board about it."

"You didn't!" said Suze.

"She most certainly did," said Maria.

"What did he say?"

"It was hard to tell with all the stuttering and back-pedaling, but he apologized and promised my dear mother that it wouldn't happen again." She finished the egg cream in a single gulp and pulled a handful of change from her purse. With a clatter she deposited two dimes on the table, then gestured to Maria to follow suit. "We've got to blow. I'll catch up with you later, Suze." She offered me a wide smile that stopped at her eyes. "See you around, Iris."

"What did I do?" I asked as soon as they were gone.

"It's not you, baby. It's Tommy. She's worried about him and she doesn't like talking about it."

I couldn't let that pass without comment. "If she's so worried about him, why has she taken up with someone else?"

"That's her pride talking. If he's safe and avoiding her,

she wants to punish him by showing him that she's moved on. The truth is, she's sick about it."

That had certainly been corroborated by what I'd over-heard. "So is that who the private eye was asking about? Tommy?"

"I wasn't there, but from what everyone else said, he was the one and only topic."

"Wow." I stirred the dregs at the bottom of my drink. It was almost solid chocolate down there. "No wonder she's upset."

"He probably just took a powder. He's done it before. Of course, those times he always told Rhona where he was going. I think that's what worries her the most."

"What could keep him away for so long?"

"It's hard to say. He could've done something bad, got-ten pinched, and decided it was better to stay gone than face his pops."

"His old man's strict?"

"Tight as a girdle. It's amazing Tommy can breathe some days. He has an older brother who wound up in the joint and his pops is convinced Tommy's going to do the same."

I wished I could take notes, but there was no way that was going to happen without drawing suspicion. Maybe that was why the Rainbows hadn't wanted to talk to Pop: they believed Tom wanted to stay lost.

"But if Tom was lying low until the heat was off him, don't you think he'd try to contact one of you?" I asked.

"That's what I'm hoping. At the very least, he'd need cash."

"What about the money from the locker thefts?"

"That was used for something else."

I was dying to ask what that something else was, but I could tell I was quickly approaching the point of asking too much. Besides, there was only so much Suze was going to be able to tell me. The person who knew Tommy, who could best guess at his whereabouts, was Rhona. She was the one I needed to talk to.

"You feeling better?" asked Suze.

"Much. Haven't thought about my pop for a half hour now."

"So come out with us on Friday. See if you feel like spreading your wings a bit. If nothing else, you'll be giving your mind a rest."

"What do you on Friday nights?" I asked.

"Dance, of course. It's the only way to end the week."

"Where do you go?" I asked.

"The land of darkness. It's the best place for it, baby girl."

A thrill passed through me. She was talking about Harlem. I'd never been there before. It was forbidden territory, not because anyone had ever told me not to go there, but because I knew that it wasn't the kind of place young white girls went. And now *I* was going there.

Rhona would be there on Friday, and maybe by then in

her eyes I wouldn't be the odd little girl following her crowd. I'd think things through between now and then— what to ask and how to ask it. I'd have a plan. I'd find out why she was worried about Tom.

"All right," I said. "Just tell me where to meet you."

8

I WAS ITCHING WITH QUESTIONS by the time I got home that day. What had Tom done with the money from the locker thefts? How could Rhona be both concerned about Tom and willing to take up with someone else to teach him a lesson? Why had she said I was Tom's type?

"Hi," I told Pop as I came in the door. His own door was open, giving him a clear view of me as I arrived. I wondered if it was deliberate; perhaps he no longer wanted to be surprised by my comings and goings.

"Hello yourself," he said. He had a stack of phone directories in front of him. "How was school?"

"Fine. What are you working on?"

"Trying to track down a missing person for an attorney handling a will. If I find her, she has quite a bit of money coming her way."

I couldn't tell if it was the truth or if he was doing something to help chase down Tom.

"You had a phone call from Grace Dunwitty. I told her I'd have you call her when you got home." He pushed a piece of paper my way with Grace's exchange scrawled on it. "She said she's called before."

"I know." I waited for him to say something more, to, at the very least, ask me if I was avoiding Grace, but it wasn't in Pop's nature to pry into my life. Besides, if he did, it might give me permission to pry into his. And then what? Would I ask him what it was like to have only one leg? Or if he missed Mama as much as I did?

"You ever see those kids you went to that club with?" he asked.

"I eat lunch with Pearl almost every day." I saw my chance and grabbed at it. "In fact, she asked me to go out again this Friday."

"Where?"

"A dance." It was sort of the truth. After all, there would be dancing.

Pop nodded. "Sounds good. They seemed like nice kids."

How would he know? He hadn't even bothered to talk to them.

He didn't ask anything else. Not where the dance was, not how late I'd be. I should've been thrilled, but I was strangely disappointed. For a man who refused to let me work for him because he was worried about my safety, he was curiously nonchalant about the whole thing. Maybe it just didn't occur to him that high school kids could get

127

themselves into trouble, despite what Tom Barney's disappearance implied.

"Here." He passed me a pile of rumpled bills he'd unearthed from his pants pocket.

"What's this?"

"What does it look like? If you're going to a dance, you need a new dress, right?"

I stared at the money, simultaneously touched and uncomfortable. Was this part of the retainer from Tom's parents? Or had he pawned something else? "Thanks, but I'm okay."

"Take it, Iris. You deserve a treat."

He turned his attention to the newspaper in front of him. War news. There were numbers on the front page, never a good sign. I knew what those digits meant: lives lost, boats sunk, planes downed. Numbers never meant anything good. Victories were reported with vague, verb-heavy language like "pushed back," "taken over," "captured," and "defeated."

"How long do you think it will last?" I asked Pop.

He looked at the front page, wondering, I'm sure, what had inspired the question. "It's hard to say. The Germans and Japanese are good fighters. It could end tomorrow." I read between the lines. They weren't just good enough to beat us; they could do it fast.

"So they're better than we are?"

"They're more prepared. They've been at this longer. We

have a lot of catching up to do. Our military wasn't ready for this."

"But we can catch up?"

"Maybe."

This was one of those moments when I hated that Pop didn't immediately think he needed to reassure me. Would it hurt him to tell one little white lie to help me sleep better at night? "Do you think the draft is a bad idea?" I asked.

"I think eighteen and nineteen is awfully young. But it won't affect me—what do you think about it?"

"I don't know."

I didn't have time to worry about it. I had other things to focus on. Things like going to a dance club in Harlem and finding out about Tom Barney.

PEARL WAS WAITING FOR ME outside the cafeteria the next day. "What happened to you yesterday? I waited for you after school."

"I'm so sorry," I told her as we entered the lunchroom and claimed our usual spot. Her lunch bag bulged with delectable offerings. What would it be today? Cake? Pie? Chocolate doughnuts? "I actually ended up going with Suze to Normandie's after school."

"Seriously?" she asked. "How did you arrange that?"

"I went into the restroom pretending I was crying. She stuck around after Rhona and Maria left and asked me what the matter was." I couldn't tell her the whole truth, but I needed to provide some sort of explanation for how I'd wrangled an invitation. "I told her I was just so lonely since starting public school. I hadn't made any friends."

"And that did it?"

I didn't blame her for her disbelief. Hollywood would've rejected that scene as too dull to be believed. "That did it."

"Wow." She let this roll about her head for a moment. I expected more questions, but she decided to let it drop. "Did she talk about Tom?"

"A little, after school. I mean, I couldn't tell her why I was asking, not if I wanted her to be open about it."

"Or honest about it. You can't trust the Rainbows. Remember that."

I don't know why, but Pearl's comment irritated me. Yes, they had a bad reputation, but the Rainbows had their good qualities.

And besides, her need to remind me that some of them were dishonest made me wonder if what Rhona said Pearl had done was true. It was hard to believe that everyone stopped talking to her just because her brother died. Being a gossip, on the other hand, might've sealed her fate.

"Do they know where he is?" she asked.

"Not yet." I chased a pea around my plate. "Did you know Tom's brother?"

She pursed her lips. They were dusted with sandwich

crumbs that I longed to tell her to wipe away. "Yeah. His name's Michael. He was in my brother's class."

Her dead brother's class. "Were they friends?"

"Not particularly. Michael was always a troublemaker. Peter was pretty straitlaced."

Peter. It was the first time she'd said her other brother's name out loud.

She pulled out a folder and slid it across the table to me. "What's this?"

She raised an eyebrow. "What do you think?"

I lifted the edge and saw Tommy's name typed on an official-looking form. "You pulled his student record?" My irritation at her instantly lifted.

Pearl put her finger to her lips, like I needed a reminder that this was on the q.t. "I need to get it back by the end of the day. Think you can do that?"

"Absolutely." The boredom I'd been expecting to face that afternoon instantly washed away. The topmost page of the file was Tom's schedule, written in Pearl's familiar sloping scrawl. "Did you do this?" I asked.

She nodded. "I thought it might be helpful for you to see what classes he was in. They keep the schedules filed separately and I couldn't get into that cabinet."

"Do you memorize everyone's schedule?"

"Of course not." She played with the lid from her milk bottle.

But she knew his, and a thousand other details about him. I couldn't believe it had taken me so long to put two and two together: Pearl liked Tom. And not just a little bit.

"So are you going to go out with Suze after school again?" she asked me.

"I'm not planning to. Actually, I'm going to go out with them on Friday to see if I can't find out more."

"Them?"

"Suze, Rhona, Maria, and those two Italian guys who are always with them."

"Oh." She unwrapped the rest of her bag's offerings. A piece of coffee cake glistening with translucent icing was among its contents. "How did that happen?"

"I don't know. She just asked if I wanted to go and I said yes."

She continued staring at her lunch. "Where are you going?"

"Dancing. At a club. In Harlem."

She looked up and her eyes grew wider than Little Orphan Annie's. "A negro club?"

"I think it's a black and tan. Otherwise, how could we get in?" I felt like an old pro, using the lingo I'd seen in the movies and read in the magazines.

She removed the cake from its waxed paper cocoon and took a bite. "That should be interesting." She licked her fingers clean and dug into the bag for a napkin. "I've always wanted to go to Harlem."

Did she expect me to invite her to go with us? I tried to ignore her fishing expedition and concentrate on my own lunch. "I'd invite you, but that might seem strange. After all, I cried about not having any friends."

"Oh, I know. I'm just saying that I'd like to go *sometime*." She took another bite of cake. I wished she'd use a fork, or at the very least stop licking her fingers after every bite. "Want some?" she asked.

"No, thanks." I needed to clear things up with her, just so if it became an issue, there wouldn't be a problem. "Were you ever friends with Rhona?"

She looked like she was about to laugh. "Um, no. You've met me, right?"

She had a point. "Did you start the rumor that Rhona was pregnant last year?"

A V formed between her eyes. "Why would you ask that?"

"She seemed to think you had."

"You talked about me?"

"She'd seen us together and asked about you."

"So you told her she's nuts, right?"

Was she? It didn't escape my notice that Pearl hadn't denied the accusation. If she had a crush on Tom and Tom had started seeing Rhona, ruining the reputation of his new girlfriend might have seemed like a great idea. "I didn't exactly know you back then, Pearl. I mean, if she was talking about something that happened last week, sure, I'd defend you. But this was a year ago."

She let the cake fall back to its wrapping. "I'm the same person I was a year ago."

That was impossible. Even if her brother hadn't died and her weight hadn't ballooned, no one was exactly the same person they were a year ago. "I just changed the subject," I told her. "But I thought you should know that Rhona thinks the story started with you. She seemed pretty upset about it."

"Well, thanks, I guess. For letting me know." She wrapped up the cake. She was done with it. Whatever appetite she'd had had been killed the minute I mentioned Rhona. "I should return the file by the end of the day. Can you meet me right after school?"

"Absolutely," I told her.

I SPENT THE AFTERNOON with Tom's file hidden inside my American History textbook. There was a lot to go through. The first pages were his attendance records, meticulously filled out in blue ink. In the past year and a half, he'd racked up almost thirty days of unexplained absences, and an equal number of tardies. Letters had been sent home, the carbon copies of which were retained for his file. After stating his concern over Tommy's extraordinary number of days away, Principal Deluca asked for an explanation and a meeting. In return he got letters that had clearly been forged. Tom's "mother" described a number of health problems plaguing her son, ranging from colds and infections to much more dire things like polio and rubella. There was also a record of at least one phone call from Mrs. Barney, though it was clear from the notes pinned to the message slip that the recipient had doubts about whom they were talking to. Whoever it was reiterated poor Tom's failing health and promised to give her son a good talking-to about the importance of completing his education.

You could almost hear the laughter those letters and that call had to cause, especially for the people writing them (Suze? Rhona? Whoever it was dotted their i's with a small circle). Eventually, the principal seemed to realize that the meetings he requested were never going to happen and the letters he sent would always be intercepted. Although he continued to write to Tom's parents, the tone in the most recent letters changed from that of one authority figure addressing another to that of a concerned administrator addressing a student whom he wasn't quite ready to give up on. "While I am sympathetic to the changes that have occurred in Thomas's life over the past year, I do hope he understands that continued absences might result in his failing to graduate with his class. I would hate for him to have to repeat a grade, especially since his work shows such promise when he does bother to step into the classroom."

He wasn't exaggerating Tom's potential. The proof was in the next several pages in the folder: Tom's report cards. Given his friends, I would've expected a slew of C's and an occasional D or F, but Tom was almost exclusively a B student. In the area that allowed for teacher commentary, instructor after instructor lauded his innate intelligence while taking him to task for not applying himself. Three years before, when he was still Paul Levine's best friend and preferred pressed pants to the zoot, his grades had been A's.

The last items in the folder were a slew of discipline reports, authored by teachers who'd broken up fights in the hall. While Tom was present at each incident, along with two other boys, he never received any disciplinary action. Why? Had his friends insisted he was an innocent bystander and saw to it that he got off?

It was impossible to tell for sure, though one teacher hinted at a possible explanation in his description of a fight Tom had been present at. "It's a shame Mr. Barney continues to associate with troublemakers and ne'er-do-wells. It's obvious that he possesses a slippery moral character that makes him fall easily under the influence and sway of others. While I have no doubt he was not a participant in the above-described activity, especially given eyewitness statements, it's clear he wishes himself to be thought a thug capable of these grievous offenses. It pains me to think what may become of him in another year or two if he continues down this path."

If that was true, maybe he had committed the locker thefts to prove he was just as tough as his friends?

It was enough to make my head spin.

So what had I learned? Tom Barney was smart, liked to skip school, and wanted to be where the action was. Even though nobody had ever seen him do anything wrong—or at least had the courage to report that they had—he wanted people to think he was as tough as the boys he associated with.

How did someone who defined himself through the opinions of others just disappear?

I MET PEARL at four o'clock on the school steps. With the kind of discretion Sherlock Holmes would've killed for, I slid the folder inside my American History book and exchanged her text for mine.

"Thanks," I said. "That was swell of you."

We fell into step together and headed toward the office. "Learn anything?" she asked.

"A lot, though I don't know that any of it has anything to do with why he disappeared. He appears in a lot of the write-ups for things two other boys were collared for, but he never got punished for any of them. Not even detention. Why do you think that is?"

"Who were the boys who got the blame?"

I checked my notes. "Benicio and Bernadino."

"Ah, Benny and Dino. They're the two Italian boys who are always with Suze and her crew." She paused near a row of lockers. Already the halls were virtually empty, but this didn't seem like the kind of conversation we should have in the vicinity of the principal's office.

"So why did they get blamed and he didn't?"

"Probably because he's pale instead of tan and his last name doesn't end in a vowel."

"Seriously?"

"That counts for a lot around here," said Pearl.

"Then why did he bother getting involved in what Benny and Dino were doing? For the thrill?"

Pearl licked her lips. "Back when Tom and Paul were pals he always seemed like he wanted to please my brother. He was that way with me, too. But then after his brother went to jail, it was like something snapped and he decided it wasn't worth trying to be perfect anymore. Paul told me Tom's father was pretty tough on him, more so after Michael was arrested. If you can't please someone no matter how hard you try, at some point it might seem easier to go ahead and become the thing they think you're going to be. Either way, you're going to disappoint them."

I knew what that was like. I'd felt that way myself a time or two. "So do you think that's why he broke into the lockers? To prove he was exactly what everyone thought he was going to be?"

"Probably." Pearl seemed distant. I got the feeling that she wanted to stop talking to me and go on her way.

"I'm sorry about what I said about Rhona," I told her. "I should've defended you."

"Why? Like you said, it wouldn't have made sense for you to stick up for me. And I couldn't care less what she thinks about me, anyway."

I doubted that was true. Pearl struck me as the kind of person who cared deeply about how others felt about her.

She thumped her chubby fingers across the top of the textbook. "Maybe on Saturday we could get together. Talk about what happened on Friday night."

"All right."

"We could sleep over at my place. You'd have to put up with Paul, but I know my mother would love to meet you."

"I'll ask my pop, but I can't imagine a reason in the world why he'd say no."

We parted ways at the office door. As she disappeared inside to return the file, I wondered if it was possible that Rhona was wrong about Pearl. Or was I being naïve because I wanted to believe that my brand-new best friend wasn't capable of lying to me like I lied to her?

CHAPTER

9

FRIDAY NIGHT WAS ALL I could think about for the next two days. My nerves were swiftly replaced by my excitement about going somewhere forbidden. What would the club be like? Would people be smoking? Drinking? Would the music be so loud that I couldn't think? Would they even let me in?

Friday at lunch, just as Pearl and I were debating whether Deanna Durbin was a better actress than Shirley Temple, Suze came over and greeted me with a wide smile. "Feeling better?" she asked.

My own smile matched hers. Was that a mistake? "Some," I said. I offered Pearl a sidelong glance. She was staring at Suze as if Rita Hayworth had just parachuted out of a plane and decided to join us.

Suze slid next to me on the bench. "No more news?"

"Not a peep." I didn't want to talk about this in front of

Pearl, so I swiftly changed the subject. "Are we still on for tonight?"

"If you're game, so are we. How about we meet at my aquarium at eight?" She gave me an address that wasn't far from where we lived.

I could sense Pearl's longing to be included. It radiated off her like heat. I think Suze sensed it, too, because she smiled Pearl's way and introduced herself.

"It's nice to meet you," said Pearl.

"Likewise," said Suze. "I better beat tracks. See you at eight." Once she left, I tried to pick up my conversation with Pearl from where we'd left off, but she wasn't having any of it.

"She wears a lot of makeup."

"Really? I hadn't noticed."

"Do you think she stuffs her bra?"

"Beats me." It didn't seem fair to talk about Suze behind her back.

"What news was she asking about?" she asked.

"What?"

"She asked if you'd had any more news."

She'd picked up on that? Boy, howdy—Pearl was a lot more perceptive than I gave her credit for. "I think it's just an expression like, 'Hey, Joe, what do you know?'"

Pearl's face made it clear she wasn't buying it, but it didn't look like she was up for pursuing it further, either. "You must be excited about tonight," she said.

I was, but it didn't seem like I should admit it. "I'm more nervous than anything."

"What are you going to wear?"

I'd spent half the night worrying over that very subject. I couldn't bring myself to spend Pop's money, not after my stripped-down tale of where I was going that night. Besides, what did girls wear to dance clubs in Harlem? "I haven't really thought about it yet."

"I can't believe your pop's letting you go." She unraveled her lunch bit by bit. Today's dessert was some sort of nut-encrusted roll that smelled of honey.

"He doesn't exactly know."

"You didn't tell him?"

"I told him we were going dancing." I didn't bother to tell her that she was part of that "we." "He didn't ask where and I didn't volunteer it."

"Oh." She looked concerned. I understood where she was coming from. Lying to a parent was a big deal, even if it wasn't lying so much as omitting important details. "I guess you didn't tell your mother, either?"

"My mother's dead."

Her sandwich fell, limply, onto its waxed paper wrapping. "Seriously? You never told me that."

"You never asked."

Her forehead furrowed. "Why would I ask something like that?"

I shrugged. "Can't we talk about something else?"

"Sure." She paused long enough to let me know that no other subject could possibly be as important as this to her. "It just seems strange. I mean, you knew about Peter. Why wouldn't you tell me about your mother?"

Because it wasn't the same? Because I thought I'd shared enough when I told her about what had happened to Pop? "I just didn't," I said.

"How did she die?"

She wasn't going to let this drop, was she? Couldn't she see how uncomfortable the topic made me? What was it going to take? "She killed herself." There. Subject closed, I hoped.

"When?"

I was reminded of Grace Dunwitty and all the other girls I used to consider my friends, circling me like sharks while they made their consolation call at our uptown apartment. After they left, Aunt Miriam had told me that they were young and didn't know any better than to ask prurient questions ("What was prurient?" I'd asked her; "Rude," she'd replied), but I knew that wasn't the case. These were good girls from good homes. They knew better. But Mama's death had devalued me in their eyes. They no longer had to be tactful to someone like me. Scandal invited inquiry.

I dropped my silverware onto my plate and gathered my things. "She did it on New Year's Eve. In a hotel room. She took a bunch of pills. I don't know why she did it. No, she didn't leave a note. She wasn't depressed that I knew of, but then after hearing that my father had lost his leg, who knows what was going through her head. I have to go." I stood to leave. Pearl put her hand on mine and gently pushed my lunch tray back onto the table.

"I'm sorry if I upset you."

"You're acting like I lied to you," I said.

"I don't think you lied. I just find it weird that you didn't tell me, that's all."

"Just like you didn't tell me that you have a crush on Tom Barney?" It felt like a low blow, but I didn't care. Her lips fluttered but she didn't respond. "There are some things I just don't want to talk about, all right?"

"All right," she said. Her voice was soft and full of regret. For a while we ate in silence, though it was obvious neither of us had any appetite left. As I sat there, trying to down the salty, greasy pasta that was that day's lunch, I felt terrible. Of course Pearl was curious. Who wouldn't be? Was it really fair to bite her head off over it? I almost said as much, but right then she looked up at me and asked, "Is that why you lied to my brother about being Jewish?"

"What?"

"It's on your school record. Suicide is forbidden by Jewish law. Were you afraid we'd judge you for that? Because those were your mother's actions, not yours."

I couldn't have been more shocked if she'd slapped me with her sandwich. I stood up from the table so quickly that my chair threatened to topple over. "You may think Suze wears too much makeup and dresses like a tramp, but at least she had the good sense to let the subject drop."

"You told Suze about your mom?"

Was she really making this a competition? I shook my head. "I've got to go."

"Wait. I didn't mean it like that." Her voice was too loud. A table of boys to the left of us caught wind of our conversation and echoed her words back at her, their own voices raised in falsetto. *Wait. I didn't mean it like that.*

I left my plate where it was and exited the cafeteria, while the table of boys exploded with laughter.

I SPENT ALL OF AMERICAN HISTORY fuming about Pearl, instead of listening to the lecture on war preparedness. To think there was a time when I felt guilty about not defending her to Rhona. No wonder Rhona thought she was the one who'd spread the rumor about her absence. Even if Pearl hadn't done it maliciously, I could see her clumsily making assumptions about Rhona's personal life and then repeating them within earshot of the wrong person.

She'd probably do the same thing to me. "Her mom committed suicide," she'd tell people. "And so now she thinks she can't be Jewish."

By the time typing class arrived, I'd spent as much energy as I could muster being mad at Pearl. I let my mind empty as we took our places at the machines and keyed *The quick brown fox jumps over the lazy dog* in time to the ticking of a metronome. When my mind wasn't tallying the number of mistakes I'd made, I let it worry over what I was going to wear that night. While my wardrobe had matured since those first, early days of school, it had by no means become fashionable. By the time class ended, I had an outfit in mind: my pencil skirt and a blouse that made me look like I had a bosom.

I half expected to find Pearl waiting for me after school, but she'd either left before me or was deliberately hanging back until she was certain I was gone. I'd overreacted and I knew it. Of course she was curious—I would be, too. In her shoes I probably would be wondering what else I was keeping from her.

I made it home and spent far too much time taming my hair. Pop was out, so I sought Mrs. Mrozenski's approval on my attire.

"You're going to a dance?" she asked.

I nodded, hoping she would have the good sense not to ask where.

"You look very grown-up. Maybe, though, something is missing." She went upstairs to her bedroom and returned a moment later, a girdle in hand. It clearly wasn't hers, but rather some castoff her daughter, Betty, had left in her possession.

I thanked her and, after a quick lesson on how to squeeze

into it, I put the garment on. Instantly, I achieved the smooth silhouette the skirt demanded. And a sudden, inescapable feeling that I couldn't breathe.

At seven-thirty I made the brief, anxious walk to Suze's house, arriving fifteen minutes early. If our home was a step down from the Upper East Side, hers was a leap. The apartment was one of many in a tenement building that hugged a thin, weed-choked sidewalk. Outside, bored children played jacks, hopscotch, and any other game they could think of that took less money than imagination. Row after row of laundry rippled in the evening breeze on lines strung between the close-set buildings. There was no attempt at maintaining privacy here. Brassieres and shorts were as prominently displayed as trousers and dresses, all bearing the telltale signs of wear and tear that were visible even from where I stood at street level.

I would've died of embarrassment, but no one here cared. This was poverty. In comparison, at Mrs. Mrozenski's house, Pop and I were on easy street.

I carefully made my way up the stairs and into a narrow hallway. Suze had told me they lived in number six, so I followed each labeled door until I reached one that didn't bear a numeral but, because of its proximity to number seven, had to be the apartment I was looking for. Inside, dishes clattered as someone washed up after dinner. A woman's nasal voice screeched at top volume. I couldn't tell if she was angry or deaf.

I leaned against the door and tried to verify that I was at the right place.

"You need to learn some respect, little girl. This isn't a hotel," said a voice from inside.

"I told you I had plans." That was Suze, or someone doing a pretty good imitation of her.

"You don't decide when you get to come and go."

"I'll stay with her tomorrow."

"I don't have to work tomorrow."

"You don't have to work now."

"I do if you expect food on the table. Who else is going to provide it?"

"I gave you my paycheck."

"Gee, a whole five dollars, Suze. Don't tell the Rockefellers."

"What do you want from me? I go to school. I go to work. And now I want to go out."

"That little girl in there needs someone to watch over her."

"Then you do it—you're her mother." Footsteps pounded across the floor, growing louder as they grew closer to the door.

"Don't you walk away when I'm talking to you! You're getting too big for your britches."

Suze responded, though her voice was so low that the words were indistinct. What came next wasn't so quiet though: it was the sound of flesh hitting flesh.

"You come back here right now!"

The door flew open and Suze emerged, unlit cigarette in one hand, pocketbook in the other. Her cheek was red, one eye partially closed. Behind her a woman in factory coveralls and a dark blue snood tried to grab hold of her arm and missed.

"I said come back here right now!"

Suze slammed the door behind her and took two steps before seeing that I was in the hallway.

"Sorry," I said. "I'm early."

"No, it's good. I need to truck out of here."

I followed her down the stairs and out of the building. At the stoop she paused and pulled a compact out of her purse. With a practiced hand she studied her reflection, assessed the damage, and then carefully covered the woman's handiwork with her powder puff. The red was lost beneath the makeup's sheen.

I tried to imagine what could bring Mama to hit me, but the idea that she could strike me was so absurd that I couldn't invent circumstances to support it.

But maybe if she had struck out at me instead of herself, she'd still be here.

"What happened?" I asked.

"What always happens? She doesn't like the way I dress, the way I talk, or who I hang out with. She's tired, we're poor, and my no-good father hasn't made an appearance for months." She held her eye open with one hand and

149

stared at the red that appeared threaded through the white.

"Maybe you should stay home tonight."

"Maybe you shouldn't beat your gums off time." She instantly regretted saying it; I could see it in her eyes. "I'm sorry, baby—I didn't mean to bust a button. She has me rattled. Look, she's sore that I won't stay home and sit with my sister. The brat's old enough to take care of herself, she's almost eleven, but the truth is Ma feels guilty for taking the swing shift, so she thinks if she can goad me into staying, she can forgive herself for working."

"What does she do?"

"Munitions work. The hours are long, but the pay's nothing to sneeze at. She's right—my little paycheck isn't even a drop in the bucket."

"Where's your father?"

"I don't know and I don't care." She added lipstick and rouge to her palette, then returned everything to her purse. Now that her own appearance was taken care of, she turned her attention to me. "Oh, baby—what's this?"

"What's what?"

Her fingers indicated my pencil skirt. "We're dancing. You can't dance in a straitjacket."

What was she talking about? I could move my feet just fine.

"Are you wearing a girdle?" she said.

"Yes."

"Boy, do you have a lot to learn. Come on." She took me by the hand and pulled me around to the side of the building, where a row of windows stared across the brief alleyway at the brick wall of the building next door. What a view. At the rearmost window she paused, pushed over a coal bin, and then hoisted herself on top of it. She threw one leg over the window's ledge and then motioned for me to follow. Seconds later she was inside the building and I was left to negotiate the tight skirt and tall bin. After a few graceless attempts, I made it up to the window and over the ledge.

We had landed in a bedroom. Instead of finding Suze, I found a young girl lying belly-down on a bed, flipping through the new Nancy Drew, *The Quest of the Missing Map*. This had to be the sister.

"Hello," I said. "Where's Suze?"

She tipped her head toward a wardrobe, where Suze was rapidly flipping through rows of clothing I recognized from school. "Here," she said, flinging a navy blue skirt my way. "Try this on."

I looked around, hoping there was a screen I could duck behind to change. Apparently, I was expected to exchange skirts in front of Suze. And this child.

"I'm Iris," I said to the little girl, because it seemed to me that if she was about to see me in Betty Mrozenski's girdle, we might as well be on a first-name basis.

"This is my kid sister, Barbara," said Suze.

"Ma's going to be mad," said Barbara.

"Ma's already mad. And she won't get any madder unless you tell her I came back here, brat."

While Barbara stared down her sister, I pulled off my clothes and pulled on Suze's. Her A-line skirt was designed to lift into the air when I twirled, which I did at that moment under Suze's orders.

"Now that's a skirt you can dance in," she told me. "Here." She passed me a necklace and a pair of earrings from a box on her bureau. They were just paste, but I felt like I was being loaned the crown jewels.

"Are you sure?"

"Absolutely. Where we're going, you have to be togged to the bricks. Now hold still." She put her hands on either side of my face and pushed my head until I was looking directly at her. From her pocketbook came the powder puff, rouge, lipstick, and mascara. While I prayed she had steady hands, she painted my face until it looked just like hers. "Perfect," she said when her work was finished.

I caught sight of myself in the tarnished mirror above her dresser. I did look good. Grown-up, almost pretty. Red cheeks, red lips, eyelashes that went on forever.

Suze turned her attention to my feet. "How big are your dogs?"

I told her and she again turned to the wardrobe and pulled out a pair of well-worn pumps. "These are small, but they'll do. Can't have you ruining the effect with saddle shoes."

I slipped on the leather loafers with Cuban heels, long-ing to see how different my legs looked. The shoes were tight, but I didn't care.

"Now you're hotsy totsy from head to toe. All right, sun-shine. We got to blow." Suze climbed out the window and instructed me to follow her.

"It was nice meeting you," I told Barbara.

She didn't bother to reply.

CHAPTER

10

I STRUGGLED TO KEEP SUZE'S PACE out on the street. It was obvious the scene with her mother had bothered her more than she was willing to let on, but I wasn't sure how, or if, I should ask any more about it. Adults didn't act that way in my world, and I had a funny suspicion that if I condemned her mother for her behavior, Suze would defend her. And the last thing I wanted to do was to put us at odds. After all, I'd been in enough arguments that day.

"So your aunt was okay with you coming out tonight?" she asked me.

It took me a minute to remember that I lived with my fictional aunt. "Absolutely."

"No curfew?"

Pop hadn't said anything about when I needed to return. "Nope."

Suze eyed me suspiciously. "Lucky dog. If I'm not home

by twelve-thirty I get the belt." She raised an eyebrow. "Of course, sometimes it's worth it."

"My aunt doesn't have any other kids, so I don't think it occurred to her that she needed to tell me when I should come home."

Suze laughed. "Enjoy it while you can. After tonight, I'll bet she gives you all kinds of rules."

We met up with Rhona and Maria outside Normandie's Pharmacy. Rhona ignored me. Maria greeted me by saying, "Nice hardware," which I realized was a reference to the jewelry Suze had loaned me. Five minutes later, two Italian boys I recognized from the Rainbows' lunch table joined us. Benny was tall and tan, both features set off by the oversized dark blue pinstriped suit he wore. His shoes were polished to a high sheen and from his waist hung a watch on a chain that he twirled as he approached us. With him was Dino. He also wore an oversized suit, only his was a butter-yellow color that made it seem even more like a costume. Neither introduced himself to me. Instead, they talked to Rhona and Maria and periodically looked my way like they were wondering why I was still there.

I was starting to wonder, too.

The plan was to pool our money and take a cab into the heart of Harlem. As we waited for a taxi to appear, everyone searched pockets and pocketbooks for enough coin to get us there and into the club. It was obvious that everyone was broke and no one was eager to pay more than their share. By the time we found a car willing to go north of 96th Street, we still hadn't sorted out how we were going to pay the bill.

I was starting to panic. What if the entire evening was canceled? "I've got it," I said, producing Pop's small wad of bills from inside my purse.

"Are you sure?" asked Suze.

She had no idea how hard it was for Pop to come up with that dough. She probably thought it was walking-around cash my aunt and uncle gave to me. "Why not? After all, you're all being so nice about taking me with you. It's the least I can do."

After that the mood toward me drastically improved.

We piled into the cab, Suze in the front seat, Rhona and Maria on the boys' laps in the back. I was wedged into the remaining space beside them, trying not to become overwhelmed by the cigarette smoke they began to fill the car with.

The cabbie drove like a madman, obviously eager to get us into Harlem and get himself on his way. I rolled down the window and concentrated on the view as the wind whipped my hair in my face. I'm not sure what I was expecting to see—crime out in the open, maybe—but Harlem looked pretty much like the rest of New York, save the skin color of most of the people living there. There were grocers and produce stands, children out playing in the dimming twilight, and couples walking hand in hand, dressed in their best getups, many of which mirrored our own attire. When we paused at a traffic light, I could hear music coming from somewhere nearby. I thought it was the radio, until I saw a man singing on a street bench, using the wooden seat as his stage. He saw me watching him and rewarded me with a smile before launching into another song and dance.

At last we came to a stop on Lenox Avenue. Brightly lit clubs lined the block, their names identified in brilliant neon that pulsed against the darkening sky. I paid the driver, adding a tip, and we all tumbled out of the car and onto the sidewalk. Suze took me by the arm and pulled me toward what looked like a large theater marquee. It read SAVOY and a huge crowd of people lingered beneath it, clearly waiting to get inside.

"What's the holdup?" I asked.

"The band's still frisking the whiskers," said Maria. "Until they're ready, we wait." I stared at the building, trying to take it all in, an impossible feat given its size. It was a block long, stretching the distance between 140th and 141st streets. Music leaked out its windows and doors— brass instruments, drums, piano, and guitar, each sounding strangely tempered as though they were saving up their energy for the real thing.

At last the doors opened and the crowd streamed inside and up the stairs, our group among them. As I followed the flow, I saw both black and white faces itching to get on the dance floor. Many of the men were outfitted in the same strange suits Benny and Dino wore. The women, by and large, were stunning. All wore skirts like the one Suze had loaned me, reaching to the middle of their calves but capable of standing straight out at the waist. Many had flowers in their hair and heavily made-up faces that told of the hours of preparation they'd endured for this evening. The air was heavy with the scent of hairspray, perfume, cigarettes, and another smoke I couldn't identify but which I found pleasantly sweet. As we at last arrived at the entrance to the ballroom itself, I could see signs reporting that the Savoy Sultans were one of two bands taking the stage that night.

"The joint is jumping. You ready to bust loose?" Suze asked me.

"As ready as I'll ever be."

The ballroom was gorgeous. The wooden floor gleamed with wax; the chandeliers twinkled in the dim light. Two bandstands populated the room, one of which was already taken up by a group playing a song I didn't recognize. I had no idea how we were expected to dance in there. The place was wall-to-wall people, except for a small cordoned-off section where a few pairs of dancers performed such feats of gymnastics that I was terrified they were going to hit the vaulted ceiling.

"What's that?" I asked Suze.

"Cat's Corner. That's where the best of the best strut

their stuff." We found a spot near the wall where we were less likely to be trampled, and I watched as these extraordinary dancers continued their demonstration. I'd heard about swing and certainly knew much of the music that fell under that label, but I'd never seen the dancing that accompanied it before. At least not like this. The men literally threw their partners around and the women let them, demonstrating such grace, trust, and athleticism that I wanted to weep for the sheer beauty of it all. How had they learned to do that? Weren't they afraid their partners would drop them? Were they embarrassed when their skirts rose into the air, showing off their garter belts? Would they be mortified to learn that every time they flipped I could see the white flash of their panties?

But it wasn't just the dancing that grabbed my gut and held me solid. The music was different. This wasn't Benny Goodman rocking the airwaves from the parlor radio. These musicians worked their instruments like they were part of themselves—trumpets grown in place of arms, pianos where there should've been legs. Instruments didn't sound like instruments here: they were animals that growled, hooted, and barked in four beats to a measure. I don't know how the musicians got them to sound that way, but it was more alive than any music I'd heard before.

"What do you think?" Suze yelled above the roar of the band.

"It's amazing!" I wished I had a chair I could sink into so I could take it all in. I felt like I'd woken up in a foreign land. All around me people talked about scobo queens, hepcats, high steppers, trucking, and tumbling. With each word I didn't understand, I turned to Suze and asked for a translation. She patiently laid out the racket for me as best she could. "Can you dance like that?" I asked her.

"No way. Half of those hoofers are working on Broadway. You ready to get in there?"

I backed away from her, instantly afraid. "Not yet."

"Relax, baby—just watch and learn. Nobody ever died from doing the jitterbug."

Before I could respond, a man took hold of Suze's arm and pulled her into the center of the dance floor. They joined the gyrating, swinging mass of humanity while I pressed myself against the wall. So this was what people did on Friday nights. They didn't stay home reading Nancy Drew novels or biding their time learning the detective business. They lived.

I caught a glimpse of Maria in the arms of a black man whose smile was sixty watts, easy. She was one of the better dancers on the floor, so comfortable in her man's arms that I had a hard time telling where he ended and she began.

"Having fun?" Rhona joined me, a silver flask in her hand. Perspiration had plastered her hair to her head.

"I'm swell. Just swell." I'd forgotten my reason for being there. How convenient that it hadn't forgotten me.

"Want a tipple?" She passed the flask my way. Desperate to make her stay by my side, I accepted her offer and took a swallow. The booze burned down my throat, and it took everything in me not to choke and cough it back up. Is that what alcohol was like? And people drank it by choice? "Where's Suze?" she asked.

I struggled to keep myself from gagging. "Dancing. I saw Maria over that way. Is that her boyfriend?"

"If he isn't yet, he will be." She took a sip and screwed the cap back on the container.

"How come you stopped dancing?" I asked. Talking suddenly seemed easier.

"I needed a rest. How come you didn't start?"

"I needed a lesson."

She laughed at that. This was good. "You should get Benny or Dino to take you for a spin. They can cut a rug with the best of them."

"Is Tommy a good dancer?" I asked. I was surprised to hear the words come out of my mouth. Apparently, whatever was in the flask had erased my ability to deliberate before talking.

"Fantastic. One of the best. He was in Cat's Corner a time or two."

"It's a shame he's not here tonight."

She raised an eyebrow, but didn't respond right away. I was being too obvious. She had to know I was up to something. "You think I don't remember you, don't you? Talking to Tommy in the hall, hanging on his every word like God himself was speaking."

"It wasn't like that, Rhona."

"Tell me another one while that's still warm. I got my boots on, girlie. I know what I saw." She shrugged and unscrewed the flask for another drink. I decided to move away from her. If she didn't like me—and it was clear she didn't—I wasn't going to prolong my misery by forcing her to talk to me.

"Wait," she said. She put her hand on my arm to stop me. "I'm sorry. I'm being a beast, aren't I?"

"You shred it, wheat," I said.

She grinned at that. I was learning their world, bit by bit. "You just remind me of her."

"Her who?

"Tommy's Upper East Side bobby soxer."

This was new. "He has a girlfriend uptown?"

"Had. You went to private school, right?" she asked. I nodded. "So did his latest obsession. He loves those girls in their prissy little uniforms who reek of old money. Tommy thinks he's too good for public school girls. Fancies himself a real B.T.O."

"Oh." Was that why Tom had asked Pearl who it was who had gone to Chapin? "I didn't realize he was seeing someone."

"You and me both. I followed him one day. Saw her with my own eyes."

No wonder she'd gotten a new man when Tom disappeared. She wasn't being callous; she was simply doing as he'd done. "So maybe he's been with her this whole time?" I said.

"Nope. She gave him the gate back in September, but he wouldn't hear it. Kept showing up at the duchess's school and her fancy apartment, hoping to win her back. It was pathetic."

I couldn't see it. But I also couldn't see Rhona lying about it. Her story dripped with truth. And jealousy.

"He told you that?"

"Nope, but he told Benny, and that's practically the same thing."

"They could've gotten back together, though."

"If they did, she's doing a fine job covering it up. I saw her out with stars and stripes on her arm just last week."

"I'm sorry, Rhona. She sounds awful."

"She is. And check this for irony—her name is Grace. You expect more from a girl with a name like that, you know?"

A chill passed through me. "What's her last name?"

She snapped her fingers as the name came back to her. "Dimwitted. What a name, right?"

It would've been, if she'd remembered it correctly. It was actually Dunwitty. Grace Dunwitty. My former best friend at the Chapin School.

11

GRACE DUNWITTY WAS THE DEFINITION of sub-deb. The daughter of a doctor, she was the third person in her family to go to Chapin. I met her my first day there, when our big sisters for the day sat us down together at lunch and introduced us. She was a year older than me and I liked her immediately. She was everything I wanted to be: pretty, blond, outgoing. The only thing I didn't envy about her was that, like her mother, she was an unapologetic snob.

She was the last person in the world that I would've paired with someone like Tom Barney. The boys Grace went with were students at our brother school, boys who came from wealthy families, spent summers at the club, and were shoo-ins for the Ivy League. She would've seen someone like Tom as cut-rate, not worth the energy it took to cross the street to avoid talking to him.

What had changed?

"I know Grace," I told Rhona.

"For real?"

"Well, I used to know her. We went to the same school." I shook my head, trying to think a clear thought despite the one-two punch of booze and music. "I can't see her with Tom."

"Neither could I, but I've seen enough with my own peepers to know it was true."

"What did he see in her?"

She was drunk enough that my curiosity didn't seem strange. Either that or she wanted someone to talk to about this.

"If I had to guess, I'd say a way out. To him a girl like Grace was a ticket out of the Lower East Side."

It didn't escape me that she was speaking in the past tense. She passed me the flask again. Before I could take a drink, a hand extended her way and she took it, allowing the man attached to the other end of it to pull her onto the dance floor.

More hits from the flask and I was ready to take on whatever the night offered me. That meant that when Benny approached and asked me if I wanted to learn to jitterbug, I told him yes without thinking about it.

The next ten minutes were a blur as he tried to show me the basic steps and I tried to follow them without running into anyone else on the dance floor. My self-consciousness was gone. It didn't matter that I stumbled or that I was as graceful as Pinocchio taking his first wooden steps. The music and the mass of humanity around me embraced me and made me feel alive for the first time in months.

"Now you're cooking," said Benny as he swung me to the left. And—boy, howdy—I was, too. I never considered myself graceful or, for that matter, athletic, but the music and the booze gave me the courage to give it my all. The steps no longer felt frenetic and strange, but as natural as walking. I could guess what Benny would do next, and rather than waiting for him to lead me, I anticipated his moves and mirrored them. "You've done this before," he said.

"Nope."

"Well, you're going at it like gangbusters." For the first time I saw how beautiful he was. It was funny thinking of a boy like that, but there was no other way to describe him as he moved about the dance floor, his grin never leaving his face. "What are you thinking?"

"Honestly, I can't believe I haven't tripped and fallen."

He threw his head back and laughed. "You're funny," he said.

"Thanks."

"So what do you think of the Savoy?"

"It's the most amazing place I've ever been."

"You're not scared?"

"Why would I be?"

"Tough neighborhood. Tough crowd. This ain't the kind of place a girl like you should be." His voice was playful. Was he flirting with me? I'd barely heard him speak two words since we'd met, so I didn't know how to gauge his sideways smile or the way he never pulled his eyes away from mine.

"Says who?"

"Me."

"You don't look so dangerous to me," I said. Pearl had to be wrong about the Rainbows. This beautiful boy with the dark eyes and the full lips couldn't be a thief.

As though he heard my thoughts, he said, "Looks can be deceiving." And then he did something very strange—he kissed me.

It was my first kiss and I was completely unprepared for it. And yet despite the fact that I hadn't had time to analyze what was about to happen, it felt like the most natural thing in the world. There I was at a Harlem dance club, a little drunk and a lot sweaty, kissing a beautiful Italian boy wearing a pinstriped suit.

He pulled away but didn't release me. I fought an urge to ask him if I'd done all right.

I didn't want our time at the Savoy to end, but eventually it did.

Suze grabbed my arm and pulled me toward the doors, freeing my hand from Benny's. "We got to make tracks, baby girl. Can you get the others, Benny?"

"I'm on it."

We entered the stairwell, where the music dropped by several decibels. "Have a good time?" she asked.

"The best ever."

"Looked like you and Benny were getting friendly."

Every part of me blushed, I was certain of it. "Is that a bad thing?"

"Not as long as you don't expect to wear his ring come Monday."

"Oh." So what happened with Benny wasn't likely to happen again. I was disappointed but not completely surprised. After all, what could he see in a girl like me?

Perhaps the same thing Tom had seen in Grace?

"You're going to be beat to the socks tomorrow." Suze leaned toward me and took a whiff. "You're lit."

"Rhona gave me something." I looked around for the flask, but it had vanished at some point during my time on the dance floor. I hoped Rhona wouldn't be mad.

"I should've warned you: never take what Rhona offers." We started down the steps, arm in arm.

A breeze greeted us outside, drying the perspiration that had turned my skin damp and clammy. As we waited for the others, we leaned against the building and took in the people still walking the streets at that late hour. Black and white, young and old, men in uniform milled about the crowd. They gave us a look that unnerved me. Didn't they know I was only fifteen years old? Or had one kiss transformed me into someone who seemed as mature as Suze?

Suze lapped up the attention and tried to get me to

return their winks and smiles. But even as looped as I was from Rhona's booze, I wasn't ready to cross that line.

"How you doing, doll?" asked a sailor as he passed us by.

"Never been better. How 'bout yourself?" asked Suze.

"Fine until it looked like you were leaving the party. Don't tell me you're cutting out."

"If I don't get home by twelve-thirty I turn into a pumpkin."

"And your friend?"

I blushed as I realized he was talking about me.

"She's my fairy godmother," said Suze. "Wherever I go, she goes."

"I ship out tomorrow. Don't you want to help me celebrate my last night?"

"What's to celebrate? You're leaving and breaking my heart."

"Maybe if you stick around I'll decide to stay."

"If you did that and we lost the war I'd never forgive myself."

He blew her a kiss and continued on his way.

"Did you know him?" I asked.

"No."

Would I ever feel comfortable talking to a stranger like that? I didn't think so. "Rhona told me Tom was seeing a Chapin School girl. Grace Dunwitty."

Suze tossed an impatient look toward the club and fished

through her pocketbook. "Is Rhona still going on about that?" She did a double take. "You like him, don't you?"

"Tom? No . . . I mean—"

"That's why you've been asking about him. Rhona warned me, but I just assumed she was overreacting."

So they'd talked about me after our chat at Normandie's. "She is overreacting. Or she was. I mean, Tom was nice to me, but I knew he had a girlfriend." She didn't look convinced. "I know Grace. That's why I brought it up just now. We went to school together. I was just surprised to hear he was dating her."

"You and Rhona both."

"So how soon after he broke up with Rhona did he start dating Grace?"

She checked the air behind us, like she was worried that Rhona was there, listening over our shoulder. "He didn't dump Rhona. She dumped him."

"Really?"

She lit a cigarette and blew smoke at the moon. "Hand to my heart. That's why she was so surprised when he hooked up with the little princess right away. Rhona thought she was worth at least a week of mourning."

"She sure seems like she regrets the breakup."

"She was hasty, for sure. But she had her reasons."

"That had to be hard, losing Rhona and then being tossed aside by Grace. Do you think maybe that's why he went away?"

She cocked her head at me. "Honestly, baby, I can't speak to what's in his mind. If it were me and my heart were broken twice, maybe I would've gone away for a while to get my head in order. It's hard to say." She narrowed her gaze. "For someone who claims not to care, you sure ask a lot of questions."

I wanted to tell Suze the truth. But there was no guarantee she'd keep quiet about what I was up to and there was no benefit in tipping your hand too soon. Besides, if I told her I was conducting an investigation, she might put two and two together and figure out my pop wasn't overseas. "Sorry," I said. "Rhona just seemed so upset tonight. I know what it's like to say something you regret and not have a chance to apologize for it."

Her face softened. "That's sweet of you, baby girl. We're not used to people giving us second chances."

The others joined us just then, their faces slick with perspiration. Benny had his coat off and slung over his shoulder. Even though we could no longer hear the band, he danced as he moved across the sidewalk, swinging his slim hips to a tune only he could hear. The motion exaggerated the strange feminine lines of the suit, and yet seemed sexual at the same time. I felt like I was watching something forbidden. And I liked it.

"You cold?" he asked me. I was all of a sudden, so I nodded. He wrapped his jacket about my shoulders. It was so large it swallowed me whole.

Maybe Suze was wrong. Maybe that kiss had meant something to Benny.

We hailed a cab and hit the road. This time, I was one of the ones seated two by two in the back—I reclined on Benny's lap while a drunk Rhona leaned out the window and tried to sober up with the fresh air. The journey was punctuated by laughter as everyone recalled the evening, describing dancers they'd seen, moves they'd made, and hot new songs the band had dragged out and filled the night with. Dino had a memory for music, and he sang snatches of the lyrics to refresh our memories when we couldn't recall the pieces that had been played. Benny joined him on the melody, my back serving as his percussion section. As he played the song's rhythm on my spine, I relaxed against him, feeling the warmth of his breath on my neck. My whole body tingled.

The trip home went much too quickly. We were dropped off in front of Normandie's, where the street was alive with other late-night partygoers. I ponied up what money I had left to cover the cab fare and relinquished the jacket to Benny, wishing I could take it home with me and sleep with it in my arms instead of my baby blanket. Rather than dispersing right away, we all continued chatting, reluctant to call it a night. Another group of soldiers and sailors passed by, and I expected them to say something to us just like the ones in Harlem. I wondered how Benny would react if one of them flirted with me. Would he tell them to back off?

Sure enough, the group paused and looked us over. Rather than addressing Rhona, Suze, Maria, or me, though, it was the men they were interested in.

"Look," said one of them. "Pachucos. Shouldn't you be back in the barrio?"

"I didn't think they had those out East," said his friend.

"They don't," said a third man. "These aren't spics, these are dagos."

"Even better," said the first guy. "We got us a bunch of fascists here."

"We don't want any trouble, man," said Dino. "There's no signifying going on here."

"You should've thought of that before you picked out your clothes for the night. Don't you know there's a war on? All that fabric, all that waste." The first guy clucked his tongue. And then he and his friends surrounded Dino. I thought they were going to beat him up, but they had something else in mind: they each grabbed ahold of his waistband and yanked down his pants.

As Dino stood on the sidewalk in his underwear, his canary pants around his ankles, the military boys turned their attention to Benny. Now that he was aware of what they were doing, he put up more of a fight. Unfortunately, he didn't stand a chance. With five of them, and Dino momentarily restrained, Benny's attempts to keep his pants on and retain his dignity only made things worse. They struck him repeatedly, the fists on his face sounding like a mallet hitting a bass drum. With his fight beaten out of him, they pulled off his pants and then, to add insult to injury, took his hat and threw it into the street.

The men howled with laughter and slapped each other on the back before turning and walking away.

I rushed to Benny's side. He looked so small and defeated, as different from the boy I'd danced with as Pop was from the handsome man in uniform whose picture used to decorate our fireplace mantel. I offered him my hand, wanting to help him to his feet, but he pushed me away, insisting on standing without my assistance.

The rejection was completely understandable, and yet it broke my heart all the same.

While Maria and Rhona tended to Dino, Suze retrieved a handkerchief from her purse and moved to mop the blood from Benny's face.

"Back off." His voice was a growl. I was secretly glad I wasn't the only one he was pushing away.

"Should we call the police?" I asked, wishing I could do something.

"No," said Rhona. "They'll only make things worse."

I didn't see how that was possible. Both boys were humiliated, and neither had done anything to deserve it. How was it fair to let the men responsible for it get away?

"Why did they do that?" I asked.

Suze met my eyes and shook her head. I got her meaning: not now. If you have to ask questions, save them for later.

174

Benny pulled his pants up and helped Dino to his feet. Without saying another word, they started their way up the block. I wanted to follow them, but I knew in my heart that it was the last thing Benny would want. Suze watched them for a moment, her weight shifting from one foot to another. "You okay getting back to your cubby?" she asked me.

"Sure."

"Be safe." She took off toward her tenement. Seconds later, Rhona also turned a corner, leaving Maria and me alone to find our way home.

We walked side by side in silence. But I couldn't stop the flow of questions welling up in me.

"I don't understand," I said. "Why would they do that?"

"They thought our boys were pachucos."

"What's a pachuco?" I asked her as we lumbered in the direction of Orchard Street.

"Mexican zoot-suiters out West. They don't mix with the military."

"Why?"

"Your guess is as good as mine."

"So they punished Dino and Benny for what boys out West are doing?"

"It's more than that. They think the zoots are unpatriotic because a ton of fabric is needed to make them—fabric that should be used to make uniforms. Here they are risking their lives, and boys like Dino and Benny are mocking them. And I'm sure they weren't happy to see them out on

175

the town with pale girls like you and Suze. Brown skin stays with brown skin. Get it?"

"But Benny and Dino are Italian."

"Where you been, little girl? The Italians aren't on our side in this war. Benny and Dino are lucky they're not being locked up like the Japs."

I felt so young and stupid. How had the evening gone so wrong? Just an hour before I'd been chalking it up as the best night of my life.

"I should've gone after them," I said.

"Benny's not yours to worry about."

"He kissed me," I said.

"And if it happens again, maybe it will mean something. Or maybe it means exactly this: there wasn't anyone else around to kiss."

For the second time in so many minutes, I recoiled in pain. I willed her to turn up the next street so I could finish my walk alone.

"I'm sorry," she said. "That was evil."

I didn't respond, terrified if I did she might take back the apology or add some comment that made her earlier re-mark cut even deeper.

"It's just hard to trust girls like you," Maria said.

I almost laughed. Did the girl in the gang of petty thieves really just tell me that I was the one they couldn't trust? "Girls like me?" I asked.

"Come on now—we all know you're Upper East Side. I'm surprised you're willing to be seen with people like us."

And here I'd been thinking that it was amazing that Suze would agree to be seen in public with me.

"This is my turn," said Maria.

I paused beside her. "Oh. Thanks for walking with me."

"No problem." She hesitated. There was something else she wanted to say, but I wasn't sure if I wanted to hear it. "Pearl Harbor was wrong, you know. That's why Rhona was so upset."

I was thrown off guard by the mention of Pearl's nickname. "Oh?"

"Rhona wasn't pregnant then. She was sick, but it was legit. See you on Monday."

"Yeah," I said. "See you."

I WAS SOBER BY THE TIME I got home. I expected to find the house dark, but a light was on in the parlor. As I passed through the room on the way to the stairs, Pop cleared his throat.

"Iris."

I turned and found him in his office, the door wide open so he could observe my comings and goings.

"Do you know what time it is?" he asked.

His tone was icy. Above his shoulder the clock tattled that it was one-fifteen.

"Just after one."

"And what made you think that that was an appropriate time to stay out until?"

I wasn't quite sure how to take the question. Was he mad? Seriously? "You didn't tell me to be back at a specific time."

He left his roost and came around to me. He had his leg on. Had he just returned from somewhere, or was he getting ready to go someplace? "That's because I thought you knew better. I've been worried sick. I went to that boy Paul's house and neither he nor his sister knew where you were."

Had Pearl squealed on me? Seriously?

"I told you—a dance."

"With who?"

"Some other friends from school."

"And just where was this dance?"

My mouth fluttered. My impulse was to lie and I wasn't sure where that was coming from. I'd never overtly lied to Pop before. Well, except for telling him who I was with that night. "It's a club called the Savoy."

"And just where is this club located?"

I hoped by giving him part of the truth, I might squeak by. "Lenox and 141st Street."

"Harlem?" asked Pop. I shrugged, like I wasn't sure what neighborhood we'd been in. "I thought it was a school dance."

"I never told you that." He couldn't fault me for his assumptions.

178

"What's that on your mouth?"

My hand went to my lips. Suze's lipstick smeared my fingers red. "Just lip cream."

"You're too young for that."

For what, I wanted to ask. *Wearing makeup or having half of it kissed off me?* "A friend loaned it to me," I said. "Everyone there was wearing it."

"Have you been drinking?"

How could he know that? "I . . ."

"My God, Iris. What's come over you? Staying out to all hours, lying about who you're with, wearing makeup, drinking. And Harlem? What could've possibly possessed you to go there?"

My mouth fluttered open but no sound came out. I couldn't tell him I was searching for Tom. Not yet.

"Who gave you the booze?"

"I . . . I don't know."

"You don't know? Do you have any idea how worried I've been? I didn't know if you were alive or dead."

It was strange to hear him being so paternal and scared. About *me*. On the one hand, I was touched to find out that he cared, but on the other, it struck me as very inconvenient. "It won't happen again, Pop."

"You better believe it won't. From here on out you go to school and you come home. That's it."

"I said I wouldn't do it again. How was I supposed to know there were rules?"

"Because you live on Planet Earth. What fifteen-year-old girl is allowed to stay out until the wee hours of the morning—in a Harlem dance hall, no less—and come home reeking of booze? Why do I have to tell you that that's forbidden?"

"Because that's what parents do," I said.

We stared at each other for a moment, each challenging the other to make the next move. I thought I had won—after all, my arguments were the most logical. But Pop had finally figured out the one essential thing about parent-child relationships: age trumps all.

"Go to your room, Iris."

"But I'm not done."

"Yes, you are. Go to your room."

Whatever courage Rhona's flask had given me had disappeared. With a huff, I turned and headed upstairs.

I didn't fall asleep for at least an hour. It wasn't the scene with Pop that kept me up. His anger would fade by morning. No, what kept my mind humming was everything I'd experienced that night: the hot jazz, the gorgeous dancers, the kiss that curled my toes, the sensation of Benny's breath on the back of my neck. And of course all I'd learned about Tom Barney and his relationship with Grace Dunwitty.

Try as I might, I couldn't picture the two of them together. Maybe that was why he'd robbed my locker and everyone else's—to get the money necessary to woo a girl he had nothing in common with.

Poor Rhona. It had to be heartbreaking to learn Tom had replaced her with someone like Grace. Especially after enduring the rumors Pearl had supposedly spread about her. No, there was no *supposedly* about it. Pearl being Pearl, she was most likely jealous as all get-out of Tom and Rhona's relationship. She had started the rumor, all right.

But Rhona wasn't pregnant. She was sick, according to Maria.

No, wait—Maria had said Rhona wasn't pregnant *then*.

I was up until sunrise pondering exactly what that meant.

12

I AWOKE WITH A BLINDING headache to the sound of the radio blaring downstairs. For a moment, as I strained against the sunlight streaming in the window, I thought I was sick. But as my eyes got used to the light, the night before came flooding back. Was this what alcohol gave you: a pounding head and a failing memory? If that was the case, I was done with it.

I put on my robe and went downstairs, worried that the radio meant that there was bad news on the war front. Mrs. Mrozenski had a habit of turning the volume up so she could continue working in the kitchen while listening to the news. She said the war got her so upset that she couldn't stand to sit still and do nothing when casualty numbers were reported. But as I came down the stairs, I realized it wasn't war news I was hearing. Someone had tuned the radio to WMCA, where *The Children's Parade* was just starting.

The living room was empty. A cup half filled with Postum, a coffee substitute Pop drank because it was cheaper than the real thing, had been left behind, as had the morning papers. The front page reported that forty-six Nazi planes had been downed. I hoped that meant Pop would be in a good mood. I knocked on his office door, expecting to find that he was already at his desk working. There was no reply from inside. I tried the knob and found the door unlocked. I opened it, praying Pop was in a better mood than the night before.

My prayers were in vain. No one was there.

I DEBATED STAYING at the house that day, but it seemed foolish to keep myself under house arrest when I wasn't sure how sore Pop was. Instead, I made myself some oatmeal for breakfast, got dressed, and took the subway uptown.

After all, I was already in trouble. What was one more infraction?

Grace lived on Fifth Avenue, in an apartment that faced Central Park. I used to think her digs were no big deal, but as I approached after all those months away, I saw for the first time how fortunate she was and how grossly out of place I had become. In my scuffed saddle shoes and Suze's skirt (smelling of smoke and who knows what else from the night before) I had to look like a servant's daughter come to pay my mother a visit during lunch. Had I ever fit in here?

I must have, and yet the idea suddenly seemed preposterous.

I approached the building and greeted the doorman. He was new, not that I would've expected the old doorman to still recognize me after so much time had passed.

"How can I help you?" He had a voice like the women at the cosmetic counter at Macy's. Even though you knew they were working for their money, they still somehow managed to communicate the idea that they were better than you. He underlined his superiority by examining me with his cold, blue eyes, choosing not to linger too long on my outfit, as though just being asked to look at it was insulting to him.

"I'm here to see Grace Dunwitty," I said. I tried to match his snobbery with my own tone, but I'd fallen out of practice. Instead of sounding rich and important, I sounded vaguely British.

He didn't have the apartments memorized yet. He glanced at the list that provided extensions for each residence and located the Dunwittys' near the top. "And who may I say is here?"

"Iris Anderson."

He picked up the receiver for the internal phone, dialed the number, and paused. As he waited to be connected, he examined his recently buffed nails. "Good afternoon, Caroline, if you could please inform your mistress that there's an Iris Anderson here to see Miss Dunwitty. Yes, *Iris*—like the flower." He covered the mouthpiece and sneered at me. I'd failed the first test—the maid didn't know who I was. She came back on the line before he could say anything to me. Whatever she said surprised him—I could see it in his face. "Really? Of course. Right away." He deposited the phone on its cradle and offered me a more genuine grin. "You may take the elevator to your right. Miss Dunwitty will be waiting for you."

I lifted my nose ever so slightly and sashayed to the waiting car. The elevator operator took me up to Grace's floor. I only had one foot in the hallway when the Dunwittys' apartment door burst open and Grace rushed out.

"Iris! Is it really you?"

"It really is. I hope you don't mind the surprise."

"Mind? I thought I was dreaming." She hugged me and for a moment things felt just like old times. She'd grown taller in the months since I'd seen her, and she'd started wearing makeup. Since it was Saturday, she wasn't wearing her Chapin uniform. Instead, she had on a cashmere twin-set and a skirt that captured the sweater's azure blue in a delicate plaid pattern. "Why haven't you returned my calls?"

"I'm sorry about that. I meant to, but it's been crazy since school started."

"Never mind. I'm just glad you're here." She stepped away and took me in, keeping her hands wrapped in mine. "Look at you, Iris." I wasn't sure what that meant. Look at how I'd changed, how shabby my clothes had become? "Come on." She pulled me into the apartment. "I've got so much to tell you."

But first there were formalities. Mrs. Dunwitty was sitting in the front room, enjoying an early afternoon tea with a woman I didn't recognize.

"What a lovely surprise. I'm delighted to see you, Iris," said Mrs. Dunwitty. Her words never sounded sincere to me, though I recognized early on that they contained the same artificial quality no matter whom she was speaking to. That meant, I hoped, that I shouldn't take it personally.

"Thank you, Mrs. Dunwitty. It's a pleasure to see you again."

"This is my dear friend, Mrs. Huckabee." She turned to her companion. "This is Iris Anderson. She used to attend Chapin with Grace."

"And where do you go now, dear?" asked Mrs. Huckabee, a woman so polished she gleamed brighter than the silver tea service.

"She attends public school now," said Mrs. Dunwitty. She said *public school* like it was something very different from its reality. This wasn't a generic term for schools one didn't pay to attend, but a lofty institution all its own. "You must tell us all about your new home," said Mrs. Dunwitty. There she was being careful again—there was no mention of it being on the Lower East Side. "How is your father?"

"Very well, thank you."

"Iris's father was one of the very first veterans of this war," said Mrs. Dunwitty. "He was injured at Pearl Harbor."

"Remarkable," said her friend.

"Iris has been a tremendous comfort to him during his recuperation. She has had so many challenges to face in this past year; she lost her mother right before he came home."

I wanted to laugh. There was much more to the story than that, and yet somehow Mrs. Dunwitty had just rescued me from further inquiry. I was the daughter of a war hero, bravely nursing him back to health as I tended my own wounds over my mother's tragic death. When they made the movie, would they cast Deanna Durbin or Shirley Temple in my role?

"You poor dear," said Mrs. Huckabee. "It is, of course, these times of trial that show us how strong we can be."

"Would you please excuse us, Mother?" said Grace. "I have ever so much to share with Iris."

"You will stay for lunch, won't you?" asked Mrs. Dunwitty.

"I would be delighted to," I said.

As I followed Grace down the hall and to her room, my words echoed in my head: *I would be delighted to.* What would Suze say if she heard me talking like that? Even Pearl would've found it queer.

We closed the door to Grace's room, and she launched herself onto the pink canopied bed. Little had changed in the last months, beyond the addition of cosmetics on the vanity top and a poster advertising a concert by Frank Sinatra and the Benny Goodman Orchestra at the Hotel Astor back in May.

"Sorry about that scene back there," she said, pulling a china doll into her chest. "Oh nausea! That woman is insufferable, but since she's in the Met Guild Mother has to put up with her twice a month."

"It was fine. She seemed nice."

"So tell me everything. I can't believe you're really here. It's too much!"

I claimed the end of the bed for myself, leaning my back against one of the canopy's posts. "There's not much to tell. Public school is awful. I feel like I learned everything they're teaching years ago. But I've made a few friends. What about you?"

"Oh, everyone is wrapped up in studying for the Slimy and Atrocious Torture. It's all too desperate." I'd forgotten about the SAT. No one at P.S. 110 ever talked about the test. Chapin girls were expected to go on to college; P.S. 110 girls had no such aspirations. The subject quickly shifted from academics to the goings-on of every girl I used to know—and a few I couldn't remember—at Chapin. When she was done telling me who had changed her hair, gained weight, planned her coming out, and gotten pinned, Grace finally turned to herself. "Of course, I'm positively bored to tears without you. Fortunately, I found someone new to keep me busy."

Tom. She was talking about Tom. Finally! I sat up a little straighter. "Really? Who's that?"

"Her name's Josephine O'Hara. She transferred to Chapin this fall and we've been inseparable ever since." Grace flipped her hair over her shoulder. "You'd love her if you met her. She's very mature and plays a mean game of Ping-Pong. All the boys think she's zazz. And not just the ones our age, either. She's always getting asked out by men who think she's older. She's just oolie droolie."

I was obviously supposed to be shocked, but after being around Suze and Rhona, I couldn't muster anything more than a nod. "And what about you?" I said. "Are you seeing anyone special?"

She stretched her legs, pointing her sock-clad feet. "Oh, you know. There's always someone who catches my eye, but I'm not going steady. Playing the field is much more fun."

What was it going to take to get her to talk about Tom? "Would you ever date someone who didn't go to private school?"

"You mean like an older boy? Absolutely."

"No, I mean like a public school boy."

She pondered the question a little too long. "The hell you yell! You know how my parents are." Her eyes narrowed. "Why? Are you going with someone?"

"No," I said. "I mean, not yet. There's this one boy I kind of like."

"Do tell," said Grace.

"There's nothing to tell. We kissed, that's all. Public school boys are just so strange. They seem rough and yet at the same time . . . I don't know . . . I'm curious about them." I followed the pattern on her quilt, trying to figure out the best way to get the conversation to go where I wanted it to.

"Just because you changed neighborhoods doesn't mean you should forget your value. Have you gone on a date with him?" she asked.

I nodded. "Sort of. It was him and a lot of his friends. We went out dancing last night."

"To a school dance?"

"Nope. To the Savoy Ballroom."

"In Harlem?" Her eyes threatened to fill her face. "Holy Joe! Your pop let you?"

"He didn't know. He does now, and believe me it won't be happening again anytime soon. I went with some girls from school. They go all the time."

"What was it like?"

I struggled to describe the night in a way that did it justice. I didn't hold back. Every drink, every dance, every wondrous sight I repeated, to Grace's shock and amusement.

"I can't believe you did all that."

"I can't either. I wish you'd been there, Gracie. The music was marvelous and the boys—I didn't know men could move like that."

"It sounds like absolute bliss."

Something in her seemed to be breaking away. I got the feeling she was close to telling me about Tom, but I had no idea what else it would take to get her there.

"You should come with me sometime," I said. "I just know you'd like Rhona and Suze, even if they aren't Chapin girls."

If she recognized either of their names, she didn't show it. Perhaps Tom had never mentioned them to her?

"That would be luscious. And I'd love for you to meet Josephine," said Grace. "I talk about you all the time." Her phone extension rang. She answered it with a bubbly "Hi there, playmate," and signaled to me that she'd be just a minute. "I was just talking about you."

I gestured that I was going to use the powder room and left her to her conversation. She was still talking five minutes later, and rather than being rude and lingering as they chatted, I walked back toward the parlor, thinking I might say hello again to Mrs. Dunwitty. Her company was still there, though, and they were deep into a conversation that I didn't want to interrupt.

Especially when I realized that it was about me.

"They found her mother dead in a Yorkville hotel. Suicide."

"No!" said Mrs. Huckabee.

"Naturally, everyone assumed that she was so distraught over her husband's injury that she couldn't bear to go on."

"That hardly makes sense."

"I'm just telling you what everyone else said," said Mrs. Dunwitty.

"But why Yorkville?"

"She was German."

"And she had family there?"

"In Yorkville? I don't think so, but they all stick together, don't they? Once a German, always a German."

A teacup rattled as it was returned to its saucer. "Perhaps she wanted to make sure the daughter didn't find her," said Mrs. Huckabee.

"I wish I could say she was that considerate, but I doubt it. If you ask me, she had something to feel guilty about, and rather than running the risk that her husband would come home and find out about it, she decided it would be better to die."

"But what on earth would make her feel so guilty?"

"I think she was seeing another man."

"What makes you think that?"

"Her husband was away. She was young and attractive. What else could she have been doing?"

I backed away from the two of them, my head growing increasingly heavy.

"There you are," said Grace. She stood in her doorway. "That was Josephine. I was telling her all about you. She's dying to meet you."

"I have to go," I said.

"Oh. I thought you were staying for lunch. Our new cook is simply marvelous. She makes the most delish desserts."

I felt sick. If I didn't get out of there soon, I was going to vomit all over Grace's plush pink carpeting. "I can't. I forgot I'm supposed to help Pop with something."

"Buzz me tomorrow, all right? Let's make plans to get together more often."

I promised I would, then bade her mother a polite farewell and left the apartment just in time to get sick in a potted plant positioned just outside the elevators.

MAMA KILLED HERSELF. That's what Uncle Adam told me after I demanded something more from him than the tired euphemisms he'd offered me as an explanation for why she wasn't coming home. It was two days before Pop was due back in the States, almost a month to the day since he'd lost his leg at Pearl Harbor. The year 1942 was so new that Christmas decorations still sparkled from shop windows along Fifth Avenue, so new that every time I saw a newspaper I was convinced the date was a misprint.

"I'm so sorry, Iris," said Adam. He crushed my hand in his. He was shaking with the force of his own grief.

"But why did she do it?"

"I wish I knew."

I was staying with Uncle Adam and Aunt Miriam. Mama had to go out of town, I'd been told. She'd be home before the new semester started. Wouldn't it be nice to spend some time with the aunt and uncle I'd always adored?

But she didn't come home. If her sudden trip seemed unusual, her failure to return was even more so. *Where had she gone?* I asked Adam and Miriam. Each time I was told it was a family matter, nothing to concern myself with. She'd explain everything when she returned. Nobody made allowances for what would happen if she didn't come back. Just like nobody prepared me for what would happen when Pop did.

When Pop joined the military I was only ten years old. From that point on in my life, he became an infrequent visitor: holidays, birthdays, and a surprise now and again that I greeted with less and less enthusiasm. After all, he was a stranger now—why all this fuss because he decided to disrupt what was starting to become a normal life without him? Mama, of course, didn't see it that way. Each return was a gift, each visit's end a tragedy that sent her to her bedroom for days on end. She wrote to him constantly and cherished each letter in return, reading and rereading them until the paper began to tear apart at its folds.

In Pop's absence, I became her focus. It's funny how much someone can annoy and smother us in the name of love and how much you miss those very same things when they're gone. Mama insisted on brushing my hair every night, no matter how late she came home, no matter how much I groused about how old I was and how stupid this little ritual of hers was to me. Her mother had done it for her, she explained, and someday I'd do it for my own daughter. She quizzed me every day about what I had eaten, comparing my recited lists with the USDA food charts we'd been given at school. "More milk," she'd say. "You are a growing girl." Over dinner I was interrogated about my friends. What did they wear? How much spending money were they given? Did they all walk to school, or did some take a hired car? Were any of them going with boys yet? Always she wanted me to be in the same league as everyone else. What they got, I got. I used to hate the way she measured my life against theirs like slices of pie, but eventually I learned to play the system, increasing their allowances when I wanted more money, inventing permissive parents when it better suited my purposes. But it didn't happen very often. At some point I began to realize that what Mama wanted for me wasn't what everyone else had so much as everything she hadn't been provided with when she was a girl. I was to live the life she'd been denied.

How had she felt about the war? I never asked her. Until that December, it wasn't something I thought about, beyond wishing she did a better job hiding her accent. And after that fateful day, when a tiny island in the Pacific became the focus of so much rage, when someone else's war became our war, there were too many things to think about to worry how she was feeling. Pop had lost his leg, resigned his post, and was coming home for good. Our lives were about to change forever. A father in the house meant less freedom. And a war . . . well, I had no idea what that meant.

I didn't have time to worry about what Mama was going through. And in fact until she disappeared, and all I had was time to worry, I didn't notice the dark circles that had appeared under her eyes in the days following December 7, the shaking hands with bitten nails, the late-night phone calls—always in German. These things came to me later, when I asked myself why she had done it, when I wondered what I had missed.

The biggest question of all was how I had gone from being her everything to not even being reason enough for her to stay alive.

CHAPTER

13

I HAVE NO IDEA how I made it back to the Lower East Side. Habit must've led me, or sheer luck. I wandered the streets for a while, unwilling to go back to Orchard Street until the sickness that threatened to return had passed. Could Mrs. Dunwitty be right—had Mama been having an affair? Pop didn't act like a man who'd been betrayed by his wife. But then Pop didn't necessarily know.

Mama loved Pop, though. I was certain of that. Every visit, every letter, was something she cherished. Maybe it was possible to desperately love someone and yet be so consumed by loneliness that you were willing to betray him with someone who was around more often. It happened all the time in the movies.

I paused and found myself standing before Normandie's Pharmacy. Through the window Suze was wiping down a table with a cloth. She looked up in time to see me watching her and offered me a wisp of a smile. Then she waved me in.

I didn't want to go home. Not yet.

The bell tinkled its welcome as I passed through the doors. A few customers lingered in the booths, but it was hardly crowded.

"How'd you know I was working?" said Suze.

"I didn't. In fact, I didn't even realize where I was until I looked up and saw the sign."

"You're pale as a sheet. How 'bout a milk shake? It's on me—it's the least I can do after you sprung for all that cab fare last night."

I agreed and slid into a booth while she told the soda jerk that I'd be having a chocolate milk shake. I realized that the only thing in my stomach was oatmeal and the remnants of Rhona's flask. No wonder I was shaking.

"You're not going to believe who showed up at my bedroom window during early bright," she said.

"Who?"

"Benny."

I'd forgotten about the night before's humiliation. What had seemed so important to me just a few hours ago had faded in significance. So Benny got humiliated—so what? His mother was alive. She hadn't possibly betrayed her entire family.

"Why'd he do that?" I asked.

"He couldn't take going home with a bloody nose. His

pop's got a temper, would've blown his top if Benny had shown up wearing someone else's bruises. So he slept on my bedroom floor."

I wondered how I would have responded to this story if she'd told it to me an hour before. Jealousy? Curiosity? Right now all I felt was numb.

"Anyway, neither of us could sleep, we were so wired from the Savoy, and once he got done telling me all the things he would do to those soldiers if he ran into them again, he started talking about you."

I felt like I was listening to this conversation over the radio. "Me?"

"Don't look so sad, baby girl. Our Benny thinks you're murder."

"Murder?" I asked.

"You know—marvelous. As a matter of fact, he was talking about taking you out sometime, just you and him."

"That's nice," I said.

It clearly wasn't the response she was expecting. "Are you all right?"

"Just beat to the socks, I guess. You were right about that."

"Sorry I didn't walk you home. You made it okay, though, right?"

"I got an earful for getting in so late, but otherwise it was fine."

"Your aunt was mad?"

I nodded. That's right, my aunt. Not Pop, or my lying, secretive mother, but my imaginary aunt who'd told me I had no curfew only to yell at me when I failed to return at a reasonable hour.

Apparently, I was just another liar in a family of many.

"You should've seen how angry my ma was," said Suze. "I didn't get it until this morning after Benny had left and her shift ended, but I swear people on Houston could hear her." She had another mark on her face, poorly covered by the heavy makeup she'd obviously applied that morning. "Is that how come you're upset? Because you got in trouble?"

If only it were something that simple. I shook my head. The milk shake arrived and I focused on stirring the thick liquid until it was thin enough to make it up the straw.

"Is it Benny? Have you changed your mind about being seen with a boy like him?"

That pulled me back. I wasn't Grace. Not even a little bit. "No. Of course not."

"Then what is it?"

Should I tell her? I needed to talk to someone. I couldn't imagine telling Pearl, not after the way she'd reacted to Mama's suicide. And it's not like I could talk to Pop about it. "I heard some things about my mother today. About why she killed herself."

Suze frowned. She'd forgotten I was the girl with the weight of the world on her shoulders. "What did you hear?"

"That she might've been having an affair."

"Ouch, baby." She put her hand on mine and squeezed. "Who told you that?"

"I overheard some women talking about her."

"What was your mama like?"

I was surprised by the question. What was she like? So often it was her death I thought of rather than who she'd been before it. "Beautiful. Generous. Smart. Stubborn. She wouldn't take no for an answer." Chapin had turned me down when we first applied, though I never knew why. Mama was the one who convinced them to change their minds. She'd marched into the headmaster's office, while I was left to wait with his secretary, and ten minutes later she emerged with the good news that they had made a mistake and I would be going there after all.

That was Mama. If she thought something wasn't fair, she'd fight to the death to make it right.

Suze smiled. "She loved your pop?"

"Absolutely."

"Then what those women said was just gravel. You can't go thinking something's true just because you heard it out loud. Maybe they were jealous of her. Or maybe they were trying to make sense of why she did what she did."

"She was a German," I said. I'm not sure why I told her. Maybe to prove that she was the last person anyone would be jealous of. Or maybe because I felt like I needed to be honest with Suze about something.

"That must've been hard for her," said Suze.

"And for me," I said.

"How so?"

"You know. Being an immigrant's kid is embarrassing enough, but being a German Jew? Nobody thinks that's a good thing."

Suze nodded. "I didn't realize you were Jewish."

"We changed our last name."

"Why?"

"I don't know." The one time I asked Mama about it, she'd said it was like how Deanna Durbin had changed her first name from Edna Mae—sometimes you had to have a name that better fit who people wanted you to be.

Suze pushed her hair behind her ear. "When people already think bad of you, it's pretty easy for them to assume the worst. You knew her, though. No matter what anyone says, you know the truth, right?"

It was like with Tom and how his father assumed he was headed down the wrong path. Actually, it was probably like that for all the Rainbows. Once people thought you were bad news, there was no hope of redeeming yourself. You either proved them right or made up your mind that what they thought of you didn't matter.

"You there, baby girl?"

I looked up and found Suze staring at me. She'd been talking this whole time, buzzing in my ear like a trapped

202

fly, and I hadn't heard a word of it. How long had I been lost in my own thoughts? "Sorry."

"No need for apologies. What I said was, if you're still worried, I bet your pop could clear everything up."

I almost laughed at the thought. Even my imaginary pop, the one still fighting the war, would never be able to talk to me about this. And who could expect him to? If the idea made me sick, it was a wonder he was able to get up in the morning.

I drank some of the milk shake and fixed a smile on Suze. "You're right."

"Where'd you hear these women talking, anyhow?"

"Upper East Side. I went to see a friend I went to school with and the minute I left the room, her mother started telling this other woman all about me." The words were out of my mouth before I realized that Suze might put two and two together and realize I'd gone to see Grace.

"What a bunch of vipers. What did your friend say?"

"I couldn't tell her. Sarah—that's her name—would've been mortified. I just made an excuse and left." So now there was an imaginary Sarah to remember.

"And she didn't come after you? Some friend." The door sounded its bell, warning of the arrival of more customers. "They're playing my song," she said with a smile. "I better get moving or get fired. You going to be okay?"

I nodded.

She slid out of the booth and straightened her uniform. "You want to come to my cave tonight? I'm watching the brat."

"I wish I could, but I think my aunt would have a conniption."

"All right. Then I'll see you Monday." She paused, like she wanted to say something else but couldn't think of what magical words it would take to make everything go away. Instead, she leaned toward me and planted a kiss on top of my head.

I WAS FEELING much better by the time I got home. Maybe Suze was right. These were bored society women, after all, who had nothing better to do with their time than gossip. And I knew Mama loads better than they did. She loved Pop, practically worshipped him, and if there was another man he was temporary at best. He certainly wouldn't have been the reason for her to kill herself, any more than Pop's return would've been the motivation for her to do herself in.

I let myself into the house and was about to go upstairs to take a nap when Pop's voice stopped me.

"Where have you been?" He was sitting on the sofa in the parlor with an ashtray full of half-smoked cigarettes resting in front of him.

It wasn't a friendly question. I wasn't in the mood for

combat, so I gave him the truth. "I went to the Upper East Side to visit Grace."

"And what made you think you could leave this house without telling anyone where you were going?"

"You weren't here and neither was Mrs. Mrozenski."

"I wasn't here because I went to get us this." He gestured toward a bakery box sitting beside his ashtray. Pastries that had once been fresh but had now begun to grow stale in the hours since he'd purchased them huddled together on a waxed paper sheet. How many sugar ration tickets had he used for those?

He'd intended them to be a peace offering. I could see that. After last night's run-in he was trying to call a truce by offering me sweets and hoping that *The Children's Parade* would bring me back to myself, or at least to the self I used to be before he went to Pearl Harbor.

"I'm sorry," I said.

My apology had no effect on him. Whatever anger had been bubbling inside him after he discovered I wasn't home rose to a full boil. "First Harlem, now the Upper East Side? New York's not your playpen, Iris. You don't get to pick and choose where you want to go without talking to me first."

His ire awoke something in me. Why was he being this way? "You. Weren't. Here."

"Then you write a note or, heaven forbid, wait until I come home and ask me if you can go."

I rolled my eyes.

He plucked a cruller from the box and tore it in two. "Something horrible could've happened to you last night."

"Why? Because there were negroes there?"

He looked like I'd slapped him. "This isn't about black and white. This is about you being fifteen years old. The world isn't a safe place."

I headed toward the stairs.

"I'm not done talking to you."

"I am."

"Get back here, Iris."

I mounted the first step. "No." I paused, expecting him to order my return even more loudly, but we'd reached a stalemate and he knew it. I was my mother's daughter, stubbornness and all.

"Go then," he said. I continued my climb. As I reached the top of the stairs, he spoke again, not to me, but to himself. I couldn't make out the words, at least not most of them. The only word I was certain I heard was my mother's name.

IT TOOK ME AN HOUR to fall asleep, even with the assistance of my baby blanket. As tired as I was, I was too irritated to doze right away. When I did finally sleep, I dreamed of Mama.

She and I are in the dining room of our old apartment, decorating it for a party. She sings as she works—"Alle

Meine Entchen," a silly little German song about ducklings that she used to entertain me with when I was very small. Pop's photo is on the mantel, two candles flickering on either side of it. He is dead and has been for a while. The party we are preparing for is to commemorate the anniversary of Pearl Harbor, when Pop was killed in action.

I awoke with a start just as the sun was going down. I wasn't sure what had jolted me awake until I heard the doorbell.

It had been ringing for a while.

Did Pop have a client? I crept down the stairs and saw his office door open and the room empty. He was gone again. No lights had been left on in the parlor and what little light was left in the day made the room look sleepy and sad. I clicked on a lamp, smoothed my hair, and approached the front door.

Grace was standing on the other side.

She'd never been to the Orchard Street house before. In fact, I was pretty sure she'd never been to the Lower East Side. As I watched her through the curtained glass panel that ran alongside the entryway, I could see her growing discomfort. She was most likely asking herself why she'd come here, and I was wondering the same thing. And while I was pretty sure it was fear that fueled her nervousness, mine was powered by embarrassment. What would she think of this house? Of Mrs. Mrozenski? Of the entire neighborhood that I now called home?

"Hello?" she called out. She must've seen the curtain move. It would be impossible to pretend no one was home now without appearing unforgivably rude. With no other choice, I opened the door and pretended to be surprised to see her there.

"What are you doing here?" I asked.

"I was worried. You left so fast today and you were acting so strange. Rolph said you got sick in the hallway."

Rolph? That must've been the doorman. I felt a jolt of pleasure that he was the one responsible for cleaning up my mess.

"You could've called," I said. "There was no reason to come all this way." My fingers found the molding around the door and worked it loose.

"I was afraid you wouldn't call me back. May I come in?"

I backed away in silent invitation. She entered the house, making no effort to hide her curiosity at the way the other half lived. I went into the parlor and sat on the sofa, one leg bent beneath my body, the other dangling over the cushion.

"What upset you?" asked Grace.

I played with the cushion's cord trim. "Nothing." She cocked her head at me. It was such an old familiar gesture that I instantly felt like I'd been fed a truth serum and had to respond honestly to her questions. "I overhead your mother and her friend talking about Mama."

"Oh." She didn't look surprised. "I thought as much. I

208

could just die. I'm so sorry, Iris. You know Mother is a terrible gossip, and Mrs. Huckabee is twice as bad."

So now I didn't need to worry just about Mrs. Dunwitty thinking these things about Mama; the entire Upper East Side would be talking about it.

"She said my mother was having an affair."

Grace sighed and took a seat on the upholstered rocker to my left. It was a comfortable chair—overstuffed and worn until its cushion was perfectly molded to fit the human form—but she sat on it stiffly, like she didn't trust that the furniture was strong enough to maintain her slight, feminine weight. In fact, everything about her seemed stiff— even the language she used in the Orchard Street house was overly formal.

How had she ever hooked up with someone like Tom? He must've hailed from a house just like this, where the furniture never got reupholstered or replaced, but instead bore the stains, scars, and burn marks it received until its working parts ceased functioning and someone put it out of its misery and left it out for the garbage collectors to retrieve.

She eyed the ashtray, still overflowing with the fruit of Pop's afternoon. "Is your father around?"

"No," I said. "He went out."

"Mind if I smoke?"

I said no only because I was so surprised by the question. What was she going to ask next? If I'd make her a cocktail?

She retrieved a cigarette from her purse and, once it was lit, inhaled it in a practiced way that made it clear that many, many cigarettes had come before it. Maybe it was an upperclassman thing. If I'd stayed at Chapin, I, too, might've learned how to blow perfect smoke rings and master the art of ashing with one hand while wielding a cheese knife with the other. "It's shameful behavior, but you must understand how your mother's death rattled everyone. Dying . . . as she did left so many questions, and I'm sure Mother was only theorizing to put her own mind at ease."

Was she really defending her mother? It didn't seem possible, and yet—

"Of course it was completely inappropriate and I'm sure she'd be mortified to learn you'd overheard her."

"Please don't tell her," I said.

"She needs to learn." She tweaked her mouth to the left, releasing a stream of smoke. "I won't allow her to upset my friends like this."

I could imagine how that conversation was going to go. Would Grace really be doing it because of me, or because of the joy she got from putting her mother in her place?

"Really, I'm fine, Grace. I know gossip is gossip. It just took me by surprise."

The front door rattled and Mrs. Mrozenski appeared, her arm filled with bags and boxes containing that week's groceries. She smiled when she saw me, then her gaze drifted over to the strange girl sitting in her chair, smoking in her house.

"Let me help you." I leaped to my feet and took two boxes from her. Grace remained sitting and smoking, completely unconcerned that an adult had arrived. "This is Grace Dunwitty, an old friend of mine from Chapin. Grace, this is Mrs. Mrozenski. She owns the house."

Grace raised an eyebrow but still didn't get up. "Nice to meet you."

"Yes, you, too," said Mrs. Mrozenski. I followed her into the kitchen and deposited the bags on the table. "Your friend is smoking," she whispered as she removed eggs, flour, and cabbage from the packages. "She is allowed to do this?"

I shrugged, uncertain how to respond. I couldn't imagine Grace doing it in her own house. But that was the point, wasn't it—she wasn't in her house.

Mrs. Mrozenski shooed me with her hand. "Go, enjoy your company. I get this."

"Are you sure?"

"Of course I'm sure."

I returned to the parlor. Grace wasn't there. She had moved into Pop's office, where she stood before his desk, examining the papers he'd left out the night before.

I cleared my throat. "That's Pop's office," I said. "It's kind of off-limits."

"Sorry. The door was open."

She gave the room another glance before returning to the parlor. Nervous energy propelled her. Instead of sitting, she approached the fireplace. On the mantel was a collection of porcelain bells, some photos, and a glass box intended for cigarettes.

"So all this stuff belongs to Mrs.—? I'm sorry, what's her name?" asked Grace.

"Mrozenski. Most of it's hers." Only the radio belonged to me and Pop, and the glassless photo of Mama sitting atop it.

"I guess she doesn't let you decorate, huh?" What she really meant was, she couldn't imagine anyone choosing to live among these cheap furnishings and belongings if they didn't have to.

"It's her house," I said.

"You know, our last cleaning lady was Polish. I don't think you met her. Mother fired her when she found out she was stealing from us." She picked up one of the bells and shook it. I half expected Mrs. Mrozenski to come running from the kitchen and demand she put it down.

When she didn't, I decided to do it myself.

"We're not really supposed to touch her stuff," I said.

"Why? It's not like it's worth anything."

I wanted her to leave. While her visit initially seemed like a kind gesture, it was starting to feel like something very different. I glanced at the mantel clock and feigned surprise. "It's getting late," I said.

"When's your pop coming home?" she asked. She put

down the bell and picked up a photo of Mrs. Mrozenski's family, letting the cigarette dangle as she examined it. A piece of ash fell from the tip and landed on the faded wool rug. I kept my eye on it, worried it would burn a hole right through, but it smoldered and disappeared before any damage could be done.

"Soon, I guess. Like I told you before, I got in trouble for the Harlem trip last night. I don't think he'd be too happy to know I had a friend over on top of it." She showed no sign of leaving. What was I going to have to do? Throw her purse out the door and hope she chose to follow it? "Do you want me to call a cab for you?"

"No need. I took the subway."

I didn't hide my shock. I'd counted on her and everyone else from Chapin being too afraid to journey this way. "Do you want me to walk you to the station?" I asked.

"Oh, I know the way. I've been there loads of times."

She seemed to be baiting me and I realized for the first time that her visit wasn't just about trying to get information about me; there was something she wanted to tell me. "Seriously?" I asked.

She nodded, a smile lingering on her lips. "Jo and I do it all the time. You can't spend your whole life on the Upper East Side, right?"

"So what do you do when you come here?"

"A little bit of this and that. Go to the USO dances, mostly. Jo can't get enough of the sailors."

"And you?"

"I prefer a man in an Air Corps uniform."

"And your parents don't mind?"

"Hell's bells—I'd never tell them. Could you imagine? And it's not like I'm serious with any of them. It's all about the chase."

"The what?"

She tilted her head at me the way Aunt Miriam used to when I said something precious and naïve. "You know— what you can make them do for you. How much you can make them spend. I haven't paid for a dinner out in two months."

I'm sure I wore my disgust like a masquerade mask. But Grace was in her own little world, where it was perfectly acceptable to go out with a boy just so she could later share the tale of what a goon he was. "And then that's it?" I said. "You never see them again?"

"What's to see? They're off to war and I'm off to school." She inhaled the cigarette. She was, mercifully, reaching its end.

"It just seems like you're using them."

"It's not like they're getting nothing in return."

I raised an eyebrow, as Pearl had done when she wanted me to understand that Rhona's past trouble had to do with sex.

"Not that!" said Grace. "Not from me, anyway. But a kiss or two and a few dances go a long way toward making them feel like they aren't being taken advantage of. Besides, you can't use someone who doesn't want to be used." She said it like it was a pronouncement written on a holy scroll. Were these her words or her new friend Josephine's?

"It seems strange to go to all that trouble for a boy you're not planning on seeing again."

"Why? Even if I really liked them, it's not like it could ever go anywhere. I might as well date a negro." She extinguished the cigarette in the ashtray, looped her pocketbook around her arm, and fluffed her hair in the mantel mirror. "You should come out with us sometime. It's a real gas. They can't get enough of private school girls. Of course, we don't have to tell them you don't go to Chapin anymore."

Because heaven forbid we be honest with them about *something*. "That would be swell."

"Let's make a plan to get together next week. I promise you Mother won't be around. I am so embarrassed about her behavior. I could just die."

"Don't worry about it," I said. "I've practically forgotten all about it."

"That's what I love about you, Iris. You're just so . . . resilient."

Resilient. That was a new one. I opened the door and held it for her as she passed through. "Be careful out here," I said. "It's a rough neighborhood."

215

14

ONCE GRACE WAS OUT OF THE HOUSE and up the street, I emptied the ashtray, picked the remnants of her cigarette from the rug, and mulled over her strange visit. I just couldn't believe that her trip to the Lower East Side was motivated by concern for me. After all, she could have called me on the telephone and accomplished just as much. Something else had sent her here. But what? If she didn't know he was missing, maybe she was hoping to run into Tom. That seemed unlikely though—she'd never mentioned him. What if Rhona and Suze had it all wrong? Maybe Tom had a crush on Grace that she never returned, and he'd exaggerated the relationship to his friends as a way of breaking free of Rhona. It wasn't hard to imagine Grace paying him a little attention one night and then tossing him aside like her military boyfriends. And if she was embarrassed to have momentarily been attracted to someone like him, she certainly wasn't going to mention it to me.

But why come here?

As I finished cleaning, Mrs. Mrozenski came into the room and smiled at my efforts.

"Your friend is gone."

"No."

"She's upstairs?"

"No, I mean she's gone, but she's not my friend. Not anymore."

She touched my hair, smoothing it with her palm. "This is good, Iris. You don't need to be around people like her." How could she tell so much about Grace in so little time? I wanted to ask her. It seemed to me that despite all the hours I'd spent learning to read people, I was still a very poor judge of character.

"She's changed a lot," I said.

"You have, too. That is life." She approached the mantel and straightened the picture Grace had plopped haphazardly back into place. "Dinner will be ready soon. I make sausages tonight."

"That sounds great."

She glanced toward the office. "Your father is not here."

"Not yet."

"You two make peace?"

So she knew about how things had been between us. Was she exercising the same sixth sense that told her Grace Dunwitty was bad news, or had Pop come to her asking for advice during the hours when I was sleeping?

"Not yet."

"He worries about you, Iris. Maybe more than most fathers. He has been through a lot."

"I know."

"We don't have to agree, but we can show respect. Sometimes that's all anyone wants."

While she returned to the kitchen, I went into the office, worried that Grace might have left some evidence of her visit during her brief time in there. Pop's paperwork lay strewn around the desk and his notes about Tom's case were on top. He had been to the prison where Tom's brother, Michael, was held. So he knew about that. According to his notes, Tom hadn't been to see him in two months, a fact Michael seemed less than happy about. "He said his brother came to see him at least once a month," Pop had written in his messy, military scrawl. "He figured either his parents had put a kibosh on the trips or Tom had a Hershey Bar that was taking up his attentions." Pop had also found out about Tom's previous disappearance. He'd talked privately with Mrs. Barney, who "seemed reticent to discuss her son's previous comings and goings, but eventually admitted he had left before and returned with a face full of fading bruises. She never learned the source of his injuries but insisted he keep them hidden from his father."

There was also an inventory of what had been found in Tom's locker: gym shoes, cigarettes, textbooks, gum wrappers, and the note Pop had told the Barneys about. It read,

"If you're serious, meet me at 240 Houston Street #7D at 4:00." Pop was no slouch. He'd checked out the address and made a note of his findings: "240 Houston #7D is a private physician's office. The occupant didn't recognize the photo of T.B., but did say the area was a popular hangout for youth because of the private back alley. No one in T.B.'s alleged group of friends copped to writing the note."

I felt a mix of pride and disappointment. Pop had done all right without me. The only thing he hadn't yet learned of, or at least made note of, was Tom's relationship with Grace.

Should I tell Pop about her? I was on thin ice with him as it was; if I told him about Grace, I would have to tell him I'd been working on the case, and who knows what would happen then. Besides, I wasn't sure Grace was involved. In fact, so far I had no proof that Tom and she even had a relationship.

So that would be my first step: verify what was going on between Tom and Grace. And maybe then I could let Pop know there was a lead he'd missed that was worth following up on.

A car door shut outside the window. I spied a yellow cab out front. Pop was home. I returned the notes to their original position, left the office, closed the door, and landed on the sofa just as Pop arrived.

"Hi," he said as he came into the house.

"Hi," I replied, my voice soft and hesitant. I wanted to congratulate him on getting so far on the case and apologize for thinking he couldn't do it alone. I could tell from the stiffness in his shoulders that our argument that afternoon was still playing in his head.

"Have a nice nap?" he asked.

"It was fine."

I didn't want to become like Grace, crabby to my parents because I thought I'd earned that right. Mrs. Mrozenski was right: I didn't have to agree with Pop, any more than he had to agree with me, but he deserved my respect.

"I'm sorry about last night," I said. "You're right: common sense should've told me that I shouldn't go to Harlem and I definitely shouldn't have drunk anything. I'm not going to apologize for coming home late because, honestly, I didn't know I was breaking a rule. The others had curfews and if I thought I had one I would've followed it, but you never told me."

"Iris—"

I held up my hand to stop him. "I'm also sorry for disappearing today. I was feeling homesick and I wanted to see Grace. I knew you were angry enough that you probably wouldn't let me go, and so I did it before you had a chance to tell me not to. That was dumb of me."

Some of the tension left his shoulders. He must've been worried I was out drinking again, or doing something else he never expected from me. The desire to see an old friend was something he could relate to.

"You can trust me," I said. "I promise. But I can't be locked up here all day every day, Pop. I'm lonely."

He sat where Grace had sat earlier, sighing as his back came in contact with the overstuffed cushion. He worked his hands into a ball, the skin reddening as he squeezed them together. "This girl you went to see was someone you went to Chapin with?" I nodded. "Good girl, good family?"

If only he knew. "The best."

He wagged a finger at me. "No more Harlem. No more drinking."

I nodded my pledge.

"Maybe I was harsh before. House arrest is over. But I want you to stay in this neighborhood. No more trips uptown. Not for the time being, anyway."

I didn't see any point in arguing with him, so I nodded my agreement.

I FIGURED SUNDAY was a lost day. Grace would be busy with church and brunch, so there was no point in trying to contact her. And besides, I had a feeling that it was best to let her come to me again. In her house, surrounded by all those silent expectations for how she should behave, she hadn't been honest with me. And while I may not have liked the girl who showed up on my doorstep, at least she was free here.

I spent Sunday lolling around the house, listening to the radio and reading the papers. On Monday I arrived at school early, hoping I might see Benny. I'm not sure what I was thinking by getting there before the morning bell. Benny wasn't the kind of boy to come to school early. In fact, it was amazing he came to school at all.

"Iris?"

As I scanned the front lawn looking for any sign of the Rainbows, Pearl approached me. Her books were wedged beneath one pudgy arm, her lunch hanging limp in her other hand.

"Hi," I said.

"How was Friday night?"

It felt like a million years ago. When I thought about explaining everything that had happened since I last saw her, I felt weary. "It was fine."

The warning bell rang. We had ten minutes to get to class.

"I missed you on Saturday."

That was right; we'd made plans to get together so I could tell her about my trip to the Savoy. Of course, that was before Pearl had squealed on me when I needed her the most.

"I kind of assumed you'd know our plans would be canceled when you told my pop I wasn't with you on Friday," I said.

"I'm so sorry for that. When he came by, my father was there. There was no way I could lie and get away with it."

That softened me. A little.

"And I'm sorry about Friday afternoon. About how I acted," she said.

I tried to remember what had bothered me so much about her behavior and couldn't. Mama. That was right. She's been mad that I hadn't told her about her death.

My good mood evaporated.

"Did you find out anything about Tom?"

I should've said no and walked away, but my desire to get back at her overruled any logic coursing through me. "Sort of. I found out he had another girlfriend right before he disappeared. A girl I knew at Chapin."

Her face grew pink. It wasn't what she had wanted to hear. "Really? Did Rhona know?"

"Rhona knew, all right. In fact, she got another boyfriend as payback."

"Was it serious with the other girl?" Her lower lip quivered.

"He thought it was. He was heartbroken when she called it off."

People pushed past us as they entered the building and headed toward their homerooms.

"I better blow," I said.

"So I'll see you at lunch?"

"Maybe."

She skulked away, clearly unhappy that her apologies hadn't made everything perfect again. But lunch with Pearl meant having to pretend I hadn't changed in the last two days, or launching into a long explanation of everything that had happened, and I just didn't want to do that.

Besides, there was a chance Benny might want to sit with me.

I spent the morning trying to figure out how I could avoid Pearl in the cafeteria. Fortunately, as I arrived at lunch, the perfect distraction landed in my lap.

"Iris! Come join us," said Suze. I looked toward the table Pearl and I usually occupied and offered the waiting Pearl a shrug. Then I followed Suze to the cluster of other Rainbows. Rhona and Maria sat together. Maria had that day's hot lunch. Rhona had an apple and an orange. An empty seat had been left next to Benny and I slid into it, trying not to stare at the mass of bruises obscuring his handsome face. No wonder he'd slept on Suze's bedroom floor. Even two days out he looked gory.

Something snapped in my head.

Bruises. Tom had had bruises that made him disappear the previous spring, that were still vivid when he came home a week later. Tom also wore the zoot. Was it far-fetched to think he'd been beaten up one night after an evening on the town and decided to lay low until the bruises faded?

"How's everything?" asked Suze.

"Better," I said. "How was babysitting?"

She rolled her eyes and took a bite of sandwich. It looked

like peanut butter. Just plain peanut butter. "Fraughty. The brat's lucky she lived through the night. Ma was happy, though. You thought any more about what I said?"

She was talking about the rumors about Mama. "Yeah. I'm not going to let it bother me. Until someone confirms it, it's not worth paying it any mind."

"Don't let it get you down, baby girl." Her bruises had also faded since Saturday, but they were still there. I wondered what it was like to live in a family that used fists instead of words to make their points. As stupid as it sounds, I almost envied her. At least she knew where she stood moment to moment. There was something so uncomplicated about basing the status of your relationship with someone on whether or not they were angry enough to hit you.

Lunch passed quickly in their company. Benny never talked directly to me, but his thigh periodically made contact with mine, and after the third time it happened, I was pretty sure it wasn't an accident. Nobody talked about the run-in with the servicemen. Instead, they recounted our evening at the Savoy and how the rest of their weekends had been dreary exercises in making money and not getting yelled at by parents and bosses.

I contributed very little beyond my tale of getting in trouble for coming home late. They were fascinated that it was the first time it had ever happened to me.

"No one told you that you had a curfew?" asked Dino.

"Nope."

"Doesn't seem right that you got in trouble then. How do you know you're breaking a rule when no one told you there was a rule to begin with?"

"That's what I told him," I said. "And he actually saw the logic. I think we reached a truce."

"Him?" asked Suze. "I thought it was your aunt."

"She's the one who caught me, but my uncle's the one who lectured me." I was amazed I could think so fast on my feet.

"So you're out of the doghouse?" asked Rhona.

"Not really. He smelled your booze on my breath, so . . ."

Rhona shook her head. "You've got to learn to cover that up. Peppermints work great. And chewing gum."

"If you can get it," said Maria. "I hear they're going to start rationing gum and most everything else."

"Disappointing high school boozers everywhere," quipped Benny.

"Don't worry," said Rhona. "I'll come up with something else. You could always kill the smell with a ciggie."

I held up my hands in surrender. "Trust me, that would only make them yell louder."

The bell signaled the end of lunch, and we all got up to throw away our trash and say our farewells. As I disentangled myself from the table, I felt a hand grab mine and gently squeeze. Warmth rippled through me and I met Benny's eyes for the first time.

"How long are you in the doghouse for?" he asked.

"I don't know. A week, I guess?"

"At least it's not forever, right?" He gave me a wink, released his grip, and with long, even strides walked away.

Should I follow him? I didn't think so. He didn't look back, anyway.

As the rest of the group dispersed, I fell into step with Dino, hoping his empathizing about my getting in trouble gave us enough of a connection that I could talk to him. There were things I needed to know. Things I didn't feel comfortable asking Benny.

"You all right by the way?" I asked, my voice almost a whisper.

"You mean after Friday? Yeah. It's no big thing."

"Maybe not to you, but I couldn't believe they'd do something like that. I mean, here they are enlisting to protect our country, and they pick a fight with one of the very people they've pledged to protect."

He looked at me like I'd just laid an egg in the middle of the hall. "Huh. Never thought of it that way."

"Does it happen a lot?" I asked.

He shrugged. "More than I'd like."

"Maria said it happened to Tom, too."

"Sure, we've all taken our licks. It's about the zoot, not about being brown."

"Did any of you ever fight back?"

"We're not chicken."

"I'm not saying you are," I said. "I'm just curious 'cause it seems like if you fought back, someone would make a big deal about how that proves you're unpatriotic. I mean, you can't hit a soldier, right?"

Another look of amazement. "Yeah," he said. "I mean, yeah. It's really unfair. They've got our backs against the wall."

"So none of you ever fought back?"

"I took a swing a time or two. But it's just easier if you go limp and let them do whatever they're going to do. Makes them mad. They want you to fight back so it'll last longer, especially if there's an audience."

"You mean the other soldiers?"

"Sure, them and the skirts. Fools thought Rhona, Maria, and Suze would be impressed if they put us in our places."

"What about Benny and Tommy? Do they fight back, too?"

"Benny usually plays possum until it passes. He's no fool. Tom learned the hard way not to stand up for himself. The one time he did, he ended up with two cracked ribs and a busted schnozzle. He was out of school for a week."

"Last spring?"

"How'd you know?"

"Rhona mentioned something about it." So I was right. The life had gotten pummeled out of him and he hadn't

228

wanted anyone to see the damage he took. If it had happened once before, it could've happened again. And maybe this time he wasn't smart enough to lie there and take it.

"I better trilly," said Dino. "See you around."

"Yeah," I said. "See you."

I ROLLED what Dino had told me around my head throughout the afternoon, barely paying attention during American History and Geography. There was one detail that had stuck in my head—Dino said that the servicemen liked to have an audience, especially a female one. They may not have been able to impress Suze, Maria, and Rhona by humiliating their friends, but that didn't mean it didn't work for other women. Like Grace and her friend Josephine.

What if Grace had been there the night this happened? It would certainly give Tom reason to lay low. It was one thing to fight back and lose, but it was another thing to fight back and lose in front of the girl you were hoping to win back. He might've been so humiliated that he took off then and there.

But would Grace have just let him run off without checking to make sure he was all right?

Probably. Especially if she was desperate to get rid of him.

I needed to see Grace. Not at my house, but in her own element at Chapin, where she didn't know she was being watched. I wanted to see how much she'd really changed since I'd left. I wanted to know why she hadn't told me about Tom.

And despite my promise to Pop to stay on the Lower East Side, I was going to do it that afternoon.

15

THERE WAS NO TELLING how quickly Grace would leave Chapin after school, so rather than waiting until the end of the day to go uptown, I decided to skip typing class.

I'd never skipped before and I had no idea what would happen when I did. Would they send a truant officer after me? Call Pop and report the absence? I couldn't take any chances, and so just before the period started, I sought out Pearl and asked for her help.

"I need to leave school," I told her.

"Now?" I nodded. She didn't ask why or where I was going. I think she was so thrilled that I was talking to her that she didn't dare risk rocking the boat.

"Can you snag the attendance records for my typing class and make sure no one knows I'm playing hooky?"

"Sure. Absolutely."

A twinge of guilt passed through me, but I didn't have time to analyze it.

"Thanks," I said.

"What are friends for?"

It was surprisingly easy to walk off campus. I called the house from a pay phone plastered with a sign that warned me to keep my calls brief so our enlisted men could use the lines. Mrs. Mrozenski answered on the third ring, her voice so out of breath that I had to imagine she had been upstairs when she first heard the call.

"Hi, it's Iris," I said.

"Everything is okay?"

"Everything's fine. I had a quick break between classes and wanted to ask if you'd tell Pop that I have to stay after school."

"You have a meeting maybe?" It was like she was feeding me a ready-made excuse because she didn't think my vague reason would be sufficient for Pop.

"Yeah, a meeting." I felt terrible about the lie. Pop and I were supposed to be honest with each other. But the pull was too strong. I needed to see Grace.

"Dinner will be at six," said Mrs. Mrozenski. "You will be back then?"

"Absolutely."

I took a train uptown, feeling like I was breaking a thousand laws along the way. What if Pop—or someone he knew—saw me? That would be it—no more second chances, no hope of one day working by his side, nothing to help me pass my time but school and Pearl.

My travel companions only made me feel worse. Enlisted men in uniforms so new you could still see the pinholes from the tags they'd removed rode the subway with the wide-eyed gaze of tourists. I thought of the men we'd encountered on Friday night and wondered if these boys shared similar thoughts about zoot suits and patriotism. But then they looked at me with such sad expressions in their eyes, like I reminded them of their sister or the girl they'd left behind, and I felt ashamed for thinking they were capable of doing anything wrong.

I got off at 86th and Lexington and walked the familiar streets, taking in the fall smells of the privileged part of the city. As I arrived at Chapin, the doors burst open and the first of the girls piled out of the main building. They weren't headed home. Chapin didn't end with its last class. Now was the time for the various sports and clubs the girls participated in to kick off their meetings and practices. In groups of twos and threes, the identically clad girls headed for Drama, Dance, Orchestra, Yearbook, Student Government, Newspaper, or the dozens of other activities they could sign up for. If I were still there, who knew what I'd be doing?

It didn't matter, I told myself. I was gone now. There would be no opportunity to excel at playing the handbells or writing poetry for the literary magazine.

Girls continued streaming out of the building, Grace among them. In her company was someone I didn't recognize. She had a mane of bright red hair that looked like it would frizz out if it wasn't tamed into the victory rolls she currently wore. This had to be Josephine.

Neither of them wore their uniform. Clad in street clothes, their faces made up with a heavy hand, their saddle shoes exchanged for pumps, they obviously weren't headed to a club meeting, rehearsal, or lacrosse match. They exited the gates and I counted to twenty and followed after them, keeping enough distance that I'd have time to react and hide just in case they suddenly turned around.

Josephine's voice was low and musical, though she made no effort to keep it quiet. "How about if we try the Wall?" she said to Grace. She meant Horn & Hardart, the automat we used to frequent after school.

Grace bowed her head in supplication. She seemed to be fighting to keep pace with her friend. "There weren't that many last time—"

"Last time we went too early."

"I suppose it's worth a try."

A group of sailors approached from the opposite direction. Josephine slowed her pace, forcing Grace to do the same. I responded accordingly, ducking to the right so I didn't walk into anyone.

"How's my hair?" asked Josephine.

"Good," said Grace.

"Lipstick?" She bared her teeth, momentarily looking like a wolf.

Grace scraped at one of her own incisors to indicate where Josephine should devote her attention. "You got a little lip cream there."

"The tall one's cute, don't you think?" As she asked the question, she waved at the sailors, fluttering her fingers like some movie coquette.

"He's zazz all right," said Grace.

"Where are you headed to, girls?" asked the sailor Josephine had just described as cute.

"Wouldn't you like to know?" she said back.

"I don't suppose you have time to show some boys from out of town where they can get a good cheap meal."

"Depends on how cheap you want it," said Josephine. "Girls like us have standards."

The boys stopped, bringing Josephine and Grace to a standstill. The crowd parted around them, me included, and continued on its way. I put a scarf over my hair and pulled up the collar of my jacket, hoping it would hide my face. I walked ten steps, then doubled back, pausing at a newsstand where I pretended to be absorbed by that day's headlines.

"What do you say, fellows?" said the tall sailor. "Would a little company make you willing to stretch your budgets?"

"How old are you?" asked one of his friends, a short boy with a nose like a beak.

Now it was Grace's turn to pipe up. She shifted her body, sticking out her chest while arching her back. "How old do you think we are?"

He stared at her for a moment. "I'm guessing you two are still in high school."

"Then you'd be guessing wrong," said Jo.

He cocked his head toward Grace. "That so?"

"Would I lie to you?" said Grace.

"No, I don't think you would."

A wind blew past, bringing with it the first hint of the approaching winter. Even though Josephine was wearing a coat, she shivered and rubbed her hands together like we'd just been hit by an arctic blast.

"You cold?" asked the tall sailor.

"Freezing. Mind if I put my hand in your pocket?" She fluttered her lashes like she was a Southern belle.

He pulled his peacoat from his body. "You go right ahead." She slid her hands into the navy wool jacket, keeping enough of a distance from the boy that her behavior didn't seem overtly improper. "So where are we taking you two for dinner?" asked the sailor.

"There's an automat a few blocks from here," said Josephine. "How 'bout we meet you there in an hour?"

"Why not walk there with us now?"

"Because I can't keep my hands in your pocket all night. I need to pop by my house and get a hat and gloves."

"How do we know you and your friend won't stand us up?"

"You don't," said Josephine. She removed her hands from his jacket. "Ta-ta." She waved goodbye to them, looped her arm in Grace's, and then continued on her way.

I stepped into place behind them as they passed the newspaper kiosk. The sailors watched them leave and then headed in the opposite direction. Josephine was silent for half a block, then tossed a look over her shoulder to verify that the sailors were gone. Once she was sure they were, she removed a wallet from her jacket and flipped through its contents.

"Fifty dollars," she told Grace. "Not bad."

"I thought we were going to get dinner with them," said Grace. She sounded irritated, though I don't think it was the fact of Jo's crime that bothered her so much as the change in plans it represented.

"I didn't like the looks of them up close. All that talk about a cheap dinner. And how dare they ask our age."

Grace pouted. "I can't believe you stole from him."

"I'm cutting out the middleman," said Josephine. "Why go through the trouble of listening to their boring war stories for a free meal when we can just take the cash and run?" Josephine removed a pack of cigarettes from her other pocket. She tapped out two, put both to her mouth, and lit them like she was Humphrey Bogart. Once both had ignited, she passed one to Grace, who greedily sucked at the slim white tube.

"It's probably his money for a month," said Grace.

"If you feel so bad about it, why don't you track him down and give him your take?" Jo removed a hunk of bills from the wallet and passed them Grace's way.

"Don't be stupid," said Grace. But she took the money.

"You're the one who's being unpleasant. I'm just trying to have a little fun." Josephine snapped her fingers as an idea occurred to her. "Speaking of fun, how about if we show up at the automat and rescue him by paying for his meal with his own money? Wouldn't that be a scream?"

"Not really. Ten to one the minute he realizes his wallet is gone he'll figure out who took it. I'm not in the mood to get arrested."

Josephine rolled her eyes. "Fine. Then what do you want to do?"

"Meet someone to take us for dinner and dancing. Like we planned."

They paused at an intersection.

I took a step backward and bent down to tie my shoe, worried that I was getting too close to them. As much as I wanted to hear how this argument played out, the last thing I wanted was to get caught.

"Iris?" Behind me, a familiar voice rang out. Two of them, actually—it was Bea and Bev.

I looked back toward Josephine and Grace. They hadn't

heard my name. They were too caught up in their own drama to pay attention to anything else going on around them. I spun around and smiled at the twins.

"Oh my gosh," said Bev. "It is you. Are you visiting your aunt again?"

"Yes," I said. So much for my disguise. I stood up, pulled the scarf from my hair and shoved it in my pocket.

"Grace said she saw you on Saturday."

"She sure did," I said. I tried to echo their polished enthusiasm even as I wondered what was fueling it. What had Grace told them about our time together?

"Are you looking for Grace?" asked Bea.

Grace and Josephine crossed the street. Their pace had picked up. Had they reached a decision about how they were going to spend their evening, or were they still arguing?

"No, I'm actually on my way home," I told Bea. I was even less comfortable seeing them now than I had been during my first stakeout. Were Bea and Bev privy to the rumors about Mama? If they were, thankfully they were too well bred to drag my scandal into broad daylight. Which wasn't to say that they didn't regularly discuss me in the hallowed halls of Chapin.

"Grace said you're going to get together again," said Bev.

"Maybe. I mean, it depends on our schedules and stuff."

"Believe me, it would be good for Grace," said Bea. "We were so glad when she told us she saw you. I'm sure she told you about you know who?"

Who was *you know who?* Tom?

I shrugged to indicate that I didn't know what they were talking about.

"Josephine O'Hara," said Bev.

"Oh, right. Yeah, she mentioned her a time or twelve. I'm surprised those two get on so well," I said. "Jo's an upperclassman, right?"

"I think that's why she likes Grace," said Bev. "She figured out she was top dog of the underclassmen and made a beeline straight for her."

"So I take it you two aren't in her band of admirers?"

"Please," said Bev with an eye roll. "She's a scholarship student." She made the word *scholarship* sound like a terrible disease, like polio. Being on aid was usually the kiss of death at Chapin. When we first discovered that Mama's money had run out, Pop offered to look for funding to pay for my schooling. I nixed the idea. I knew word would get out that my family could no longer afford the school and along with it would come the cooed remarks that everyone liked me just the same and don't worry, my secret would never get out.

Except it always did. Those girls whose families had experienced reversals of fortune became social outcasts. At least the girls who'd always been on scholarship knew they were different and didn't expect to fit in. For the rest of us, there were constant digs that the only reason you were there was because everyone else's parents could afford to pay for them and by golly you better be grateful for that.

There was no way I would have let them do that to me.

"Does Grace know that?" I asked.

"She just found out," said Bea. "Can you imagine? Josephine takes the subway to campus each day. The *subway*."

Did she mean that thing I was getting ready to board to go back to the Lower East Side? How shocking.

"So have you met any cute boys this year?" I asked.

"Not really," said Beatrice. "Besides, who has time? Between studying and extracurriculars, we hardly have a moment to eat."

And they certainly didn't have time to travel across town to visit their aunt, she seemed to be saying. I decided to take a shot in the dark. "Grace seems to have made the time," I said.

"Don't tell me that's still going on," said Bev.

"I heard she dumped him," said Bea. "After the *incident*."

"Thank God," said Bev. "I would've died of embarrassment if I were her."

"Do tell," I said.

Bea stepped toward me and lowered her voice. "She was going with this boy from one of the public schools. Or at least *he* thought so, anyway. One day he showed up at Chapin wanting to talk to her. And the way he was dressed—"

"In a bright red suit," said Bev. "Like he was a colored boy. And he had those flowers."

"Carnations," said Bea. Couldn't he afford nicer flowers with the money he'd made from the locker thefts? Or had that money been used for something else? "She tried to breeze past him, but he kept calling out her name in that accent of his. It was just awful. I mean, it's one thing to be attracted to a boy like that, but to be seen in public . . ."

"Oh, come on—it was kind of sweet," said Bea.

"Are you off your nut?"

"Remember what the note said."

"There was a note?" I asked.

"He dropped it," said Bea. "It was a love letter. Diana Fox found it and by the next morning there were copies all over the school."

"And what did it say?"

Bev fluttered her lashes, obviously not seeing the romance her sister did. " 'I can't live without you. I'll do anything for you. You're Juliet to my Romeo.' It just went on and on. The most notable thing about it was that he actually spelled everything correctly, though I'm sure someone helped him with that. I really thought it was going to ruin her for life. Girls were quoting it for weeks."

"When did this happen?" I asked.

"About a month ago," said Bea. "Of course, eventually everyone stopped talking about it, Grace being Grace."

"The gossip may be gone, but the relationship could still be on if Grace told Iris about him," said Bev.

"She barely mentioned it," I said. "I'm sure the only

reason she said anything to me is because Tom and I go to school together. She probably wanted to warn me that he was bad news."

"Lord and butler," said Bev. "You go to school with him? You poor thing."

"He's not so bad."

They exchanged another look. Judgment had been rendered: Grace may have been able to resurrect her reputation, but I was a lost cause.

"How'd she meet him, anyhow?" I asked. "She never told me."

"Who knows?" said Bea. "I'm sure Josephine had something to do with it. She's always dragging Grace to unsavory places. I've heard they've even gone to USO dances in Brooklyn."

I was half tempted to tell them about my night in Harlem just to see them faint. "I'm surprised Tom gave up on her so easily. He's pretty persistent from what I've heard. There was a girl he dated in public school who practically had to get the police to step in to get him to leave her alone." Poor Tom. It was bad enough that they were dragging his name through the mud; did I have to invent stories about him now, too?

Bea shrugged. "All I know is one day he's showing up at Chapin, and the next day Grace is gushing over how she won't have to worry about ever seeing him again."

A chill passed through me. Was her choice of words

standard sub-deb exaggeration, or was it a clue that whatever happened to Tom Barney was more permanent?

"I better go," I told Bea and Bev. "My pop busts a gut if I'm late for supper."

"We should get together sometime," said Bev. "We miss you."

"That would be swell," I said. "Anytime either of you want to come to the Lower East Side, give me a buzz. Grace knows the number."

They told me that they'd be in touch, but I knew better than to hold my breath. The Lower East Side was Mars, and I was now a Martian as far as they were concerned.

16

I WAS LATE TO DINNER, but fortunately so was Pop. Mrs. Mrozenski sat by herself at the table, smoking a cigarette in front of a full plate of something that had been wrapped in cabbage and then cooked for hours in tomato sauce. "Sorry," I said as I came in. "Things went longer than I expected."

She wasn't mad. Mrs. M rarely ever got mad. But I could see worry creasing her face. I wasn't sure if it was fear that something had happened to me or concern about what punishment I'd face if I hadn't gotten home before Pop had. And I knew she'd never tell me unless I asked her flat out. As nice as she was to me, she was an intensely private person. And while I appreciated that most of the time, there were moments when I wished there was at least one person in this house who didn't keep their worries bottled up inside.

Her face seemed long and sorrowful. Had something

happened to her son? Letters arrived regularly from him, snatched from the postman's hand and whisked away to her room upstairs, where I imagine she read them in privacy. She never shared their contents, though I often saw a piece of V-mail sticking out of her apron pocket, and more than once I'd caught her rereading his missives like a page of Scripture you toted around and turned to when you needed reassurance.

She did so much for us: cooking, cleaning, putting up with delayed rent. And yet I never thought to ask her about her own life. "Are you all right?" I asked her.

She cocked her head to the right, as though she was trying to prevent her surprise at being asked the question from leaking out the other side. "They released new casualty numbers today for the Navy and the Marines." She passed the newspaper my way. It was folded so that the article in question appeared on top: "14,466 Casualties in Sea Service."

Not even a year had passed yet and we'd topped five figures, and that was for only a portion of the armed forces.

Surely the new, lowered draft age would pass now. And if that happened, every boy in the senior class could be gone in one fell swoop. Including Benny.

I pushed the paper away. "It'll end soon," I said.

"This I pray for every night."

I dug into the meal with as much excitement as I could muster and was pleasantly surprised to find the cabbage full of meat and rice, delicately seasoned to better meet Pop's and my unadventurous taste buds. "This is delicious," I told her, hoping my enthusiasm seemed genuine.

"Is halupki. From my mother's recipe."

I cleaned my plate and dug into a second helping. Rather than letting my mind linger on how massive a number fifteen thousand really was, I forced myself to mull over my conversation with Bea and Bev. I could almost guarantee that the last thing those two were thinking about was the war.

"You are awfully quiet," said Mrs. Mrozenski.

"I'm just tired." I thought about talking it over with her, but given the enormity of what weighed on her mind, my problems seemed ridiculously lightweight in comparison. So Grace didn't tell me about Tom. So what? It's not like she valued my opinion anymore. But it was strange that everyone at Chapin knew about him and she didn't say one word to me. Could it be that she wanted to keep up the illusion that she was superior to me and wouldn't lower herself to trawl the Lower East Side for a boyfriend? Or had she figured out that Tom and I went to the same school and decided it would be wiser not to mention him to me?

But why would it matter if I knew they were connected . . . unless she was somehow responsible for his disappearance. I shook the thought out of my head. As much as Grace had changed—and I had to face that she was now a shadow of the girl I once knew—there was no way that I could believe she would physically harm someone.

We finished dinner, and still no Pop. Was he following a lead in the Barney case, or was there some new job demanding his attention? I went to my room to tackle my homework, which would take all of five minutes if I extended any kind of effort at all. I wondered how much work Bea and Bev were facing. The workload at Chapin was legendary, especially for upperclassmen. They wanted to prepare you for college. Chapin girls didn't just go to university to meet men. They actually went to get degrees.

And me? What would I be doing in four years? Working for Pop, tending my own family, or spending my days as a secretary in some dingy Lower East Side office?

The phone rang, causing me to jump.

"Iris?" Mrs. Mrozenski called up the stairs. "Is for you."

Who would be calling for *me*? I took the steps two at a time, my heartbeat matching the pace of my feet.

Maybe it was Benny. That would explain Mrs. Mrozenski's smile as she handed me the receiver. A boy calling the house for me would be a historic event.

"Hello?" I said.

"Hello, Iris," said a decidedly female voice. "It's Grace."

My heartbeat picked back up. Had she seen me tailing Josephine and her that afternoon?

"Hi," I said. "Is everything all right?"

"Oh, it's fine. I was just thinking about how nice it was to see you on Saturday."

There was something pulled and strained about her voice. Clearly she had another reason for calling, but she wasn't willing to own up to it yet.

"How's school?" she asked.

"Fine. How about for you?"

"Oh, marvelous. But I'm absolutely shattered. You know what a chore Chapin can be."

We both paused and listened to the hum of the line.

"I'm curious about something," she said when the silence began to approach awkwardness. "It occurred to me that I might know someone you go to school with. His name's Tom Barney?"

"Tom Barney?" I repeated, hoping to buy myself some time. What was the best way to proceed? Admit that he had disappeared and garner her reaction? Or pretend all was fine and do the same? What would Pop do? "Sure," I said. "I know him. He's kind of hard to miss. In fact, he used to hang out with the group I went to the Savoy with."

"Really? What do you mean 'used to'?"

"It's the strangest thing. He's been missing for almost a month."

Her breathing deepened. Even over the lousy connection, I could hear the tension strangling her.

"So how do you know him?" I asked.

"We went out a time or two."

"Seriously? I mean, don't get me wrong, he's dreamy, but not exactly the kind of fellow I would figure you for. I guess that's why it ended, huh?"

"Sort of." Another pause. I could picture her in her massive apartment, looping the pigtail cord around her arm. "Has anyone said where he might've gone?"

"No. I don't think anyone knows. He's taken a powder before, but he always let people know where he was going. This time he didn't, and it has everyone pretty upset."

"Do they think something happened to him?"

"They seem to be leaning that way."

I thought I heard a tiny gasp escape from her end of the line. "I think I'm in trouble, Iris."

"What kind of trouble?"

"I think I know what happened to Tommy and it's not good."

It took me a moment to regain my composure. Of all the things that I pictured happening that night, Grace confessing to a crime was at the bottom of the list. "What did you do?" I finally said, hoping the anger I was feeling wasn't apparent in my words.

"It wasn't me, I swear. It was that girl I told you about. Josephine."

"What did she do?"

She sighed heavily, so heavily that it almost sounded a bit theatrical, but that might've been the connection.

"She didn't like that I was going out with him. Thought he was beneath me."

"And you didn't?"

"Honestly, I did at first. But the more I got to know him, the less it seemed to matter."

"Did you tell her that?"

"You have to understand Josephine." That imperious sound was back in her voice, the one she'd used when she was at my house, schooling me on the ways of the world. "It wasn't just about my reputation. She wasn't happy with how he was taking me away from her. I thought she'd get over it, but then she gave me an ultimatum. Told me I had to break up with him, or—"

"Or what?"

"Or she'd tell people what we'd been doing. With the enlisted men."

"Right," I said. She was talking about the favors in exchange for nice dinners and little gifts. Those weren't the kinds of things nice Chapin girls did, and while there was a fine line between a girl being friendly and being fast, there was no way anyone wouldn't have thought Grace had crossed it. If word got out, Grace would be marked as a girl who had ruined herself in exchange for goods and services.

"I told her that I didn't care. I was in love with him, but she swore she would tell. I was so scared, Iris." Was she really? It was hard to tell from her voice, but perhaps enough time had passed that she'd managed to quell the emotion

251

the way I could distance myself from the agony of learning about Mama's death. "I stopped returning his calls, told him it was over. But he showed up at school one day, begging me to take him back. I couldn't stand it, how hurt he was. And so that night I told Josephine that if it was really so important to her that I stop seeing him, she would have to break it off for me. And after that I never heard from him again."

So that's what she'd meant when she told Bea and Bev that she didn't have to worry about seeing him again. "Why do you think Jo did anything more than tell Tom to take a hike?"

"Jo was really strange afterward. She refused to talk about what happened with him. Got upset whenever I brought him up. She made me promise that I wouldn't tell anyone that she'd gone to talk to him."

This was new. Why ask someone to make such a promise unless you needed an alibi?

"Honestly, I didn't think anything would keep Tommy away for good. What we had—it wasn't just a puppy-love thing. I really thought we would be together forever. So as the weeks passed and he didn't try to contact me, I started to get worried. And then on Saturday—"

"This past Saturday?"

"Yes. I went to all the places I knew he used to hang out. I even went by his house. And there was no trace of him anywhere." So that was why she'd really come to the Lower East Side—to find out about Tom. I was her cover in case anyone asked her where she'd gone or, God forbid, saw her entering or exiting the subway.

"Did you go to 240 Houston Street?" I asked her. Maybe Grace had left the note Pop had found in Tom's locker.

"Where?"

"It's just a place I heard some of the kids hang out."

"I've never heard of it."

There was nothing in her voice that made me think she was lying. "Do you think Josephine is capable of hurting someone?" I asked.

"I don't know. There have been stories—rumors really— about things that happened at her old school. She's a scholarship student at Chapin. She lives alone with her mother. Her father is supposedly overseas, though I think she made that part up. She told me once that they moved to Manhattan to get away from something that happened where she used to live. This was supposed to be a fresh start for her family. She . . . she's done things before that make me think she's rougher than she wants me to believe."

"With the servicemen?"

"Yes. She's stolen from them. And I've seen her shoplift. She may not be capable of physically hurting someone, but I wouldn't be surprised if she knew someone who could do it for her."

What I'd witnessed that afternoon certainly corroborated that. "What do you want me to do about this, Grace?"

"I don't know. I just wanted someone to know what was going on. I don't like who I'm becoming. I realized that after I left your house on Saturday. I've become this ugly, awful person because of Josephine. I want it to stop, but mostly I want to know that if she did do something to Tom, she'll pay for it."

Who was the real Grace Dunwitty? Was it the girl who was thrilled to see me on Saturday afternoon, or the cool cat who needed me as her alibi on Saturday night? Or could it be this girl, who seemed genuinely scared and remorseful? I wanted to believe the last one was the version of Grace that counted, but she'd mixed me up too much the last few days for me to completely trust her.

And yet— "I should probably tell you something, Grace. My pop has been hired by Tom's parents to try to find him."

"Oh." She was quiet for a beat while she struggled to take this new information in. "His parents must be pretty worried."

"His mother is. His father is more angry than anything. He seems to think Tom's nothing but a big screwup who they should write off."

"That's terrible. So I guess you're going to have to tell your father everything I just told you?"

"I won't if you tell me not to." Why did I say that?

Because I wanted Grace to like me. Because even after her weird behavior this past weekend, I wanted her to be my friend.

"No, I think you should tell him everything. Especially if it will help Tom." She sighed heavily into the line. "Thanks for listening, Iris. I feel so much better getting that off my chest. You're a true friend, you know that?"

I told her I did.

WE SAID OUR FAREWELLS. I hung up the phone and went into the parlor. There I turned on the Philco and listened to the war news while flipping through *Calling All Girls*. I wasn't reading it, though. I was replaying Grace's words in my head. If Josephine was as manipulative as she said, it wouldn't be hard for her to convince some sailor making eyes at her to hurt a small-time thug on her behalf. And if Tom was wearing the zoot on the night it went down, any number of servicemen would've been happy to humiliate him, just like the scores of others who'd done it before. Only this time, maybe Tom fought back too hard and ended up with something a lot worse than his pants around his ankles.

Where was Pop? I desperately wanted to talk to him. It was time for me to come clean before I got in over my head. It wasn't like him to stay out without telling us when he'd be home. Could he have made his own headway on the Barney case? Was he working on something new? If he was on the tail of someone, he wouldn't necessarily have a chance to call home and express his regrets over being late for dinner. But would a stakeout really last this long? He'd been gone since I'd skipped out of school, longer, in fact, since he hadn't been home when I called Mrs. Mrozenski. He couldn't keep up that kind of pace for hours on end. His stump would grow sore, even if he'd been sitting in one place the entire time. And what about his pain pills? He probably hadn't taken any with him, thinking he'd be home before the throbbing demanded another dose.

I fell into a fitful sleep on the sofa, integrating the chilling news of what was happening overseas into my dreams. In my dream Pop is hidden in the shadows of a submarine, trying to keep himself from being spotted in a space no larger than his office closet. His wound is pulsing, his stump tired of being held in the same position. Slowly, it begins to vibrate, the motion worsening the more he tries to still it. His thigh is centimeters from striking a metal support pole whose top screw has come loose and will rattle when set off by the slightest movement. Pop knows that when that happens, his hiding place will be given away and he'll be a dead man . . .

I awoke with a jolt, uncertain where I was, but doubly glad I hadn't had to experience whatever was about to happen in my dream. What woke me? The parlor was cold, the radio had turned to static, and the front door stood closed. Had Pop returned and bypassed me, assuming it was better

256

to leave me asleep than to make me climb upstairs to my room? No. If he had come home, he would've silenced the Philco, extinguished the lamp, tossed the orange-and-brown afghan over my body to keep away the chill.

Maybe it was the radio signing off for the night that roused me. I switched it off and wrapped a blanket around my shoulders, preparing myself for the cold climb to my room.

A sound came from the kitchen—rattling, like someone was at the back door. Was that what I'd heard? There was no way to know for sure. The back door worked on a skeleton key and was always locked from the inside. Pop used it to haul coal inside and Mrs. Mrozenski used it to take the garbage out of the house, but we were forbidden from using it as a main entrance. Pop said it was because Mrs. Mrozenski's mother had been a maid who was always restricted to the rear door of the house, and Mrs. M never wanted to feel like a servant in her own home. I thought it was funny at the time, especially given that she spent her days cooking and cleaning, but I was suddenly grateful for that little nugget of knowledge, because if someone was at that back door, I knew it wasn't someone who was supposed to be.

Maybe what I'd heard was the wind or the vibration a car created as it passed through the alley. I continued up the stairs, convinced it was nothing, when I heard the unmistakable sound of glass breaking. That wasn't the wind. Someone had just broken one of the small rectangular panes at the top of the kitchen door—I was certain of it. It wouldn't do the culprit much good. The key was never left in the lock. It hung from a hook above the stove. He would realize that soon enough and move on to the kitchen window. It, too, would be locked, but if he broke it, it would be large enough for a grown man to pass through.

My mouth was dry. I wanted to call to Mrs. Mrozenski, but her bedroom was suddenly a million miles away. I didn't want to alert the burglar that we were here and vulnerable. I needed to call the police.

With leaden legs, I went into Pop's office, leaving the door open so I could still hear what was happening in the kitchen. I picked up the receiver and told the operator to get me the police. The dispatcher responded to my calm recitation that someone was breaking in by telling me to lock myself in a closet and a patrol car would be there shortly. From the kitchen more glass broke. I wished Mrs. Mrozenski wasn't so conscientious and had, for once in her life, left a sink full of dirty dishes to slow his progress, but I knew there would be no such thing waiting for our robber. Still, it seemed to take an eternity from the time I heard the window break to when any other sounds came from the kitchen. I turned off the lights in the office and slipped into the small closet that Pop used for file storage and client coats, leaving the door cracked open just a sliver. There, among his galoshes and umbrellas, I sat with my knees pulled up to my chest and waited.

Footsteps left the kitchen and entered the parlor. Then, presumably finding nothing of value, he entered the office and clicked on a lamp.

I was certain my heart was thumping so loudly that, like in my dream about Pop, he'd hear it and uncover my hiding place. I desperately wanted to see him with my own eyes, not only so I could identify him later, but to cement for myself once and for all that this wasn't a new scene in the awful dream I'd been having the moment before.

What would you have done if they had a gun? Pop had asked me after I'd taken the photos of Mrs. Wilson. I prayed I wasn't about to find out the answer to that question.

A desk drawer slid open and papers rustled. Another drawer opened, and another one, though it was clear that whatever he was seeking wasn't conveniently showing itself. From the minute space left by the open closet door, I could see that his back was to me. I longed to open the door just a little more, enough to see the color of his trousers or the shape of his shoes, but I was certain that the hinges would creak, giving me away.

He turned and approached the forbidden locked cabinet, where Pop kept his gun. He rattled the lock and found it immovable. Something new was produced—perhaps an object from the desk? He banged it against the cabinet with enough force that I could hear the wood splinter. Just as I was recovering from that jarring noise, a siren wailed outside the house, announcing the police's arrival.

The culprit cursed. I'm not trying to be a goody two-shoes by not repeating what was said. I honestly don't remember which forbidden word it was because the voice caught me so off guard.

Our intruder was a woman.

In a flash, she was out of the office and running toward the kitchen. I pushed out of the closet, confirmed that the cabinet was broken, and took off after her, just in time to see the edge of her skirt as it turned the corner into the kitchen. Someone was pounding on the front door and demanding, "Open up, it's the police," but I didn't have a moment to spare. I made it into the kitchen and found the back door wide open, the skeleton key protruding from the lock. I rushed out the door and found the alley empty.

CHAPTER

17

"WHAT TIME DID YOU HEAR the glass break?"

Mrs. Mrozenski and I were seated at the kitchen table along with Officer Dignam, a man with jowls so pronounced he could have been mistaken for a bulldog. "I'm not sure," I told him. Mrs. Mrozenski wrapped her arm around me. In her other hand she clutched a rosary. "Maybe an hour ago?"

He checked his watch and I stole a look at the time. It was one o'clock in the morning.

"And you're certain the perpetrator was female?"

"Absolutely. I heard her curse. And I saw part of her skirt. It was black, wool maybe. A-line, so it flared when she ran."

He seemed to be attempting to write down everything I said, but I'd lost him somewhere around "A-line."

"It means that the skirt can open up really full, so that you can dance in it."

A commotion came from the front of the house, where two other officers had been left to assess what had taken place in the office. A familiar voice rose above their gruff, officious tones—Pop was home.

He rushed into the kitchen, looking like death warmed over. His face was gray, his hair a greasy mess, and his leg, as predicted, had reached a point where he could no longer put weight on it.

"Oh my God—Iris. Are you hurt?"

"I'm fine."

He wasn't just exhausted and sore; there was something else off about him, though I couldn't quite put my finger on it. Despite his obvious physical agony, he launched himself at me and took me in his arms. I took in a whiff of body odor and something else. He was drunk.

So not only had I wasted an evening worrying about him, I also got to confront a burglar all by myself so he could—what? Get sloshed?

"You're Arthur Anderson?" asked Officer Dignam.

Pop struggled to keep the slur out of his words while I tried to keep him a safe distance from the cop. "Yes. I'm Arthur."

"Where were you tonight, sir?"

His mouth worked like a hand puppet's, but no sound came out.

"He was meeting with a client," I said.

"Have you been drinking?"

"No," said Pop. "I haven't." His hands remained entangled in my hair, squeezing my head with such force that I worried he might pop it off if he wasn't careful.

Pop had nothing but respect for the police, but I knew it wasn't a two-way street. Private eyes, even properly licensed ones, were viewed as meddlers who took advantage of people who were too impatient to let the law do its job. Uncle Adam used to bribe the officers that worked his beat to keep them on his side, but Pop had made no such effort. If we barely had money for rent, how could we be expected to grease the mitts of local law enforcement?

"You sure about that?" asked Officer Dignam.

He walked toward Pop. Another step and he'd have all the olfactory confirmation he needed. And then what? Having caught Pop in one lie, would he insist that meant there were others to uncover? Probably. And then what had started as a simple break-in investigation would turn into a close examination of Pop's business practices.

"It's his leg," I said.

"What?"

"Go on, Pop. Show him. You must be in awful pain."

From across the room, Mrs. Mrozenski nodded encouragingly. "I'll get your pills, Arthur." While she left to retrieve the vial from his room, I helped Pop wiggle the leg loose. It dropped to the floor with a thud. His thigh was hot to the touch.

"He's a Pearl Harbor vet," I said. "And quite frankly, he doesn't know his limits."

"Now, Iris—"

"Don't *now Iris* me. Ten hours on your feet? And for what? So some fat cat can get proof that his wife is cheating. And now you're going to be bed-bound for a day. It's not worth it."

He waved me off, aware that the less he said, the better.

"Show some respect, young lady," said Officer Dignam.

"Yes, sir," I said. Mrs. Mrozenski returned with the pills and gave Pop a strong cup of Postum to wash them down with.

"It looks like your business office was the focus of the break-in, Mr. Anderson. We'll need you to let us know what, if anything, is missing. Perhaps it would be easier for you to wait until morning?"

"Yes, I'd appreciate that," said Pop.

"She broke into your cabinet, Pop," I said.

"She?"

"Your daughter said the intruder was a woman. What's in this cabinet?"

"Nothing really," said Pop. "Just personal papers and some case files."

My eyebrows went up at that. Since when had he started locking up case files? "People assume if there's a lock, there's a reason," said Officer Dignam. "Your would-be robber probably assumed that's where you stashed your cash."

264

Pop smiled. "If I had cash to stash, it would be in a bank."

"Still, take a look around when you feel up to it. If something is missing, no matter how small, you'll want to report it, just to be safe."

THEY WERE GONE by two a.m. By then, the Postum had eradicated all signs of Pop's evening activities and I'd cleared the kitchen of every shard of glass I could find. One of the officers helped us secure the broken window and door panes with boards and then left us alone to sort out why this had happened.

"I'm sorry," said Pop when the police had left. "I'll fix the windows."

"Is not your fault," said Mrs. Mrozenski.

"I should've been here."

She clicked off the overhead light, leaving only the fixture above the kitchen sink burning. "Everyone is safe. Is all that matters."

"Thank you," he whispered. She left and Pop and I sat in the near darkness for a while, listening to the kitchen clock count down the minutes until dawn.

"Why were you drinking tonight?" I asked.

"I don't know," he said. But he did know. I could hear it in his voice. And then it dawned on me why he'd chosen tonight of all nights to get soused.

"The Navy casualty numbers are out," I said.

"How do you know that?"

"Mrs. Mrozenski told me."

"That's not something she should be sharing with you." Even as he condemned her for it, I thought I could hear the slightest hint of relief in his voice that I was privy to the same information he was, even if it didn't weigh on me in exactly the same way.

"Fifteen thousand already dead or wounded. That's a lot of men in a short time," I said. He nodded at his drained mug. "You must know some of them, right?"

"The odds are good." Where I saw an enormous figure that might one day eclipse the lives of the boys I went to school with, he saw the individual faces of men he'd served with. How agonizing that had to be. It was one thing to have to commemorate Pearl Harbor every single time you tried to take a step, but to know that you weren't the only one who suffered, but just one of the first ones? I would've gotten drunk, too.

"I'm so sorry, Pop."

He reached out and smoothed a strand of hair out of my face. "God, you're so much like her." It was so rare that he mentioned Mama that it took my breath away. "She would've been proud of you tonight, protecting me like that. Thank you. I promise you, I won't leave you alone like that again." He left the table and hobbled over to the stove to refill his cup. "You must've been terrified."

"It all happened so quickly." Was I really like Mama?

266

"You did everything right: calling the police, hiding."

I had, hadn't I? I might not have had the right instincts when I tailed Mrs. Wilson all those weeks before, but I'd grown wiser since then. And—boy, howdy—Pop had noticed!

"You should get to bed, Iris."

"What about you?"

"I need to check the office."

I told him good night and headed out of the kitchen. Rather than going to my room, though, I lingered at the top of the stairs and watched him limp into the office. He cursed beneath his breath as he surveyed the damage.

I couldn't help myself. I went downstairs and joined him.

"Is something missing, Pop?"

He was looking at the broken cabinet. Some of the papers that had once been inside it had spilled onto the floor, including his notes on the Barney case.

"I'm not sure."

"Do you think it's related to one of your cases?"

"I don't know." He slowly bent to retrieve the scattered pages. "You get to bed. You look exhausted."

I told him I would, though I was certain there was no chance I was going to sleep that night.

I STARED AT THE CEILING, trying to sort through who would've broken into our house. Clearly it had to do with Tom Barney. If nothing was missing, then whoever it was wanted a good look at the case file to see what it contained. And that meant whoever it was had to know Pop was working on the case.

I took in a breath so sharply that it pierced my lungs. Grace had gone into Pop's office when she visited and was looking at what was sitting on his desk. I'd also told her he was investigating the case. She could've come back here, hoping to get a longer look at his files. Or perhaps she'd told Josephine about them and she was the one I'd heard swearing as the police arrived.

I eventually slept, much to my amazement. When I finally awoke, the light coming in my bedroom was so bright I winced in pain. I turned to look at my bedside clock and was shocked to discover it was almost noon.

I threw on a robe and rushed down the stairs. Pop wasn't there, but Mrs. Mrozenski was.

"So you finally wake. What a night we had."

"I'm missing school," I said, just in case the rest of the world had forgotten it was a weekday.

"Your father called the school this morning, said you were sick. He did not think you would be up for classes after last night."

"Oh." I sat on the sofa arm, unable to process having a whole day with nothing to do. I was touched that Pop let me sleep in. Could we finally be turning a corner? "Where is he?"

"He went to get glass to fix windows. He be back soon. I make breakfast. You must be starved."

I admitted that I was and let her ply me with fried eggs and toast. When the meal was done and the dishes washed, I changed into clothes and went into Pop's office. My plan was clear: I wanted to see if anything was missing from Tom Barney's folder. The cabinet was open when I entered the room, the contents gone. Pop had wised up and moved everything while I slept.

AS I WAITED for Pop to return, I tried to decide the best way to come clean to him. I could claim that I'd stumbled into the case, not realizing that the boy I'd met at school and who had gone missing was someone Pop had been hired to find. But how to explain Grace? He would have to know I'd started an investigation on my own. No, maybe instead I should tell him that my dear friend Grace was in trouble and I needed his help before someone got hurt. She was dating this guy I went to school with named Tom Barney . . .

The front door opened and Pop came in. He was toting something large and flat that had been wrapped in brown paper and secured with twine—no doubt glass he'd just had cut at the glazier. "This way," he directed someone traveling behind him. "It goes in the room to your left. Let's put it on the floor of the closet."

Two men entered behind him, weighted down by a

heavy black object it took every ounce of their shared strength to carry.

"You're up," said Pop with a smile directed my way. "Good."

No, I would be totally honest with him. It was time. "What's that?"

"A safe," he said as the men grunted their way into the office. "I think last night proved that we need to be a little more secure around here."

"Can we afford it?"

"We don't have a choice." He leaned the glass against the wall. "There's something that I want to talk to you about."

Had last night proven to him that I could be trusted to help him work on his cases?

"What's the story, morning glory?" I said, aping Suze.

He gave me a funny look. "Where were you yesterday afternoon?"

"What do you mean?"

"I called the school this morning to tell them you were sick, and they said they were glad to hear that since you missed your last class yesterday."

I couldn't have been more surprised if he'd told me that he and Uncle Adam had kissed and made up. By catching me off guard, he gave me no time for a lie, which I'm sure he knew. "I went to Chapin."

"Why?"

"To see Grace."

Mrs. Mrozenski, hearing the fuss caused by the two men with the heavy safe, appeared in the parlor doorway and watched the scene.

"And you had to cut class to do this?" said Pop.

"I was afraid if I waited until after, I'd miss her."

One of the men in the office cursed as the unforgiving steel box landed on his foot. Pop tossed a look their way, then redirected his attention to me.

He took in what I'd said and rolled it about his head. "I thought we agreed you'd stay on the Lower East Side."

Oh no. I'd blown it and for no good reason. After all, Grace had called me and told me everything. There'd been no need for me to follow her and Jo. "I know, but it was important. She got bad news. About her father." I couldn't believe I'd chosen that as my cover story. What was wrong with me? "He's missing in action."

He frowned and I waited for him to point out the holes in my story. How did I hear about Grace's dad? If she was so upset, why was she in school? But he didn't point out any of my inconsistencies. I wish he would've. Maybe then I could stop myself from digging a deeper hole.

"They were having a vigil after school yesterday for him and all the other relatives of students who were missing, injured, or killed. I wanted to show my support."

"Then you ask for permission to do so."

"I tried to. I called before I went. Ask Mrs. Mrozenski."

271

My eyes flashed toward the older woman and I pleaded with every ounce of my being that she'd confirm my story.

"Did Iris call here yesterday afternoon?" Pop asked.

She left my gaze and latched onto Pop's. "Yes. She ask for you, but you were gone. I tell her it was all right to be late but to be home by supper. When I think you be home, too." There was an undercurrent to her words that Pop couldn't have missed: maybe if you hadn't been out drinking, you could've talked to your daughter and told her this was a bad idea. "She come home, just like she said." Unlike her father, whose expected arrival time had passed with nary a word.

"I'm sorry," I said. "I shouldn't have skipped. That was a stupid decision."

"School comes first," he said.

"You go to the principal," said Mrs. Mrozenski. "You tell them you play hooky."

A thought occurred to me: the only way the office would've known that I was missing was through the attendance records. Pearl hadn't helped me like she'd said she would.

I guess I knew who my real friends were.

"You don't need to do that," said Pop. "I told them you came home sick yesterday. Being new, you didn't realize you were supposed to report to the office before leaving."

"Thanks."

"Mr. Anderson? Is this where you want it?" One of the

272

men stood in the office doorway, pointing toward the open closet.

"It looks great. Thanks."

While they continued talking, I followed Mrs. Mrozenski into the kitchen. "Thank you," I told her.

"I don't lie for you."

"I won't ask you to do it again."

"No, I don't *lie* for you."

It took me a minute to register what she was saying. What she meant was she'd stuck to the letter of the truth in what she'd told Pop. I had called. I had said I'd be late. Fortunately, he'd never asked her if I'd told her why.

"Be a good girl, Iris. Okay?"

I promised her that I would.

CHAPTER

18

POP SPENT MOST OF THE AFTERNOON behind the closed office door, presumably shifting what had once been in the cabinet into the safe. I watched the door like a hawk, promising myself that as soon as he opened it, I would tell him the truth about everything: why I'd gone to Chapin, how the break-in might have been my fault, my connection to Tom Barney. But as the afternoon wore on and the door remained shut, my courage dwindled. I finally decided to go to him.

"Can I come in?" I asked him after I knocked.

"Sure." He was behind the desk examining a stack of papers. I couldn't tell if it was Tom's file or someone else's.

"Did you figure out if anything was missing?" I asked.

"No. I should've made an inventory of the file contents. I'll know better next time."

I chewed on my lip as I pondered how to proceed. "Were there a lot of case files in there?"

"No, just one."

Either he was only working on the Barney case or none of his other cases were important enough to keep under lock and key. "Are you close to solving it?" I asked.

"Close to closing it. The clients called and told me they don't want me to proceed any further."

"Why?"

"They're pretty sure the missing person is missing by choice and they don't want to spend any more money tracking him down." That had to be Mr. Barney talking. I couldn't imagine Mrs. Barney agreeing to halt things until Tom was home safe.

"Do you agree?" I asked.

"I might've until the break-in. Now I'm not sure what to think."

"Did you tell them about it?" I asked.

"Yes. They've agreed to give me until Monday. If I come up with something, I get paid for my time; if I don't, we call it a wash."

I couldn't believe Pop had agreed to that. All that work he'd done and he was just going to walk away empty-handed?

"It's a goodwill gesture," he told me. "I'd rather have them happy than telling everyone who will listen that I took their money and left them with nothing to show for it."

"Maybe you'll solve it," I said. I needed to tell him what I knew. And I would tell him, in five, four, three, two—

"This isn't something you need to worry about, Iris. Mrs. Mrozenski isn't going to throw us out on the street. I promise."

He shifted the paperwork in front of him and knocked a second stack of paper with his elbow. It slid off the desk and scattered across the floor.

He cursed beneath his breath and surveyed the mess like a climber facing a mountain.

"Let me help," I said. I kneeled and began cleaning up the mess. As I pushed the paper into a stack, Tom's name leaped out at me. I recognized Pop's notes and the inventory of what had been in the locker. Everything seemed to be present and accounted for . . . except for the note that mentioned 240 Houston Street.

I double-checked the stack and surveyed the floor beneath his desk. The note was definitely missing.

"Thanks," he told me as I returned the files to him.

"Anytime," I replied.

I GOT TO SCHOOL EARLY the next day and immediately went to the newspaper room. Paul was there, but Pearl wasn't. In her place was Denise Halloway, the girl he'd been with at the Jive Hive, struggling to type up hand-scrawled notes with one finger.

"Where's Pearl?" I asked them as I entered the room. Denise shrugged and looked toward Paul. He was going through another batch of photos, a dust pen clenched between his fingers, his tongue darting in and out of his mouth as he readied himself to wet the tip.

"She said she had better things to do than help me. And right before our deadline, too."

"Any idea where she's doing these better things?"

He shrugged and flipped to the next picture. "Your guess is as good as mine."

I shifted my weight from side to side as I debated what to do next. "How's the Jive Hive?"

"Hopping. You thinking about coming out again?"

"Maybe." A theory was bubbling to the surface. Maybe the note in the locker had been from Josephine. Perhaps she had lured Tom to Houston Street to do whatever she had done to him. "I heard about another hangout: 240 Houston Street. You ever been there?"

Paul frowned. "Are you serious?"

Uh-oh. What had I stepped in? "Why?"

"Um, it's not a hangout, Iris. It's a place for girls who are *in trouble*."

I had no trouble understanding what *in trouble* meant this time.

I stammered an excuse that I must've heard the address wrong and left them to their work. While I mulled over why Tom would have that address in his locker, I prowled the halls, looking for Pearl's short, dumpy form. What classes did she have? I'd never asked her. All I knew was that she worked in the office during her study hall.

I didn't find her. Instead, I went to Personal Hygiene and then to each subsequent subject, staying after class each time to find out what I'd missed the day before and what I needed to do to catch up.

At lunch I looked for Pearl at her usual table, but didn't see her there. She had to be hiding. She must've known I'd be furious about the attendance thing. I was about to give up my search and join the Rainbows at their table when I realized Pearl had been right in front of me the entire time. She was sitting between Suze and Rhona.

How had that happened? Had Suze seen her sitting alone the day before and invited her to join them?

I walked, tentatively, toward the table. I tried to lock eyes with Benny, but he was deep in conversation with Maria. That was okay. I'd talk to him later. "Hi, Pearl," I said to her. She looked up at me with cold, uninterested eyes. That wasn't the only thing that was different about her. She was wearing a sweater that day that turned her soft, overly padded body into gentle, feminine curves. A scarf was knotted at her neck, in the same style that Rhona wore hers.

"Oh, hi," she said, like I was someone she hadn't seen for a while that she didn't immediately recognize.

I turned to Suze and smiled. "Hey, Joe, whaddya know?" She didn't meet my gaze. Her eyes drifted to the scarred tabletop, where one student after another had carved their initials into the wood. "Mind if I join you?"

"You better scat, pussycat," said Rhona. "There's no room for you here."

"Seriously?" I said.

"You either leave, or we make you leave," said Dino.

"Find the door, drizzle puss," said Maria. She tossed a glance Benny's way. His eyes, like Suze's, were locked downward.

"I don't understand. What's going on? Suze? Benny?"

"Don't make me make you leave, little girl," said Rhona. "Dig?"

I was completely taken aback. What had happened in the twenty-four hours since I'd been gone? I wanted to ask, but—boy, howdy—the way Rhona was glaring at me made it clear that if I didn't leave immediately I'd be suffering from a lot more than sore feelings.

I backed away from the table, humiliated. On Monday, everything had been fine. Suze had been concerned about me, about how upset I'd been by Mrs. Dunwitty's gossip, but I'd assured her I'd put all that behind me. Dino had opened up to me about Tommy. Benny had squeezed my hand and asked me how long I was grounded for. And now not one of them wanted anything to do with me.

Pearl. Pearl must've done something. Telling Pop I wasn't with her and then reporting my absence was only the first of the things she planned to do to sabotage me. Rhona was right—she was evil.

The afternoon passed in a bitter haze. I desperately wanted to leave school, go home, and sulk and ponder, but my promise to Pop that I wouldn't skip class hung heavily over my head, especially now that I knew any move I made would be carefully monitored.

Two thousand hours later, four o'clock arrived and with it the final bell of the day. I gathered my books and started the long walk home. To add insult to injury, a cold heavy rain began and I had nothing aside from my light mackintosh to protect me. I thought about ducking underneath an awning to wait it out, but I was so desperate to get home that I slogged through the downpour, willing to face the humiliation of looking like a drowned rat if it meant I could hide out in my bedroom a little sooner. I was only a block away from home when a sound interrupted the torrential rush of water. What I thought was a hiss was actually my name.

I turned and found Pearl running to catch up to me. She'd had the good sense to bring an umbrella to school, and the combination of being dry and better dressed made her look almost pretty.

"There you are," she said as she arrived at my side. "I've been trying to find you since final bell. You're soaked."

You don't say, I almost said, but that would've required my speaking to her.

"Here," she said, stretching the umbrella out so it covered both of us. "It's big enough for two."

"Keep it to yourself. What do you want?"

She looked taken aback, which was pretty funny, considering. "To talk to you. To make sure you're okay. I heard you were sick."

"Just to my stomach. I've got to go." I stepped back into the rain, instantly regretting my decision. Had it gotten colder? At this rate, I really was going to be ill.

"Iris—wait."

"For what?"

"I need to talk to you. About the Rainbows. Can we go someplace dry? Like maybe your house?"

We were almost there. If I didn't give her a chance to say her piece, I'd wonder about it all night. "Fine," I said.

I refused her umbrella's shelter the whole way there. Unfortunately, the rain picked up, not only giving me a thorough soaking, but making it impossible for her to know that I was still giving her the cold shoulder and deliberately choosing not to speak. We arrived at the Orchard Street house and I let us in. As Pearl shook out her umbrella and left it on the stoop, I kicked off my ruined shoes and entered the parlor.

"You should change," said Pearl.

"I'm fine." I slumped onto the sofa and wrapped the afghan around me. A fire crackled in the hearth, setting the room aglow with reds and oranges. "So what did you want to tell me?"

"I messed up." She took a seat in the rocker, and her eyes danced around the room. Unlike Grace, she didn't judge her surroundings. If anything, she seemed delighted in their familiarity. "We have a table just like this," she said, her hand stroking the wooden cocktail table beside her. Her fingers traced the edge of the lace doily at its center like it was a childhood dress she hadn't seen in years.

"You are home, Iris," said Mrs. Mrozenski as she entered the room. She took in the state of my hair and clothes and jumped. "You are soaked."

"I'm fine. The fire and blanket are warming me up. This is Pearl Levine."

Pearl leaped to her feet and offered Mrs. Mrozenski her hand. "Is this your house? It's lovely."

They made small talk that I struggled to ignore. Unlike Grace, Pearl was sincere, her questions genuine inquiries. It turned out Mrs. Mrozenski knew her mother. Her daughter, Betty, had sat for Pearl and Paul when they were small.

"I was so sorry to hear about your brother. Is tragedy. There is no other word."

"Thank you," said Pearl.

Mrs. M left to make us cocoa, a rare treat since rationing had started. Pearl returned to her seat.

"So how did you mess up?" I asked.

"Monday. After school. I ran into Suze. She was looking for you. I told her that you'd left before your last class and she asked me if you'd left because you'd gotten more news about your father."

I could see the writing on the wall: Pearl didn't know

that Suze thought Pop was overseas. And so, innocently, she'd corrected her, not realizing that by doing so she was also branding me a big fat liar.

Pearl acknowledged that this was exactly what had happened. "As soon as I said that your pop was fine, you could see all the blood rushing out of her face. I wanted to fix it, so I said that he *had* been injured in the war, he'd lost his leg at Pearl Harbor, but that just made things worse."

"Oh God."

Her face was bright red with excitement and fear. She'd had to wait two long days to tell anyone this story. "Rhona and Dino showed up just as I was telling Suze this. And then Rhona asked me your last name." The leg had tipped her off. Who knew Rhona was that observant? "I told them—I didn't think it was a big deal—and Rhona tells Suze that it's the same surname the detective with the bum leg had. They asked me if your dad was a cop. I said I didn't know, and right then Paul shows up, wanting to know if I was coming to the journalism office . . ."

I was going to throw up. "He told them, didn't he?"

"I know my brother's a drip, but he honestly didn't know what was going on. And by then they were laying it all out, all the questions you'd asked about Tommy—they would've put it together eventually, Iris."

It was worse than I could've imagined. Not only did they know I'd lied about Pop, but now they knew I was the detective's daughter. There was no coming back from this. My cover was blown and so was any hope I might have had of being friends with Suze and anything more with Benny.

"I didn't know what to do, Iris. I was really afraid they'd hurt you. Not Suze, but Rhona was so angry. I needed to distract them and so I decided then and there to become a double agent."

I didn't think I'd heard her right. Had she snapped? Gone goofy? Was her grief over her dead brother so pronounced that she thought she was living in a Humphrey Bogart film? "What are you talking about?"

"I knew I'd messed things up for you, that you weren't going to find out anything else about Tommy from them, so I thought I would try to become their friend and maybe they'd tell me." Her voice droned on. As soon as Paul left, Pearl told Rhona and Suze that I'd been using her to get information from the attendance office and that I'd pretended I was her best friend until other people began talking. "I cried," said Pearl. "I just stood there in the hall and bawled about how you were the first friend I'd had since my brother died and how much it hurt to find out you were using me. Suze invited me out then and there—we went for milk shakes at Normandie's. And then yesterday Rhona took me shopping and helped me pick out this." She plucked at her sweater. "I felt so bad at lunch today. I wanted to warn you, but there was no way I could without them seeing me talk to you."

I was shocked Pearl had it in her. Who knew she could be so duplicitous? "What about Rhona?" I asked.

"I apologized to her."

So Pearl *had* started the rumor? At least that question was answered once and for all. "So why didn't you fix my attendance record on Monday?" I asked.

"They told me not to. They said I had to stop letting you use me."

The funny thing was, they were right.

Since the beginning, I had been taking advantage of Pearl, seeing her first as a way to stop being thought of as the strange, friendless new girl and later relying on her access to information to get me what I wanted. Yet for all my selfishness, I don't think Pearl saw things that way. Even as she cried to Rhona and Suze about the way I'd mistreated her, I had no doubt she really believed she was inventing my misbehavior.

Mrs. Mrozenski appeared with twin cups of hot chocolate and a plate of cookies and disappeared just as quickly. I wrapped my hands around the hot mug and finally felt the chill start to leave my body.

"Did you get in trouble?" asked Pearl.

"No," I said. "It's fine. It wasn't fair of me to ask you to do that to begin with."

"Why didn't you come to school yesterday?"

I told her about the break-in. I didn't stop there. I also told her about my visit to Chapin on Monday, about my old friend Grace Dunwitty and her new pal Josephine O'Hara. She listened intently, picking at the cookies with enormous restraint.

"Wow," she said when I'd paused in my recitation. She honestly didn't know what to tackle first. "You don't really think he's dead, do you?" Her eyes started to water.

Dead? Hearing the word said out loud shocked me. But it was what I was thinking, wasn't it? It was the only explanation for his absence that made any sense.

"I don't know what to think," I told Pearl. "It doesn't make sense that he would've stayed away this long unless something is keeping him from returning."

"Bu . . . but there must be loads of other reasons for that." *Like what*, I wanted to ask, but it was clear that wouldn't help things. "What does your pop think?"

If Pearl and I were going to be friends, I needed to be honest with her. About everything. "I don't know. Look, I kind of lied before. I'm not working with my pop. He won't let me. Everything I've been doing I've been doing on my own. We're broke, Pearl. I don't know what's going to happen if Pop doesn't solve this case." That wasn't all I told her. I also told her about Mama, about the rumors of the affair, and what Suze had said to calm me down.

"I'm so sorry, Iris. I think Suze is right, though. People make up awful stories for the dumbest reasons." I could tell she was itching to say more, but wanted to hold back for my sake. "Do you think Josephine and the break-in at your pop's office are related?"

"Definitely."

"So what are you going to do about Josephine?"

I checked to make sure Mrs. Mrozenski wasn't about to appear in the room. "I don't know yet. For Pop to convince the Barneys that Tom didn't run away, I need proof, which means I need her to confess. The question is—how?"

Pearl thumped her forefinger against her cocoa mug as she pondered the problem. "If she's as awful as Grace claims, do you know who I'd love to see her get cornered by? Rhona."

"That'd be a scream."

"Think about it—Rhona's not scared of anyone. She's tough. She could be Josephine's match."

The more I thought about it, the less absurd the idea seemed. If we somehow let on to Rhona that Josephine was the last person to see Tom alive, she might be able to force a confession out of her.

"But how would we ever get those two together?"

"Josephine likes dangerous places, right? What if you invited Grace and her to go with you to the Savoy Ballroom?"

There would be a lot of witnesses at the Savoy—not just Rhona and Suze, but a whole dance floor of people who could observe what was being said. "But if Rhona and Suze see me there, they'll know something's up."

"So we make sure they don't see you."

"We?"

"I could get Suze and Rhona to take me to the Savoy. We synchronize things to make sure your friends and mine run into each other." *Her* friends. Would Benny be there, too? Would he dance with Pearl and kiss her right before the evening ended? "Rhona knows what Grace looks like, right? And that she used to be your friend?"

"Yeah. So she said. But how are you going to get them to take you to Harlem?"

Pearl shrugged. "I got them to invite me to lunch, and I never thought that would happen. How hard could it be to wrangle an invitation to go dancing?"

19

I USED THE TIME before Pop got home to call Grace. I told her Pop couldn't do a thing without more evidence and then explained how I proposed to get that evidence. She didn't seem thrilled with the plan, but when I explained it was the only way I could think of to convince the Barneys to go after Josephine, she gave in.

The next afternoon I met up with Pearl at my house, far from prying eyes, and reviewed her progress on getting an invite. She was being very careful with how she played things, making sure not to drop hints that would be too obvious (I was impressed that she was aware that she had a habit of doing this). Unfortunately, that gave Rhona and Suze no reason to even make the offer. By Friday we were in a panic: the weekend was upon us and no invitation was in sight. I decided I was going to have to do something to force their hand.

During lunch, which I now ate alone, I approached their

table. I lingered on the sidelines for a little while, listening as Pearl laughed at their jokes. My heart ached at how easily she fit in with them. It was so strange how she could go from being the girl they all made fun of to being one of them. Sure, I had made the transition just as swiftly, but until I left Chapin, I'd always had oodles of friends. This was a new experience for Pearl and as badly as I envied her, I admired her, too. I didn't want her to have to go back to the way things were once we got the information we needed. Pearl deserved this. Even if it meant I was alone and friendless from here on out.

"You need something, girl detective?" asked Rhona, snapping me out of my reverie.

"I wanted to talk to Pearl."

"So go on and beat your gums," said Maria.

Everyone at the table stared at me, waiting for me to make the next move. Everyone, that is, except Benny.

"I was hoping I could talk to her alone."

"And I was hoping to be a natural blonde," said Rhona. "Looks like neither one of us is going to have our wishes come true."

"What do you want?" asked Pearl. Her voice contained a snappishness that sent me off balance. Even though I knew she was acting, it still hurt.

I shuffled my feet, making it clear exactly how uncomfortable it was to have to talk to her in front of everyone.

"I was wondering what you were doing this weekend. I thought maybe you could come and stay at my house."

Pearl rolled her eyes. "And what made you think I would want to do that?"

"Because we talked about it last week."

"Last week was last week. Seems to me a lot's changed since then."

She was good at this. Too good. "So what are you doing?" I asked.

"I'm going to the Jive Hive tonight."

"So you're free on Saturday?" I asked.

Pearl's mouth dropped open, but no sound came out. She had rehearsed this nicely. Her tough exterior melted away as she came to realize that in fact she had no plans.

Suze picked up on it immediately. "As a matter of fact, Pearl's going out with us tomorrow," she said. I wished it were Rhona who was speaking up. Having Rhona and Maria be mad at me was nothing new, but knowing how hurt and sore Suze was made me sick to my stomach.

"I am?" said Pearl.

"Of course you are," said Rhona. "You're coming to Harlem with us, remember?"

"I'm going to teach you how to jitterbug," said Dino.

At least it wasn't Benny who'd made the offer. I had that to be grateful for.

"All right," I said. I backed away slowly, like I was hoping they'd change their mind and invite me along, too. And the sad thing was, I really was hoping that. I would much rather spend the evening with them than trying to worm a confession out of Josephine. "Have fun," I told Pearl. "If you change your mind, you know where to find me."

I increased my speed, but I wasn't fast enough to make it out of the cafeteria before they started laughing at me.

GRACE CALLED ME that night to make plans. We would meet at her house at seven to get ready for the Savoy. It would be a whole lot easier to sneak out of her house than to try to justify to Pop why we were leaving mine so late.

I just needed to convince Pop that me going anywhere was a good idea.

"Is it all right if I stay over at Pearl Levine's tomorrow night?" I asked him that evening.

"Will you really be staying at Pearl's this time?" he asked.

"Yes." And I would, too. As soon as everything was over in Harlem, I'd go home with Pearl to her house. So it wasn't really a lie.

"It's Halloween, Iris. I don't know if that's such a good idea. Who knows what sort of mischief will be going on?" Mayor La Guardia had appealed by paper and radio for people to keep the peace that weekend. There was enough blood and gore happening abroad; we didn't need even the pretend stuff cluttering our streets.

"We're not doing anything. We'll just be at her house."

He pondered this. I should have said we were going to a movie, just in case he tried to check on me again. "I want to talk to her parents," Pop said.

"Seriously?"

"Yes, seriously. You've been making some bad decisions lately, and I think it's my right. It's either that or an automatic no."

I was close to laying into him for that, but I knew it would get me nowhere. "All right," I said. "I'll have her mother call you tomorrow."

"Then you'll have your answer tomorrow."

I obviously couldn't get Pearl's mother to call him. My only option was to take a page out of Rhona's book and have someone impersonate Pearl's mother. I didn't feel comfortable asking Pearl to do it, not after everything else she'd done for me. Instead, I turned to someone who was bound to be much less conflicted about lying to an adult: Grace.

She called Pop late Saturday morning, posing as Mrs. Levine. She apparently has quite a future as an actress, because when he hung up with her he didn't hesitate to give me permission to spend the night.

Pearl came to our house after lunch to talk about what she should wear to the Savoy. Pop greeted her at the door and told her how much he'd enjoyed talking to her mother. Pearl played along with the same cool conviction she'd shown me when she was sitting with the Rainbows.

"Sorry about that," I told her when we were safely in my room, away from Pop's prying ears.

"You should've had me call him," said Pearl. "I do a great imitation of my mother."

"I didn't want to make you lie for me."

She frowned. "But you just did."

I hadn't thought about that.

"Should I drink?" asked Pearl.

"At the Savoy? It's your choice, but I wouldn't if I were you. In the first place, it's not like you think it's going to be."

She lifted her head, as though to reinforce that she was more mature than I was giving her credit for. "I've had Manischewitz at Passover before."

The overly sweet kosher wine had nothing in common with the hooch Rhona toted around. "Then you're definitely not ready for real booze." The truth was, we had no idea how alcohol would affect Pearl and I wanted her at her most present that night, just in case something went terribly wrong.

"What do I do if someone asks me to dance?"

"It's a ballroom, Pearl. Not a bond drive. You're going to have to dance."

"But I don't know how."

To reassure her, I put a Glenn Miller platter on the phonograph and showed her the basic moves that I remembered from my trip to the Savoy. I imagine it was a bit like watching Pop dance—stiff, awkward, and more basic than a loaf of white bread—but seeing things broken down into simple steps was what Pearl needed. She'd learn soon enough how complicated dancing could be when people who could really hoof it shared the floor.

At five o'clock we said our farewells to Pop and set out for Pearl's house. I lugged an overnight bag packed with the skirt and shoes I hadn't returned to Suze, cosmetics I'd borrowed from Mrs. Mrozenski, and a comic book to keep me occupied on the subway. Once we turned the corner, we parted ways, and I headed to the station. By five-forty-five I was uptown and en route to Grace's apartment. Fear made me walk too fast and I ended up in front of her building earlier than I wanted to be. I decided to walk around the block to calm myself down. As I passed the park, someone called out my name. I slowed and glanced over my shoulder, dreading which person from my former life I was about to run into. It was Aunt Miriam.

"Iris, is that you?"

It was too late to deny it. I stopped walking and tried to match her smile for smile. "What are you doing here?" I asked. While Uncle Adam and Aunt Miriam lived uptown, their apartment was nowhere near where Grace lived.

"I came with friends to their temple for services. Now I'm bound for home." And it was still the Sabbath, at least according to the strict laws Miriam followed. That meant no cabs and no subway. She either legged it home or waited until three stars appeared in the sky, lifting the ban on work. I felt guilty for my own easy trip uptown. While she never criticized how Mama and Pop lived, she couldn't have been happy with how completely they'd abandoned their religion. "The question is, what are you doing here? Is your father with you?"

"I'm staying at a friend's tonight. Pop's at home."

"A Chapin friend?"

I answered right away, such was the power Aunt Miriam still wielded over me. "Yes, Grace Dunwitty."

"Good for you, Iris. I always liked Grace. You need to keep up with girls like that. That's where you belong."

That's where I belonged? Among thieves and murderers? If only she knew. "I better go. She's expecting me." I turned, hoping that was the end of it, but she caught me on the shoulder and wouldn't let me leave.

"We miss you, you know. You're always welcome in our home."

"Thanks," I said. "I miss you, too. We both do." I liked Aunt Miriam and I knew deep down Pop did, too. I didn't want her to take Pop's decision to cut off from Uncle Adam as a personal slight.

"Your father talks about us?" she asked.

"Sometimes."

She smiled. The relief was evident in her eyes. "What's happened between your uncle and your father, it doesn't have to change things between us. This is your father's

296

choice, but it doesn't have to be yours." She spoke slowly and deliberately, nodding when she completed her sentence, as though she needed my acknowledgment that I'd understood her.

"I know," I said. I felt guilty, for some reason. It was like we were criticizing Pop, and how was that fair?

"Your father's business is good?"

I felt like I needed to stick up for Pop in some way, even if I hadn't exactly betrayed him. "Very good."

"He's able to handle the work with his leg?"

"Most of it. When he needs help, he asks for it."

"From whom?"

I don't know why I lied. I guess I wanted to prove that Pop and I were a team. "Me."

She frowned. "You help him in the business?"

I nodded.

She took both of my hands in hers and smiled. "You be a good girl, Iris. Come to see us. Please."

I promised I would, if only because it meant I could escape her hold and hurry on my way.

I was ten minutes late to Grace's house. The same doorman who'd been on duty on my last visit greeted me, though his demeanor was considerably warmer this time. I expected him to remark on the present I'd left in the plants outside the elevator, but he'd either forgotten about my mountain of upchuck or decided that since I was an invited guest, I deserved a little discretion. I arrived at Grace's floor, hoping

297

to find her waiting for me, but it was Mrs. Dunwitty who stood at attention as the elevator doors slid open.

"Iris. I'm glad you were able to come. I was so excited when Grace said she'd invited you over."

I couldn't meet her eyes. The wound was still too fresh. Her voice instantly conjured that other conversation, the one in which my mother had been having an affair.

But that wasn't true. It was just gossip.

"I was hoping I could have a word with you before you go inside," said Mrs. Dunwitty. Was she going to throw me out? Repeat her tale and explain why it was the truth?

"All right."

She fixed a grin on her face, as carefully considered as the twinset she wore with pearls. "I understand you may have overheard some things last weekend. Please forgive me for anything inappropriate I may have said. I want you to always feel welcome in our home. Of course, what you overheard was just that: a private conversation that I certainly wouldn't have chosen to make public to you or to anyone else."

There was an air of blame in her voice that I couldn't miss: it was my fault for eavesdropping, not her fault for saying these things. Grace had made her apologize and she was following the letter of the law without really accepting any blame for what had occurred.

"Your mother was a lovely woman. We all miss her terribly."

"Thank you," I muttered. "I should probably get inside."

I pushed past her before she had a chance to say anything else.

Grace was seated at the vanity in her bedroom. She was alone.

"Oh, you're here! Thank goodness—I was starting to worry. Did Mother apologize to you?"

I nodded, not having the strength to repeat what she'd said. "Where's Josephine?"

"She'll be along shortly, once Mother leaves. Those two are oil and water, so Jo tries to time her entrances and exits accordingly."

She may have been a thief and potentially a murderer, but Josephine was also a good judge of character.

Grace took me in with her eyes for the first time. "You look beat up. Everything all right?"

I tried the truth on for size. "I ran into my aunt on the way here. And then that scene just now with your mother."

"Hell's bells. Grownups can be so taxing, can't they? I do hope Mother didn't say anything else to upset you." She fluffed her hair in the mirror. I got the feeling that if I did own up to Mrs. Dunwitty's apology being light on sincerity, Grace would make a big stink out of it, and I didn't have the energy to face that on top of everything else.

I needn't have worried. Grace quickly forgot what we were talking about and stood up to model her outfit. She twirled in front of me, showing off the dress she'd bought just for tonight's expedition. From the way she was acting, you would've thought she really was just going out for a night on the town, not hoping to trick her supposed best friend into confessing to her role in a murder. "What do you think?"

"It's swell. You'll fit right in."

"I hope so. There's nothing worse than going someplace new and sticking out like a sore thumb." She took me in top to tail and turned up her lip slightly. "Is that what you're wearing?"

"Only part of it. The rest of it's in here." I patted my overnight case.

"Clever girl—I guess you didn't want to get wrinkled on the subway."

I sat on her bed as she returned to the vanity stool. "I'm surprised you're not nervous," I said.

She concentrated on plucking an errant eyebrow hair. "Oh, I am, but I figure it's out of my hands now. Whatever's going to happen is going to happen, right?"

"You never said how Josephine reacted to tonight's plan."

"Oh, she was thrilled with the idea. She's always wanted to go to Harlem. Especially when I told her there'd be loads of servicemen there." She moved on to the other eyebrow. How had she shaped them so perfectly? My own brows looked like uneven hedgerows.

"Don't you want to hear my plan?" I asked.

"I don't have to do anything, do I?"

"Not exactly, but I think it would be helpful for you to know what to expect. Just in case."

She spun around on the vanity stool and set her hands on her lap. "All right—I'm all ears."

Unfortunately, I never got to tell her. Right then her bedroom door flew open and Josephine O'Hara walked in.

HER EYES, CLOSE UP, were a pale blue-gray. I used to think Rhona had dead eyes, but after seeing Josephine's, I realized Rhona's were simply chilled by her manner. Josephine had peepers that were completely soulless.

"You're early," said Grace.

"My mother was driving me crazy. Another minute with her and I swear I was going to snap. You must be Iris."

"I must be. Nice to meet you," I said from my perch.

"Likewise," said Jo. "So are we ready to cut out?" Her red hair had been tamed into curls, her face painted with a careful hand. Her clothes were expensive and, given her background, most likely paid for with money she'd lifted from soldiers' wallets or coerced them into ponying up after an evening of freebie dinner and dancing. From a distance, she was a dead ringer for Rita Hayworth. But up close she was just another high school girl playing dress up.

It was hard to see her as a killer. But then did anyone with the capacity for such things really look like a murderer?

"It's really up to you two," I said. "There's no point in

getting to Harlem before nine. Not unless you just want to walk the streets and take in the sights."

"That doesn't sound very wise," said Jo. "I say we wait to leave until at least eight-thirty. That okay with you, Gracie?"

She had returned to her vanity and her tweezing. "Sure."

"So Grace says you're in public school now," said Josephine.

While everyone else talked about my descent in euphemisms and soft voices, Josephine made no such allowances. After all, she had been a public school girl herself until recently.

"That I am."

"That must be . . . interesting."

"The school's terrible and the people who go there aren't much better. But I'm stuck."

She lifted her chin slightly and I got the impression that I'd just passed some sort of test. "Grace says you have a fellow there."

Benny. What was he doing right then? Putting on his zoot suit and slicking back his hair? Or had last weekend scared him into donning more conservative rags? Whatever his choice, I hoped for his sake no one bothered him that night.

"Had. I don't think we'll be announcing our engagement anytime soon."

"What happened?" asked Grace.

I thought carefully before I spoke. As much as I hated to think about everything that had happened that week, I could put my loss to good use here. "I wised up. I realized that fixing my wagon to a public school boy wasn't going to do me any favors. I may be trapped at a public school for the next four years, but I don't have to become one of them, you dig?"

"That I do," said Josephine.

"You don't think that sounds snobbish?" I asked. I wanted to get on the topic of her own time in public school, hoping to find out why she'd had to make a clean break before she came to Chapin.

"More like wise," said Josephine. "You tie yourself to the wrong balloon and you might find yourself grounded for the rest of your life."

"You sound like you're speaking from experience."

"I figured out that if I want to go anywhere I've got to put myself first."

It was actually good advice. I wasn't prepared to hear wisdom coming out of her mouth. Did that make me just as vulnerable to her as Grace was?

"Are you seeing anyone now?" I asked.

"Jo prefers a band to a soloist," said Grace with a wink.

"Just because I don't want to be tied to the wrong fellow doesn't mean I don't want to have fun. And the safest way to do that is to make sure your dance card is always full," said Josephine. "And you're one to talk. You get this girl around an Army Air Corps uniform and she'll offer to take back things she didn't steal."

"The hell you say!" Grace tossed a cotton ball her way, intending it to be a reprimand. It fell ineffectually to the ground.

"You know it's true, Grace." She pointed her thumb Grace's way. "She comes off like butter wouldn't melt in her mouth. I even bought her act for a while. But this girl has the devil in her."

Grace pushed her lips into a pronounced pout. "So I like to have fun. So what?"

"My point exactly," said Josephine.

Someone knocked on the bedroom door. "Grace? It's Mother. I'd like to have a word with you before I leave."

Grace excused herself and left Josephine and me alone.

"I like you," said Josephine.

"Thanks."

"When Grace first told me about you, I was worried you were going to be like all those other squares from Delaware."

"I have my moments. Funny how public school changes what you're willing to do, but then you probably know that. Grace said you were at a public school before Chapin."

Josephine fished a brass cigarette case out of her bag and popped it open. With one hand she struck a match, with the other she offered me the contents of the case.

I considered the offer carefully. I might've been betraying Pop in a thousand different ways that night but I wasn't about to add smoking to the list. "No, thanks."

She tweaked her mouth to the left and exhaled a stream of smoke. "Yeah, I did my time."

"How'd you end up at Chapin?"

"Fell in with the wrong crowd. Bunch of bad influences, the lot of them. It was either private school or a reformatory. Fortunately my grades were good, so I got a scholarship instead of a sentence."

"Lucky you. And so now you get to be the bad influence?" I meant it as a joke, but as soon as I said it, I worried she wouldn't take it that way.

She narrowed her eyes. "How much has Grace told you?"

"Not nearly enough, I'm afraid. She clams up if she thinks she'll look bad. She doesn't realize how much I've changed and that I assume she's changed, too."

"That's Grace all right."

It was obvious she wasn't going to tell me anything unless I offered her something first. "She said you two like to play the soldiers you meet. Get a few gifts and a nice meal or two and pay as little as possible in return."

"You think that's bad?" she asked.

"I think it's clever. You can't use someone who doesn't want to be used."

I don't think she knew I was parroting Grace. Only that I was echoing a philosophy she happened to share.

"So are you game?" she asked me.

I hadn't considered the possibility that they might want me to join in on their scheme. "I might be willing to give it a try."

Jo relaxed. "I'm surprised Grace owned up to it. Like you said, she doesn't like to be associated with anything that makes her look bad. So you know she traded in her halo for a pair of devil's horns?"

"I'm not sure she ever had a halo."

Another exhale of smoke, this one aimed right for me. "Funny, I think you and I are the only two people who've figured that out."

I took a chance. "What about Tom Barney?" I said. "Surely he knows."

Surprise flashed through her eyes. "The sad part is, he doesn't. And that means the joke's on him."

Grace appeared in the bedroom door, her face long and serious.

"Is everything all right with your mother?" I asked.

"Fine. She's gone now, thank goodness."

We took turns at the mirror, getting ourselves ready for our evening out. As I slipped on Suze's skirt and pumps, I wondered what she would think of me wearing her clothes. I'd make it up to her somehow.

Josephine whipped out a tube of magnet-red lipstick,

and we took turns putting it on. She then disappeared into the bathroom, leaving Grace and me to finish our preparations by ourselves.

"What did you two talk about while I was gone?" asked Grace once she was sure we were alone.

"You, mostly. She seemed awfully eager to make sure I knew that you were just as bad as she is."

"She knows something's up. That's why she came early and braved Mother. I wouldn't be a bit surprised to find out she was listening outside my door for a half hour before she announced her arrival. She doesn't trust you."

How could that be? She seemed to not only trust me, but to actually *like* me. "How can you tell?"

"Little things. Like how she asked you about the boy you're seeing. I never told her you were seeing anyone. That was a test."

"Of what?"

"I'm not sure, but it's not good. You need to be careful, Iris. She knows she's being played and she's going to do everything possible to turn the tables on you tonight. This could get ugly."

I found it impossible to wrap my head around that. I had been starting to think Josephine wasn't as bad as we'd made her out to be, but if anyone knew the real Josephine, it was Grace. This girl was clever—clever enough to get into private school instead of juvie. Clever enough to make my once straitlaced friend go along with her schemes. And clever enough to make sure Tom Barney disappeared for good. I couldn't afford to let my guard down with her.

Josephine reappeared with her hair carefully pinned into place. She seemed to have matured during her brief time in the bathroom. Or maybe it was just my understanding of her that had changed.

"Let's blow," she said. "I'm in the mood for some dancing."

IT WAS EVEN HARDER to find a cabbie on Fifth Avenue willing to take you to Harlem than it had been on Delancey Street. After four failed attempts, Josephine offered to double the driver's rate for the lift. He was still reluctant, but the promise of twice the cash at least gave us the chance to hear about his reluctance on the drive there.

Of course, Josephine didn't actually have the money in hand. She might've pocketed enough from her latest marks, but it seemed her intention all along was to make Grace pony up for the bill. So, in addition to being a manipulator, she was also a moocher. And Grace did exactly as she asked, pulling the crisp bills out of her wallet with absolutely no hesitation. She would do the same when we got to the Savoy, paying for all three of us like it was her obligation.

The Savoy was the same as on my first visit: packed to the gills, the music loud, the hoofing hot. I tried to navigate the place like I was well acquainted with it, and did a pretty good job schooling them on where to wait before the doors opened, and where to go once they did. As we entered the ballroom, I pointed out the sights the way they'd been pointed out to me, using the same lingo Suze had, although I misused half the words and made up new ones to replace the ones I couldn't recall. It was all right, though; it wasn't like Jo and Grace would know any better. Nor did they care. As I rambled on about this band and that dance step, they both took in the amazing world swirling around them. I wanted to stare and gawk, too, but I was too nervous to play tourist. We had a plan I had to follow: at midnight, everyone needed to be in front of the building, where Josephine and Rhona would have their showdown and what happened to Tom would finally come to light.

That was hours away. I had no idea how I was going to occupy myself until then.

Josephine had no such concerns. We weren't in the ballroom five minutes before someone hauled her onto the floor and engaged her in a whiplash-inducing jitterbug. For a girl who was supposedly so calculated, she knew how to let go and give in to the music.

"She really comes on like gangbusters," I said to Grace.

"She knows it, too," she replied. We stood near the wall, a couple of wallflowers waiting to be picked. Grace's eyes danced over the crowd, looking for who knows what. Just when I thought we'd both be stuck there forever, a man grabbed her hand and pulled her onto the floor. I receded further into the wall, torn between wanting to dance and wanting to hide. I combed the crowd, looking for Pearl, but there were far too many people for me to be able to spot her. I stepped away from my hiding spot, hoping to get a better view of the room, when a sailor took my hand and asked me to dance.

I said yes. After all, I might get a better vantage of the ballroom.

It wasn't like dancing with Benny. Oh, my partner was light on his feet, but I was as stiff as a Popsicle stick. I still knew the dance steps I'd been taught the week before (and had taught to Pearl just that afternoon) but the fluidity I'd experienced dancing with Benny had vanished.

"Relax, doll," said the Fred Astaire to my Ginger Rogers.

Maybe it was him. He was nice-looking, but he wasn't Benny. Instead of wearing the zoot, he wore Navy dress blues. His hair wasn't slicked back with Brylcreem, but cut close enough to his scalp that the skin showed pink beneath it. He wasn't the only enlisted man in the club that night. The Savoy was teeming with them. The sea of brightly colored dresses and suits was broken up by a uniformed stream of khaki, blue, and white.

Fortunately, though, the enlisted men were outnumbered by the regular attendees. There would be no humiliating the men wearing zoot suits here. This wasn't their turf.

Josephine caught my eye from across the floor. She pinched her forefinger and thumb into an O to let me know what she thought of my partner. She nudged her head to the left and I followed her line and found Grace in the arms of yet another soldier. Poor Grace with her ballroom lessons and impeccable posture simply couldn't give in to the Lindy Hop. She was the exact opposite of her name.

"You come here a lot?" asked my partner. I thought I smelled alcohol on his breath. Whatever it was, it wasn't pleasant.

"No. I'm only in high school," I said. "How about you?"

"First time in New York. The boys and I decided to do it up right and come here tonight. We ship out Monday."

I tried to relax, but it wasn't working. My reason for being there weighed too heavily. "Do you know where they're sending you?"

"Nope." He slid to the right and tapped his foot. "How old are you?"

If I'd been trying to impress him, I would've lied. "Fifteen. Bet I look like a baby, huh?"

"Want to know a secret?" I nodded, though I didn't, not really. "I'm only sixteen."

"How can that be?" I said. "Don't you have to be eighteen to enlist?"

"That's why it's a secret."

"Why do you want to go off to war? What's the hurry?"

"It's a lot better than wasting away learning about things

that have already happened and memorizing dates and names, right? I'd rather be part of history than spend my time learning about it."

He obviously thought the news would impress me, but I couldn't find it in me to gush over how brave he was. After getting caught in my own deception, I was hardly going to reward someone else for theirs. Besides, weren't rules about what age you had to be to enlist there for a reason? Even under the best of circumstances, people were getting killed. I hated to think we were banking on our freedom being protected by a bunch of boys with guns who were too young to know how to use them.

The dance ended and I exchanged one partner for another, and then still another. No one asked me for a second dance. I might've looked like I could cut a rug, but it only took a measure or two before they figured out my legs were as stiff as the cuffs on their slacks. But the activity made the time pass quickly and gave me a chance to survey the room from one side to another. It wasn't until my last partner pulled me into his arms that I spotted Rhona. She was partnered with Dino, whose bright yellow suit turned into a blur of color as he spun around the dance floor. I almost waved when I saw them, but then I remembered what I was there for. Instead, I tried to lead my partner toward the other side of the room, where I was less likely to be recognized.

"What's the matter?" he asked me.

"Leg cramp," I said. I broke our hold and hobbled away, hoping my lousy acting skills weren't drawing any more attention to me than necessary. As I slinked toward the wall, I saw Suze spinning toward Benny. Both of them were grinning from ear to ear as he tossed her into the air for a hip to hip.

"Iris?"

I turned and found Pearl just over my left shoulder. She waved me over to the wall, where she was cooling herself and drinking out of a flask.

Rhona's flask. Oh no.

She saw my panic as I took in that silver portent of doom and shook her head. "Relax. I dumped it out when she wasn't looking and filled it with water. Want a swig?"

I chugged the container half empty and passed it back to her. "How's it going?"

"Fine so far. I got worried when I couldn't find you."

"Me, too. Having fun?"

She was trying to be calm and collected, but I could feel the excitement that bubbled beneath the surface. "I've danced twice—once with Benny and once with Dino. I thought for sure I'd trip and that would be the end of it, but I actually was able to keep up with them."

"Good for you." Jealousy burned through me the way Rhona's booze had passed down my throat the week before.

"Where's Josephine?"

I gestured toward the other side of the room, where most of the military men were gathered. "Over there some- where. I'm not sure how useful tonight's going to be. Grace seems to think she's on to us."

"Rhona's in a beastly mood. I say we still let her have at Josephine."

"Suit yourself."

Another hour to kill, and my dogs were barking. I'm not sure how many times I danced, but each time I felt a little less pleasure. Maybe it was the fear of how much closer we were to events coming to pass, or maybe it was simply that the Savoy lost its magic when I wasn't there with the Rain- bows.

At ten to twelve, I found Grace, and together we tracked down Josephine. She reeked of booze and a sweet smoke that I learned was from reefer. She'd discarded her shoes and switched to dancing in her bare feet.

"We've got to make tracks," I said.

"But the evening's young," she slurred. "This is Ran- dolph." She clung to the arm of an Army sergeant. "He's talking about buying me a steak dinner."

"Can she get a rain check?" I asked. I pulled her away, strongly enough that her hold on his arm broke.

"Are you kidding?"

"I'm bleeding," I said.

"Then get a bandage and sit the next one out."

"Not that kind of bleeding." I raised an eyebrow, hoping she'd catch my meaning. "I don't mean to be a pill, but I'm dying here and I want to go home."

I was worried she'd just send me on my way to deal with it by myself. In fact, Grace had warned me as much when I'd suggested the strategy to her. But something in my face must've sold my pain as real, and the possibility of my humiliation—and hers and Grace's—was great enough that she gave in.

"Oh, bother. What timing. All right, we'll go."

While she said her farewells to Randolph, we tracked down her pumps. We hit the stairs just as the clock chimed twelve. I hadn't seen Pearl round up her crew, but knowing Suze they were already outside looking to hail a cab. She didn't mess around with her curfew, not when the punishment was a hit to the mouth.

Just as we arrived outside, I spotted them. They were near the wall where we had waited the week before, already analyzing their night while Dino sang the songs everyone else had forgotten. Pearl spotted me. Before anyone else had a chance to eyeball me, I turned back to Josephine and Grace and whispered, "I'll be back. I need to hit the ladies' one more time."

I missed the first five minutes of what came to pass, but Pearl was happy to recap it for me later on.

Right after I left, Pearl turned to a very drunk Rhona

and remarked that Grace looked familiar to her. "Does she go to our school?"

Rhona said no, but immediately recognized that this was the girl Tom had been seeing. The others urged her to leave it alone, but Rhona, as Pearl had warned me, was breathing fire that night. Rather than attacking Grace with words, she walked right up to her and slugged her.

Grace's nose gushed blood and she fell to her knees in shock. Rhona's behavior must've stirred something in Josephine, because she immediately leaped to defend her friend's honor. I came back outside right then, but stayed in the background, hoping no one would notice me.

"What is your problem?" Josephine screamed.

"I want to know where Tommy is," said Rhona.

"I don't know," howled Grace from the ground.

"The hell you don't. You did something to him. You made him go away!"

Grace began to sob in pain. Boy, howdy—I felt terrible. Never in a million years did I think Rhona would hit her. And while Josephine was doing everything she could to make sure Rhona didn't do it again, the one thing she wasn't doing was confessing to a crime.

So I stepped out of the shadows and tried to speed things up.

"Grace had nothing to do with it," I said. I tried to help her to her feet, but she'd gone limp.

"What are you doing here, girl detective?" asked Rhona.

"You want to know what happened to Tom?" I said. "Ask her." I pointed at Jo, who looked at me like the world had just gone topsy-turvy.

"What are you talking about?" she said.

"You're the one who told Tom that Grace didn't want anything to do with him anymore. And you're the last one who saw him before he vanished. Why don't you tell everyone here what exactly you did to make him go away?"

Even in the half light created by the neon sign, her eyes burned bright. "I told him what Grace told me to tell him. That she wasn't interested. That military men were her thing now."

The rest of the Rainbows formed a circle around us. "And then let me guess," I said. "You had one of your boyfriends step in and teach him a lesson."

"Is that what she told you?" asked Josephine.

"Never mind what Grace said or didn't say. It's true, isn't it?"

"You've been had, little girl," said Jo. "I liked Tom Barney. I liked him a hell of a lot more than your pal Grace did. Problem was, he was too good for her. She wanted danger, and he wanted a debutante who wouldn't be embarrassed to take him to the country club. I told him that and everything else I thought he needed to hear to get out from under her. But what I didn't do was force him to break up with her."

"She's lying," said Grace from the ground. "She did

something to him. I know it. Make her tell you where she took him that night."

But I didn't get a chance to. Just then a familiar voice called my name and I spun around in time to see Pop getting out of a taxi.

IT WAS AN UGLY SCENE. It always is when you're caught somewhere you're not supposed to be.

"Get in the cab," said Pop.

He took in the sight of Grace on the ground and the blood still pouring between her hands. He saw the crowd gathered around her, just seconds from becoming an unruly mob. And among all those white faces he saw the residents of Harlem who just wanted to spend Halloween night celebrating with hot jazz and the best hoofing in town.

"Pop—"

"Get. In. The. Cab."

There was no option. I slid into the backseat and joined him for a silent ride home.

21

POP HAD TRIED TO START the same sentence four times, but the words wouldn't come. I'd never seen him that angry before. Finally, the words made their way out of his mouth.

"What were you thinking? Lying to me like that?"

I desperately wanted to know how Pop had tracked me down, but it was clear it wasn't my turn to ask questions. "I didn't mean to lie."

"And yet you've done it again and again over the last few weeks. Is it so awful here, Iris? Is that it? Are you punishing me for moving us here?"

"No."

He paced the parlor floor as he spoke, his limp growing more prominent with each lap he took around the room. "I can't help that we don't have the money for Chapin."

"I don't care about that."

"Apparently you do. Otherwise, why would you go back there? Why would you lie to your aunt?"

And that's when it dawned on me: Miriam had called him. That's how he'd found out that I wasn't where I was supposed to be.

"Do you have any idea how foolish you made me look? Not only was it clear to your aunt that I had no idea what you were up to, I had to spend ten minutes assuring her that we weren't so bad off that I was asking my child to work for me."

So that was why she'd called. "I wanted her to know you were doing okay."

"By claiming I needed a fifteen-year-old's assistance?"

"Maybe you do. One of those girls was with Tom Barney right before he disappeared. That's why I was there tonight. She knows what happened to him."

All movement in the room stopped. Even the mantel clock ceased its ticking. "What do you know about Tom Barney?"

"I went to school with him, Pop. I know his parents hired you and I know you hit a dead end."

A flash of maroon started at his chin and pooled up his face. "I told you I didn't want you involving yourself in anything having to do with my business."

"I wanted to help. I know you didn't have any other work. You said yourself that if you didn't come up with something fast they weren't going to pay you."

"That wasn't an invitation for you to meddle."

"I was careful this time. I got to know his friends—the group who wouldn't talk to you." There was no point in explaining how I'd blown that. "I followed leads. I asked the right questions. And I'm telling you, that girl Josephine knows what happened. If someone did something to him, Pop, shouldn't they pay for that?"

Something in his face changed. Had I struck a chord?

"No one's done anything to Tom," he said.

"How can you say that? I have a witness. Grace was dating Tom. Josephine didn't like that and so she did what she could to get rid of Tom permanently."

"According to Grace?"

I didn't understand why he kept going back to her. Of course it was according to Grace. "Yes."

"That's not proof, Iris. That's one person's imagination."

"I know. That's why I was trying to get Josephine to confess."

He put his fingers to his eyes like Mama used to whenever she was starting to get a headache.

"Something's happened to him, Pop. It's not right. She needs to pay."

"Go to bed, Iris."

"So that's it? You're just going to let his parents believe he ran away when we know otherwise?"

"I know you think I'm not capable of doing this job, but I know what I'm doing." He sighed heavily. "I don't think he just ran away." His voice softened, his anger at me no longer important. "I know Tom's dead."

For the second time the room stood stock-still. Had I heard him right? "Someone found his body?"

"No. Iris, Tom wasn't murdered. He was killed during an Army training exercise."

I didn't understand. Tom Barney had joined the Army? "But he wasn't eighteen."

"He lied to join up. I spoke with a recruiter several days ago who remembered meeting him. After that it wasn't hard to track down where he went."

He'd lied, like the boy I'd danced with at the Savoy. But why? "You knew he joined up a while ago?"

"It was an avenue to pursue, like checking hospitals and morgues. It just so happened this one panned out."

"It can't be true. Grace told me—"

"I know what Grace told you. And I'm sure she believes it's the truth, but nothing nefarious is going on. He was just a boy who made a bad decision and paid for it with his life."

I was going to be sick. All these weeks, all this work, and Tom really was missing by his own hand. And now this: dead because of the war, only not really, since he'd died before ever seeing a battle.

"I'm sorry, Iris."

Grace was going to be devastated. I should've stayed out of it. "So what are you going to do now, Pop?"

"There's nothing to do. I'm going to write up my report and tell his parents what I learned. Then the case is closed."

"But won't they want to know why he joined up?"

"They have a son in jail and one they were pretty sure was fast on his way there. They'll probably assume Tom wised up and wanted to turn his life around. So he enlisted."

I could see why the Barneys might want to believe that, but I just couldn't see Tom leaving everything behind to join the Army. And Grace had been so certain Josephine was behind his disappearance—there had to be a reason for that.

"It's over, Iris," said Pop.

"I know."

But despite the fact that the case was over, I couldn't let it go. I needed to know the end of the story, starting with what happened at the Savoy after I left. Pearl would let me know. And if not her, then Grace.

SUNDAY POP REMAINED locked in his office. Lunch was a silent affair, despite Mrs. Mrozenski's best efforts. At one, Pop left the house. He didn't say where he was going, but I could guess: he was going to see the Barneys.

While he was gone, I performed one last act of disobedience. I headed uptown to Grace's apartment to break the news about Tom. As I walked the forbidden Upper East

Side streets I heard a deep laugh that sounded oddly familiar. I turned toward the sound and saw a woman with her arm intertwined with a soldier's. She laughed again and kicked up one of her scuffed high heels. It was Mrs. Wilson, the woman I'd photographed all those weeks before. But her companion wasn't the man I'd caught her with. This was someone new.

She didn't look any worse for wear. In fact, from the way she was carrying on it seemed like she was having the time of her life. She looked my way and smiled. If she recognized me, it didn't show on her face. I was just another Upper East Side kid, going about my business.

As I made it to Fifth Avenue I couldn't shake the image of her out of my head. She didn't look like a woman who'd been destroyed by my photos. Maybe I'd been incorrect in thinking she was the one being wronged. Like Pop said, sometimes it's not so easy to know who's good and who's bad. We really never know the whole story.

Mrs. Dunwitty greeted me at the door when I arrived. Grace was in her room, resting, I was told. She'd been attacked by a mugger the night before.

I feigned shock and outrage. Wasn't anyplace in the city safe? Then I waited for the inevitable questions about why I hadn't been at Grace's side when she was attacked, but they never came. Grace had already prepared my alibi.

"Is your father better? Grace was so disappointed you had to leave last night. She was so looking forward to spending the evening with you. And of course all this nastiness probably could've been avoided if she'd stayed in as you girls intended. I told her that Josephine was nothing but trouble."

"My pop's going to be fine," I said. "Can I see Grace?"

I was escorted to her room, where I found her sitting up in bed, her face swaddled in white bandages. A lunch tray sat at the end of the bed awaiting retrieval, and the radio was tuned to WEAF for *Parade of Stars*.

We waited until Mrs. Dunwitty left before speaking.

"How are you?" I asked.

"Sore. They set my nose last night, but who knows if it's ever going to be the same. Your pop looked fit to be tied."

"He was. In fact, I can't stay." I knew I needed to break the news about Tom, but given what Grace had already gone through, I wanted to delay it as long as possible. "I really just wanted to get my things and check on you. What happened after I left?"

"Not much. Jo huffed away, calling me a liar. Your friend Pearl got me a cab."

"So no confession?"

She shook her head. "I know it's terribly disappointing. And that was our one chance, too."

There was no point dragging this out any longer. "Actually, I don't think we're going to get anything out of her. They found Tom."

"Really?" Grace's face was a mixture of surprise and

326

something that I couldn't quite read. Could that be relief? "Where is he?"

I took a deep breath. "He's dead, Grace."

The life drained from her face. "Oh."

"That's what you expected, right?"

Her fingers trembled like keys on a piano. "Of course. I just hoped that it wasn't true. How did you find out?"

"Pop told me."

Her mouth formed a small O. "So then he must be going after Josephine."

I put my hand on hers, hoping to comfort her. "Josephine didn't do it. It turns out he enlisted. He was killed during a training exercise."

"Well, then, she must've convinced him to enlist."

"That's my thought, too. Unfortunately, Pop doesn't think his parents will care. Either way he's dead."

She winced as pain worked through her face.

"Are you all right?"

"I don't know. I need a moment alone. Would you help me to the bathroom?"

I did as she asked, lending my arm for support. I left her there and returned to her room. Poor Grace. Like me, she'd been led to believe that something darker was behind Tom's disappearance. And then, to make matters worse, Tom had done this thing no one understood. Why did he enlist? What motivated him? Had Josephine convinced him to do it? Was there something about him that none of us had been able to uncover, something that made him want to defend his country? Or were his parents right that joining up was his way of making a fresh start?

I moved the dirty dishes to the dresser and fluffed Grace's pillows. Beneath them was a shoebox full of letters— V-mail, I realized, the kind that had come from soldiers overseas. I picked up the box, intending to find its lid and store it. But the topmost note caught my eye. It was signed by Tom.

"Dear Grace," it began. "Basic training is pretty much what you'd expect. The food is awful, the company worse, but thinking about your smiling face is getting me through it. I'm going to make you proud, I promise you that. If you want a soldier, I'll be a soldier."

It was dated almost a month before. And it wasn't the only one. A more recent letter written by a friend in his platoon told the sad tale of his death.

So she knew. All this time she had known exactly what had happened to him.

"What are you doing?" Grace came into the room and launched toward me.

"I was trying to tidy up the room. This was under your pillows."

She grabbed for the box. "Give me that."

I relented. After all, I didn't need the box anymore. "I don't understand—you knew? Why didn't you say something?"

"He asked me not to."

I felt like I was trying to work out a math problem someone had posted on the chalkboard at Chapin. My brain just wasn't prepared for work that difficult. "So then why say anything to me about him?" She'd been in Pop's office. The Barneys' file had been out in plain sight. She must've suspected that Pop had been hired to find him, and her visit to the Lower East Side had been an attempt to confirm that. And then the break-in—that had been her coming back to get a better look at things without my interrupting her. "You knew Pop was looking for him, didn't you? Before I told you?"

She slid the box onto a bookshelf beside a copy of *Little Women*. "I suspected as much when you showed up at my house. The coincidence was too much, especially since we hadn't talked in so long."

"If you knew what Tom was up to, why the big act? Help me out, Grace."

Her eyes blazed beneath the shadows cast by the bandages. "There's nothing to help you with. What Tom did, he did on his own."

"Then why this big charade?" She didn't respond. Something still wasn't adding up, and she knew I knew it. "Josephine was telling the truth, wasn't she? You were never in love with Tom. You're the one who gave him the ultimatum, not her. You told him that if he wanted to be with you, he had to put on a uniform and pick up a gun." I was shaking. How could someone who was once so close to me turn out to be such a liar?

Perhaps the same way that I had.

"Why did you break into Mrs. Mrozenski's house? Did Pop find something that tied you to Tom?"

"What are you talking about? I didn't break into your house."

"Still, you hoped he'd go away and that would be the end of it. You made him enlist."

"I didn't make him do anything. If he thought he had to join up to be with me, he reached that decision on his own."

"But you did nothing to stop him."

"Oh, bother! He wouldn't leave me alone. You don't know what it was like with all the calls, the letters, the visits. It was humiliating, Iris. So I told him the only way I would ever be with him was if he enlisted. It was his choice to follow through on it."

I stared at her—I couldn't help it. Who was she? The Grace I'd known had never been this self-absorbed. Or maybe she had been, but I'd been too self-absorbed myself to notice. "He's dead, Grace. Don't you feel anything?"

"Of course I'm sorry about that, but it's not like I killed him. Half those boys I danced with last night are going to die in this war. That's what war is. It's sad and awful but it's not my fault."

She was right. No matter how much I wanted to blame

her for Tom's death, she wasn't the only cause. Even if he hadn't gone, there was no guarantee that when he turned eighteen his number wouldn't have come up in the draft. Maybe it wouldn't have been a training accident then, but he could've been killed all the same.

"Why would you try to blame Josephine? I thought she was your friend?"

She rolled her eyes. "Hardly. She's a scholarship student."

"So?"

She crossed her arms. "So I didn't know that when I first met her. She should've told me from the get-go. You know what Chapin's like."

I was wrong that Rhona and Josephine were cold. In that moment I'd never seen anyone colder than Grace Dunwitty.

"Who are you?" I said.

A smile bloomed across her face. "The same girl I've always been. You're the one who's changed."

I WAS SO DISTURBED by my meeting with Grace that I went straight to the Barneys' house, hoping to find Pop. He was still inside as I arrived, his familiar silhouette seated in the parlor with Mr. and Mrs. Barney. I remained outside sitting on the curb until he was done.

"What are you doing here, Iris? Is everything all right?"

I stood and went to him. This wasn't the kind of thing to

331

talk about on the street and yet I knew if I waited a moment longer to get it out, I'd explode. "Grace made him do it."

"Made who do what?"

"She made Tom enlist. She said she wouldn't continue dating him if he didn't."

He took my arm and pulled me away from the house. "Are you sure?"

"Positive. She has letters from him where it's clear he's doing it for her."

He lowered his voice and seemed to be imploring me to do the same. "How do you know this? Did you go see her?"

I could see what was coming: another lecture about how disobedient I was. "Damn it, Pop—this isn't about me." I shocked him with the profanity, I could see that. "Yes, I went there. I thought I owed it to her to tell her what really happened to Tom. I was going to console a friend who was about to find out the boy she loved was dead. And if that makes me a bad kid in your eyes, then I guess that's what I am." I shook free of his grip and started up the Barneys' walk.

"Where are you going?"

"I have to tell the Barneys."

He gently took my hand in his. "No, Iris. They don't need to know the why behind this."

"But he'd be alive if she hadn't manipulated him."

His other hand found mine and squeezed. "And she's

going to have to live with that. But as awful as what she did was, it's not a crime."

"But still—"

"Honey, right now they think their son was trying to turn his life around. Whether they know the truth or not, the outcome is still the same. He's still dead. Understand?"

I nodded. He was right. What good could come from letting them know that Tom did what he did to please a spoiled rich girl? All it would do would increase the sense that his loss was absolutely pointless.

I let Pop pull me toward the street. As we started home, I thought about Mr. Barney, about how easily he'd given up on his own flesh and blood. Tom wasn't perfect, but he was hardly the terrible boy he made him out to be. And while no crime may have been committed, beyond Tom's insatiable need to please people who didn't deserve the effort, I had to wonder if Tom's desire to make Grace happy wasn't rooted in some similar desire to please his pop.

"Have you given up on me?" I asked Pop.

"Why would you ask that?"

I shrugged, unable to put what I was thinking into words.

"I wish you were more cautious, Iris. But I can't say I'm surprised that you're not, given who your mother was." He winked at me. "When we first met she took me to a Yorkville dance hall. It was supposed to be for Germans only, but she paraded me inside with a look on her face that dared anyone who had a problem with me being there to challenge her. No one did. I asked her later why she took me there and she told me that she figured if she could get me into someplace restricted to Germans, it would be a lot easier to get people to accept that she was marrying me when the time came."

I'd never heard the story before, but it didn't surprise me. Mama claimed she knew she wanted to be Pop's wife from the first second she saw him. "If you understand that I'm like Mama, why can't you let me help you?"

He didn't answer me.

"I'm going to keep at it, Pop. I can keep doing it behind your back and making mistakes, or you can teach me how to be safe. The choice is yours."

He was silent for half a block. Just as I was starting to think that he was never going to respond, he paused before a row house with a low wrought-iron fence. "If I agree to this, will you follow my rules and only do exactly what I tell you to?"

"Absolutely."

He rubbed his chin, where that day's beard growth peeked through the smooth skin, adding contour and dimension to his face. He may not have known me, but I was kidding myself if I thought I knew him. "Maybe we can give it a try. But you play by my rules. No more lies and no more secrets. I can't work with you if I can't trust you."

"All right," I said.

"And I need you to trust me. I promise you we won't

starve to death or end up on the streets. Things are hard right now, but they're not desperate." That was good to know. "I don't pretend to know what it's been like for you, Iris. I know it's been hard. I know I'm not the parent you would've chosen if it had been left up to you."

I didn't argue with him. After all, I'd made a pledge to be honest. "Why did she do it, Pop?"

"I wish I could tell you. I don't think we'll ever know, and that's the worst part, isn't it? That she could do something so terrible and not even leave us understanding why."

Tears squeezed past my nose and landed on the sidewalk in front of me. "Do you think I did something that upset her?"

"No. Absolutely not. This had nothing to do with you, I'm certain of that."

"I've heard things—"

He fished a handkerchief out of his pocket. "Idle gossip, Iris. That's all. Everyone wants a reason, and sometimes they come up with the worst explanations possible, even when there's no basis for it. To them, any answer is better than no answer."

I mopped at my eyes and wiped my nose. "I don't think I can forgive her if I don't know why she did it."

"That'll change," he said. "You'll see."

"I dream about her," I said. "In my dreams she's always alive."

He nodded. "Mine, too."

I was surprised. I had no doubt that Pop missed her, but it never occurred to me that he dreamed about her, too.

He put his hand on my head and ruffled my hair. "You know how when you dream Mama is still alive and then you wake up, you have to suffer her loss all over again? In my dreams I'm running. And then when I wake up—"

He didn't finish the sentence. He didn't have to.

22

I CALLED PEARL and let her know the ugly end to the story of Tom Barney. She cried at the news. Like me, she didn't want to believe something tragic could happen to someone our own age. Just because it was the war that had done it, or the desire to be part of it at least, didn't make Tom's end any easier. Just more inexplicable.

There were more people I had to talk to.

I found Rhona at Normandie's after school. She sat at the counter drinking an egg cream while Suze divided her time between her and a booth filled with other customers. Rhona started when she saw me, but quickly recovered, setting her jaw in a way that made it clear she wasn't going to let me ruffle her. "Well, if it isn't the girl detective."

"I need to talk to Suze and you," I said.

"Suze is busy. And I'm not in the mood for your off-time jive."

On cue, Suze eyeballed me and darted into the restroom.

Boy, howdy—they weren't going to make this easy. "I thought you might want to know about Tom."

Rhona squared her shoulders. "Go on."

"He's dead, Rhona."

The tough-girl act vanished. "Was it that girl Josephine?"

I shook my head. "He enlisted in the Army. He was killed during a training exercise."

Her eyes looked wet. Anger flashed behind the tears. "Tommy enlisted? Why?"

I searched my pockets for a handkerchief, as Pop had done for me. "He did it for Grace. She convinced him it was the only way she'd continue seeing him."

She took the handkerchief, but didn't use it. Instead, she mashed it in her hands and twisted it until I expected the fabric to tear in half. Grace would get hers. Rhona would make sure of it.

"Thanks for telling me," she whispered. It was obvious she wanted me to leave so she could be alone with her thoughts, but I wasn't done yet.

"I've been trying to figure something out," I said. "How did you put together who my pop was?"

"Your friend Pearl Harbor told me."

"But see, I think you knew before then and she only confirmed it. You were at my house, weren't you?"

Her expression said it all. She'd been there all right, going through Pop's files.

"You came to get the note. The one you'd written the

doctor's address on. 240 Houston Street." It was the i's dot-ted with circles that had given it away. The same i's that had been in the notes to Principal Deluca that Rhona had forged for Tom.

She stared at me and I could see how surprised she was that I'd put it together.

"You were pregnant," I whispered. "Not last year when Pearl started the rumor, but this fall, right before Tommy started breaking into lockers. He'd never done anything outright illegal until then. He did that for you, didn't he? He wanted to get money to help you. And then you dumped him."

"I didn't want him tied to a girl like me. I'm nothing. I'm always going to be nothing. He was better than that, even if he didn't know it yet."

It was funny how a girl everyone thought was bad news saw the potential in Tom, while someone like Grace couldn't wait to tear him down.

"So why did you steal the note?" I asked.

"I was worried your pop would put it together and word would get back to Tom's old man. If he did come back, I didn't want that hanging over him." What was it like to fear the people you were supposed to love? I hoped I never found out. "So I guess you're going to tell everyone."

Did she really think I was that kind of person? "You al-ready suffered plenty of humiliation last year. I won't put you through that again." I started to leave, then stopped myself. "Of course, I could go to the police about the break-in."

The little weakness I'd seen in her disappeared. "What do you want from me?" she hissed.

"I want you to make Suze forgive me."

"Oh, little girl—I'm afraid you're going to have to do that on your own."

I WAITED UNTIL SUZE was off work to talk to her. As she exited Normandie's and started for home, I rushed to catch up with her. She didn't seem surprised to see me. Or happy about it.

"Rhona already broke the news," she told me.

That was good. At least I was spared from having to do it twice. "Could I talk to you for a second?"

"If you make it fast. I'm meeting Maria." Her pace slowed slightly. I no longer had to jog to keep up with her.

"I'm so sorry. About Tommy. About everything." I had no idea what else to say. "Here." I passed her a bag with her skirt, shoes, and jewelry in it. She checked the contents and then tucked the sack under her arm.

"I bet you got it good when your pop found you in Harlem."

"It wasn't pretty."

"How'd he find out where you were?"

"My aunt told him."

She raised an eyebrow.

"My real aunt," I said. "I ran into her near Grace's apartment. She called him and he realized I wasn't where I told him I'd be. I guess once he realized I lied about that, he figured he better check all the places I'd been lately without permission, including the Savoy."

"So I'm not the only one you lie to?"

That hurt. Not that it wasn't true. "I didn't mean to lie about my pop. That first day I was so desperate to make a friend, and so when you assumed my pop was at war, I just let you. And by the time Tom disappeared and Pop got involved, it was too late for me to make things right."

She lit a cigarette. "And what about your mother?"

"That was true. Every word of it. I know you don't trust me, and you have every reason not to, but please believe me when I say I didn't mean to hurt you. I like you, Suze. I liked all of you." I felt naked standing there on the sidewalk with her.

She tweaked her mouth to the left and exhaled. "I like you, too, baby girl."

"You coming, Suze?" Maria appeared up the street. In the shadows behind her I could see Benny and Dino.

"I'm on my way," said Suze. "You better head home while the sun's still up," she told me. "You don't want your pop to blow another gasket."

"Will do."

She took two steps and turned back to me. "And remember, baby girl—be good."

I watched them walk away and then headed toward the Orchard Street house. The local businesses were winding down for the evening. Signs in English and Hebrew lured passersby to stop and buy day-old loaves of pumpernickel bread, hand-rolled cigars, and fish piled into barrels. Women called out to one another from the line outside Kamiskey's butcher shop, wishing each other a good evening and asking after their families. The sun started its descent and the air filled with the sounds of children finishing their last games of hopscotch and kick the can before their mothers called them inside. As I rounded the corner, my stomach growled in hunger. With any luck, dinner would be waiting for me and so would Pop and Mrs. Mrozenski. There would probably be a fire burning in the parlor and the radio would be tuned to the evening news.

I quickened my pace, eager to reach home.

More Talking of Shakespeare

More Talking of Shakespeare

EDITED BY JOHN GARRETT

THEATRE ARTS BOOKS

NEW YORK

© LONGMANS, GREEN AND CO. LTD. AND
CONTRIBUTORS 1959
PUBLISHED BY THEATRE ARTS BOOKS
333 SIXTH AVENUE
NEW YORK 14, N.Y.

Library of Congress Catalog Card Number: 59–13240

Printed in Great Britain

TO

GLEN BYAM SHAW

CONTENTS

FOREWORD

THE twelve lectures brought together in this volume have nothing more in common than the fact that they were delivered at the Shakespeare Memorial Theatre's Summer Schools on Shakespeare between the years 1954 and 1958. These courses are designed primarily to serve as stimulus and refreshment for teachers whose responsibility it is to introduce young people in schools, colleges and other places of learning to Shakespeare, and to make available to them some of the fruits of contemporary scholarship in their particular field of study. If by becoming themselves excited by the performances of the plays in the theatre, they can make their pupils enthusiastic to see the plays on the stage as opposed only to studying them as texts in the classroom, so much the better. As no particular theme is imposed on any course, it follows that no pattern or continuity is apparent in this volume. Each lecture stands on its own merit and has been selected for no better reason than that it made immediate impact when it was delivered, provoked discussion, and seemed to merit a more permanent form than the ephemeral life of the spoken word. A first volume of these Stratford lectures was published in 1954, under the title *Talking of Shakespeare*. Here is more talking of Shakespeare. It is hoped that it will give pleasure and profit.

JOHN GARRETT

I

WAGS, CLOWNS AND JESTERS

by NEVILL COGHILL

AMONG the less exalted orders of the Shakespearian populace there are three that tend to shade off into a kind of class, whose main functions, mannerisms and idiosyncrasies are easy to recognize, though they tend to merge and mingle, or at least to overlap: they are the Wags, the Clowns and the Jesters.

Mainly they are meant to be funny, whether as wits or butts or both: but they have other functions and qualities too. Time has dealt unkindly with many of their jokes, and some have not survived the footnotes that expound them. Not their jokes only, but their very being, in some cases, may call for explanation. We still meet with rustics in the modern world, with clown-policemen and bull-calf recruits; a yokel needs no footnote. But where are now the pert boys whom Shakespeare shows us paging their young masters from Verona to Milan, from Pisa to Padua, and throwing out a barrage of waggery in choplogic, cross-purpose, paronomasia and arch comment upon the love-affairs of their betters? And where are the professional fools, those privileged jesters, men like Will Sommers, who called Henry VIII 'Harry' to his face, and could make him roar with laughter on damp days?

Some pictures of the Jesters remain. Richard Tarlton was a snub-nosed smiler, with wide-set eyes, a curly moustache and a little chin-beard; he could play tabor and pipe together, a difficult art. Watteau has left us the melancholy face of Gilles, Court Jester to the King of France, and there is, I learn from Professor Davis, an epitaph in Beckley Church, to the last of all the Jesters, Dicky Pearce, the Earl of Suffolk's Fool, who died in 1728. It is ascribed, for what good reason I do not know, to Jonathan Swift:

> Here lies the Earl of Suffolk's Fool
> Men call'd him Dicky Pearce:
> His folly served to make men laugh
> When wit and mirth were scarce.

I

Poor Dick, alas! is dead and gone,
What signifies to cry?
Dickys enough are left behind
To laugh at by and by.[1]

Wags and Jesters are now denizens of a museum world and there they lead their fancy-dress existence; it may well be that this is a factor which helps us to achieve that never-never-landish state of mind suited to a comedy of Shakespeare's golden world, a state in which it is easy to cross the frontiers of Illyria or Arden, and bid lullaby to our social consciences for an hour or two, for the refreshment of their foolery.

What a fantastic foolery it is! It has an extravagance in which, for once, Ben Jonson has outdone Shakespeare, who has nothing to match the macabre trinity of twisted creatures or grotesques, Nano the dwarf, Castrone the Eunuch, and Androgyno the Man-Woman, who are Volpone's household monsters, his kept Fools. Each of them is a museum piece, a creature of great rarity, quaintness and cost: their collective function in the play is more than that of entertaining their master: it is to appear as further items in, and emblems of, his inordinate wealth and connoisseurship. They are the *trouvailles* of a collector.

When we first meet with them, whether in the text or on the stage, we have to open our mouths wide to swallow them; we teach ourselves to accept them as a deliberately stomach-turning Jonsonian hyperbole, in scale with the huge scope of his satire, with the allegorical stature of Volpone himself. And yet I can recall a paragraph in a newspaper, at the time when Benito Mussolini was waging war in Abyssinia: it described the vast and curious wealth of a certain Abyssinian Prince, Ras Tafari, a cousin of the Emperor. Among his more fabulous possessions, he also kept a little human zoo; it contained a monk, a eunuch and a hermaphrodite. It would seem that Ben Jonson's fantasies are not entirely out of this world.

Half-wittedness, deformity and abnormality, seem to have been (historically speaking) the usual qualifications for the Fools or 'naturals' that, from time to time, were kept for a whim, or for the amusement of great households—a use for the village idiot.

At what time cunning, intelligence and talent took over from cretinism in the making of the Court Fool, it is hard to say. The Fool by Nature and the Fool by Art have always existed, and which is the more in vogue will depend on the taste of the age. In a civilized Court,

[1] Samuel Palmer, *Epitaphs and Epigrams* (London 1869).

like that of Richard II, we find that entertainment came from poets like Chaucer and Gower, and from tregetours such as those we read of in the *Franklin's Tale*. In a semi-barbarous Court, like that of Henry VIII, we find Will Sommers. It is hard to understand how educated people could relish the company of a freak of nature, and keep him, so to speak, as a pet. Shakespeare lifted the whole company of such Fools out of the slough of imbecility; his jesters have wit, pithiness; they can dance and sing and extemporize, their presence has point. It seems to say 'as, in the midst of life, we are in death, so, in the midst of sanity, we are in folly'.

But no actual Tudor Fool I ever heard of had such gift or quality. A good loud laugh or an agreeable gibe was as much as could be hoped for from Sommers, or even perhaps from Tarlton, except when he took to his tabor and pipe. If Will Sommers had no better jokes than those that Armin records of him, what are we to think of the taste and intelligence of Henry VIII?

We read in Armin's *Nest of Ninnies*, that the king, when sad, would cheer himself up by rhyming and riddling with this melancholy moron. The stooping, hollow-eyed figure would squinny at his monarch: ' "Now tell me," says Will, "if you can, what it is that, being borne without life, head, lippe or eye, yet doth runne roaring through the world until it dye?" "That is a wonder," quoth the King, "and no question; I know it not." "Why," quoth Will, "it is a fart." At this the King laught hartely and was exceeding merry.'

Richard Tarlton's verbal gifts seem to have been very little better, such, at least, as have come down to us in *Tarlton's Jests* and *News Out of Purgatory*; yet Fuller tells us that, 'when Queen Elisabeth was serious, dare not say sullen, and out of humour, he could undumpish her at his pleasure'. But he brought a frown to her face when he said of Sir Walter Raleigh, 'See, the Knave commands the Queen.' He was famous for his powers of extemporal rhyme, like Touchstone: but alas his published vein is no better than what one would expect to find in a ballad sold at a fair by Autolycus. Here is a sample:

> By rushing rivers late,
> In Bedford town, no nay,
> Ful many a woeful state
> May yeeld to fast and pray.

> At twelve oclock at night
> It flowed with such a hed,

> Yea, many a woful wight
> Did swim in naked bed
>
> Among the rest there was
> A woful widow sure,
> Whome God did bring to passe
> The death she did procure.
>
> Widow Spencer by name
> A sleep she being fast,
> The flood so rashly came
> That she aloft was cast.
>
> Which seeing started up,
> Regarding small her pelf
> She left beside her bed,
> And so she drowned herself.[1]

And so on for thirty-six verses. Contrast them with Touchstone's lilting extemporizations:

> If the cat will after kind,
> So, be sure, will Rosalind. . . .

But before I go on to Shakespeare's imagination of Jesters, let me show you a few more authentic Tudor ones, for it is hardly possible to realize how much Shakespeare transfigured the whole tribe, if one does not know how raw his raw material was.

There was Jack Oates, Fool to a countrified knight.[2] Oates was a 'natural' given to almost senseless rages and jealousies whenever attention was paid to any entertainer other than himself. He broke a fiddle on a fiddler and beat up a bagpiper and burnt his bagpipes, not out of musical feeling, but out of envy. But his vendetta with the cook was crazier and more malicious. Sir William was particularly addicted to quince pies, and so, acting on an imperfectly thought-out plan to get the cook into trouble, Oates stole a quince pie. But it was too hot to hold, so the Fool jumped into the moat to cool it. Sir William's first reaction was to roar with laughter and sack the cook (presumably for having allowed the theft of the pie; he seems to have been almost as big a fool as Oates himself), but on learning that there was malice be-

---

[1] Tarlton's *Jests and News out of Purgatory*, ed. J. O. Halliwell, Shakespeare Society, 1844.

[2] See *Fools and Jesters*: with a reprint of Robert Armin's *Nest of Ninnies*, with an Introduction by J. P. Collier, Shakespeare Society, 1842

hind the incident, he 'bid the Cook enjoy his place againe'. Oates's best recorded joke is that he ran in to his master and some assembled guests, to announce that a country-wench in the servants' hall had eaten garlic, and seventeen men had been poisoned kissing her.

Then there was Jemy Camber, a fat Scotch dwarf, said to have been a yard and a nail high, and two yards round, with a small head, long hair, one ear bigger than the other, flaming eyes, a flat nose, a wide mouth, few teeth, short legs, pretty little feet and enormous hands. He seems to have been more butt than wit: ' "No," says Jemy, "the sun blowes very colde." "No," says the King, "the wind shines very hot." So simple hee was that he knew not whether it was the sunne or the winde made him sweat.'

Perhaps Edward Atienza had read this account of Jemy Camber in Armin's *Nest of Ninnies* when he contrived to perform Lavache in *All's Well That Ends Well* as a tubby dwarf—a miracle of costume, make-up and acting—at Stratford in 1955. There is, of course, no suggestion in Shakespeare that Lavache was a dwarf, but he is described as suffering from another inconvenience which he certainly shared with Jemy, namely a pressing sexual appetite.

'My poor body, Madam, requires it,' says Lavache when asking permission of the Countess to marry, 'if I may have your ladyship's good will to go to the world, Isbel the woman and I will do as we may.' Jemy Camber was sub-intelligent and could never so have expressed himself; nevertheless he got quite a long way towards seducing the laundress. She, however, was too much for him. She stuffed a heap of nettles under her bed; then, having lured him in beside her, she knocked the wall with her hand, as if someone were at the door. Jemy, terrified at being caught in the act, dived naked under the bed and found himself among the nettles.

One might think I had chosen my illustrations from specially oafish jests and jesters, but they are a disappointing lot; even Henry Pattensen, household Jester to Thomas More, was a crude-witted fellow; jokes about the size of a nose were about his level. Only More's charity can explain Pattensen's membership of the household.

What a world away from all such dolts and deformities are the Fools in Shakespeare! What a civilization breathes from Arden and Illyria, compared with what issues from Hampton Court! Armin's book shows us something of the actuality of Jesterdom, Shakespeare shows us jesters in the ideal, not what they were, but all they could never be.

Yet it was Armin who made this possible. Not his book, but himself, as an actor; *for* him, *through* him, Shakespeare created the witty Fool, the singing Fool, the fey, the tragic Fool. Armin joined Shakespeare's Company just before the turn of the century, in 1599; and from that moment began Shakespeare's vision of the Fool and his high art.

For the moment, however, let me return to the Wags and the Clowns. As I have already said, the three sub-categories of comic actor merge into one another in some of their tricks; what distinguishes the Wag is to strut along behind or beside his master. Some are blockish like the Dromios; some, like Launce and Speed, are fond of their own wit and ever ready to risk their bottoms for their tongues. The secret of their comedy is simple: word-play and horse-play. A good friendly knockabout or thrashing of the 'knock-me-on-the-door' style, for instance, is after all what everyone enjoys.

It may have been John Lyly who taught Shakespeare the dramatic charm of this master-to-boy relationship, from which it is so easy to create dialogue, catechism-wise when all else fails. Lyly's boys seem all to be in the top form of some Prep. School to Parnassus; they have been taught to utter in imagery. Here, for example, is young Half-penny, in *Mother Bombie*:

HALFPENNY: Nay then, let me come in with a dream, short but sweet, that my mouth waters ever since I waked. Methought there sate upon a shelf three damask prunes in velvet caps and pressed satin gowns, like judges; and that there were a whole handful of currants to be arraigned of a riot, because they clung together in such clusters: twelve raisins of the sun were impannelled in a jury, and, as a leaf of whole mace, which was bailiff, was carrying the quest to consult, methought there came an angry cook, and gelded the jury of their stones, and swept both judges, jurors, rebels and bailiff into a porridge-pot; whereat I being melancholy, fetched a deep sigh that waked myself and my bed-fellow.

This is excellent fooling. Youngest and smallest of Shakespeare's Wags, in a vein even more delicate and poetical, is Moth, servant to Don Adriano de Armado. Their happy sparring-partnership, so full of affectation, and, which is more, of affection, is a large part of the verbal magic of the play:

ARMADO: Warble, child; make passionate my sense of hearing.
MOTH (*singing*): *Concolinel.* . . .

ARMADO: Sweet air! Go, tenderness of years; take this key, give enlargement to the swain, bring him festinately hither; I must employ him in a letter to my love.

MOTH: Master, will you win your love with a French brawl?

ARMADO: How meanest thou? brawling in French?

MOTH: No, my complete master; but to jig off a tune at the tongue's end, canary to it with your feet, humour it with turning up your eyelids, sigh a note and sing a note, sometimes through the throat, as if you swallowed love by singing love, sometime through the nose, as if you snuffed up love by smelling love . . . with your arms crossed on your thin belly-doublet like a rabbit on a spit. . . . These are complements, these are humours, these betray nice wenches. . . .

ARMADO: How hast thou purchased this experience?

MOTH: By my penny of observation.

Lovely nonsense of this kind is a subliming of Lyly's dialogue, and indeed of the 'conceit' itself; the speakers feed each other with question and answer, and their relationship, of master and boy, is as if mellowed out of that between Sir Tophas and Epiton in Lyly's *Endymion*. An impudent variation of it is seen in Falstaff and his page:

FALSTAFF: Sirrah, you giant, what says the doctor to my water?

PAGE: He said, sir, the water itself was a good healthy water; but, for the party that owed it, he might have more diseases than he knew for.

This is a *visual* as well as a *verbal* use of the relationship—the enormous Falstaff, the infinitesimal page; verbally, it is amusing to see the first comic (might I say Dickensian?) use of the word *party* that I know of.

The main of Shakespeare's serving-boys are yokels in the egg, peasants like the Dromios, not gentry-pages like Moth; they are meant to be funny, not poetical; but they shade upwards socially, via Launce and Speed, to Biondello and to Tranio, who is well-enough bred to pass for his master Lucentio. But it would seem that there was a limit, even for Shakespeare, to what could be done with comic serving lads by way of stage effect; perhaps he found he was repeating himself; the soliloquies and name of Launce have much in common with those of Launcelot. The species seems to disappear from Shakespeare's work towards the turn of the sixteenth century; chronological order in this matter is not certain, but perhaps the last of the comic pages were the two imps who appear out of nowhere in the forest of Arden, sing, 'It was a lover and his lass . . .', and vanish as suddenly as they came.

B

But the Clown class goes right through Shakespearian comedy: and not only through the comedies, but through the histories and the tragedies. One of his first and most memorable is a tragic clown. He comes in at the height of the agony in *Titus Andronicus*, when the storm of passion is frothed with hysteria. Titus is as mad as the sea, but the tide is beginning to turn; hitherto he has only suffered, now he is beginning to act. As if to mark this moment, Shakespeare brings in a clown carrying a basket of pigeons, and the tension seems to be released a little; at last there will be something to laugh, or at least to smile, at. Titus mistakes the clown, in his crazy way, for a messenger from Jupiter: 'Shall I have justice? What says Jupiter?' 'Jupiter' however is a new word to the simpleton; he mixes it up, in baleful ignorance with 'Gibbet-maker': 'O! the gibbet-maker? He says he hath taken them down again for the man must not be hanged till the next week.' It is grim word-play, the beginning of Shakespearian malapropism, but grimmer is to come.

> TITUS: Why, didst thou not come from heaven?
> CLOWN: From heaven! alas! sir, I never came there. *God forbid I should be so bold to press to heaven in my young days.*

Could there have been, when this was first produced, experienced Shakespearian playgoers, they would have scented irony in airs such as these. Titus sends the fellow with a letter, demanding justice, to his enemy, the Emperor Saturninus: 'And when you come to him, at the first approach you must kneel; then kiss his foot; then deliver up your pigeons; and then look for your reward.' The simpleton moons off on his errand, the scene changes to the Emperor's court.

> TAMORA: How now, good fellow! wouldst thou speak with us?
> CLOWN: Yea, forsooth, an your mistership be emperial.
> TAMORA: Empress I am, but yonder sits the Emperor.
> CLOWN: 'Tis he. God and Saint Stephen give you good den.
>   I have brought you a letter and a couple of pigeons here.
>   (*Saturninus reads the letter.*)
> SATURNINUS: Go, take him away, and hang him presently.
> CLOWN: How much money must I have?
> TAMORA: Come, sirrah, you must be hanged.
> CLOWN: Hanged! By'r lady, then I have brought up a neck to a fair end.
>   (*Exit, guarded.*)

Here is Shakespeare's first juxtaposition of madman, fool and death; his first use of comedy to heighten horror with surprise. The mention of Saint Stephen may put the fancy into one's mind that this clown is a first martyr to irony. But he has the last word: '*I have brought up my neck to a fair end.*' These effects are above what can be achieved with Wags. It is the *simplicity*, not the waggishness, of the clown that touches the scene with tragic feeling in its unique blend of lunacy and evil and rustic innocence.

Shakespeare's last tragic clown, if the clown that brings the asp to Cleopatra be he, is also a death-clown, also a simpleton; and in this case, that shimmers with ironies even more intense, his simpletonism is underlined by his attempts at waggery: 'You must not think I am so simple but I know the devil himself will not eat a woman.' He, too, has the last word in the interchange: 'I wish you joy of the worm.'

Apart from their vacuous innocence, these two tragic clowns have no 'character'. They do not need it. But most of the great clowns in Shakespeare are highly individual; they are among the most humanly perceived of all the members of their little worlds. One has only to think of Bottom and his companions.

It may be that we have to thank Will Kempe for this; we know, from the 1599 quarto of *Romeo and Juliet*, that he played Peter: from the Folio we know he played Dogberry too. If we unbridle our imagination a little, we may see him as a chief stimulus to Shakespeare's comic invention until Robert Armin took over from him, about 1599. Whatever quirks of individuality Shakespeare invented to give scope to the antics of Kempe, all the clowns have the great foundation-stone we have already noted, of simpletonism. Bottom is a simpleton who is also a genius. Suppose him, for a moment, anything but the pure innocent he is; suppose him a knowing wag; how intolerable would his relation with Titania become! But, as with the clown with the asp, such waggery as he has is the index of his innocence: 'And yet, to say the truth, reason and love keep little company together now-a-days. The more the pity, that some honest neighbours will not make them friends.' Bottom and the clowns of his class have, in their making, a hint of the aphorism of St Augustine that Langland quotes in *Piers Plowman*: '*Ecce ipsi idioti rapiunt celum, ubi nos sapientes in inferno mergimur.*' See! very fools take Heaven by assault, where we, the wise, are sunk into the pit.

On this foundation of innocence, Bottom's genius as an artist is superimposed. I believe it was Mr J. B. Priestley who first noted that Bottom was essentially an artist, among companions whose only thought was for sixpence a day from the Duke. But Bottom cares about *style*; he knows how to distinguish—'in the *true* performing'—between the 'condoling' style of the lover and the cat-tearing manner needed for the part of Ercles. His first thought is his make-up: 'Well, I will undertake it. *What beard were I best to play it in?*' and he rattles off half a dozen plausible alternatives from a glowing imagination. When, later, problems in production arise, he overflows with exciting suggestions, and he rejects the proposal of Quince that the Prologue shall be written in the trite metre of 'eight and six', preferring the full dignity of octosyllabics: 'Let it be written in eight and eight.' Certainly style is a great preoccupation with him, and inventiveness his special talent. One would like to see a tapestry woven by Bottom the Weaver.

Dull and Elbow, the constables in *Love's Labour's Lost* and *Measure for Measure*, are simpletons, both of them, too; but they have no genius. They have character, however, far beyond what is needed for their minimal plot-function. Dull is a model of obstinacy well-based in ignorance. 'I said the deer was not a *haud credo*; 'twas a pricket,' he asserts to Holofernes, and he can hold his own in a debate:

HOLOFERNES: . . . The allusion holds in the exchange.
DULL: 'Tis true indeed; the collusion holds in the exchange.
HOLOFERNES: God comfort thy capacity! I say the allusion holds in the exchange.
DULL: And I say the pollution holds in the exchange. . . .

Elbow, whose plot-function is the arrest of Pompey and Mistress Overdone, is a product of the same constabulary, an adept in word-mismanagement; but his endearing incompetence as an officer is used not only to make us smile, but to show the patient tact of Escalus, who, after a tiring morning with him and Pompey Bum, sees that Elbow will have to be replaced and manages to make arrangements for this without hurting his feelings. The patient justice and good feeling of Escalus are, in turn, juxtaposed to the contemptuous attitude of Angelo, who cannot be bothered with such matters and has left them, with a sneer, to Escalus to handle. Thus the insufficiency of a comic Constable is used by his creator to show the insufficiency of a protagonist.

The idea 'that out of the mouths of babes and sucklings hast thou ordained strength', however, is more directly presented to us through Dogberry, Verges and the Messina Watch in *Much Ado About Nothing*. Once again we have a feast of malapropism and a good deal of ordinary clowning ('We will rather sleep than talk; we know what belongs to a

Watch'); on top of that there is a sudden overflow of character in Dog-berry's last speech which instantly places him as a person—that is, as more than a Constable, in the social context of Messina: 'I am a wise fellow; and, which is more, an officer; and, which is more, a house-holder; and, which is more, as pretty a piece of flesh as any in Messina; and one that knows the law, go to; and a rich fellow enough, go to; and a fellow that hath had losses; and one that hath two gowns, and everything handsome about him.'

Pompey Bum, and his fellow-pander, Boult, in *Pericles*, are spirits of another sort, and yet the same actor may play them; they are in the Kempe tradition. To them are also allowed supererogatory moments of intimacy, brief glimpses of disarming candour, touches of grace. Pompey is brought to admit that his profession 'does stink in some sort': Boult, about to make the old and obvious joke about roses and prickles, suddenly stops short and says, 'O! sir, I can be modest.' Lysimachus retorts, 'That dignifies the renown of a bawd.'

Clowns make a class but Jesters are only a guild; that Shake-speare would ever have thought of that guild as a rich mine of drama without the advent of Robert Armin, seems unlikely. Yet his first Jester had been created some years before Armin replaced Kempe, and he sprang out of the Wag tradition, the tradition of the imp-servant in mischievous mood. It was Puck, court-fool to fairyland: 'I jest to Oberon, and make him smile. . . .'

The boy who played Moth could no doubt have played Puck too, but Touchstone is imagined for a matured actor: breathlessness and brio will carry Puck through his part, but Touchstone calls for timing. His lines are a study, an *étude*, for a professional, full of antitheses, alternatives, conditionals and qualifications: 'By my knavery, if I had it, then I were; but if you swear by that that is not, you are not fore-sworn; no more was this knight, swearing by his honour, for he never had any; or if he had, he had sworn it away, before he ever saw those pancakes or that mustard.' This and so many of his speeches depend for their effectiveness on infinitesimal changes of tone and tempo. Shake-speare seems to have discovered Armin's range gradually; it looks as if he did not at first know that he could sing, for the songs in *As You Like It* go to Amiens and the pages; but what he seized upon was the power of pulling off a set-piece in prose: and that means timing, and cadencing—the precise degree of emphasis required for the two demonstratives, for instance, *those* pancakes and *that* mustard. Touch-stone is a shallower, or at least a less complex character than Feste; he is the jester of prepared witticisms, the raconteur with a repertory. The story of Jane Smile, and the recital of the Seven Degrees of the Lie have evidently been made perfect by many previous repetitions. One feels he may even have tried out his dialogue with Corin on some previous occasion too, with some other shepherd, the reasons he gives fall so pat; court versus country was a stock debate, and Touchstone was prepared for it; indeed he initiates it. He is playing on home ground.

TOUCHSTONE: Wast ever in court, shepherd?
    CORIN: No, truly.
TOUCHSTONE: Then thou art damned.
    CORIN: Nay, I hope——
TOUCHSTONE: Truly, thou art damned like an ill-roasted egg, all on one side.
    CORIN: For not being at court? Your reason.
TOUCHSTONE: Why, if thou never wast at court, thou never sawest good manners; if thou never sawest good manners, then thy manners must be wicked; and wickedness is sin, and sin is damnation. Thou art in a parlous state, shepherd.

There is no bitterness in Touchstone: bitterness (mild though it be) in *As You Like It* is given to Jaques. Touchstone is there to be a blithe wit, and he knows it; he takes pleasure in it; he is a great exhibitionist. His name, no doubt, is chosen to tell his function—a debunker of romantic nonsense, whose triumphant common sense leads him to espouse Audrey. Jaques never made a worse guess than when he hazards that their loving voyage 'is but for two months victual'd'. An audience may well imagine it will outlast that of Rosalind and Orlando, even in that romantic world. Professor Hotson has reminded us that Armin had been apprenticed to a jeweller, and that may have given Shakespeare a hint for the Fool's name: for a touchstone is 'a piece of black quartz or jasper, used for testing the quality of gold and silver alloys, by the colour of the streak produced by rubbing them upon it'.

Feste does not seem to rely on set-pieces, but on extemporal wit; he has a repertory not of jokes, but of songs. He is a great reader of character; the first service he does for the audience in this regard is to make them realize that the Countess's 'mourning' for her brother is simply a mask she has assumed, in order to keep the Duke Orsino at arm's length. No one but Feste perceives this; he not only perceives it, but thinks the best way back into her favour is to tease her about the very man for whom she is so ostentatiously in grief:

FESTE: I think his soul is in hell, madonna.

COUNTESS: I know his soul is in heaven, fool.

FESTE: The more fool, madonna, to mourn for your brother's soul being in heaven. Take away the fool, gentlemen.

COUNTESS: What think you of this fool, Malvolio? doth he not mend?

But a melancholy, not unlike the melancholy given to Jaques in *As You Like It*, is in *Twelfth Night* allowed to tinge the wit of Feste; undaunted co-operative jollity, such as we see in Touchstone, is exchanged for touches of controlled, critical derision: 'Vent my folly! he has heard that word of some great man, and now applies it to a fool; vent my folly!' He is also coldly, wittily *mercenary*; no one ever hears Touchstone ask for money, but Feste is an adept:

CLOWN: Would not a pair of these have bred, sir?

VIOLA: Yes, being kept together and put to use.

CLOWN: I would play Lord Pandarus of Phrygia, sir, to bring a Cressida to this Troilus.

VIOLA: I understand you, sir: 'tis well begg'd.

Above all he is malicious, a grudge-bearer, who has it in him to gird at Malvolio, tormented and defeated as he has been; but the whirligig of time brings its revenges even to Feste, for, at the end, he is left out of things. When all the rest have moved off to the joyful *solemnitas* of their journey's end, Feste, who has no Audrey to serve his turn, who does not even seem to have a turn to serve, is left alone to sing his melancholy song of the wind and the rain, the song he has in common with the Fool in *Lear*. Feste seems to me the most complex of all the Armin-Fools, the subtlest and bawdiest and coldest, the most attractive, the most musical, the most talented; he has it in him to glitter in the golden world, and yet to throw across it the long and deepening shadow.

Having drifted into the romantic way of thinking about Touchstone and Feste—as if they were real people, not characters in a play—let us note that this is what the old magician so unfailingly contrives, and his spell is a simple one; he gives his characters more character than they actually need for the purposes of their play. This is the bamboozling touch, that makes one think it is life, not a play; for in life the characters of men and women have similar surprises for us. Let us therefore, for a moment, submit to the illusion, go the whole hog; the truth is that Touchstone could easily become rather a bore, but Feste never. You would be lucky if Feste even liked you. But then, of course, you could always buy his liking—or a perfect imitation—and if you went on buying it, it would stay bought.

One has to try to keep one's head over Shakespeare's greatest Fool, the Fool in *Lear*; for, as Granville-Barker has warned us, it is possible to etherialize him to such a point that any actor would be a disappointment in the part. There are three things about him that differentiate him from all the other Jesters in the canon. First, he is a half-wit; that is, he is in the tradition of the 'natural' which, as we have seen, is the historic Tudor household-fool tradition, the village idiot taken into the family. Lear's Fool is an idiot of genius, just as Bottom is a simpleton of genius. Secondly he is a fierce critic of his master—no other 'allowed Fool' is allowed so much, because no other is a half-wit—and thirdly he is in total dependency on Lear; and this is also the effect of his native imbecility. He must be protected.

Lear's Fool thus does two things for an audience, both of which stem from his helpless, feeble-minded nature. It enables him to satisfy one of the strongest of an audience's wishes during Acts I and II, which is to hear someone give the insensate King a piece of their minds, for his treatment of Cordelia and trust of Goneril and Regan. It is true that Kent's gruff, bluff rebukes offer some expression to the indignation of an audience; but Kent cannot hit the King where it hurts most, because Kent's attack is *from outside*. Kent's attack can be repelled, and is so. Kent is banished. But the Fool is *inside*, under Lear's guard.

Because he is a helpless dependent, the Fool's attack cannot be repelled; he is inside Lear's armour, grafted to his compassion. He can, of course, be threatened with the whip, but what good is that? Lear would only be whipping himself for having heard and rebelled against the truth, as excellent a whipping as he advises later to the rascal beadle. The Fool's crazy versicles, riddles and proverbs sting Lear inwardly, and therefore give an 'I could have told you so' satisfaction to an audience; these are the satisfactions for which the Fool is so much beloved:

FOOL: The reason why the seven stars are no more than seven is a pretty reason.
LEAR: Because they are not eight?
FOOL: Yes, indeed: thou wouldst make a good fool.

The second great thing he does for us is to make visible the charity of Lear. This again is a consequence of the Fool's helplessness, of the *nuncledom* of their relationship.

Come on, my boy. How dost, my boy? art cold?
I am cold myself. Where is this straw, my fellow? . . .
Poor fool and knave, I have one part in my heart
That's sorry yet for thee. . . .

The action that must go with these lines makes one perceive the sincerity of Lear's prayer for the misery of others, the naked wretches,
wherever they may be, that bide the pelting of the pitiless storm. His
new-found charity and humbleness of heart are made manifest, are
actable, are *seen*, in his tenderness towards the Fool. Seeing is believing.

That yet a fourth Fool, wholly different from all the others, and
almost as dominating a figure, should have followed is one more
example of a dramatic invention that seems never to repeat itself; the
singing rogue-fool Autolycus, who has in his time been a gentleman
and worn velvet, and is now reduced to the theft of lesser linen from
farmers' wives, has to be considered. He is there to contribute an
explosion of energy and rejuvenation at the very moment when
The Winter's Tale needs the vigorous impulse of a new start. So he
comes in singing, '*When daffodils begin to peer*'.

He has, of course, an infinitesimal part in the plot by which Camillo
helps the escape of Florizel and Perdita; Florizel borrows his clothes.
This could easily have been contrived in some other way, and it seems
probable that Shakespeare made that rather mechanical use of Autolycus, to give countenance to his presence in the play, for a further, more
significant purpose. Autolycus, it seems to me, is there not only for his
energy but also for the stiffening of *roguery* he gives to what, without
him, might have been indicted of pastoral sentimentality. Shepherd
and shepherdess idealism and the pure airs of the country are all very
well, but Shakespeare had always taken care to moderate such raptures.
Silvius and Phoebe are brought to their senses even in Arden; Touchstone shows William off, and gets Audrey. One is kept down to earth.
This earthiness is what Autolycus exists to provide, and with his
earthiness he brings his country music; it has all the air of an Armin
part.

Trinculo is the last and most deboshed of the race of Jesters. He
is as different from those that preceded him as they are from each
other; he seems only there to be bullied, to sink in the esteem of Caliban, to be jester to a drunken butler. He can just manage to sing a
catch, but he seems to have no other talent; if he were not listed as 'a
Jester' in the cast-list at the end of the play in the Folio, one might
almost take him for a Clown, and a cowardly one. Unlike most of his

fellow-fools in other plays, he has sunk into the sub-plot; he is even less than Lavache, the Fool in *All's Well*.

Trinculo, like the others, however, fits into his own play. Touchstone would have made rings round Caliban; Feste would have deserted Lear. Only Lavache, Jester to the old Countess of Roussillon, has moments which seem to qualify him for something better than his part and play. His actual function is to be a time-sandwich, that is, to keep a scene going which has no other purpose than to indicate a lapse of time between the scene before and the scene to follow, or to deliver a letter from one part of France to another. He has two or three creative touches lavished and lost upon him, for in spite of them he never comes into full view as a character. He builds no sympathy for Helena, as Lear's Fool does for Cordelia. He does little for the old Countess and nothing for Bertram. He is unimportantly rude to Parolles on two occasions, but whenever the play gets going, he is forgotten, or laid aside as not-for-the-moment necessary.

And yet this character which barely exists is given a lovely snatch to sing, one that deepens the enigma of what Shakespeare thought about the tale of Troy, which haunted him so long:

> Was this fair face the cause, quoth she,
>   Why the Grecians sacked Troy?
> Fond done, done fond,
>   Was this King Priam's joy?
> With that she sighed as she stood,
> With that she sighed as she stood,
>   And gave this sentence then;
> Among nine bad if one be good,
> Among nine bad if one be good,
>   There's yet one good in ten.

and he has one speech that rings strangely in the mouth of a jester: 'I am for the house with the narrow gate, which I take to be too little for pomp to enter; some that humble themselves may; but the many will be too chill and tender, and they'll be for the flowery way that leads to the broad gate and the great fire.'

'A shrewd knave and an unhappy' is Lafeu's wise comment on Lavache. He is an extreme example of what one finds in so many of Shakespeare's creations—there is more to them than they actually need for the plays in which they appear—they spill over into life.

2

'AS YOU LIKE IT'

by HELEN GARDNER

A s its title declares, this is a play to please all tastes. It is the last play in the world to be solemn over, and there is more than a touch of absurdity in delivering a lecture, particularly on a lovely summer morning, on this radiant blend of fantasy, romance, wit and humour. The play itself provides its own ironic comment on anyone who attempts to speak about it: 'You have said; but whether wisely or no, let the forest judge.'

For the simple, it provides the stock ingredients of romance: a handsome, well-mannered young hero, the youngest of three brothers, two disguised princesses to be wooed and wed, and a banished, virtuous Duke to be restored to his rightful throne. For the more sophisticated, it propounds, in the manner of the old courtly literary form of the *débat*, a question which is left to us to answer: Is it better to live in the court or the country? 'How like you this shepherd's life, Master Touchstone?', asks Corin, and receives a fool's answer: 'Truly, shepherd, in respect of itself, it is a good life; but in respect that it is a shepherd's life, it is naught. In respect that it is solitary, I like it very well; but in respect that it is private, it is a very vile life.' Whose society would you prefer, Le Beau's or Audrey's? Would you rather be gossiped at in the court or gawped at in the country? The play has also the age-old appeal of the pastoral, and in different forms. The pastoral romance of princesses playing at being a shepherd boy and his sister is combined with the pastoral love-eclogue in the wooing of Phoebe, with the burlesque of this in the wooing of Audrey, and with the tradition of the moral eclogue, in which the shepherd is the wise man, in Corin. For the learned and literary this is one of Shakespeare's most allusive plays, uniting old traditions and playing with them lightly. Then there are the songs—the forest is full of music—and there is spectacle: a wrestling match to delight lovers of sport, the procession with the deer, which goes back to old country rituals and folk plays, and finally the masque of Hymen, to end the whole with courtly grace and dignity. This is an image of civility and true society, for Hymen is a god of cities, as Milton knew:

> There let *Hymen* oft appear
> In Saffron robe, with Taper clear,
> And pomp, and feast, and revelry,
> With mask, and antique Pageantry.

The only thing the play may be said to lack, when compared with Shakespeare's other comedies, is broad humour, the humour of gross clowns. William makes only a brief appearance. The absence of clowning may be due to an historic reason, the loss of Kempe, the company's funny man. But if this was the original reason for the absence of pure clowning, Shakespeare has turned necessity to glorious gain and made a play in which cruder humours would be out of place. *As You Like It* is the most refined and exquisite of the comedies, the one which is most consistently played over by a delighted intelligence. It is Shakespeare's most Mozartian comedy.

The basic story is a folk-tale. The ultimate sources for the plots of Shakespeare's greatest tragedy and his most unflawed comedy are stories of the same kind. The tale of the old king who had three daughters, of whom the elder two were wicked and the youngest was good, belongs to the same primitive world of the imagination as the tale of the knight who had three sons, the eldest of whom was wicked and robbed the youngest, who was gallant and good, of his inheritance. The youngest son triumphed, like Jack the Giant Killer, over a strong man, a wrestler, joined a band of outlaws in the forest, became their king, and with the aid of an old servant of his father, the wily Adam Spencer, in the end had his revenge on his brother and got his rights. Lodge retained some traces of the boisterous elements of this old story; but Shakespeare omitted them. His Orlando is no bully, threatening and blustering and breaking down the doors to feast with his boon companions in his brother's house. He is brave enough and quick-tempered; but he is above all gentle. On this simple story Lodge grafted a pastoral romance in his *Rosalynde*. He made the leader of the outlaws a banished Duke, and gave both exiled Duke and tyrant usurper only daughters, as fast friends as their fathers are sworn enemies. The wrestling match takes place at the tyrant's court and is followed by the banishment of Rosalynde and the flight of the two

girls to the forest, disguised as shepherd and shepherdess. There the
shepherd boy is wooed by the gallant hero, and arouses a passion of
love-sickness in a shepherdess who scorns her faithful lover. The repentance of the wicked brother and his flight to the forest provide the
necessary partner for the tyrant's good daughter, and all ends happily
with marriages and the restoration of the good Duke. Shakespeare
added virtually nothing to the plot of Lodge's novel. There is no
comedy in which, in one sense, he invents so little. He made the two
Dukes into brothers. Just as in *King Lear* he put together two stories of
good and unkind children, so here he gives us two examples of a
brother's unkindness. This adds to the fairy-tale flavour of the plot,
because it turns the usurping Duke into a wicked uncle. But if he invents no incidents, he leaves out a good deal. Besides omitting the
blusterings of Rosader (Orlando), he leaves out a final battle and the
death in battle of the usurping Duke, preferring to have him converted
off-stage by a chance meeting with a convenient and persuasive hermit.
In the same way he handles very cursorily the repentance of the wicked
brother and his good fortune in love. In Lodge's story, the villain is
cast into prison by the tyrant who covets his estates. In prison he
repents, and it as a penitent that he arrives in the forest. Shakespeare
also omits the incident of the attack on Ganymede and Aliena by
robbers, in which Rosader is overpowered and wounded and Saladyne
(Oliver) comes to the rescue and drives off the assailants. As has often
been pointed out, this is both a proof of the genuineness of his repentance and a reason, which many critics of the play have felt the want of,
for Celia's falling in love. Maidens naturally fall in love with brave
young men who rescue them. But Shakespeare needs to find no
'reasons for loving' in this play in which a dead shepherd's saw is
quoted as a word of truth: 'Whoever lov'd that lov'd not at first sight.'
He has far too much other business in hand at the centre and heart of
his play to find time for mere exciting incidents. He stripped Lodge's
plot down to the bare bones, using it as a kind of frame, and created no
sub-plot of his own. But he added four characters. Jaques, the philosopher, bears the same name as the middle son of Sir Rowland de Boys
—the one whom Oliver kept at his books—who does not appear in the
play until he turns up casually at the end as a messenger. It seems possible that the melancholy Jaques began as this middle son and that his
melancholy was in origin a scholar's melancholy. If so, the character
changed as it developed, and by the time that Shakespeare had fully
conceived his cynical spectator he must have realized that he could not

be kin to Oliver and Orlando. The born solitary must have no family: Jaques seems the quintessential only child. To balance Jaques, as another kind of commentator, we are given Touchstone, critic and parodist of love and lovers and of court and courtiers. And, to make up the full consort of pairs to be mated, Shakespeare invented two rustic lovers, William and Audrey, dumb yokel and sluttish goat-girl. These additional characters add nothing at all to the story. If you were to tell it you would leave them out. They show us that story was not Shakespeare's concern in this play; its soul is not to be looked for there. If you were to go to *As You Like It* for the story you would, in Johnson's phrase, 'hang yourself'.

In an essay called 'The Basis of Shakespearian Comedy'[1] Professor Nevill Coghill attempted to 'establish certain things concerning the nature of comic form, as it was understood at Shakespeare's time'. He pointed out that there were two conceptions of comedy current in the sixteenth century, both going back to grammarians of the fourth century, but radically opposed to each other. By the one definition a comedy was a story beginning in sadness and ending in happiness. By the other it was, in Sidney's words, 'an imitation of the common errors of our life' represented 'in the most ridiculous and scornefull sort that may be; so that it is impossible that any beholder can be content to be such a one'. Shakespeare, he declared, accepted the first; Jonson, the second. But although *As You Like It*, like *A Midsummer Night's Dream*, certainly begins in sadness and ends with happiness, I do not feel, when we have said this, that we have gone very far towards defining the play's nature, and I do not think that the plot in either of these two lovely plays, or in the enchanting early comedy *Love's Labour's Lost*, which indeed has hardly any plot at all, can be regarded as the 'soul' or animating force of Shakespeare's most original and characteristic comedies. Professor Coghill's formula fits plays which we feel rather uneasy about, *The Merchant of Venice* and *Measure for Measire*. It is precisely the stress on the plot which makes us think of these as being more properly described as tragi-comedies than comedies. Neither of them is a play which we would choose as a norm of Shakespeare's genius in comedy. In *As You Like It* the plot is handled in the most perfunctory way. Shakespeare crams his first act with incident in order to get everyone to the forest as soon as he possibly can and, when he is ready, he ends it all as quickly as possible. A few lines dispose of Duke Frederick, and leave the road back to his throne

---

[1] *Essays and Studies* (English Association: John Murray, 1950).

empty for Duke Senior. As for the other victim of a wicked brother, it is far more important that Orlando should marry Rosalind than that he should be restored to his rights.

Mrs Suzanne Langer, in her brilliant and suggestive book *Feeling and Form*,[1] has called comedy an image of life triumphing over chance. She declares that the essence of comedy is that it embodies in symbolic form our sense of happiness in feeling that we can meet and master the changes and chances of life as it confronts us. This seems to me to provide a good description of what we mean by 'pure comedy', as distinct from the corrective or satirical comedy of Jonson. The great symbol of pure comedy is marriage by which the world is renewed, and its endings are always instinct with a sense of fresh beginnings. Its rhythm is the rhythm of the life of mankind, which goes on and renews itself as the life of nature does. The rhythm of tragedy, on the other hand, is the rhythm of the individual life which comes to a close, and its great symbol is death. The one inescapable fact about every human being is that he must die. No skill in living, no sense of life, no inborn grace or acquired wisdom can avert this individual doom. A tragedy, which is played out under the shadow of an inevitable end, is an image of the life pattern of every one of us. A comedy, which contrives an end which is not implicit in its beginning, and which is, in itself, a fresh beginning, is an image of the flow of human life. The young wed, so that they may become in turn the older generation, whose children will wed, and so on, as long as the world lasts. Comedy pictures what Rosalind calls 'the full stream of the world'. At the close of a tragedy we look back over a course which has been run: 'the rest is silence'. The end of a comedy declares that life goes on: 'Here we are all over again.' Tragic plots must have a logic which leads to an inescapable conclusion. Comic plots are made up of changes, chances and surprises. Coincidences can destroy tragic feeling: they heighten comic feeling. It is absurd to complain in poetic comedy of improbable encounters and characters arriving pat on their cue, of sudden changes of mind and mood by which an enemy becomes a friend. Puck, who creates and presides over the central comedy of *A Midsummer Night's Dream*, speaks for all comic writers and lovers of true comedy when he says:

> And those things do best please me
> That befall preposterously.

This aspect of life, as continually changing and presenting fresh

[1] Routledge, 1953.

opportunities for happiness and laughter, poetic comedy idealizes and presents to us by means of fantasy. Fantasy is the natural instrument of comedy, in which plot, which is the 'soul' of tragedy, is of secondary importance, an excuse for something else. After viewing a tragedy we have an 'acquist of true experience' from a 'great event'. There are no 'events' in comedy; there are only 'happenings'. Events are irreversible and comedy is not concerned with the irreversible, which is why it must always shun the presentation of death. In adapting Lodge's story Shakespeare did not allow Charles the wrestler to kill the Franklin's sons. Although they are expected to die, we may hope they will recover from their broken ribs. And he rejected also Lodge's ending in which the wicked Duke was killed in battle, preferring his improbable conversion by a hermit. But why should we complain of its improbability? It is only in tragedy that second chances are not given. Comedy is full of purposes mistook, not 'falling on the inventor's head' but luckily misfiring altogether. In comedy, as often happens in life, people are mercifully saved from being as wicked as they meant to be.

Generalization about the essential distinctions between tragedy and comedy is called in question, when we turn to Shakespeare, by the inclusiveness of his vision of life. In the great majority of his plays the elements are mixed. But just as he wrote one masterpiece which is purely tragic, dominated by the conception of Fate, in *Macbeth*, so he wrote some plays which embody a purely comic vision. Within the general formula that 'a comedy is a play with a happy ending', which can, of course, include tragi-comedies, he wrote some plays in which the story is a mere frame and the essence of the play lies in the presentation of an image of human life, not as an arena for heroic endeavour but as a place of encounters.

Tragedy is presided over by time, which urges the hero onwards to fulfil his destiny. In Shakespeare's comedies time goes by fits and starts. It is not so much a movement onwards as a space in which to work things out: a midsummer night, a space too short for us to feel time's movement, or the unmeasured time of *As You Like It* or *Twelfth Night*. The comedies are dominated by a sense of place rather than of time. In Shakespeare's earliest comedy it is not a very romantic place: the city of Ephesus. Still, it is a place where two pairs of twins are accidentally reunited, and their old father, in danger of death at the beginning, is united to his long-lost wife at the close. The substance of the play is the comic plot of mistakings, played out in a single place on a single day. The tragi-comic story of original loss and final restoration provides a frame. In what is probably his second comedy, *The Two Gentlemen of Verona*, Shakespeare tried a quite different method. The play is a dramatization of a *novella*, and it contains no comic place of encounters where time seems to stand still. The story begins in Verona, passes to Milan, and ends in a forest between the two cities. None of these places exerts any hold upon our imaginations. The story simply moves forward through them. In *Love's Labour's Lost*, by contrast, Shakespeare went as far as possible in the other direction. The whole play is a kind of ballet of lovers and fantastics, danced out in the King of Navarre's park. Nearby is a village where Holofernes is the school-master, Nathaniel the curate, and Dull the constable. In this play we are given, as a foil to the lords and ladies, not comic servants, parasitic on their masters, but a little comic world, society in miniature, going about its daily business while the lovers are engaged in the discovery of theirs. Shakespeare dispensed with the tragi-comic frame altogether here. There is no sorrow at the beginning, only youthful male fatuity; and the 'putting right' at the close lies in the chastening of the lords by the ladies. The picture of the course of life as it appears to the comic vision, with young men falling in love and young women testing their suitors, and other men 'labouring in their vocations' to keep the world turning and to impress their fellows, is the whole matter of the play. Much more magical than the sunlit park of the King of Navarre is the wood near Athens where Puck plays the part of chance. Shakespeare reverted here to the structural pattern of his earliest comedy, beginning with the cruel fury of Egeus against his daughter, the rivalry of Lysander and Demetrius and the unhappiness of the scorned Helena, and ending with Theseus's over-riding of the father's will and the proper pairing of the four lovers. But here he not only set his comic plot of mistakings within a frame of sorrow turning to joy, he also set his comic place of encounters apart from the real world, the palace where the play begins and ends. All the centre of the play takes place in the moonlit wood where lovers immortal and mortal quarrel, change partners, are blinded, and have their eyes purged.

Having created a masterpiece, Shakespeare, who never repeated a success, went back in his next play to tragi-comedy, allowing the threat of terrible disaster to grow through the play up to a great dramatic fourth act. *The Merchant of Venice* has what *The Two Gentlemen of Verona* lacks, an enchanted place. Belmont, where Bassanio goes

c

to find his bride, and where Lorenzo flees with Jessica, and from which Portia descends like a goddess to solve the troubles of Venice, is a place apart, 'above the smoke and stir'. But it is not, like the wood near Athens, a place where the changes and chances of our mortal life are seen mirrored. It stands too sharply over against Venice, a place of refuge rather than a place of discovery. *Much Ado About Nothing* reverts to the single place of *The Comedy of Errors* and *Love's Labour's Lost*; and its tragi-comic plot, which also comes to a climax in a dramatic scene in the fourth act, is lightened not by a shift of scene but by its interweaving with a brilliant comic plot, and by all kinds of indications that all will soon be well again. The trouble comes in the middle of this play: at the beginning, as at the end, all is revelry and happiness. A sense of holiday, of time off from the world's business, reigns in Messina. The wars are over, peace has broken out, and Don Pedro and the gentlemen have returned to where the ladies are waiting for them to take up again the game of love and wit. In the atmosphere created by the first act Don John's malice is a cloud no bigger than a man's hand. And although it grows as the play proceeds, the crisis of the fourth act is like a heavy summer thunder-shower which darkens the sky for a time but will, we know, soon pass. The brilliant lively city of Messina is a true place of mistakings and discoveries, like the park of the King of Navarre; but, also like the park of the King of Navarre, it lacks enchantment. It is too near the ordinary world to seem more than a partial image of human life. In *As You Like It* Shakespeare returned to the pattern of *A Midsummer Night's Dream*, beginning his play in sorrow and ending it with joy, and making his place of comic encounters a place set apart from the ordinary world.

The Forest of Arden ranks with the wood near Athens and Prospero's island as a place set apart, even though, unlike them, it is not ruled by magic. It is set over against the envious court ruled by a tyrant, and a home which is no home because it harbours hatred, not love. Seen from the court it appears untouched by the discontents of life, a place where 'they fleet the time carelessly, as they did in the golden age', the gay greenwood of Robin Hood. But, of course, it is no such Elysium. It contains some unamiable characters. Corin's master is churlish and Sir Oliver Martext is hardly sweet-natured; William is a dolt and Audrey graceless. Its weather, too, is by no means always sunny. It has a bitter winter. To Orlando, famished with hunger and supporting the fainting Adam, it is 'an uncouth forest' and a desert where the air is bleak. He is astonished to find civility among men who

> in this desert inaccessible,
> Under the shade of melancholy boughs,
> Lose and neglect the creeping hours of time.

In fact Arden does not seem very attractive at first sight to the weary escapers from the tyranny of the world. Rosalind's 'Well, this is the forest of Arden' does not suggest any very great enthusiasm; and to Touchstone's 'Ay, now I am in Arden; the more fool I: when I was at home, I was in a better place: but travellers must be content,' she can only reply 'Ay, be so, good Touchstone.' It is as if they all have to wake up after a good night's rest to find what a pleasant place they have come to. Arden is not a place for the young only. Silvius, for ever young and for ever loving, is balanced by Corin, the old shepherd, who reminds us of that other 'penalty of Adam' beside 'the seasons' difference': that man must labour to get himself food and clothing. Still, the labour is pleasant and a source of pride: 'I am a true labourer: I earn that I eat, get that I wear, owe no man hate, envy no man's happiness, glad of other men's good, content with my harm; and the greatest of my pride is to see my ewes graze and my lambs suck.' Arden is not a place where the laws of nature are abrogated and roses are without their thorns. If, in the world, Duke Frederick has usurped on Duke Senior, Duke Senior is aware that he has in his turn usurped upon the deer, the native burghers of the forest. If man does not slay and kill man, he kills the poor beasts. Life preys on life. Jaques, who can suck melancholy out of anything, points to the callousness that runs through nature itself as a mirror of the callousness of men. The herd abandons the wounded deer, as prosperous citizens pass with disdain the poor bankrupt, the failure. The race is to the swift. But this is Jaques's view. Orlando, demanding help for Adam, finds another image from nature:

> Then but forbear your food a little while,
> Whiles, like a doe, I go to find my fawn
> And give it food. There is a poor old man,
> Who after me hath many a weary step
> Limp'd in pure love: till he be first suffic'd,
> Oppress'd with two weak evils, age and hunger,
> I will not touch a bit.

The fact that they are both derived ultimately from folk-tale is not the only thing that relates *As You Like It* to *King Lear*. Adam's sombre line, 'And unregarded age in corners thrown', which Quiller-Couch said might have come out of one of the greater sonnets, sums up the fate of Lear:

> Dear daughter, I confess that I am old;
> Age is unnecessary: on my knees I beg
> That you'll vouchsafe me raiment, bed, and food.

At times Arden seems a place where the same bitter lessons can be learnt as Lear has to learn in his place of exile, the blasted heath. Corin's natural philosophy, which includes the knowledge that 'the property of rain is to wet', is something which Lear has painfully to acquire:

> When the rain came to wet me once and the wind to make me chatter, when the thunder would not peace at my bidding, there I found 'em, there I smelt 'em out. Go to, they are not men o' their words: they told me I was everything; 'tis a lie, I am not ague-proof.

He is echoing Duke Senior, who smiles at the 'icy fang and churlish chiding of the winter's wind', saying:

> This is no flattery: these are counsellors
> That feelingly persuade me what I am.

Amiens's lovely melancholy song:

> Blow, blow, thou winter wind,
> Thou art not so unkind
> As man's ingratitude. . . .
>
> Freeze, freeze, thou bitter sky,
> That dost not bite so nigh
> As benefits forgot. . . ,

is terribly echoed in Lear's outburst:

> Blow, winds, and crack your cheeks! rage! blow!
> .   .   .   .
> Rumble thy bellyful! Spit, fire! spout, rain!
> Nor rain, wind, thunder, fire, are my daughters:
> I tax not you, you elements, with unkindness;
> I never gave you kingdom, call'd you children. . . .

And Jaques's reflection that 'All the world's a stage' becomes in Lear's mouth a cry of anguish:

> When we are born, we cry that we are come
> To this great stage of fools.

It is in Arden that Jaques presents his joyless picture of human life, passing from futility to futility and culminating in the nothingness of senility—'sans everything'; and in Arden also a bitter judgment on human relations is lightly passed in the twice repeated 'Most friendship is feigning, most loving mere folly.' But then one must add that hard on the heels of Jaques's melancholy conclusion Orlando enters with Adam in his arms, who, although he may be 'sans teeth' and at the end of his usefulness as a servant, has, beside his store of virtue and his peace of conscience, the love of his master. And the play is full of signal instances of persons who do not forget benefits: Adam, Celia, Touchstone—not to mention the lords who chose to leave the court and follow their banished master to the forest. In a recent number of the *Shakespeare Survey* Professor Harold Jenkins has pointed out how points of view put forward by one character find contradiction or correction by another, so that the whole play is a balance of sweet against sour, of the cynical against the idealistic, and life is shown as a mingling of hard fortune and good hap. The lords who have 'turned ass', 'leaving their wealth and ease a stubborn will to please', are happy in their gross folly, as Orlando is in a love-sickness which he does not wish to be cured of. What Jaques has left out of his picture of man's strange eventful pilgrimage is love and companionship, sweet society, the banquet under the boughs to which Duke Senior welcomes Orlando and Adam. Although life in Arden is not wholly idyllic, and this place set apart from the world is yet touched by the world's sorrows and can be mocked at by the worldly wise, the image of life which the forest presents is irradiated by the conviction that the gay and the gentle can endure the rubs of fortune and that this earth is a place where men can find happiness in themselves and in others.

The Forest of Arden is, as has often been pointed out, a place which all the exiles from the court, except one, are only too ready to leave at the close. As, when the short midsummer night is over, the lovers emerge from the wood, in their right minds and correctly paired, and return to the palace of Theseus; and, when Prospero's magic has worked the cure, the enchanted island is left to Caliban and Ariel, and its human visitors return to Naples and Milan; so the time of holiday comes to an end in Arden. The stately masque of Hymen marks the end of this interlude in the greenwood, and announces the return to a court purged of envy and baseness. Like other comic places, Arden is a place of discovery where the truth becomes clear and where each man finds himself and his true way. This discovery of truth in comedy is made through errors and mistakings. The trial and error by which we come to knowledge of ourselves and of our world is symbolized by the disguisings which are a recurrent element in all comedy, but are particularly common in Shakespeare's. Things have, as it were, to become worse before they become better, more confused and farther from the proper pattern. By misunderstandings men come to understand, and by lies and feignings they discover truth. If Rosalind, the princess, had attempted to 'cure' her lover Orlando, she might have succeeded. As Ganymede, playing Rosalind, she can try him to the limit in perfect safety, and discover that she cannot mock or flout him out of his 'mad humour of love to a living humour of madness', and drive him 'to forswear the full stream of the world, and to live in a nook merely monastic'. By playing with him in the disguise of a boy, she discovers when she can play no more. By love of a shadow, the mere image of a charming youth, Phoebe discovers that it is better to love than to be loved and scorn one's lover. This discovery of truth by feigning, and of what is wisdom and what folly by debate, is the centre of *As You Like It*. It is a play of meetings and encounters, of conversations and sets of wit: Orlando versus Jaques, Touchstone versus Corin, Rosalind versus Jaques, Rosalind versus Phoebe, and above all Rosalind versus Orlando. The truth discovered is, at one level, a very 'earthy truth': Benedick's discovery that 'the world must be peopled'. The honest toil of Corin, the wise man of the forest, is mocked at by Touchstone as 'simple sin'. He brings 'the ewes and the rams together' and gets his living 'by the copulation of cattle'. The goddess Fortune seems similarly occupied in this play: 'As the ox hath his bow, the horse his curb, and the falcon her bells, so man hath his desires; and as pigeons bill, so wedlock would be nibbling.' Fortune acts the role of a kindly bawd. Touchstone's marriage to Audrey is a mere coupling. Rosalind's advice to Phoebe is brutally frank: 'Sell when you can, you are not for all markets.' The words she uses to describe Oliver and Celia 'in the very wrath of love' are hardly delicate, and after her first meeting with Orlando she confesses to her cousin that her sighs are for her 'child's father'. Against the natural background of the life of the forest there can be no pretence that the love of men and women can 'forget the He and She'. But Rosalind's behaviour is at variance with her bold words. Orlando has to prove that he truly is, as he seems at first sight, the right husband for her, and show himself gentle, courteous, generous and brave, and a match for her in wit, though a poor poet. In this, the great coupling of the play, there is a marriage of true minds. The other couplings run the gamut downwards from it, until we reach Touchstone's image of 'a she-lamb of a twelvemonth' and 'a crooked-pated, old, cuckoldy ram', right at the bottom of the scale. As for the debate as to where happiness is to be found, the conclusion come to is again, like all wisdom, not very startling or original: that 'minds innocent and quiet' can find happiness in court or country:

> Happy is your Grace,
> That can translate the stubbornness of fortune
> Into so quiet and so sweet a style.

And, on the contrary, those who wish to can 'suck melancholy' out of anything, 'as a weasel sucks eggs'.

In the pairing one figure is left out. 'I am for other than for dancing measures,' says Jaques. Leaving the hateful sight of revelling and pastime, he betakes himself to the Duke's abandoned cave, on his way to the house of penitents where Duke Frederick has gone. The two commentators of the play are nicely contrasted. Touchstone is the parodist, Jaques the cynic. The parodist must love what he parodies. We know this from literary parody. All the best parodies are written by those who understand, because they love, the thing they mock. Only poets who love and revere the epic can write mock-heroic and the finest parody of classical tragedy comes from Housman, a great scholar. In everything that Touchstone says and does gusto, high spirits and a zest for life ring out. Essentially comic, he can adapt himself to any situation in which he may find himself. Never at a loss, he is life's master. The essence of clowning is adaptability and improvisation. The clown is never baffled and is marked by his ability to place himself at once *en rapport* with his audience, to be all things to all men, to perform the part which is required at the moment. Touchstone sustains many different roles. After hearing Silvius's lament and Rosalind's echo of it, he becomes the maudlin lover of Jane Smile; with the simple shepherd Corin he becomes the cynical and wordly-wise man of the court; with Jaques he is a melancholy moralist, musing on the power of time and the decay of all things; with the pages he acts the lordly amateur of the arts, patronising his musicians. It is right that he should parody the rest of the cast, and join the procession into Noah's ark with his Audrey. Jaques is his opposite. He is the cynic, the person who prefers the pleasures of superiority, cold-eyed and cold-hearted. The tyrannical Duke Frederick and the cruel Oliver can be converted; but not Jaques. He likes himself as he is. He does not wish to plunge into the stream, but prefers to stand on the bank and 'fish for fancies as they pass'. Sir Thomas Elyot said that dancing was an image of matrimony: 'In every daunse, of a most auncient custome, there daunseth together a man and a woman, holding eche other by the hande or the arme, which betokeneth concorde.' There are some who will not dance, however much they are piped to, any more than they will weep when there is mourning. 'In this theatre of man's life', wrote Bacon, 'it is reserved only for God and angels to be lookers on.' Jaques arrogates to himself the divine role. He has opted out from the human condition.

It is characteristic of Shakespeare's comedies to include an element that is irreconcilable, which strikes a lightly discordant note, casts a slight shadow, and by its presence questions the completeness of the comic vision of life. In *Love's Labour's Lost* he dared to allow the news of a death to cloud the scene of revels at the close, and, through Rosaline's rebuke to Berowne, called up the image of a whole world of pain and weary suffering where 'Mirth cannot move a soul in agony.' In the two comedies whose main action is motivated by hatred and with malice thwarted but not removed, *The Merchant of Venice* and *Much Ado About Nothing*, Shakespeare asks us to accept the fact that the human race includes not only a good many fools and rogues but also some persons who are positively wicked, a fact which comedy usually ignores. They are prevented from doing the harm they wish to do. They are not cured of wishing to do harm. Shylock's baffled exit and Don John's flight to Messina leave the stage clear for lovers and well-wishers. The villains have to be left out of the party at the close. At the end of *Twelfth Night* the person who is left out is present. The impotent misery and fury of the humiliated Malvolio's last words, 'I'll be reveng'd on the whole pack of you', call in question the whole comic scheme by which, through misunderstandings and mistakes, people come to terms with themselves and their fellows. There are some who cannot be 'taught a lesson'. In Malvolio pride is not purged; it is fatally wounded and embittered. It is characteristic of the delicacy of temper of *As You Like It* that its solitary figure, its outsider, Jaques, does nothing whatever to harm anyone, and is perfectly satisfied with himself and happy in his melancholy. Even more, his melancholy is a source of pleasure and amusement to others. The Duke treats him as virtually a court entertainer, and he is a natural butt for Orlando and Rosalind. Anyone in the play can put him down and feel the better for doing so. All the same his presence casts a faint shadow. His criticism of

the world has its sting drawn very early by the Duke's rebuke to him
as a former libertine, discharging his filth upon the world, and he is to
some extent discredited before he opens his mouth by the unpleasant
implication of his name. But he cannot be wholly dismissed. A certain
sour distaste for life is voided through him, something most of us feel
at some time or other. If he were not there to give expression to it, we
might be tempted to find the picture of life in the forest too sweet. His
only action is to interfere in the marriage of Touchstone and Audrey;
and this he merely postpones. His effect, whenever he appears, is to
deflate: the effect does not last and cheerfulness soon breaks in again.
Yet as there is a scale of love, so there is a scale of sadness in the play. It
runs down from the Duke's compassionate words:

> Thou seest we are not all alone unhappy:
> This wide and universal theatre
> Presents more woeful pageants than the scene
> Wherein we play in,

through Rosalind's complaint 'O, how full of briers is this working-
day world', to Jaques's studied refusal to find anything worthy of
admiration or love.

One further element in the play I would not wish to stress, because
though it is pervasive it is unobtrusive: the constant, natural and easy
reference to the Christian ideal of loving-kindness, gentleness, pity and
humility and to the sanctions which that ideal finds in the commands
and promises of religion. In this fantasy world, in which the world of
our experience is imaged, this element in experience finds a place with
others, and the world is shown not only as a place where we may find
happiness, but as a place where both happiness and sorrow may be
hallowed. The number of religious references in *As You Like It* has
often been commented on, and it is striking when we consider the
play's main theme. Many are of little significance and it would be
humourless to enlarge upon the significance of the 'old religious man'
who converted Duke Frederick, or of Ganymede's 'old religious uncle'.
But some are explicit and have a serious, unforced beauty: Orlando's
appeal to outlawed men,

> If ever you have look'd on better days,
> If ever been where bells have knoll'd to church. . . ;

Adam's prayer,

> He that doth the ravens feed,
> Yea, providently caters for the sparrow,
> Be comfort to my age!

and Corin's recognition, from St Paul, that we have to find the way to
heaven by doing deeds of hospitality. These are all in character. But the
God of Marriage, Hymen, speaks more solemnly than we expect and
his opening words with their New Testament echo are more than
conventional:

> Then is there mirth in heaven,
> When earthly things made even
> Atone together.

The appearance of the god to present daughter to father and to bless the
brides and grooms turns the close into a solemnity, an image of the
concord which reigns in Heaven and which Heaven blesses on earth.
But this, like much else in the play, may be taken as you like it. There
is no need to see any more in the god's appearance with the brides than
a piece of pageantry which concludes the action with a graceful
spectacle and sends the audience home contented with a very pretty
play.

3

A CLASSICAL SCHOLAR LOOKS AT SHAKESPEARE

by H. D. F. KITTO

I F A classical scholar is asked to look at Shakespeare, and does it, let no state of rage and disappointment be declared if he sees no more than what is seen, perhaps more clearly, by everyone else. I am not come professing to bring any new ideas, and as I am no Shakespeare scholar there must be many excellent old ideas of which I am ignorant.

Both for my convenience and for yours, I am not going to look at the whole of Shakespeare. I shall say nothing about Greek comedy and Shakespearian comedy; and among the Shakespearian tragedies I am going to limit my view to *Hamlet* and the series of historical tragedies that begins with *King John* and ends with *King Richard the Third*. If I ventured into *Lear*, *Othello* and the rest, I think that the generalities I shall offer would be much the same, and I know that my task in organizing one single paper out of the more abundant material would have become much more difficult.

On turning from the Greeks to Shakespeare, one is at first impressed, naturally, by the differences between them—differences of style, structure, presentation; Shakespeare so varied, so rich, the Greeks so austere. Within the art of tragic drama, they seem to be the polar opposites. It might be extremely interesting to discuss these differences: Shakespeare with his freedom; the Greeks with their maximum of three actors, their omnipresent Chorus, and the famous Three Unities of which the neo-classics were so much more conscious than the classical dramatists themselves. But all this I shall pass over, except in so far as these differences may become relevant incidentally; I wish to discuss what is to me at least the much more interesting topic of their resemblances. The formal differences are relatively superficial.

Since what one sees whether in Shakespeare or in anything else depends very much on the point from which one looks, it is only fair that I should at once try to give you some rough idea of the point from which this particular classical scholar is looking, for not all Greek scholars look at Greek tragedy in the same way. Our lives would be duller if we did.

There is one major question, I think, that the interpretative critic of tragic drama must settle with himself before he ventures to hang out his sign: what balance was struck, in his judgment, by the dramatist between his preoccupation with individuals and particulars, and his preoccupation with universals? In Greek drama, this question involves our taking one of several possible views about the gods, who in one way or another play so large a part in it. We can say, at one extreme, that it is a grim drama of implacable Fate, one in which the human actors are little more than puppets, going through motions that omnipotent gods decree. A recent editor of the *Agamemnon*, taking this view, maintains that Paris, Agamemnon and the rest had no choice; all was decreed for them. To me, this is nonsense—and I claim credit for Hellenic restraint that to my word 'nonsense' I prefix no objurgatory epithets. I will not argue this; I am not defending, but only trying to indicate my own point of view. The opposite extreme is to give one's best attention to the individual characters—and they do indeed deserve and reward it; to admire the splendour of Clytemnestra or Antigone, to speculate about hidden motives and conflicts, to call Euripides' *Medea* 'a profound psychological study'—which in my opinion it isn't; and, doing all this, to treat the gods as an obligatory religious appanage to what was, *ex officio*, a religious art.

A short survey of the *Antigone* will illustrate this; it will also give us material that will come in handy later on.

Classical scholars, from time to time, criticize adversely the structure of this play: to some extent, we are told, it lacks unity, since for most of the play our attention is concentrated, naturally, on the heroine, but in the concluding scenes—the last 150 verses or thereabouts—she is not mentioned; what is more surprising, when Sophocles brings back Creon from the cavern he brings with him the body of Haemon, Creon's son, but not the body of Antigone. A recent critic has said that his interest in the play is very much attenuated when Antigone disappears from it; Sophocles leaves us with Creon and his troubles, and Creon, as a dramatic character, is small beer after the splendid Antigone.

It is no doubt possible that Sophocles, though an experienced and not incapable dramatist, made an elementary blunder of this kind; it is also possible that a modern critic has taken hold of the wrong end of the stick. It is clear to me that the critics, in this case, commit a simple

fallacy—a typically modern one: they strike the wrong balance between preoccupation with the particular and preoccupation with the
universal. I will restate the criticism in this form: 'I find Antigone one
of the most sublime characters in dramatic literature. I find her resis-
tance to Creon one of the most moving of all tragic conflicts. When
her tragedy is consummated and I am left with the second-rate Creon,
I lose interest.'

The fallacy lies not in the estimate of the two characters, but in the
assumption that the play is, first and foremost, a play about Antigone.
The interpretation which I have summarized leaves out the gods as
actors in the piece. It allows for the fact, of course, that Antigone is doing what the gods approve; it takes no account of the part in the
action which Sophocles allots to them, and therefore throws the play
off its balance. It gravely attenuates the amplitude of the action; it
makes the play too small. Let us look, with all brevity, at these gods. I
mention them in the order of their coming on.

The first ode is a triumphant hymn of thanksgiving for the deliverance of the city: the traitor's foreign army has been repelled. One
part of the ode runs like this:

> For the arrogant boasts of an impious man
> Zeus hateth exceedingly. So, when he saw
> This army advancing in war-like flood
> In the pride of their golden equipment,
> He struck them down from the rampart's edge
> With a fiery bolt
> In the midst of their cry of 'Triumph!'

The last words of the play—in that part of the play which is not so very
interesting—refer to Creon, now a broken man, confessing that he has
brought his disasters on his own head by his own obstinate folly. The
chorus observes:

> Proud words of the arrogant man, in the end,
> Bring punishment, great as his pride was great,
> Till at last he is schooled in wisdom.

The parallel may be significant; at all events, let us bear it in mind for
the present.

I move on to the point where the Watchman comes in with his news
that the body has been buried; he is terrified what Creon may do to
him, and he stands first on one leg then on the other before he can
bring himself to tell his story. When he has told it—that someone has

cast dust on the body, and that no animals have touched it—the chorus-leader says:

> My lord, I have been pondering on this:
> Do we not see in it the hand of God?

Creon flies into a rage at the idea: 'What, you old fool? You think the gods have any concern for the body of a traitor who came to destroy their city and temples?' No, he says; it is some political enemy who has done it. Presently, he will learn better.

Antigone is caught and condemned to death. They say to Creon: she is betrothed to your son; are you really going to kill her? His reply is coarse and brutal: 'There are plenty of women about; he can go to bed with another.' I invite your attention to the way in which Sophocles uses the love-theme here. Haemon, the lover, arrives, hoping to reason with his father, doing his best to control himself. Once more, Creon is coarse and brutal; the result is that his son rushes out in despair and rage. Then Sophocles does an interesting thing: he writes a short ode for the Chorus about the power of Aphrodite; she sits enthroned beside the other great gods and has sway over gods, men, animals. No one can defy her. 'A comment,' we say, 'on the preceding scene, in which, because of his love, a son has threatened his father.' —No doubt; but let us remember it, for it is a comment also on what is going to happen to Creon later.

Antigone at last is led off to her death. Then, unexpectedly, a prophet arrives—and I may remind you that Shakespeare too uses prophecy quite a lot. The prophet and what he says deserve attention. Very elaborately, he describes certain unnatural happenings: birds have been tearing each other to pieces, with unnatural cries; the fat of sacrifice, dripping into the flames, will not catch fire. To the prophet, the cause of this perturbation in nature is plain enough: 'You are to blame,' he says to the King; 'you have angered the gods—the gods of the upper world because you have buried one who is alive, the gods of the nether world because you will not bury one who is dead. For the life that you are wantonly destroying, you will soon have to pay with the life of one of your own; the Erinyes, the Avengers of the gods, are lying in wait for you.'

So it happens—though there is no divine intervention, no onset of black-robed Erinyes. Indeed, Sophocles makes it plain that the ruin of Creon comes in the most natural way imaginable: Creon has decided that he must release Antigone; arriving at the cavern, he finds that he has been forestalled by his son; Haemon himself, however, had been forestalled by Antigone, for she, passionate creature that she was, had hanged herself rather than wait for death by starvation. When Haemon sees his father, in his mad rage he tries to murder him; failing in this, he kills himself. The Queen, hearing of the disaster, also kills herself; she has lost one son already; she cannot endure the loss of the other; and she dies, cursing Creon.

> Proud words of the arrogant man, in the end,
> Bring punishment, great as his pride was great.

But it is a complete misconception to say that the gods have not intervened and have done nothing, that events have simply taken their natural course. Indeed, it would be nearer the truth to say that the gods have done everything, since the gods, collectively, *are* the natural course of things. This is the point at which we may recall the ode on the power of Aphrodite, and the folly of trying to oppose it. Creon told his son that one girl is as good as another; he was wrong. When the maddened Haemon turned on his father, sword in hand, we see the power of Aphrodite in action. In several ways Creon has presumed to defy certain of the deep sanctities of life: the instinctive respect that we pay to a dead body, the loyalty of a sister towards a brother and towards her whole family, the love that joins a man and a woman. All these things are, in the Greek sense, divine. Creon defied them, and inevitably they recoil on him and crush him. It is dangerous to anger the gods.

Now perhaps we see how superficial is the complaint that the play is deficient in unity, and that the dramatist leaves us in the last scenes with a character, Creon, much inferior in interest to Antigone. It is a criticism that misses the true dimensions of the play, which is so much more than simply a play about the tragic heroine Antigone. Creon may be a second-rate man, but the spectacle of such a man defying the gods in his ignorance, and being overwhelmed by them, is not a second-rate dramatic spectacle. The fallacy is the belief that tragedy has to do with exciting and tragic individuals. It has indeed, but in so wide a setting; with the gods, so to speak, keeping the ring. They do not control the actions of the individuals; rather do they work in and through the actions of individuals. Their power, their laws, are the unalterable framework of the universe within which we have to live our lives. The decisions are ours; the results, in the long run, will work out in accordance with certain laws. In the action of a Greek play, the activity of

gods is always interwoven; that is to say, the Greek dramatist consciously sets his tragic action within a universal framework.

I have said so much about one Greek play in order to indicate the
point of view from which this particular Greek scholar looks at Shakespeare. I am reluctant to go on talking about Greek plays, but perhaps
I ought to say a word about the *Oedipus*, because this play is usually
cited to prove the puppet-theory: Oedipus was doomed before ever he
was born to kill his father and to marry his mother. Well, *what* about
Oedipus? Sophocles expressly makes the play a defence of religion, and
that puzzles us. As Sophocles handles it, it is a story in which the
parents of Oedipus are told, 'If you have a son, this and that will
happen.' But they say, in effect, 'Oh, we will look after *that*.' Then we
have Oedipus before us: intelligent, resolute, Man at his most splendid
and self-confident. He too is told, 'You are going to murder your
father and marry your mother.' But Oedipus will look after *that*. He
knows where his father and mother are: they are in Corinth—though
in fact he has had a straight hint that the king and queen of Corinth are
not his parents. He will not go back to Corinth; he makes his way to
Thebes—and he does, for all his wisdom and resolution, precisely what
was predicted. Now, Sophocles was writing in an age in some ways
like our own: an age of triumphant intellectualism, new techniques,
intoxicating self-confidence. It perturbed Sophocles; for him, there
were more things in Heaven and Earth than were dreamed of by this
new and cocksure philosophy. He was for more humility, more piety,
less confidence that human confidence can take control. Therefore he
wrote the *Oedipus*.

Let me jump straight into Shakespeare from the *Oedipus*, into
Hamlet; there is, I think, an impressive resemblance in one not unimportant detail. The main argument of this paper will be that when
one turns from Greek tragedy to Shakespearian tragedy, one is impressed more and more with the feeling that they have one thing in
common—and it is the great thing: the spaciousness or amplitude that
I tried to bring out by discussing the *Antigone*; a sense that the action is
being played out with reference not simply to exciting and tragic individuals, but to the whole framework of our universe. The resemblance may be put negatively also: that as the *Antigone* is both attenuated and slightly distorted in structure so long as we approach it in a
quasi-romantic way, with our eyes glued upon the heroine, so too are
certain tragedies of Shakespeare distorted or attenuated, by some
critics and producers, though not of course by all. Thus *Hamlet* has

often been reduced to the study of the fascinating character of Hamlet
—and this has been read in very diverse ways. The real dimensions of
the play have sometimes, in consequence, not been suspected. You will
remember the very respectable film of the play, and its sub-title: 'The
tragedy of a man who could not make up his mind.' But if *this* is what
Shakespeare thought he was writing, there is an indecent disproportion
between the size of his theme and the structure which he designed to
hold it; for the action of the play concerns two houses, that of King
Hamlet and that of Polonius, and by the end of the play both of them
are wiped out, and the Crown of Denmark passes to a comparative
outsider. Rather a large penalty for the crime of not being able to make
up one's mind! As in that criticism of the *Antigone*, the real amplitude
of the play has not been perceived.

But I was speaking of the *Oedipus*. At the beginning of the play,
Thebes is being ravaged by a plague, and Sophocles makes much of it.
Apollo declares the source of it: the city is polluted by the two unnatural, though innocent, offences against natural sanctities—and the
nature of the plague is nicely proportioned to its cause, for it is sterility;
crops, animals, the human kind, are afflicted with barrenness. The
dramatic imagery is the same as that which we have met already in the
Antigone, where Creon's offences against the laws of Nature and the
gods issue in the unnatural behaviour of the birds and of the fat which
will not burn. It is the same as that with which *Hamlet* opens: murder
most foul, foul and unnatural, causes that to happen which is quite
outside the ordinary course of Nature:

> The sepulchre,
> Wherein we saw thee quietly inurn'd,
> Hath op'd his ponderous and marble jaws,
> To cast thee up again—

making night hideous, so different from that holy night, 'Wherein our
Saviour's birth is celebrated'. Evil is abroad, Nature herself is in revolt
against it. We do not even begin to see the dimensions of *Hamlet* until
we see that it begins with foul sin, which, gathering head, spreads
corruption everywhere.

This is one familiar thing which one Hellenist sees, or thinks he sees,
when he turns to Shakespeare. Let us look a little further in *Hamlet*. Did
Sophocles or Aeschylus ever contrive more terrible tragic irony than
the scene in which Claudius is at his prayers? Both in effect and intention it is, I think, very like some of the most awful strokes of irony in

D

the *Oedipus*; and again, it is easily made nothing in particular, as it is by those who turn Hamlet into an irresolute procrastinator; as it was by the last actor I saw in the part, who did melodramatic stuff with a sword and so distracted one's attention from the irony. The speech of Claudius: 'O! my offence is rank. . . . May one be pardon'd, and retain the offence?' offers a terrifying spectacle, and one which has nothing to do with the tragedy of a man who could not make up his mind: it is the spectacle of a man who knows that he is bound for everlasting damnation, and cannot do the only thing that may save him. (His speech, incidentally, ends with the same delusive words, 'All may be well,' which are used in the *Agamemnon*, twice by the doomed King, and once by the doomed Queen.) On top of this, '*Enter* Hamlet'. The poet has so designed the play that it is the only chance Hamlet is to have of killing Claudius in security; moreover, the chance comes when he has just found all the proof that he could possibly desire of Claudius's guilt; also, when his passions are attuned to it: 'Now could I drink hot blood.' Why does he *not* do it? A Laertes would have cut his throat i' the church; Horatio, one suspects, would have gone straight to his point; but Hamlet has a finer mind than these, as Oedipus has a finer mind than the sober Creon of that play—but it is Creon who survives. Hamlet will not be satisfied with the mere death of Claudius; he will have him damned as well; he will therefore not 'take him in the purging of his soul'. He is arrogating to himself—a man—the judgment which must be left to God; and, like Oedipus time after time, he is using 'god-like reason' in disastrous ignorance of a material fact:

> My words fly up, my thoughts remain below:
> Words without thoughts never to Heaven go.

One reason for looking forward to Heaven is the possibility of hearing Sophocles and Shakespeare discussing tragic irony.

We speak of the 'inevitability' of Greek tragedy. It rests on the belief, which experience does not wholly contradict, that as in the physical universe certain laws manifestly prevail, so that a basic Order is maintained—an Order, or a general Balance between things—so do certain comparable laws in that other Universe of human action and suffering; as, for example, the law that underlies the *Agamemnon*, that violence will provoke counter-violence, until the inevitable end comes: chaos. The student of Greek drama finds this same inevitability in *Hamlet* also; he is, after all, on familiar ground. In Shakespeare's imagery here, the poison which Claudius poured into King Hamlet's ear spreads everywhere, corrupting everything, especially friendship, loyalty, and love, until at the end it emerges again from a metaphorical to a literal poison, and destroys Claudius and Gertrude, Laertes and Hamlet. Here one thinks of Aeschylus, who also uses imagery like this: Paris the sinner is described as one who 'treads underfoot the beauty of holy things', and then, later, we see Agamemnon entering his palace, trampling underfoot the crimson tapestry which he knows should be offered to gods. Again, the chorus, singing of Agamemnon's destruction of Troy, tells us that Zeus cast such a net around the city that none could escape—and later we see Agamemnon lying dead in the net that was cast over him by Clytemnestra, a 'net woven by the Erinyes'.

The whole of the second part of *Hamlet* is strongly marked by this tragic inevitability. To say nothing about the way in which Claudius is driven from one crime into another, there is the opening of Act IV, Scene 2—surely one of the greatest of tragic openings: 'I will not speak with her.' It is certainly one of the important themes of the play that so many in it wish to keep the evil hidden; Shakespeare wrote one of his most extraordinary scenes, of the Ghost in the cellarage, to emphasize this very point. But it is impossible; in the end it is proclaimed to all:

> Foul deeds will rise,
> Though all the earth o'erwhelm them, to men's eyes.

Just as the foul deeds of Oedipus could not remain hidden, so here. Gertrude tries to hide the evil from herself: 'I will not speak with her,' —but she must:

> 'Twere good she were spoken with, for she may strew
> Dangerous conjectures in ill-breeding minds.

At one point this feeling of inevitability is concentrated in a stroke of dramatic irony which has its exact parallels in Sophocles. One of the things corrupted by Claudius's poison, as we have seen, is Friendship. Rosencrantz and Guildenstern are at least old associates of Hamlet's, on friendly enough terms with him, at the beginning. There is already irony when, on his arrival, Guildenstern says to the King and Queen:

> We both obey,
> And here give up ourselves, in the full bent,
> To lay our service freely at your feet,
> To be commanded.

Giving oneself up to the service of such as these is some danger, as they discover. But it is a later irony which is so Sophoclean. In the *Antigone*, Sophocles regularly puts into the mouth of his wise chorus observations about Antigone which are true, but only when we refer them to Creon; for example, 'To the one whom God will ruin, evil seems good.' So is it with that speech made by Rosancrantz to Claudius:

> The cease of majesty
> Dies not alone, but, like a gulf doth draw
> What's near it with it; it is a massy wheel,
>   . . . which, when it falls,
> Each small annexment, petty consequence,
> Attends the boisterous ruin:

This is said to King Claudius; but how much more pertinent when we refer it to the death of King Hamlet; and realize that Rosencrantz himself is a small annexment whom sin will engulf.

It is high time we escaped from this inexhaustible play, lest we never escape; but there remains one point so interesting to a Hellenist that it may not be passed over: the pirate-ship. About this, Bernard Shaw somewhere makes the illuminating comment that it is a threadbare device that would be scorned by a second-rate melodrama, but the magnificent Shakespeare didn't mind. What the comment illuminates is not Shakespeare but Shaw, among whose gifts imagination is not notable. Again the student of Greek drama knows at once where he is —or thinks he does; for the Greek too did this: namely, uses an incident that looks like pure chance in order to make us feel that the gods—that is, some universal order—is visible in the events. Twice—for example, in his *Electra* and in the *Oedipus*—Sophocles uses this sequence: the Queen makes a solemn sacrifice and petition to Apollo; when the prayer is ended, a messenger arrives with news—good news, for the Queen. He comes apparently by chance; yet the dramatic timing of his arrival is such that we, the audience, cannot but feel that it is the god's answer to the prayer; in Clytemnestra's case, at least, a blasphemous one; in each case, the message leads directly to the Queen's death. Heaven is ordinant. But the plot does not *need* the gods at all; the gods move along with the human actors, but they do nothing to help them, still less to command them. One could cut them out, here and from many another Greek play, and the play would still be intelligible and stage-worthy. But it would be much smaller; it would become only an exciting play of character and intrigue; a particular, and not a universal.

The half-hidden presence of the gods forces us to see that the ven-
geance is the recoil upon Agamemnon's murderers of their own crime; a
grim universal law is at work. The pirate-ship is a Shakespearian equi-
valent—and he has others, such as prophecy. His plays, too, are universals: Heaven is ordinant; certain unchanging laws can be discerned in
the succession of events. The course of evil begun by Claudius will
destroy the two chief houses in Denmark, but it will not be given to
Claudius to destroy Hamlet and himself to escape.

But there are other plays than *Hamlet*, and it is time to look at them.
A few years ago—if I may for a moment be autobiographical—I took
advantage of a brief and blessed illness to do what I had never done
before: to read right through the Histories of Shakespeare in order.
Naturally, I had read and seen some of them, and certain things lived
in the memory: the villainy (rather overdone, as it had seemed) of
Richard III, the tragically misguided Richard II, the splendid rhetoric
in *Henry V*; but I had no firm grip on the whole series, only the general
impression that is conveyed by the common phrase 'a grand pageant of
English history'. I read them all straight through, and the effect was
overwhelming; a 'pageant' if you will, but one which has that same
tragic amplitude of which we have been speaking. The margins of my
Shakespeare are now full of scribbles like, 'Cf. Aeschylus, *Agam*.', or
'See *Trachiniae*', or '*Trojan Women*, chorus'; on one passage, the word
'*Iliad!*'

What sent me back to the *Iliad* was the scene in the Temple Garden
in *King Henry VI*, Part I. You will recall how Richard Plantagenet has
quarrelled violently with young Somerset. These two are in the Garden
with Suffolk, Warwick, Vernon, and—a most interesting addition—a
Lawyer to whom Shakespeare does not bother to give a name; he is
just 'A Lawyer'. What the quarrel is about we are not told, but
Somerset plucks a red rose, asks that those who think with him shall do
the same, and agrees to abide by the decision of the majority. Only
Suffolk plucks the red; Warwick and Vernon pluck a white rose with
Plantagenet, and the Lawyer says to Somerset:

> Unless my study and my books be false,
> The argument you held was wrong in you,
> In sign whereof I pluck a white rose too.

Not very Homeric—not yet; but Plantagenet says, 'Now, Somerset,
where is your argument?' and the reply is, 'Here, in my scabbard.'—
So much for Law.

At the end of the scene, Warwick says:

> And here I prophesy: this brawl today,
> Grown to this faction in the Temple garden,
> Shall send between the red rose and the white
> A thousand souls to death and deadly night.

The *Iliad* begins like this:

> Sing, goddess, of the anger of Achilles the son of Peleus, that baleful anger which brought endless misery to the Achaeans, and sent the souls of many brave heroes to Hades, and left their bodies to be devoured by dogs and birds; and the plan of Zeus was fulfilled. Begin where Agamemnon the King and great Achilles came to strife and enmity.

The *Iliad* is a tragic poem, and it has a strong unity, because, in spite of its length and the richness of its episodes it does keep to its central theme, announced in these opening words: an outburst of hot wrath between two violent men not only sends 'a thousand men to death and deadly night', but also brings shame to Achilles, and such bitter grief too, over the death of his dear Patroclus, that when at length Agamemnon is ready to make extravagant amends Achilles finds them hardly worth the taking, for Patroclus is dead. And the 'plan of Zeus' does not mean that Zeus, for inscrutable reasons of his own, stirred up this quarrel, but that such violence is bound to have such results. Warwick's prophesying means the same.

The Histories are full of prophecy, and so are Greek plays, and in neither case is prophecy a mere dramatic ornament or convenience. Its real purpose is to relate the particular instance to a general law; to give it amplitude. We have seen how Teiresias prophesied to Creon what the gods, in their anger, were going to do with him; the purpose of the prophecy is not merely to break Creon's obstinacy; it is, much more, to make us feel that what happens to him is not merely bad luck, but is a typical recoil on a man of his own inhumanity and folly. Prophecy is possible only because there are general laws which operate in these things. Take, for example, King Richard's prophecy, as recollected by Henry IV:[1]

> But which of you was by,—
> You, cousin Nevil, as I may remember,—
> When Richard, with his eye brimful of tears,
> Then check'd and rated by Northumberland,

[1] *King Henry IV*, Part 2, III. i. 65 ff.

> Did speak these words, now prov'd a prophecy?
> 'Northumberland, thou ladder, by the which
> My cousin Bolingbroke ascends my throne;'
> Though then, God knows, I had no such intent,
> But that necessity so bow'd the State
> That I and greatness were compelled to kiss:
> 'The time shall come', thus did he follow it,
> 'The time will come, that foul sin, gathering head,
> Shall break into corruption:'—so went on,
> Foretelling this same time's condition
> And the division of our amity.

It is one difference between Comedy and Tragedy that comedy depends on surprise while Tragedy, on the whole, avoids it; that is to say, there may be surprise at the magnitude of the disaster, but not at the disaster itself. The tragic poet will discount surprise by prophecy; and his prophecies are not arbitrary, but have their roots in universal human experience.

Let us pursue this matter of prophecy a little further; Shakespeare gives us examples in plenty. In *King John*, Constance, whose cause has been taken up by King Philip and Austria, is thrown over by them when they strike their bargain with John—the bargain by which the Dauphin is to marry Blanche. Constance is beside herself with fury and despair, and presently cries:[1]

> Arm, arm, you heavens, against these perjur'd kings!
> A widow cries; be husband to me, heavens!
> Let not the hours of this ungodly day
> Wear out the day in peace; but, ere sunset,
> Set armed discord 'twixt these perjur'd kings!
> Hear me! O, hear me!

Immediately, in comes Pandulph the Papal Legate; he, by excommunicating John, causes Philip to renounce the bargain. A battle ensues, and by sunset Austria is dead. So is the prayer answered; Heaven has passed its own judgment on the perjured Kings. It is an exact parallel, in technique, effect and purpose, with what Sophocles does in the *Electra* when he brings in his Messenger pat upon Clytemnestra's prayer to Apollo. Another Greek example, though one which works in reverse, can be found in the denouement of Euripides' *Medea*—a scene which the logic of Aristotle failed to understand. When Medea has murdered her children, the Chorus, in horror, sings a stanza in

---

[1] *King John*, III. i. 107 ff.

which it calls upon the Sun-god, as the source of purity, to avenge the crime. But what the Sun-god does is to send an airborne chariot to rescue the murderess and take her safe to Athens. This is one reason why the play makes no sense if we try to turn it, in our modern way, into something of a psychological study of Medea; from this sequence we must infer either that Euripides could not make a decent plot, or that he could, and wanted to suggest that Medea's wild cruelty is something elemental which is not alien from the nature of Man and of the universe.

There is one form of prophecy, namely the ironic, the apparently mocking prophecy, at which we may look a little more closely. It is fairly common in folk-lore; a classical instance is the tale about Croesus the King of Lydia: that he, contemplating an attack on Persia, consulted Delphi and was told that if he crossed the River Halys he would destroy a mighty empire; so he did cross the river, and did destroy a mighty empire. Unfortunately, it was his own. What this type of story signified to the minds of those who invented them must remain a matter of speculation; but Sophocles and Shakespeare also used the type, and here we can do more than speculate.

I have mentioned the *Trachiniae*, the play which deals with the death of Heracles. In this play, he is a hero whose whole life is encompassed with oracles. The one that will concern us is that the Labour on which he is at present engaged is to be his last; it will end either in his death or in unbroken peace. He returns from it in safety; therefore all will now be well. Before he reaches his home, having fallen violently in love with a young Princess, and having failed to persuade her father to let him have her as his mistress, he storms and sacks her city, destroys all its men, takes the girl, and sends her home where his faithful wife is awaiting him. She, to win back his love, sends to him the robe which she has anointed with a love-charm. She does not know that the love-charm, given to her years back by an enemy of Heracles, is deadly poison. It destroys him; and so is the oracle fulfilled: this recent Labour does end in lasting peace, but it is the peace of death.

The classical scholar now present is forcibly reminded of this in reading *King Henry IV*, with its prophecy about Jerusalem; but before discussing that, we might glance at one or two others which are at least similar, even if not the same. In *King Richard III*, Buckingham is executed on All-Souls' Day—that same day, as he says, on which he had falsely sworn loyalty to Edward, 'his children, and his wife's allies':

> That high All-Seer which I dallied with
> Hath turn'd my feigned prayer on my head,
> And given in earnest what I begg'd in jest.[1]

We speak sometimes of the mocking irony of the gods; in this case at least the gods were doing more than simply amuse themselves at Buckingham's expense. It is a typical instance of the meaningful way in which the tragic poet will use coincidence. In *King John* the ironic fulfilment of prophecy is used in reverse. Peter of Pomfret, a rude and turbulent fellow, prophesies that on Ascensiontide ere noon John will have delivered up the crown; which John duly does, though it is in submission to the Papal Legate, from whom he immediately receives it again. *King John* I find a difficult play to understand, but as it ends in peace, with Pandulph—in spite of his not very edifying conduct earlier in the play—appearing as an anticipation of Prospero:

> It was my breath that blew this tempest up
> Upon your stubborn usage of the Pope;
> But since you are a gentle convertite,
> My tongue shall hush again this storm of war—[2]

I assume that the function of the prophecy is to underline the re-establishment of order in the kingdom by the acceptance of the Pope's authority, a kingdom in which form has been formless, order orderless.

Henry IV is very close to Sophocles. At the opening of Part I we find Henry looking forward to the end of civil tumult, and planning a Holy War, 'As far as to the sepulchre of Christ'. But Northumberland's rebellion intervenes, with all its treachery and bloodshed—treachery on both sides—and it is not until near the end of Part 2 that the dream recurs:

> We will our youth lead on to higher fields
> And draw no swords but what are sanctified.[3]

To this theme, the full-close is the illness, and then the death, of Henry in the Jerusalem-chamber:

> It hath been prophesied to me many years
> I should not die but in Jerusalem,
> Which vainly I suppos'd the Holy Land.

[1] *King Richard III*, v. i.   [2] *King John*, v. i.
[3] *King Henry IV*, Part 2, IV. iv.

> But bear me to that chamber; there I'll lie:
> In that Jerusalem shall Harry die.[1]

The resemblance to the oracles given to Heracles is unmistakable; how deep does it go? Deep enough, I think. As for Heracles, it is made quite plain that he falls because of his habitual and violent disregard of the rights of others—in this instance, of a loyal and understanding wife, whom, without a thought, he is going to supersede with the beautiful young girl Iole. We may reflect—and I think Sophocles intended us to reflect—that it was open to Heracles to return from this final Labour and live henceforth in peace; but his ungovernable passion, not for the first time, got the better of him, so that his wife was induced to use the love-charm. It was his own action which determined that the promised peace should be the peace of death. It might have been otherwise; the gods were not simply mocking him. The fulfilment of the Jerusalem-prophecy is no less tragic; but this fact is not to be seen except in its full context, and this embraces *King Richard II* as well as the two parts of *King Henry IV*.

It is, no doubt, possible to think of *King Richard II* as being the tragedy of a young king led into evil courses and then to disaster by bad advisers. It is possible to think of the *Antigone* as the tragedy of the heroic young Antigone. Both Sophocles and Shakespeare were pretty good at portraying character. But if we think of either play on this level only, we gravely diminish its importance. From such a point of view we might object to *King Richard II* what has been objected to the *Antigone*, that it lacks unity, inasmuch as the last scenes concern Bolingbroke quite as much as Richard; to which, I suppose, one answer might be that this is one of the Chronicle-plays, and one must not expect them to be very good in construction. (This answer, I may say, is not mine.)

Richard, at the beginning of the play, is under grave suspicion of having caused Gloster's death. Gaunt speaks about this, though with more restraint, as Constance speaks about her wrongs in *King John*:[2]

> When law can do no right,
> Let it be lawful that law bar no wrong . . .
> For he that holds his kingdom holds the law:
> Therefore, since law itself is perfect wrong,
> How can the law forbid my tongue to curse?

[1] *King Henry IV*, Part 2, IV. v. 235 ff.   [2] III. i. 185 ff.

Gaunt does not conclude, with Constance, that when law can do no right, no law can bar wrong; Gaunt, indeed, is the only important character in this tragic series of plays who does *not* agree with Constance. He has every incentive to stir against Gloster's butchers, but he will not take Heaven's justice into his own hands; it will be the tragedy of his son Henry that he does. You will recall Gaunt's reply to the Duchess:[1]

> Since correction lieth in those hands
> Which made the fault that we cannot correct,
> Put we our quarrel to the will of heaven;
> Who, when they see the hours ripe on earth,
> Will rain hot vengeance on offenders' heads.

Gaunt, in fact, agrees with Socrates, that it is better to suffer than to do wrong.

In the matter of the accusations which pass, on this score, between Hereford and Mowbray, I am on unfamiliar ground, but I assume that the formal ordeal by battle is the symbol of Heaven's judgment; and not only does Richard prevent this, but also he metes out his own justice to Hereford and Mowbray in a singularly capricious manner. Perhaps it is not over-subtle to see some tragic irony in the reason which Richard gives for preventing the duel; it is:

> For that our kingdom's earth should not be soil'd
> With that dear blood which it hath fostered.[2]

At the end of the play it is Richard's own blood that soils his kingdom's earth.

Having given a partial judgment on this quarrel, Richard goes on to plunder Gaunt's estate—that is to say, Hereford's—to farm his kingdom, to reduce England to chaos; to give Hereford every apparent justification, barring its lawlessness, to reclaim his dukedom and estates by force, with the support of others, like Northumberland, who can tolerate Richard no longer; with the result that, almost by force of circumstances, Bolingbroke is led to assume the crown. Henry is speaking truly when he says, in a passage that I quoted earlier:

> Though then, God knows, I had no such intent,
> But that necessity so bow'd the State
> That I and greatness were compelled to kiss.

[1] *King Henry IV*, Part 2, I. ii. 4 ff.   [2] *King Richard II*, I. iii. 125 f.

This 'necessity' is very like one in the *Agamemnon* which has puzzled some commentators: the 'yoke of necessity' to which Agamemnon submitted at Aulis when, to prosecute his war, he sacrificed his daughter to Artemis. Why did the gods present him with so bitter a choice? What primitive theological ideas was Aeschylus entertaining? Primitive ideas very like those of Shakespeare: that to avenge wrong through blood and violence can leave behind it only a legacy of more blood and violence. Both poets live in the same world. In the *Agamemnon*, Aeschylus calls the first crime of the long chain of crime in the house of Atreus the πρώταρχος ἄτη, the blind sin that began it all; a like succession has been started by the lawlessness of Richard; it leads directly to his deposition, and you know very well how that deposition re-echoes in the plays that are to follow. Richard, in his extremity, is willing to adopt Bolingbroke as his heir and to yield the high sceptre freely, but it is too late for the voice of reason and peace to be heard. As the uncomfortable Bishop of Carlisle observes: 'What subject can give sentence on his King?' Richard himself says:[1]

> I find myself a traitor with the rest;
> For I have given here my soul's consent
> To undeck the pompous body of a king.

Now, nothing can stop it. Bolingbroke may do his best to be moderate towards Richard: 'Urge it no more, my lord Northumberland.'[2] But Richard's crimes and follies have produced the crime of crimes, deposition; the consequences must follow. Even before the coronation the Abbot of Westminster is speaking to Aumerle and Carlisle about laying a plot against Henry; Henry can be magnanimous enough to pardon Aumerle, but he says, 'Have I no friend will rid me of this living fear?' —and the officious Exton murders Richard. For his service he receives from Henry the curse of Cain, and Henry says:[3]

> I'll make a voyage to the Holy Land,
> To wash this blood from off my guilty hand.

But the blood is not so easily to be washed off, either from Henry or from his kingdom. Blood spilt on the ground, as Aeschylus also knew, invokes fresh blood.

It is the first announcement of the Jerusalem theme; the new king is already beginning to take on the lineaments of a tragic figure.

One point I have passed over, and I think it is a not unimportant one;

[1] *King Richard II*, IV. i. 248 ff.   [2] IV. i. 271.   [3] V. vi. 49 f.

it relates to Shakespeare's handling of Richard in the second part of the play. That he becomes a tragic figure goes without saying, but Shakespeare also writes some rather good poetry for him, and perhaps we may be in some danger of thinking that he was merely characterizing Richard as a poetic soul. Perhaps he was; but there is something more. I am thinking in particular of the scene of Richard's return from Ireland.[1] He says:

> I weep for joy
> To stand upon my kingdom once again.
> Dear earth, I do salute thee with my hand. . . .

Carlisle reassures him:[2]

> Fear not, my lord: that Power that made you king
> Hath power to keep you king in spite of all.

This, no doubt, is true; what bishops say must be believed. Richard's reply, as you will remember, contains the passage:[3]

> Not all the water in the rough rude sea
> Can wash the balm from an anointed king;
> The breath of worldly men cannot depose
> The deputy elected by the Lord.
> For every man that Bolingbroke hath press'd
> To lift shrewd steel against our golden crown,
> God for his Richard hath in heavenly pay
> A glorious angel: then, if angels fight,
> Weak men must fall, for Heaven still guards the right.

True; but Richard is pitifully deceiving himself. The Power that made him king does not choose to keep him king; the Angels do not turn up. The breath of worldly men *can* depose the deputy anointed by the Lord—though they must pay the inevitable price for doing it. Richard did not enjoy the advantage of having read Aeschylus. He might have learned from the *Agamemnon* that the gods are stern and inflexible; from the *Suppliants* of Aeschylus that the gods do not automatically protect the wronged if they themselves are in the wrong; from the *Electra* of Sophocles that the prayers of one who is a criminal may be answered in devastating fashion. To all Richard's fine poetry Heaven is remarkably insensitive: Heaven is concerned, in these sombre plays, to visit upon men the inevitable consequences of what they have done—upon them, and (as in the *Agamemnon* too) upon the innocent as

---

[1] *King Richard II*, III. ii. 4 ff.   [2] Ib. 27 f.   [3] Ib. 54 ff.

well, as is so terribly portrayed in *King Henry VI*, Part 3, in those antistrophic scenes, reminiscent of some of the choruses in the *Trojan Women*, of the Son who has killed his Father, and the Father who has killed his Son.

Such is the context in which we should consider Henry's dream of a holy war against the infidel, and the ironic fulfilment of the prophecy that he should die in Jerusalem. It could not be, not in a world in which foul sin, gathering head, has broken into corruption; a world in which there is always argument why an oath should not be kept, an offer of friendship and forgiveness not trusted; 'Form formless, order orderless.'

The tragic thought of Sophocles is based on the conception of a universe which is grounded on Dikê, principles of Order, which, when violated, will reassert themselves, maybe just as violently. The Shakespearian basis appears to be not very different. It is said by Faulconbridge, in his speech on Commodity: 'the world . . . is peized well, made to run even upon even ground'. When it does not run even, the fault is in those who have made it uneven.

As for the unevenness, it is notable how many times in these plays a character is given only the choice between two evils, placed in a dilemma. There is Blanche, in *King John:* her marriage-feast must be stained with blood; she can, she says, wish success neither to husband nor uncle, nor to father nor grandmother. There is the good York, in *King Richard II*:[1]

> Both are my kinsmen:
> The one is my sovereign, whom both my oath
> And duty bids defend; the other again
> Is my near kinsman, whom the King hath wrong'd,
> Whom conscience and my kindred bids to right.

There is Henry VI, who time after time vainly tries to end the strife by composition, to whom Clifford harshly says:

> My gracious liege, this too much lenity
> And harmful pity must be laid aside;[2]

for Henry can avoid war only by disinheriting his own son. The same sort of thing happens in the Greek plays, and for the same reason: not that the President of the Immortals is malignant, but that human conduct has made the ground uneven. There is Agamemnon, faced with

---

[1] II. ii. 111 ff.   [2] *King Henry VI*, Part 3, II. ii. 9 f.

his choice at Aulis—because he is obeying a violent conception of justice. There is King Pelasgus in the *Suppliants* of Aeschylus: because, away in Egypt, violence is offered to certain women who are of Greek descent, they fly for refuge to Greece and invoke the rights of suppliants; the King therefore has to choose: will he, on behalf of unknown women, lead his subjects into war with the Egyptians, or will he reject the suppliants and thereby brave the wrath of the offended gods?

The classical scholar looking at Shakespeare finds at least one other point of interest which I should like to discuss, however briefly. There is extant only one Greek play, *The Persians*, which in the strict sense is a historical tragedy. It deals with events which were only eight years old, events in which most of his audience must have been involved actively. Yet in some important ways his plot diverges from history—to the occasional embarrassment of ancient historians, who think that the poet should have done better. But it can be shown, I think, that the divergences are purposeful, and, when we see what the play is really about, very effective: Aeschylus was not writing a patriotic chronicle-play, but a tragedy about a king who defied the gods. Now, my domestic *Shakespeare* is a pleasant Victorian edition, and in it I find, at *King Henry VI*, Part III, iii, 2, the following note: 'This seems a needless departure from fact. Sir John Grey fell in the second battle of St Albans, fighting on King Henry's side; and his lands were not seized by the Queen [Queen Margaret], who conquered in that battle, but by King Edward after the battle of Towton. Shakespeare has the matter correctly in *King Richard III*, i, 3.' Shall we look for a moment at this scene, in which Shakespeare contradicts not only history, but also himself?

It is the scene in which Lady Elizabeth Grey appears before Edward IV to ask for the restoration of her late husband's lands. By pretending that Grey had suffered in defence of the House of York, Shakespeare lays Edward (as he admits) under a debt of honour to Lady Elizabeth. Nevertheless, Edward will not at first repay this debt of honour unless she will accept a proposal of dishonour, upon her rejecting of which he persuades her to become his Queen, although in fact he has already sent Warwick to Paris to ask for the hand of the Lady Bona. Clearly, Shakespeare wished to suggest that Elizabeth became Queen in circumstances of folly and dishonour. This is the reason why he gets his history wrong here.

In the tragic poets, I think, close parallels are not accidental. I therefore go back to *King Henry VI*, Part I, v, 5; to the remarkable scene in which de la Pole takes prisoner at Angiers a beauteous maiden, decides that he can hardly make her mistress, being married, and so decides to make her young Henry's Queen. This he does, although Gloster the Lord Protecter is against it—for an interesting reason:

> So should I give consent to flatter sin.
> You know, my lord, your Highness is betroth'd
> Unto another lady of esteem;
> How shall we then dispense with that contract,
> And not deface your honour with reproach?

The parallel with Edward IV is fairly close; Shakespeare makes it closer. Queen Margaret he represents as turning out an implacable and vindictive stirrer-up of civil war; and as for Edward's Queen Elizabeth, he makes the advancement of her relatives—Rivers and the rest—a potent cause of dissension and bloodshed. Folly, dishonour and concupiscence bear their natural fruit. Finally, we have those appalling scenes in *King Richard III* in which these two discarded and bereaved Queens, like a band of Furies, join in cursing both each other and everyone else; and in order to engineer these scenes, Shakespeare again departs from history: he pretends that Queen Maragaret was not either in the Tower or in France, but at large in London. Both *The Persians* and these plays of Shakespeare are good illustrations of Aristotle's dictum that Poetry is more serious and philosophical than History.

Therefore, to sum up: the classical scholar, when he journeys from Athens to Stratford-on-Avon—or rather to the Globe Theatre—though indeed he has to accustom himself to a different style of dramatic architecture, to different clothes and different manners, very soon finds himself at home; for these are great tragic poets. They speak the same language, though in different dialects: those in Greek, this one in English. They speak about the same things; whether they tell us of an Agamemnon or a Creon, or of a King Richard or a Hamlet, they are speaking in the same grave and spacious way of nothing less than the terms on which the gods will let us live; and though each of them speaks in his own voice and with his own accent, about this one thing they do not speak differently.

4

THE QUESTION OF CHARACTER IN SHAKESPEARE

by L. C. KNIGHTS

LET me begin with an unashamed bit of autobiography. In 1932 I was asked to give a paper to the Shakespeare Association in London. I was a comparatively young man, dissatisfied with the prevailing academic approach to Shakespeare, excited by the glimpses I had obtained of new and, it seemed, more rewarding approaches, and I welcomed the opportunity of proclaiming the new principles in the very home of Shakespearian orthodoxy, whilst at the same time having some fun with familiar irrelevancies of the kind parodied in my title, *How Many Children had Lady Macbeth?* I gave my paper and waited expectantly for the lively discussion that would follow this rousing challenge to the pundits. So far as I remember, nothing happened, except that after a period of silence an elderly man got up at the back of the room and said that he was very glad to hear Mr. Knights give this paper because it was what he had always thought. The revolution was over, and I went home. It was hardly a historic occasion, and the only reason for mentioning it is that when my paper was published as one of Gordon Fraser's Minority Pamphlets it obtained a certain mild notoriety that has never since entirely deserted it: only a few years ago a writer in *The Listener* called it 'the Communist Manifesto of the new critical movement'. Well of course it was nothing of the kind. *How Many Children had Lady Macbeth?* has earned its footnote in the history of modern criticism partly, I like to believe, because it says a few sensible things about *Macbeth*, partly because of its sprightly title (which was suggested to me by F. R. Leavis), and partly because it reflected the conviction of an increasing number of readers that the prevailing language of Shakespeare criticism didn't quite fit what seemed to them of deepest importance in the experience of Shakespeare's plays. In the last twenty-five or thirty years there has certainly been a movement away from the older type of 'character' criticism which had for so long held the field and which culminated in

E

55

A. C. Bradley's *Shakespearean Tragedy*.[1] But so far as any one book can be said to herald the new movement it was G. Wilson Knight's *The Wheel of Fire* (1930), shortly to be followed by *The Imperial Theme* (1931).[2]

Now what I am here to do today is to try to get one aspect of that movement into perspective; more specifically I want to ask, after some twenty-five years of Shakespeare criticism that has not on the whole been on Bradleyean lines, what we now understand by the term 'character' when we use it in giving an account of Shakespeare's plays, to what extent—and within what limitations—'character' can be a useful critical term when we set out to define the meaning—the living and life-nourishing significance—of a Shakespeare play.

I don't want to burden you with a history of Shakespeare criticism, ancient or modern, but a few historical reminders are necessary. Since Shakespeare criticism began, people have praised Shakespeare for the lifelikeness of his characters. But it was not until the end of the eighteenth century that Shakespeare's remarkable power to make his men and women convincing led to a more and more exclusive concentration on those features of the *dramatis personae* that could be defined in terms appropriate to characters in real life. The *locus classicus* is of course Maurice Morgann's *Essay on the Dramatic Character of Sir John Falstaff* (1777). Twelve years before, in 1765, Dr. Johnson, in his great Preface, had given the more traditional view:

> Nothing can please many, and please long, but just representations of general nature. . . . Shakespeare is above all writers, at least above all modern writers, the poet of nature. . . . His persons act and speak by the influence of those general passions and principles by which all minds are agitated, and the whole system of life is continued in motion. In the writings of other poets a character is too often an individual; in those of Shakespeare it is commonly a species.
>
> It is from this wide extension of design that so much instruction is derived. . . .[3]

[1] Macmillan, 1904.
[2] Methuen.
[3] We may compare Johnson's characteristic comment on *Macbeth*: 'The play is deservedly celebrated for the propriety of its fictions, and solemnity, grandeur, and variety of its action; but it has no nice discriminations of character, the events are too great to admit the influence of particular dispositions, and the course of the action necessarily determines the conduct of the agents. The danger of ambition is well described. . . .' Johnson, it is true, also says of Shakespeare, 'Perhaps no poet ever kept his personages more distinct from each other.'

Morgann, on the contrary, is interested in what is uniquely individual in the character he describes, and these individual traits, he affirms, can be elicited from the stage characters in much the same way as one builds up the character of an acquaintance in real life: 'those characters in Shakespeare, which are seen only in part, are yet capable of being unfolded and understood in the whole'.

> If the characters of Shakespeare [he goes on] are thus *whole*, as it were original, while those of almost all other writers are mere imitation, it may be fit to consider them rather as Historic than Dramatic beings; and, when occasion requires, to account for their conduct from the *whole* of character, from general principles, from latent motives, and from policies not avowed.

It is this principle that allows him to distinguish between 'the *real* character of Falstaff' and 'his *apparent* one'. What R. W. Babcock, in his useful book, *The Genesis of Shakespeare Idolatry, 1766–99*,[1] calls 'the psychologizing of Shakespeare' was well established even before Cole-ridge gave his lectures; and Coleridge's influence, though of course more subtly, worked in the same direction. It seems true to say that in the nineteenth century Shakespeare's characters became 'real people', and—with varying degrees of relevance—the plays were discussed in terms of the interaction of real people for whom sympathy or antipathy was enlisted. Bradley's tremendously influential *Shake-spearean Tragedy* was published in 1904, and, for Bradley, 'the centre of the tragedy . . . may be said with equal truth to lie in action issuing from character, or in character issuing in action': 'action is the centre of the story', but 'this action is essentially the expression of character'.

Now Bradley had the great virtue of being thoroughly immersed in what he was talking about, and I am sure that his book has helped very many people to make Shakespeare a present fact in their lives. Also there is no need to make Bradley responsible for all the vagaries of the how-many-children-had-Lady-Macbeth? kind, which mostly lie on the fringes of criticism. But Bradley's book did endorse a particular kind of preoccupation with 'character', and once 'character'-criticism became the dominant mode of approach to Shakespeare, certain im-portant matters were necessarily obscured, and people's experience of Shakespeare became in some ways less rich and satisfying than it might have been. For one thing genuine perceptions became entangled with irrelevant speculations—'How is it that Othello comes to be the com-panion of the one man in the world, who is at once able enough, brave

[1] University of North Carolina Press, 1931.

enough, and vile enough to ensnare him?'; Macbeth's tendency to ambition 'must have been greatly strengthened by his marriage'. And if the critic who accepts too naïvely the character-in-action formula is liable to disappear down by-paths outside the play, he is almost equally likely to slight or ignore what is actually there if it does not minister to his particular preoccupation—witness the ease with which the old Arden edition of *Macbeth* dismissed as spurious scenes that do not contribute to the development of character or of a narrowly conceived dramatic action. Even at its best the focus is a narrow one. Shakespearian tragedy, says Bradley, 'is pre-eminently the story of one person, the "hero", or at most of two, the "hero" and "heroine" '; and the mark of the tragic hero, besides his greatness, is that there is a 'conflict of forces' in his soul. I suppose, if you look at matters in this way it doesn't necessarily mean that you idealize the hero as Bradley does Othello, missing the critical 'placing' determined by the play as a whole. But it does mean that you are likely to ignore some important matters, such as the structure of ideas in *Macbeth*. After all, in his greater plays, Shakespeare was doing more than merely holding a mirror up to nature, more even than representing conflict in the souls of mighty characters: he was exploring the world and defining the values by which men live. In short, Shakespearian tragedy, any Shakespearian tragedy, is saying so much more than can be expressed in Bradleyean terms. It was some such perceptions as these—combined with an increasing knowledge of Elizabethan dramatic usage and convention—that prompted exploration of Shakespeare, not necessarily in opposition to Bradley, but to a large extent outside the Bradleyean frame of reference.

Simplifying for the sake of clarity, I would say that as a result of critical work done in the last quarter of a century, the approach to Shakespeare of an intelligent and informed reader to-day is likely to differ in three important respects from that of the intelligent and informed reader of a generation ago. To start with, he is likely to take it for granted that any one of Shakespeare's greater plays is very much more than a dramatized story; that it is, rather, a vision of life—more or less complex and inclusive—whose meaning is nothing less than *the play as a whole*. This is what Wilson Knight meant when he sometimes referred to his work in terms of 'spatial analysis', as distinguished from the analysis of a series of steps in time. Ideally, we try to apprehend each play as though all its parts were simultaneously present: there is an obvious analogy with music, and criticism of this kind tends to describe

Shakespeare's meanings in terms of 'themes' rather than in terms of motive, character-development, and so on. Wilson Knight speaks of cutting below 'the surface crust of plot and character', and remarks that in *Macbeth*, for example, 'the logic of imaginative correspondence is more significant and more exact than the logic of plot'. He also, of course, told us that 'we should not look for perfect verisimilitude to life, but rather see each play as an expanded metaphor, by means of which the original vision has been projected into forms roughly correspondent with actuality', and the fact that this remark has been quoted in innumerable examination papers shouldn't obscure its crucial importance in determining the kind of approach to Shakespeare that I am trying to define.[1] In the second place, our contemporary reader is likely to take for granted that the essential structure of the plays is to be sought in the poetry rather than in the more easily extractable elements of 'plot' and 'character'. I think our age is more aware of the complex structure, of the depth of life, of Shakespeare's verse, than any of its predecessors. Critics have written at length about his imagery, his ambiguities and overlaying meanings, his word-play, and so on; and there is no doubt that such studies have sharpened our sense not only of the tremendous activity of Shakespeare's verse—its generative power—but of the strong and subtle interconnections of meaning within the imaginative structure of the plays. It is significant that 'interpretation' relies heavily on extensive quotation and detailed analysis.[2] Finally—abandoning my hypothetical intelligent reader—I should say that our whole conception of Shakespeare's relation to his work, of what he was trying to do as an artist whilst at the same time satisfying the demands of the Elizabethan theatre, has undergone a very great change indeed. The 'new' Shakespeare, I should say, is much less impersonal than the old. Whereas in the older view Shakespeare was the god-like creator of a peopled world, projecting—it is true—his own spirit into the inhabitants, but remaining essentially the analyst of 'their' passions, he is now felt as much more immediately engaged in the action he puts before us. I don't of course mean that we have re-

[1] 'And Shakespeare's was a mind that thought in images, so that metaphor packs into metaphor, producing the most surprising collocations of apparently diverse phenomena: he thought of time, and death, and eternity, in terms of a candle, a shadow, and an actor. Is it not likely that the large and composite image of the story as a whole would serve him as a metaphor or symbol for his attitudes to certain aspects of experience?'—S. L. Bethell, *Shakespeare and the Popular Dramatic Tradition* (Staples, 1948), p. 115.

[2] A method that has its dangers, for we sometimes seem to run the risk of having the play read for us.

turned to Frank Harris's Shakespeare, engaged in drawing a succession of full-length portraits of himself, but that we feel the plays (in Mr. Eliot's words) 'to be united by one significant, consistent, and developing personality': we feel that the plays, even if 'in no obvious form', 'are somehow dramatizing . . . an action or struggle for harmony in the soul of the poet'.[1] We take it for granted that Shakespeare thought about the problems of life, and was at least as much interested in working towards an imaginative solution as he was in making a series of detached studies of different characters, their motives and their passions. Here again, specialist studies are indicative: we think it reasonable that a scholar should inquire what evidence there is that Shakespeare had read Hooker, and if so what effect it had on his plays; we inquire into Shakespeare's political ideas and their background; we are prepared to examine *Shakespeare's Philosophical Patterns*[2] (which is the title of a book by the American scholar, W. C. Curry). In short, we take seriously Coleridge's remark that Shakespeare was 'a philosopher'; the vision of life that his plays express is, in a certain sense, a philosophic vision. But at the same time we remember—at least, I should like to be able to say we remember—that the plays are not dramatizations of abstract ideas, but imaginative constructions mediated through the poetry. If Shakespeare's verse has moved well into the centre of the picture, one reason is that linguistic vitality is now felt as the chief clue to the urgent personal themes that not only shape the poetic-dramatic structure of each play but form the figure in the carpet of the canon as a whole.[3]

This short and imperfect account may serve as an indication or reminder of the main lines of Shakespeare criticism since 1930, or thereabouts. Happily my job is not to award marks of merit to different critics, and I don't intend to offer a list of obligatory reading. We all have our own ideas about the recent critics who have helped us most in our understanding of Shakespeare, and I don't suppose that we should all agree about all of them. But I think we should agree that there have been some books offering genuinely new insights, and that where criticism has been most illuminating it has usually been on quite non-Bradleyan lines. At the same time let us recall certain facts. If 'plot' and 'character'—mere 'precipitates from the memory'—sometimes seem to be described in abstraction from the full living im-

---

[1] See T. S. Eliot's essay on John Ford.

[2] Louisiana State University Press, 1937.

[3] A few sentences in this paragraph are borrowed from my essay on the Tragedies in the Pelican Guide to English Literature (ed. Boris Ford), 2, *The Age of Shakespeare*.

mediacy of our direct experience of the plays, and therefore to lead away from it, so too 'themes' and 'symbols' can be pursued mechanically and, as it were, abstractly. Whereas it is equally obvious that criticism in terms of 'character' can be genuinely revealing; John Palmer's *The Political Characters of Shakespeare*[1] is an example. And of course you can't get away from the term. Not only does the ordinary theatregoer or reader need it to explain his enjoyment, but even critics least in sympathy with Bradley at times naturally and necessarily define their sense of significance in terms appropriate to living people. Clearly the critical field has not been given over to those whom J. I. M. Stewart calls 'the new Bowdlers, whom man delights not, no nor woman neither, and who would give us not merely *Hamlet* without the Prince but the Complete Works without their several *dramatis personae*'. The notion of 'character', in some sense, has not disappeared, and is not going to disappear, from Shakespeare criticism. What we need to do is simply to clear up our minds about it, to make our handling of the term both more flexible and more precise.

Before I go on to give my own simple summing up of things as I see them I should like to mention two books that have a direct bearing on the matters we are pursuing. The first is J. I. M. Stewart's witty, entertaining and instructive *Character and Motive in Shakespeare*.[2] Stewart not only has some shrewd knocks at those who over-play the element of Elizabethan dramatic convention in Shakespeare and those who would tailor the plays too closely to the pattern of their own proprieties, he has some illuminating comments on particular plays. But his main interest, in the present connexion, lies in the way he develops the conception of character-presentation beyond the bounds of naturalism. To the extent that Shakespeare is concerned with character and motive—and he does 'present "man" and reveal psychological truths'—he works not through realistic portrayal but through poetry—that is, through symbolism and suggestion as well as by more direct means; and in this way he makes us aware not—or not only—of what we normally understand by character but of its hidden recesses.

The characters, then (but I mean chiefly those major characters with whom the imagination of the dramatist is deeply engaged), have often the superior reality of individuals exposing the deepest springs of their action. But this superior reality is manifested through the medium of situations which are sometimes essentially symbolical; and these may be extravagant or merely fantastic when not interpreted by the quickened imagination, for it is only

[1] Macmillan, 1945. [2] Longmans, 1949.

during the prevalence of a special mode of consciousness, the poetic, that the underlying significance of these situations is perceived. (pp. 9–10)

Of just what Shakespeare brings from beyond this portal [of the depths of the mind], and how, we often can achieve little conceptual grasp; and often therefore the logical and unkindled mind finds difficulties which it labels as faults and attributes to the depravity of Shakespeare's audience or what it wills. But what the intellect finds arbitrary the imagination may accept and respond to, for when we read imaginatively or poetically we share the dramatist's penetration for a while and deep is calling to deep. (p. 30)[1]

The other book I want to refer to is *Character and Society in Shake-speare*[2] by Professor Arthur Sewell. It is a small book but, I think, an important one. Briefly, Mr Sewell's contention is that the characters of a play only exist within the total vision that the play presents: 'in Shakespeare's plays the essential process of character-creation is a prismatic breaking-up of the comprehensive vision of the play' (p. 19). There is, therefore, an absolute distinction between a dramatic character and a person in real life whose conduct can be accounted for 'from general principles, from latent motives, and from policies not avowed'. 'We can only understand Shakespeare's characters so long as we agree that we cannot know all about them and are not supposed to know all

---

[1] This insistence on the imaginative—on the non-rational but not therefore irrational—portrayal of character, and on the need to respond to it imaginatively, is important, and, as I have said, Mr. Stewart can be illuminating. But it also seems to me that his method, as he pursues it, can sometimes lead outside the play, as in his use of psycho-analytic concepts to define Leontes' jealousy. The main criticism of any psycho-analytic account of Shakespeare's characters is not simply that it is irrelevant—though it may be—but that it reduces the material it works on to a category that can be known and docketed. To accept it is to feel that you know about a character something of importance that has been simply handed over, and that can be received alike by every reader, whatever the degree of his concern, the extent of his actual engagement, with the plays. It obscures not only the uniqueness but the *activity* of the work of art; whereas any play only exists for you to the extent that *you* have grappled with its meanings. Thus Mr. Stewart's account of Leontes' repressed homosexuality (reactivated by the presence of Polixenes, and then 'projected' on to Hermione) is relevant inasmuch as it points to the presence in what Leontes stands for of unconscious motivations, of motives beyond conscious control. But within the context of the play as a whole their exact nature is irrelevant: they are simply an X within the equation which is the play. What the play gives us is the awakening of new life that can enlist the same impulses which, in the first part, have been shown as the material of an unruly aberration. All we need to know of the aberration is that it is a representative manifestation: to pin it down exactly as Mr. Stewart does, is to make Leontes' jealousy something that we *know about* instead of something we *respond to* as part of the total generative pattern of the play.

[2] Clarendon Press, 1951.

about them' (p. 12). What is relevant for us is not an assumed hinterland of motives but simply the particular 'address to the world' that is embodied, with different degrees of explicitness, in the different characters. In the comedies the characters tend to be static and, so to speak, socially conditioned: they represent attitudes and modes of judgment that serve for the presentation and critical inspection of our everyday world. In the great tragedies the characters speak from out of a deeper level of experience—'metaphysical' rather than social, though the distinction is not absolute; the vision they embody is transformed in the full working out of the attitudes to which they are committed; and their reality is established by our own active commitment to the drama's dialectical play. Of both comedy and tragedy it can be said that 'unless Shakespeare had set our minds busy—and not only our minds—on various kinds of evaluation, his characters could never have engaged us and would have lacked all vitality' (p. 18). And again, there is the suggestion 'that character and moral vision must be apprehended together, and that when character is understood separately from moral vision it is not in fact understood at all' (p. 59).

Where, then, at the end of all this, do we come out? Perhaps only among what many people will regard as a handful of commonplaces. Let me start with the most thumping platitude of all: in Shakespeare's plays *some* impression of character is constantly being made upon us. It is likely to begin as soon as a major character is introduced.

> Why, I, in this weak piping time of peace,
> Have no delight to pass away the time,
> Unless to see my shadow in the sun
> And descant on mine own deformity.

> Though yet of Hamlet our dear brother's death
> The memory be green, and that it us befitted
> To bear our hearts in grief and our whole kingdom
> To be contracted in one brow of woe,
> Yet so far hath discretion fought with nature. . . .

I pray you, daughter, sing; or express yourself in a more comfortable sort.

Here, and in innumerable other instances, we have what Mr. Sewell calls the 'distillation of personality into style'. We know these people by the way they speak; as Mr. Stewart puts it, 'In drama the voice *is* the character'—though we also have to add that often Shakespeare speaks *through* the person with a meaning different from, or even contrary to, that apparently intended by the character.

At the same time we have to admit that our sense of character—of a complex, unified tissue of thought and feeling from which a particular voice issues—varies enormously not only as between different plays, but as between the different figures within a single play. *All's Well That Ends Well* is nearer to a morality play, and is less concerned with characterization, in any sense, than is *Othello*. In *Measure for Measure* 'analysis of character' may take us a long way with Angelo; it is utterly irrelevant as applied to the Duke.

Let me give another example—which will serve to illustrate Mr. Sewell's remark about the characters embodying 'an address to the world', in case anyone should have been left uneasy with that phrase. Here is Don John introducing himself in conversation with Conrade in Act I of *Much Ado About Nothing*.

> I wonder that thou, being—as thou say'st thou art—born under Saturn, goest about to apply a moral medicine to a mortifying mischief. I cannot hide what I am: I must be sad when I have cause, and smile at no man's jests; eat when I have stomach, and wait for no man's leisure; sleep when I am drowsy, and tend on no man's business; laugh when I am merry, and claw no man in his humour.

Conrade advises that he should apply himself to winning the good opinion of his brother the Duke, with whom he is lately reconciled, and Don John goes on:

> I had rather be a canker in a hedge than a rose in his grace; and it better fits my blood to be disdained of all than to fashion a carriage to rob love from any: in this, though I cannot be said to be a flattering honest man, it must not be denied but I am a plain-dealing villain. I am trusted with a muzzle and enfranchised with a clog; therefore I have decreed not to sing in my cage. If I had my mouth, I would bite; if I had my liberty, I would do my liking: in the meantime, let me be that I am, and seek not to alter me.

A good many things are plain from this—Don John's exacerbated sense of superiority ('I . . . I . . . I . . . .'), his particular kind of 'melancholy', and his affectation of a blunt, no-nonsense manner. Clearly he is related to Richard of Gloucester and to Iago. Their common characteristic is an egotism that clenches itself hard against the claims of sympathy, and that is unwilling to change—'I cannot hide what I am; I must be sad when I have cause . . . let me be that I am, and seek not to alter me.' It is, in short, the opposite of a character 'open' to others and to the real demands of the present. That is all we know about Don John and all we are required to know: we are not asked to consider his bastardy or his other grievances. He is simply a perversely 'melancholy' man who serves as villain of the piece, the agent of an otherwise unmotivated evil.

What is true of a minor figure like Don John is true of all the characters of Shakespeare: we know about them only what the play requires us to know. Even to put the matter in this way is—as we shall see in a minute—over-simplified and misleading, but it serves to remind us that however we define for ourselves a character and his rôle, there is a strict criterion of relevance: he belongs to his play, and his play is an art-form, not a slice of life. The fact that this at least is now a commonplace is a guarantee that we shall never again have to waste our time on the complete irrelevance of some forms of character-analysis as applied to Shakespeare's *dramatis personae*.

But we still haven't got to the heart of the matter. What is the 'play as a whole', to which we say the characters are subordinate? To this question there is no simple answer, but we can at least attempt an answer that will help our reading.

Poetic drama offers a vision of life, more or less complex, more or less wide-embracing, as the case may be. Shakespeare's poetic drama as a whole is different from Jonson's or Racine's; and within Shakespeare's poetic drama as a whole there are many different kinds. Even at its simplest there is some degree of complexity, of dialectical play, as persons embodying different attitudes are set before us in action and interaction. Of course when we are watching them we don't think of them as the embodiment of attitudes—of different addresses to the world: we say simply, Rosalind is in love with Orlando. Yet while we know that two addresses to the world can't fall in love, we also know —and this knowledge moves from the back of our minds and comes into action when, having seen or read the play several times, we try to bring it into sharper focus—that Shakespeare is doing something more significant with Rosalind and Orlando than showing us how interesting it is when boy meets girl. *As You Like It*, which is a fairly simple play, will help us here. *As You Like It* is of course a romantic comedy, with its own interest and entertainment as such. But the plot and the structure of the incidents point to an interest in the meaning of a life lived 'according to nature'. Duke Senior's idyllic picture ('Hath not old custom made this life more sweet Than that of painted pomp?' etc.) is an over-simplification, as the play makes plain; but it is a possible attitude, put forward for inspection, and as the play goes on it is clear that we are meant to take an intelligent interest in the varying degrees of naturalness and sophistication—each playing off against the other—that are put before us. *As You Like It*, in short, rings the changes on the contrasting meanings of 'natural' (either 'human' or 'close down to the life of nature') and 'civilized' (either 'well nurtured' or 'artificial')—all especially pointed with reference to the passion of love. It is largely an entertainment; but at the same time it is a serious comedy of ideas—not abstract ideas to be debated, but ideas as embodied in attitude and action. So that by playing off against each other different attitudes to life, the play as a whole offers a criticism of various forms of exaggeration and affectation—either 'romantic' or professedly realistic—with Rosalind as arbiter, although of course she is not above the action but involved in it herself.[1]

What is true of *As You Like It* is also true of greater plays, such as *Measure for Measure*, *King Lear*, or *Antony and Cleopatra*, though here of course the play of varied sympathies and antipathies, of imaginative evaluation as different possibilities of living are put before us, is more complex, and the experience handled is more profound. But of all the greater plays it is true to say that *all* the characters are necessary to express the vision—the emergent 'idea' or controlling preoccupation—and they are necessary only in so far as they do express it. Gloucester's part in *King Lear* is not to give additional human interest, but to enact and express a further aspect of the Lear experience; for with Gloucester, as with Lear, confident acceptance of an inadequate code gives place to humble acceptance of the human condition, and there are glimpses of a new wisdom:

> I have no way, and therefore want no eyes;
> I stumbled when I saw.

The striking parallels between the two men are proof enough of deliberate artistic intention in this respect.

What *King Lear* also forces on us, even when we are prepared to see the different characters as contributing to a pattern, is the inadequacy of terms relating to 'character'. What character has Edgar in his successive transformations? In the storm scenes, where Lear's vision of horror is built to a climax, we are acted on directly by the poetry, by

[1] See James Smith's excellent essay on *As You Like It* in *Scrutiny*, IX. i. June, 1940, reprinted in *The Importance of Scrutiny*, ed. Eric Bentley (Grove Press, New York, 1957).

what is said, in some respects independently of our sense of a particular person saying it. So too in the play as a whole, and in the other
greater plays, our sense of the characters—of what the characters stand
for in their 'address to the world', their 'moral encounter with the
universe'—is inseparable from the more direct ways in which, by
poetry and symbolism, our imaginations are called into play. To take
one simple example. When Macbeth, on his first appearance, says, 'So
foul and fair a day I have not seen,' he does far more than announce
himself as a character—tired, collected, brooding; echoing the Witches'
'Fair is foul, and foul is fair', he takes his place in the pattern of moral
evaluations which make the play so much more than the story of a
tragic hero, which make it into a great vision of the unreality, the
negative horror, that evil is. In reading Shakespeare our sense of
'character', defined and limited as I have tried to define and limit it, is
important; but so is our responsiveness to symbolism (the storm in
Othello and Othello's trance, Lear's bare heath and Gloucester's Dover
Cliff, Hermione's moving statue), and so is our responsiveness to
imagery (the imagery of darkness conveying spiritual blindness in
Macbeth), to verse rhythm, and to all the inter-acting elements of the
poetry: it is from these that there emerges a controlling direction of
exploratory and committed interests—of interests involving the personality as a whole—that we indicate by some such word as 'themes'.

Mr. John Holloway has recently objected to the use of 'theme' in
Shakespeare criticism:[1] it is a sign that the work in question is to be
reduced to a generalized moral reflection, whereas literature does not
provide us with general truths, only with particular instances. 'What
Macbeth does . . . is to depict for us, in great and remarkable detail, one
imagined case and one only.' 'Narrative', he suggests, is 'the fundamental quality of the full-length work', the essential principle of
imaginative order. Now both these conceptions of the work of art as
'one imagined case and one only', and of 'narrative' as the controlling
principle, seem to me to be, in their turn, open to objection. But I
think we are dealing with something far greater than the particular
question—Is Shakespeare most profitably discussed in terms of
'character' or 'theme' or 'narrative'? What has come into sight, what
we must take account of, is nothing less than the depth of life of any
great work of art, its capacity to enter into our lives as power. What do
we mean when we say that a great work of art has a universal appeal?

[1] 'The New "Establishment" in Criticism', *The Listener*, September 20th and
27th, 1956.

Surely something more than that it tells a story likely to interest everybody. We mean that the special case (and I grant Mr. Holloway the artist's 'passion for the special case') brings to a focus a whole range of awareness, that it generates an activity of imaginative apprehension that illuminates not only the 'case' in question but life as we know it in our own experience: it can modify, or even transform, our whole way of seeing life and responding to it. It is this capacity to generate meanings that is the 'universal' quality in the particular work of art. And it is the presence of the universal in the particular that compels the use of such generalizing terms as 'themes' or 'motifs'. Of course, like other critical terms, they can be used mechanically or ineptly, can harden into counters pushed about in a critical game. But as simple pointers their function is to indicate the *direction* of interest that a play compels when we try to meet it with the whole of ourselves—to meet it, that is (using De Quincey's term), as literature of power.

To read Shakespeare, then (and in reading I include seeing his plays performed), we need to cultivate a complex skill. But there is no need to make heavy weather of this. That skill can be largely intuitive; we can reach it in many ways, and there is no need (especially if we are teachers) to be too insistent on any one approach. In 'Demosius and Mystes', a dialogue appended to *Church and State*, Coleridge refers to a mighty conflict between two cats, 'where one tail alone is said to have survived the battle'. There is always a danger of critical squabbles becoming like that; and I for one would rather see among my pupils an honest and first-hand appreciation of what is offered by way of 'character' than a merely mechanical working out of recurrent imagery and symbolic situations. We should remember also that the life of the imagination runs deeper than our conscious formulations. T. S. Eliot (in his Introduction to S. L. Bethell's book on Shakespeare), says of the persons of the play of a modern verse dramatist,

> they must on your stage be able to perform the same actions, and lead the same lives, as in the real world. But they must somehow disclose (not necessarily be aware of) a deeper reality than that of the plane of most of our conscious living; and what they disclose must be, not the psychologist's intellectualization of this reality, but the reality itself.

'They must somehow disclose (not necessarily be aware of) a deeper reality': I think that what Eliot says of the persons in verse plays like his own, applies—*mutatis mutandis*—to the spectators of poetic drama. To the extent that a Shakespeare tragedy truly enlists the imagination (and this means enlisting it for what is in the play, not for a display of virtuosity) it is precisely this deeper level of apprehension—the hidden potentialities, wishes, and fears of the individual spectator—that is being worked on, even though the spectator himself may not be conscious of it, and thinks that he is simply watching someone else's 'character issuing in action'.

All the same, even when this is admitted, there is no reason why the common reader should not be encouraged to see rather more. For it is in our imaginative response to *the whole play*—not simply to what can be extracted as 'character', nor indeed to what can be simply extracted as 'theme' or 'symbol'—that the meaning lies; and Shakespeare calls on us to be as fully conscious as we can, even if consciousness includes relaxed enjoyment and absorption as well as, sometimes, more deliberate attention to this or that aspect of the whole experience.

5

SHAKESPEARE'S PASTORAL COMEDY

by MARY LASCELLES

CRITICISM bearing on the pastoral strain in Shakespearian comedy belongs to two widely separated groups: that of the distant past, broadly based, both as to what it asserts and what it takes for granted—which is why I mean to begin with it; and that, more pointed and particular, of the immediate present. It is this which poses a problem for me. When you have been teaching for more years than you care to reckon, a piece of fresh criticism will sometimes make its impact in successive waves. First: 'Why yes, but isn't this what I have been trying to say all this while?' Second (in the voice of conscience): 'Trying is the operative word—when have you succeeded in formulating this idea?' Nevertheless, the conclusion must always be: 'For me, it is never completely uttered until I have said it myself—or said what arises from this encounter of old and new ideas.' Thus, while it is the least I can do, to acknowledge indebtedness (bluntly, for brevity's sake) to a number of writers whose work has appeared of late—notably, in the eighth and eleventh volumes of the annual *Shakespeare Survey*[1]—it is also the most. For it still remains for me to find my own way forward, asking such questions as I can frame, and seeking answers for which I can find words.

Hazlitt prompts the first of these questions, by what he says about Shakespearian comedy. The immediate context is *Twelfth Night*, but I think that his comments on this play apply—and that he would have been willing that they should apply—more widely; at least to include all those of Shakespeare's comedies that are called romantic. 'This,' he says, '. . . is perhaps too good-natured for comedy. . . . It makes us laugh at the follies of mankind, not despise them, and still less bear any ill-will towards them.' And, after contrasting it with the artificial and

---

[1] Cambridge University Press. I must single out for special gratitude Professor Harold Jenkins (on *As You Like It*, in *Shakespeare Survey* 8).

satirical comedy of the Restoration, he proceeds to generalize: 'Shakespeare's comedy is of a pastoral and poetical cast. Folly is indigenous to the soil, and shoots out with native, happy, unchecked luxuriance. Absurdity has every encouragement afforded it; and nonsense has room to flourish in.'[1]

I propose to consider what these conjunctions mean: comedy *but* good-natured; inviting laughter that is free from contempt, and of a pastoral, poetical cast. Why, in the first place, did Hazlitt plant that (implied) *but* between comedy and all these agreeable things—the laughter of sheer enjoyment, poetry, the world of the pastoral?

Perhaps I may be allowed a personal illustration. I happened once to be lecturing on *Henry IV*—to an audience that was, or chose to appear, decidedly non-committal. Therefore I was the more surprised when one member of it—a particularly grave-looking graduate from overseas—joined me as I walked back and told me that he had never really thought Falstaff funny until he listened to me. I replied with proper modesty that it was George Robey he should have heard. No, that was not what he meant. All the literary, all the learned people he had met hitherto had been insistent that comedy was meant to do something beneficial to you—to make you better, not to make you laugh. Now, if this seems far-fetched, let me point out that, according to some eminent scholars and critics, Falstaff *cannot* have been meant to amuse the judicious, since he is merely the traditional figure of Riot misleading Youth—an interpretation which, as Miss Gardner points out, has had an enervating effect on some recent productions of the play, 'in which Falstaff has seemed so oppressed by awareness that he is temptation incarnate that he has hardly had the spirit to present any serious temptation.'[2]

Were we meant to enjoy the rogues and fools of Shakespearian comedy? And does that enjoyment touch hands with liking? (Enjoyment and liking must, surely, go along together in actual life; but I think that they need not in art; we can enjoy the representation of what we by no means like—and that, in most other kinds of comedy, is what we are invited to do.)

Coleridge's theory of comedy may help: he was hardly likely to devise one which would exclude Shakespeare. He calls it 'poetry in unlimited jest'. It entails, he says, 'the apparent abandonment of all definite aim or end, the removal of all bounds in the exercise of the

---

[1] *Characters of Shakespeare's Plays*: 'Twelfth Night'.
[2] Helen Gardner: *The Limits of Literary Criticism* (O.U.P. 1956).

F

mind'. It is (he continues) 'a display of intellectual wealth squandered in the wantonness of sport without an object'.[1]

Now I believe that such comedy as this description comprises asks certain conditions, a particular climate of the imagination. The world in which this pure comic spirit can operate must be at once like and unlike our own. Thus, there are in this world laws of cause and effect; but, against their very nature, they act intermittently. Here, as in our world, you may, if you touch fire, burn your fingers; for it is not a world in which fire never burns, but, rather, one in which it sometimes forgets to burn—or even burns the wrong man, the one who has kept well out of its way. Retribution is not, as in satire, inexorable; the dispenser of justice may be entreated—or may prove absent-minded. The proper consequence of an act is sometimes suspended—now in favour of the fox, now on behalf of the goose. (Suspended only; where would be the sport if all law were annulled?)

Here, a doubt occurs. This is all very well so long as we are concerned with pure comedy: a game in which there is no finality—if the players desist, it is only because they wait for the impulse to renew itself; a country dance tune, whose last phrase is an irresistible invitation to a new beginning. It is natural and reasonable to contrast this 'intellectual wealth squandered in the wantonness of sport' with satire, which closes with a clang—the villain punished, the fools frightened into prudent behaviour. But what are we to make of romantic comedy? It also has its close, much like a resolution of discord in music. Theseus turns back to Athens with the words:

> . . . in the temple, by and by, with us,
> These couples shall eternally be knit.[2]

Moreover, the knitting follows a pattern of poetic justice—or purports to do; we may have to exercise a little kindly forgetfulness in favour of Demetrius—and even of Helena. He was unfaithful before ever the magic juice touched his eyelids; she has made us wonder whether faithfulness is really a virtue. After all, it is Shakespeare's way to overlook shortcomings; and the total impression stands: romantic comedy closes on true love rewarded. But will not its rewards be as alien to 'the abandonment of all definite aim or end', to 'sport without an object', as are the punishments of satire? So there *is* a problem involved in the conjunction of qualities which Hazlitt remarked—a conjunction

---

[1] *Lectures and Notes on Shakespeare*, ed. T. Ashe (1884), p. 188.
[2] *A Midsummer Night's Dream*, IV. i. 186, 7.

peculiarly Shakespearian: comedy; good nature; pastoral—which, for the Elizabethan dramatist, signified first and foremost pastoral romance, a literary species brought from abroad, but naturalized with the good gardener's intuitive skill and boldness. It was (I believe) by way of this very Elizabethan approach to the pastoral way of writing—and thinking, and feeling—that Shakespeare attained what Milton calls 'heart-easing Mirth', and Johnson 'the greatest end of comedy—making an audience merry'. For the qualities which set Shakespearian comedy apart from all other kinds are Elizabethan qualities, though raised to a higher power. The men who were born not far from the middle of the sixteenth century and grew up in the sixties, seventies and eighties, rediscovered the lost land of pastoral on their own frontiers, recognizing that its language and customs were not strange. This discovery, like a fine early morning, was too good to last; it had to give way to the sultry brilliance of Jacobean romantic fashions; but Shakespeare never wholly relinquished his vision—even his last plays, which have provoked such a variety of explanations, ranging from boredom to theophany, are best understood in the light of this pastoral morning.

To support this proposition I should need the space of a sizeable book. For example, why 'lost'? Why 'rediscovered'? I can only say that what I assume to be the true significance of pastoral must have been overlaid by the use as a school textbook of Mantuan's Eclogues—satiric diatribes, attributed to shepherds, but resembling the original pastoral eclogues no more than a lecturer on drama resembles a dramatist—and seven worlds away from pastoral romance. What, then, was recovered, and where, and in what form? To answer this I shall have to ask your patience while I trace one tradition of pastoral writing a little way back towards its source.

Pastoral romance (as the Elizabethans practised it) derives—at some distance—from those long, leisurely, extravagant prose tales written in the decline of the ancient world, among the Greek colonies in the islands and on the farther shore of the Mediterranean. One alone can truly be called pastoral—*Daphnis and Chloe*; yet all had something to contribute to the tradition of pastoral romance. Revived in the Renaissance, given currency in Latin and vernacular translations, they gained an influence out of all proportion to their merits, and took new life from better men than their original authors. (So it may happen that some vigorous future writer will derive inspiration from this or that group of minor novels which to our eyes shimmer only with the phosphorescence of decay—and a still more distant critic will wonder what he found in them.) Intricately patterned stories—the theme of love prevailing in Italy and France, of chivalry in Spain—captured the imagination of courtly audiences and were presently popularized. We, of course, expected to have it all ways: hence our mingling, on the stage and in print, of conventions proper to tales of both love and chivalry, to exotic and to homely narrative art. There was indeed some warrant for this boldness. I count it significant that three seminal pieces of Renaissance story-telling—Boiardo's *Orlando Innamorato*, Monte-mayor's *Diana*, and Sidney's *Arcadia*—were left each at the death of its author in a state to invite completion. For such romance, with its hint of improvisation to please a particular audience, seems to engage our imagination in such a way that, if the narrator cannot finish, it becomes an office of friendship to dream out his dream for him. (Imagine Walter Scott dying in his early thirties, with *The Lay of the Last Minstrel* incomplete—who but would wish to carry it further?) The *Arcadia*, which Sidney had relinquished in the midst of revision, owed its ending, as the Elizabethans knew it, partly to his sister. It has the air of an unfinished building which loving care and some regard for the original design have made habitable, and indeed elegant, but which still guards the secret of that full purpose which was growing in the builder's mind even as he worked. For this reason, and also because it has lately been studied in particular relation to Shakespeare, I prefer to use for my principal illustration that other romance which may have been Sidney's initial inspiration, and was surely one of Shakespeare's: the *Diana* of Montemayor. About a year after its first appearance in print, its author was killed, leaving his slight but intricate tale with some threads still to be tied up—and therefore (like Boiardo's) at the mercy of continuators. What they added tended to stick, and, by the time that an English translation appeared,[1] Montemayor's pretty little book had become a bulky folio.

How am I to describe in a few words the total impression left in my own mind by the *Diana*—let alone its intrinsic character? If I assert—where I should rather suggest, substantiate and so persuade—it is because I am forced to take the nearest way to a place which, when I reach it, will be no more than my point of departure. First, then: never believe those travel-weary historians of literature who tell you that this romance is unreadable—nor that its English dress is an ungainly make-shift. The translator, Bartholomew Young, has been hardly used. His original, like most of its kind, was a medley of prose and verse, and the

---

[1] In 1598—it had, however, been completed in 1583.

ill luck of inclusion in an Elizabethan miscellany has made some of his songs familiar; for them I will not enter the smallest plea. But his prose, which is often tart and fresh, and never insipid, has come to us only in those well-meaning, insidious, unavoidable extracts called Shakespearian sources—there must be few notable romances of his age which Shakespeare did not know and lay under contribution. But, here, as so often, virtue resides in the whole, not in the part he can be shown to have used.

The pattern of the stories which (folded one within another) compose this whole can be intimated thus: A loves B, but B loves C—who loves nobody until, mistaking D for E, and being mistaken by G for H, he endeavours to extricate himself by feigning love for A, supposing her to be—well, you see how it goes, and with no more reason than that, as Puck says, 'Cupid is a knavish lad.' All this is set in a world where we may reckon with some three or four *constants*. The pastoral region is a place of refuge, and the dominant symbol of relief from danger, weariness, want, every ill, is water. By stream or spring forlorn lovers may linger, recounting their former vicissitudes, until the completion of a prescribed cycle, the fulfilment of some oracular prediction, brings lost opportunity round again, and they—wiser than before —reach out and take it. Thus, time has a strange circular movement; it accords with the rhythm of the revolving seasons. True, the pastoral poet has often lamented that, while nature renews itself, man goes his way once for all. (This is, of course, mere human make-believe—the pretence that it is last year's rose or nightingale come back to us.) In pastoral romance, however, man may sometimes share in this self-renewal. It is as though, tilting the hour-glass (a much more vivid symbol than our clock), he could give himself, not the next hour, but the past hour over again. And so, surprisingly, the oracle, which in Greek myths of the prime had signified the inescapability of a man's destiny, and had usually been charged with tragic implications, has now, in the silver age and in tales deriving from it, assumed an almost contrary character and become a symbol of the second chance. In such a world, the shepherd boy may well pipe as though he should never be old, and the parents of a lost child make light of the years of waiting.

Here is another constant in such romance: loss and recovery—identity itself is very easily lost or mislaid, to be reassumed when the time is ripe. (The deserted girl who seeks redress in boy's disguise is much older than the need to provide fitting parts for boy actors.) Where none is known until he chooses to disclose himself, the odds are strongly in

favour of an unknown champion proving a woman—or, if a man, one
alienated from his rights, or his very name. And, where many do not
know themselves for what they are, a shepherdess may well find herself
a queen, or an outlaw the heir to a kingdom.

So far, you might truly say, the characteristics I have described could
belong equally to romance or pastoral—and indeed these are not very
easily distinguished in their Elizabethan forms. But there is this difference. Whereas, in romance, the final pattern is composed of rewards
and punishments, ideally distributed, pastoral has a variant of its own.
Here innocence is a protection, and contentment, set high among the
virtues, is in a special sense its own reward, since the contented mind
receives no injury from the blows of adverse fortune. An ideal world
—yes; but not the world of enervating daydream.

I have now in my hands the main threads of my argument, and can
gather illustrations (particularly from the *Diana*), and weave in Shakespearian analogies. Montemayor's story is, as you will have inferred,
too cobweb-like to bear retelling, but one strand may be followed to
its conclusion. Felismena, whose birth was attended by dark sayings, is
deserted by her lover, follows him in boy's dress (as Julia follows
Proteus) and serves him in his courtship of Celia (as Viola serves
Orsino). Parted from him once more, she takes to arms and, champion-
ing the oppressed, finds herself in the midst of a shepherd community.
After many exchanges of tale and song among these pastoral people
gathered round a spring, all of them resolve on visiting the wise lady
Felicia and the temple of Diana. For some lovers of small consequence,
Felicia has magical remedies, not unlike Oberon's. To another, the man
she mourns is restored; his death, which she believed herself to have
witnessed, was an eye-cheating trick—one very common in the Greek
romances. For Felismena, however, according to the oracular Felicia,
further trials and greater happiness are reserved. Setting out on her
quest again, she comes among other shepherds—gentle, dark-skinned,
and speaking Portuguese, her native tongue, and Montemayor's likewise, though he wrote in Castilian. On an island in the river by whose
banks they live, she rescues a hard-pressed knight. He is, of course, her
lost love, and Felicia has only to give him the water of remembrance to
bring about a perfect reconciliation. How much of all this (my general
propositions and particular instances) may we, without ever labouring
a point, relate to Shakespeare? I suggest that refuge among unworldly
people and resort to a benevolent oracular power recur significantly in
his pastoral comedy.

When Le Beau, in *As You Like It*, warns Orlando of the enmity of the usurping Duke, he is to all appearance acting out of character. Shakespeare can be very peremptory with one of his minor *dramatis personae* if he wants something done and there is nobody else at hand to do it. But the words in which this apparently shallow and time-serving courtier takes leave of the man whose life he has saved at some risk to his own are even more surprising than his action:

> Hereafter, in a better world than this,
> I shall desire more love and knowledge of you.[1]

And what else can this 'better world' be than Arden? And what is Arden but a pastoral region where lost children are found, parted lovers reunited, dispossessed men come to their own again, and repentance and reconciliation grow like the leaves on the trees? To support this I must ask your patience while I reach back and draw in yet another strand of argument.

I believe, first, that exotic myths will most readily take possession of minds familiar from childhood with story-patterns that in some way resemble them; and, secondly, that the English counterpart of that pastoral world in which

> earthly things made even
> Atone together[2]

was a legendary forest: Sherwood Forest, ruled by the gentle outlaw. It is evident that Shakespeare was familiar with the Robin Hood ballads and pageants and popular plays—these may have been the 'Whitsun pastorals' Perdita recalled—and the recollections he cherished of them seem to have been pleasant. The references to them are, it is true, given to disreputable characters or spoken in jest; but so are those to all figures of popular, native story in his plays, and this I take to be no more than a concession to the clever young men in the audience. It is certain at least that an undercurrent of allusion to the dispossessed man and the gentle outlaw runs through no fewer than three plays: *The Two Gentlemen of Verona*, *As You Like It* and *Cymbeline*.

The first is a mere sketch: bold, even careless. Valentine, 'in disgrace with fortune and men's eyes',[3] is welcomed by the outlaws; he is the very man they have been waiting for, and he undertakes to lead them on condition that none shall offer violence to women or mere travellers. (So Robin Hood in the ballad claims:

---

[1] I. ii. 301, 2.   [2] v. iv. 116, 7.   [3] Sonnet 29.

> I never hurt woman in all my life,
> Nor man in woman's company.)

He muses on life in the forest, as Duke Senior will teach his followers to do in Arden. And, again as in Arden, when the end comes it will compass the three conditions necessary to a happy ending in Shakespearian comedy: truth will be revealed; those on whom this revelation casts an ugly light will repent; the oppressed and the oppressor will be reconciled. Indeed, Valentine has but to find his enemy at his mercy to forgive him freely. Even the outlaws turn out to be 'men endu'd with worthy qualities'—or so Valentine tells the Duke.[1] Had he forgotten their original confessions, or did he claim that his brief rule had reformed them? Perhaps the forest had worked its magic.

Now in *As You Like It* we find such a strange mixture of the old Robin Hood legends and the newly rediscovered pastoral romance that I must remind you briefly of its origins. The oldest to survive is the *Tale of Gamelyn*: a lay (longer and more circumstantial than a ballad; more downright and homely than a romance) belonging to the second quarter of the fourteenth century, but, from the fifteenth onwards, attributed to Chaucer; shining, therefore, with a borrowed lustre. Rough it certainly is, probably representing an early phase in the development of that legend whose outcome is the cycle of Robin Hood ballads. It is a tale of rights lost and recovered; taken by cunning, regained by strength. The youngest of three brothers (hardy, bold, but something of a simpleton) is cheated of his due by the eldest, and calls into the balance against him other simple, wronged men. Their fortunes swing to and fro; but right finally gets the upper hand in that forest world where the outlaws have established a rule of their own. They have been driven from their homes by oppression; and, even if they are not quite so gentle as the foresters of later tradition, they know how to maintain order: that is, they are ruled by a king, not by force, fraud or fortune. Before him Gamelyn is summoned to give an account of himself—together with Adam, his brother's steward, who has helped him to escape, and shared his wanderings and hardships.

> Than seide the maister kyng of outlawes,
> 'What seeke ye, younge men under woode-schawes?'
> Gamelyn answerde the kyng with his croune,
> 'He moste needes walke in woode that may not walke in towne.'[2]

---

[1] v. iv. 153.   [2] Ed. Skeat (Oxford, 1926), ll, 669–72.

At the end, it is by summoning his friends the outlaws that he redresses the balance of justice—in an episode suggesting the outlines of a popular cartoon: the poacher on the bench, the squire and parson in the dock. And, with a flourish of legality, the King of England himself makes Gamelyn and Adam justices of the peace, and hangs all their enemies.

Presently, the Robin Hood ballads bear this story some way down towards the rich lowland pastures of romance. There, the knight who has fallen into the clutches of the Church (by bankruptcy, not heresy) wanders gently and disconsolately about the forest, until the outlaws (rather by show of strength than outright violence) regain his lands for him. (It is strange to consider that, when we reach the broad plains of Elizabethan romantic comedy, the Church—once the most powerful landowner in all England—will be reduced to a few friars and hermits who offer sensible advice, perform convenient but slightly irregular marriage ceremonies and convert usurping dukes in forest glades.) The ballads vary, of course, in tone; but their general tendency is towards a softening of the Gamelyn story, and this continues into Elizabethan drama, and probably the Robin Hood pageants also—which, with a touch of sentimental archaism, glorified the old English long-bow while it was falling out of use as a weapon of war. (Contrariwise, that mercenary soldier, Falstaff, carries a pistol—long before it was invented.)

Lodge's *Rosalynde*, the immediate precursor and substantial source of *As You Like It*, is a gay and graceful mixture of the old stories of Sherwood justice with the new, fashionable, pastoral romances. Lodge, an adventurous reader, was familiar with *Gamelyn*, Sidney's *Arcadia* (probably in manuscript) and, we may be sure, popular versions of the Robin Hood legend. And he had his share of the authentic Elizabethan magic, 'gilding pale streams with heavenly alchemy'. He has caught the happy timelessness of pastoral; any of his characters might say with Orlando: 'There's no clock in the forest.'[1] It has become the realm of 'love in idleness'. Replacing the 'wife good and fair' whom Gamelyn married in the last line but four—and a line is all she is allowed—princesses and shepherdesses (the princesses disguised as shepherdesses, the shepherdesses as courtly in their bearing as the princesses) await the approach of their suitors, sonnet in hand. And these are better love-poems than Orlando's. Was it Shakespeare's whim, or was it his wisdom, to give us the very poetry of love—and not allow so much as one

[1] III. ii. 321.

of his lovers to write a respectable piece of verse? Perhaps his motive
was akin to Chaucer's, when he took for himself the Tale of Sir Thopas.

These unreckoned riches of pastoral leisure belong rather to narrative
than to drama, and I think there are signs that Shakespeare recognized
this as a problem confronting him. Orlando, though he is driven from
his brother's house within the narrow compass of the play, is indeed
the lost child of traditional romance: he has been reared as though a
foundling; nevertheless 'he's gentle, never schooled and yet learned,
full of noble device'.[1] Then, time-inconsistencies have been apparent
to the critics, and by some set down to revision:[2] the rightful Duke's
banishment seems to be news when Charles tells it to Oliver—yet, by
Celia's account, it happened when she was too young to plead for her
cousin; and the Duke himself speaks of his forest life as though it had
endured the season's change. Presently, the usurping Duke gives Oliver
a year in which to find his brother, though our impression of the play's
duration is a few fleeting days. (The change from winter to summer, in
a recent production, was—to my thinking—an innovation enjoyable
while fresh, but not fit to establish a new theatrical tradition). Is it
fanciful to suggest that Shakespeare, when he began to write, had
hardly counted the cost of the alterations he must make and, if he later
noticed discrepancies, did not care to efface them, preferring a *past-
indefinite* tense? The passage of the seasons, especially as it is reflected in
the talk of the older men (Duke Senior and Adam), signifies an acceptance of the terms of mortal life:

> my age is as a lusty winter,
> Frosty, but kindly.[3]

The condition of this acceptance of change is the contented mind. In
Arden, love fosters its own peculiar impatience, but those who are
free 'fleet the time carelessly, as they did in the golden world'.[4] Their
contentment extends even to little things: Jaques' failure to disturb the
equanimity of any but the lovers—and *they* give as good as they get. I
suspect that a small illustration of this has been swept away in the process of tidying the text, and I would plead for its restoration. Who
should sing the third stanza of 'Under the greenwood tree'? Jaques
offers it to Amiens who, according to the First Folio, agrees to sing
and launches into it with the words, 'Thus it goes.' But the subsequent
Folios and modern editions and (so far as I can tell) stage tradition have

---

[1] I. i. 175.   [2] Notably by the New Cambridge editors.
[3] II. iii. 52.   [4] I. i. 127.

transferred those three words, together with the stanza, to Jaques—
only the New Cambridge editors offering a hesitant defence of the
Folio text in a note. Now, the actor who plays Jaques is rarely a singer,
and the stanza is usually declaimed to a little audience (Amiens and
anyone else who can be mustered) with such acrimony that Amiens'
subsequent question loses its point. But, let Jaques put a paper into
Amiens' hand, and let *him* sing innocently this parody of his own two
stanzas, asking with unruffled good humour, at the close, 'What is
Ducdame?'—and there is some reason for Jaques' exasperated retort:
''Tis a Greek invocation to call fools into a circle.'[1] The satirist is
baffled by the world of comedy.

Unexpectedness ranks high among the distinctive qualities of *As You
Like It*. The play tingles with questions. I deny altogether the claim that
it is a satire on pastoral convention. True, it returns an echo to the
pastoral idea; but the tone of this echo has not the heart-searching
melancholy of Raleigh's:

> If all the world and love were young,
> And truth in every Sheepheards tongue,
> These pretty pleasures might me move,
> To live with thee, and be thy love——

nor the scorching irony of Donne's:

> Come live with mee, and bee my love,
> And wee will some new pleasures prove. . . .

It is the tone rather of a brisk challenge—one to which the sequel may
yet be: 'Pass friend, and all's well;' and, if the pastoral idea is challenged, that is because it *is* an idea, a pattern for living laid up in the
mind, and such ideas are in full flight, and the people of the play in full
cry after them, all up and down the glades of Arden. Everything is set
off by contrasts; and the alternations are so swift that we might as
well try to tell the colour of a field of ripening barley combed by the
wind as capture any of the successive moods by definition. If the
idealism of the Duke is called in question by Jaques, why, so is the
cynicism of Jaques by the Duke. Rosalind, herself 'many fathom deep
in love' and pursued by Celia's keen raillery, undertakes to turn every
convention of love-making inside-out; and against her romantic
friendship with Celia is set her astringent treatment of Phoebe. None
of the disputants has the last word; but, with the possible exception of

[1] II. v. 48–58.

Jaques, none of them wants it. The pursuer lets the quarry escape, sure that he will not go far, for fear of ending the pursuit. This is indeed Coleridge's 'intellectual wealth squandered in the wantonness of sport without an object'. How is it to be reconciled with the need inherent in romance, to resolve all discords in a full close?

In the first place, it is necessary that all the characters should go back where they belong. Do not quarrel with this; it is required by the pattern of loss and recovery. Dekker confuses this issue when—turning the story of patient Griselda into a play—he makes her father's home, to which she returns bringing her children, a place of pastoral felicity, where the loveliest of all his songs is sung. Only her brother, a spoiled scholar and a character of Dekker's own invention, is ignorant of what Griselda knows:

> . . . adversity
> Dwells still with them that dwell with misery,
> But mild content hath eas'd me of that yoke;
> Patience hath borne the bruise, and I the stroke.[1]

Thus, when the story is pulled back into its course, we are haunted by remembrance of his pastoral world and would be glad to return to it. But the ring which is the proper symbol of pastoral romance is not rounded into completion until each of the characters has fulfilled the destiny to which he, or she, was born; and, to this end, the Duke must reassume his office—in a court where (as Professor Jenkins points out)[2] goodness has been restored and Jaques' occupation's gone, Rosalind must reign after him with Orlando, the dispossessed man come to his own again, and benignant powers must operate.

Now, I freely admit that Hymen is not a very impressive counterpart even of the *romantic* oracle. Nevertheless, I find it significant that Shakespeare should have employed, for the ending of *As You Like It*, these three agents: a symbolical figure, speaking such archaic verse as he gives to Jupiter and the ghosts in *Cymbeline*, Juno and Ceres in *The Tempest*; a mood of half-belief in Rosalind's tale of her uncle the magician ('most profound in his art and yet not damnable'); and a pattern of riddling stipulations, propounded by Rosalind in her character as *magician's boy*, to which the lovers must subscribe—and which, being fulfilled, resolve all discords.

The oracle in *Cymbeline* has proved a stumbling-block; and—not to

---

[1] *Patient Grissill* (attributed to Dekker, Chettle and Haughton), v. ii.
[2] *Shakespeare Survey* 8, p. 45.

pursue this question further than our purpose requires—it performs its function awkwardly: it bears no intelligible relation in time to those confessions by which the skein of the plot will presently be unravelled, nor any in place to that ideal country which Imogen has found and lost again, where outlaws offer refuge to the oppressed, and recognize an imposter, even in a true man's clothes. And yet I believe the use of this device to be in keeping with those pastoral intimations—with Imogen's wish, before ever she set out on the journey which led to the outlaw's cave, that she and Posthumus had been herdsmen's children; with the mountain-bred boy's victory over the court-bred ruffler and braggart. Suppose that Shakespeare was finding his way back to a source of imaginative fulfilment which had charmed him some years earlier, but was cumbered with too weighty and intricate a story, and had to rest content with something short of his full purpose.

Within a year or so, he recognized what he sought, hidden away in that old-fashioned and unprepossessing little tale, Greene's *Pandosto*. It had something he needed: an oracle which, as a source of infallible truth, could be credited with authority, even sanctity; which would inevitably punish the unbeliever and yet—so far had tragedy given ground to romance—let punishment teach repentance, and repentance cherish hope; and shepherds, the traditional guardians of that place of refuge in which hope might be realized.

To show why I believe that *The Winter's Tale* transcends the models on which it is framed by obtaining their ultimate purpose, I shall have to ask a question which must sound very simple and matter-of-fact: in those ancient tragic stories which turn upon oracular prediction, what would have happened if the people whom it threatens had taken no notice of it? If King Acrisius, warned that he would be killed by his grandson, had not imprisoned his daughter, nor, when her child was born, put them both to sea in an open boat, Perseus would not have caused the death of an unknown man, and found himself the slayer of his grandfather. For the point of these stories seems to be that it is a man's efforts to avert his fate which fasten it upon him. We are therefore (I take it) to understand that a man so visited can no more desist from struggling than could an animal caught in a trap. Does Shakespearian pastoral comedy shirk this knowledge, or see beyond it?

All I can now attempt is to point out some ways in which oracular truth—absolute truth regarding past, present, even future events—operates in *The Winter's Tale*. Notice, first, that Leontes no sooner acknowledges his suspicions than he sends to the oracle, supposing that he will obtain confirmation of them—a departure from *Pandosto*, in which the Queen asks that Apollo be consulted. Next, the crucial scene representing the messengers on their way back from 'the Isle of Delphos' is set as prelude to Hermione's trial: in some twenty lines it conveys an extraordinary impression of serenity and sanctity. Cleomenes and Dion are unshakeably convinced of the truth of the sealed statement they carry; convinced, also, that it will clear the Queen.[1] It is evidently established that, while we remain in Sicily—that is, until the end of Act III, Scene ii—things are what they seem, to us and to everyone in the play, *except* Leontes.

Now, if I may revert to my simple question: what would have happened if Leontes had accepted the truth thus delivered? The prediction that 'the king shall live without an heir' would have been inexplicable; indeed, at the time when it was entrusted to the messengers, Leontes would still have a wife and two children with him. But, possessed by the insane conviction that he and oracular truth are ranged together against false seeming, he does not wait for the revelation: he condemns the child he supposes Polixenes' to death. It is Shakespeare's way to accept character as the ultimate source of event. Therefore, when truth is revealed and he finds himself standing alone, Leontes is already committed to the utterance of his final, fatal blasphemy: 'There is no truth at all i' the oracle.'[2] Immediately and inexorably, the wheels begin to turn: word comes of Mamilius's death, and he interprets it as divine retribution:

> Apollo's angry; and the heavens themselves
> Do strike at my injustice.

Paulina's 'this news is mortal to the Queen' threatens complete fulfilment of the prediction, and Leontes' public confession and vow of amendment are answered by her passionate cry that repentance prolonged beyond the span of mortal life would not atone. Nothing further is said of reparation, nor is the oracle's stipulation, 'if that which is lost be not found', remembered again until the very eve of finding. It is mere critical officiousness to demand an oracular injunction against second marriage; Leontes has accepted the full implications of his misdeed.

Presently, a speaker only less august than the oracle intervenes. Time, in appropriately archaic verse, explains his own function as composed of contrarieties:

[1] III. i.   [2] III. ii. 141.

> . . . it is in my power
> To o'erthrow law, and in one self-born hour
> To plant and o'erwhelm custom.[1]

He is alike founder, destroyer, renewer. He cannot (in the agonized words of Lucrece) 'return and make amends'; but, given time and kindly shelter, the seed will yield next year's harvest, and we have but now seen the lost child received into the pastoral refuge.

> I turn my glass . . .
> . . . but let Time's news
> Be known when 'tis brought forth.

From now on, growth proceeds underground: things will not be what they seem; honest characters (Paulina and Camillo) will be involved in a tissue of subterfuge; the truth, if it is told, will be uttered uncomprehendingly—as when Polixenes tests Perdita with gardeners' talk of crossing strains, and she maintains that like must mate with like. One certainty alone holds: in the pastoral world, the promise of the oracle will be fulfilled as surely as were its threats, and the lost will be found.

What, then, does this pastoral world signify? Not 'wish-fulfilment' —a new name for an old misuse of the imagination. *That* requires obliteration of the boundary which separates the imagined from the actual. But the world of true pastoral is always known for a country of the mind, to be attained only by force of the imagination. This, doubtless, holds good for all great imaginative story-telling (whether cast in narrative or in dramatic form). Pastoral fiction, however, has a distinction of its own to observe, and this may best be indicated in terms of time and space. Tragedy shakes us with its tremendous *here* and *now* (no matter how remote its subject). History (Shakespearian history, at least) makes a sharp impact of *there* and *then*—the sun rising on St. Crispin's day over the field of Agincourt. But pastoral romance is, and must always remain, *elsewhere* and *some other time*. Thus, though it is simply and immediately enjoyable, in a kind and degree beyond that of other story-telling, it no more invites us to identify ourselves with its happy people than the rainbow invites us to climb. In its realm, Shakespearian comedy is free to flourish. Its happy endings are not flattering fantasies, but tokens of a fulfilment to be imagined only, not hoped for. In this fulfilment, the partial and piecemeal returns and

[1] Prologue to Act IV.

renewals which life grants us are capable of completion; not only does the future stretch before us, with its assured rhythm of the seasons and the generations—the past itself is no longer irretrievably lost. Not Perdita alone comes back, but Hermione also.

6

THE HEIGHTS AND THE DEPTHS:
A SCENE FROM 'KING LEAR'

by HARRY LEVIN

PEAKING of depths and heights, I hope that my title has not provoked a wider curiosity than can be sharply focused by my sub-
title. I shall not be talking about the periods of Shakespeare's
development, or looking for his autobiography in his dramaturgy, or
assuming—with Edward Dowden and others—that he wrote his
tragedies out of some private grief and later, when he felt mellower,
turned back to comedies. The moods and changes that continue to
interest us today are not those which we attribute to the artist in person, but those which we experience through his art. Its characteristic
transitions from splendour to torment, from O *altitudo* to *de profundis*,
seem to accord with a basic principle of tragic vicissitude. What I
propose to discuss, in some contextual detail, is one extremely specific
illustration of that principle, a text often cited but seldom re-ex-
amined, probably because our modes of stagecraft have strategically
changed.

'Gain Shakespeare's effects by Shakespeare's means when you can.'
Such was the sound advice of Granville-Barker for the modern interpretation of Shakespeare. However, there are times when the theatrical
interpreter cannot use Shakespearian means, even though the academic
interpreter may know how a certain Shakespearian effect was accomplished. We cannot cast a boy as Cleopatra, though Shakespeare did;
very few actresses are up to the part in our time, even after a long and
respectable career in the theatre. Shakespeare would never have been
able to spread his drama of *Antony and Cleopatra* through forty-two
scenes, crossing and recrossing the Mediterranean, had he been forced
to compress it within a proscenium, relying upon a succession of back-
drops or a revolving stage. Working within an adaptable but permanent structure—mainly a forestage flanked by adequate exits or

entrances, backed by some sort of curtained area and an upper balcony
—Shakespeare achieved unlimited effects by limited means.

These were primarily verbal. To one with his gift for turning words
into pictures, the absence of scenery was a stimulus to the pictorial
imagination. Hence Shakespeare did his own scene-painting, verbally.
'This castle hath a pleasant seat,' says Duncan, praising the air; and
Banquo goes on to enlarge our mental picture of Glamis Castle with
his lyrical speech about the temple-haunting martlet, the pendent bed,
and the heaven's breath. This delicate imagery has the quality of repose
in painting, or so Sir Joshua Reynolds has commented. Repose indeed!
for here the gentle Duncan will all too soon be taking his last repose;
before morning that heavenly courtyard will be all the drunken porter
fancies, when he envisages it as a gateway to hell; and we shall have
been transported, as it were, from the heights to the depths.

Shakespeare used no programmes, and does not seem to have put
much faith in locality-boards.

> Alack! the night comes on, and the bleak winds
> Do sorely ruffle,

says Gloucester, thereby setting the time and place at the end of the
Second Act of *King Lear*:

> for many miles about
> There's scarce a bush.

And with a clatter of doors being closed and shutters banged, the clang-
ing of gates and other sound effects which are actually verbal, the stage
is set—that vastest and barest of stages—for the storm scenes of Act III,
which alternate between the indoors and the open air, and gain the
effect of wind and rain by means of the old King's efforts to outscorn
them. Granville-Barker's preface to *King Lear* is a practical refutation
of A. C. Bradley's influential and paradoxical argument that, though it
may be Shakespeare's greatest achievement, it is too huge for the stage.
This, in turn, was a philosophical rationalization of Charles Lamb's
opinion that performance was unbearable. Now Lamb was more of a
theatre-goer than Bradley, but he could only have witnessed the play in
productions which were cruelly cut and badly adulterated. He therefore
concluded that the spectacle of an old man, tottering about in a storm
with a stick, could only be painful or disgusting.

Other critics have recoiled more strongly from that terrifying scene
where Gloucester's eyes are put out *coram populo*, not behind the scenes

as in *Oedipus Rex*, but in full view of the audience and in complete violation of classical decorum. It is a deliberate and definitive breach, a more flagrant gesture of indecorum than the Elizabethan intermixture of hornpipes with funerals, or the abasement of kings to the level of clowns in the companionship of Lear and his Fool. Yet even that horrendous act has a certain propriety as a literal climax to a whole train of metaphors involving eyesight and suggesting moral perception, the lack of which is so fatal for Gloucester and Lear. None so blind as those who have eyes and see not. Their eyes may be open, but—like those of Lady Macbeth in her sleep-walking scene—their sense is shut. This visual metaphor is generalized into *hybris*, the pride that goes before a tragic fall, with the self-denunciation of Antony:

> But when we in our viciousness grow hard—
> O misery on't!—the wise gods seel our eyes;
> In our own filth drop our clear judgments; make us
> Adore our errors; laugh at's while we strut
> To our confusion.

When we become too intimately involved in the tragic experience, we tend to feel pain and disgust as Lamb did, rather than pity and fear. *Catharsis*, if it clears the mind through those classic emotions, does so by placing the object at an aesthetic distance from the spectator. He must, of course, apprehend it through sympathy, empathy, or some sort of identification with it. But he also achieves a sense of perspective through his detachment from it. Recent dramatic theory would stress this latter stage, which Bertolt Brecht terms estrangement, as the most important aspect of the emotional process. But long ago Lucretius evoked the intellectual pleasure of looking out on troubled waters when one was safe ashore, of looking down on the violent conflicts of men from the heights of philosophy. Tragedy presents such knowledge, not in philosophic abstraction but in concrete exemplification. Thus, though it cries to us out of the depths, it offers us a way of temporarily detaching ourselves from the human predicament, and rising above those situations in which it has vicariously involved us.

The example for which I should like to claim your particular attention is neither the pitiful involvement of Lear in the storm nor the terrible blinding of Gloucester. It is a subsequent and incidental episode, the sixth scene of Act IV, a curiously didactic scene best known for its purple passage describing Dover Cliff. How near we really come to Dover Cliff is a moot question, as I shall try to show in my attempt to recover an unique effect which could only have been attained through Shakespearian means. Elsewhere in drama it has certain precedents and analogies, but none of them comes very close to the matter at hand. In the *Plutus* of Aristophanes, the others threaten to throw the blind god over a precipice, and the threat is averted when he reveals his name. In the repertory of Japanese Kabuki, the dance-drama *Shakkyo* concerns an old lion who pushes a young one off a cliff as a kind of test: by climbing back, the cub proves his manhood—or, rather, his lionhood.

That would seem to be the normal relationship between the two generations, father and son. Shakespeare reverses it, when Edmund accuses Edgar of maintaining that 'the father should be as ward to the son'. The accusation will come true ironically, when the disguised Edgar leads the blinded Gloucester. 'In this play,' Dame Edith Sitwell has aptly observed, 'we see the upheaval of all Nature, the reversal of all histories.' Tragedy always seems to hinge upon a reversal, or peripety. Here a peripety is the starting-point, when the King reverses his traditional role by stepping down from the throne. As the tragedy broadens, moving out of the realm of history into the sphere of nature, it sets off a series of further reversals. The antagonism between crabbed age and flaming youth, always a latent tension in Shakespeare's plays, breaks into overt conflict in *King Lear*. It was implicit in classical comedy, to be sure, and terribly explicit in the dire prophecy of Matthew: 'And brother shall deliver up brother to death, and the father his child: and children shall rise up against parents, and cause them to be put to death.'

This abrogation of the most fundamental commitments, straining family ties beyond endurance and turning simple affections into complex hatreds, is still a major source of power in literature. Filial ingratitude is an obsessive theme with Proust, just as parricide is with Dostoevsky. Like the sons of old Karamazov, Edgar and Edmund incarnate the good and evil of their father's character. Science, natural philosophy, 'the wisdom of nature can reason it thus and thus, yet nature finds itself scourged by the sequent effects', the superstitious Gloucester laments at the outset, anxious to blame his fate upon the stars. The worst of the many symptoms of upheaval that he enumerates is 'the bond cracked between son and father'. In Gloucester's own case, it is 'son against father', though he suspects the wrong son as it turns out. In the King's case, it is 'father against child', and Gloucester underlines the parallel. Shakespeare never made bolder use of the double plot than when he matched the dynastic struggle of the main plot with its domestic counterpart, the Gloucester underplot. To take a *donnée* so exceptional, to hit upon so unheard-of a set of circumstances and double them, was to call the entire moral order into question, as A. W. Schlegel pointed out.

The story in outline harks back, far beyond the old play that Shakespeare adapted, through chronicle and legend, to the mounds of British prehistory and the fens of Druidical myth. But Shakespeare, shrewd folklorist that he was, found the same archetype at work in the most fashionable book of romantic fiction among his contemporaries, Sir Philip Sidney's *Arcadia*. Two heroes of that romance, in the course of their princely adventures, had encountered the blind King of Paphlagonia begging his dutiful son to lead him to headlong death from the top of a rock because, as he put it, 'I cannot fall worse than I am.' From the doleful speeches of father and son, it emerged that a bastard son and brother had betrayed them both through his 'unnatural dealings'—a protesting phrase which Gloucester echoes at the moment when the two plots first come together in the play. The interpolated narrative ends in a battle and a reinstatement, with the blind King dying joyfully and the rightful heir forgiving his perfidious half-brother.

Sidney devotes a single chapter to this minor encounter; yet he tells us it is 'worthy to be remembered for the unused examples therein, as well of true natural goodnes, as of wretched ungratefulnesse'. Edgar and Edmund, then, are exemplary figures, models of filial conduct, for better and worse. The worse of the two has an obvious dramatic advantage. It is always easier to portray an effectual villain than a young man of simple-minded goodwill. Some of Milton's critics have sympathized more with his Satan than with his Son of God. Yet the title-page of the First Quarto leaves no doubt as to who, after Lear himself, is the male protagonist: who is, so to speak, the *jeune premier*. It reads in part: '*With the unfortunate life of Edgar, sonne and heire to the Earle of Gloster, and his sullen and assumed humor of Tom of Bedlam.*' Instead of remaining just a nice young man, rather pallid and timid, Edgar is allowed to rival Shakespeare's dynamic villains by assuming a dangerous and colourful role.

Edmund has played his part from the beginning, though he already looks toward a *dénouement* of some sort when he summons Edgar from hiding: 'and pat he comes, like the catastrophe of the old comedy'. Even while Edmund is soliloquizing, he is rehearsing his initial interview with his half-brother, and the notes he sings—*mi contra fa*—significantly form the forbidden interval known as *diabolus in musica*. His

own 'cue', as it happens, will become Edgar's: 'a sigh like Tom o'
Bedlam'. But Edgar, at this point, is no less credulous than their father.
With Gloucester he falls into Edmund's trap, is suspected of parricidal
intentions, and proscribed as an outlaw. In his fugitive soliloquy, he
determines

> To take the basest and most poorest shape
> That ever penury, in contempt of man,
> Brought near to beast.

He will disguise himself, paradoxically, by taking off his clothes and
exposing himself to the elements. 'With presented nakedness', when
we next see him, he will be attempting to

>   outface
> The winds and persecutions of the sky.

And Edgar seems to anticipate the storm, even as Lear seems to conjure
it up with his imprecations of blast and fog.

As Edgar goes on to describe the role of Poor Tom, we can understand why it made him so popular on the Elizabethan stage. But,
though it is quasi-comic, we can scarcely regard it as comic relief;
rather, with its vagrant grotesquerie, it intensifies the tragic pathos.
Those Bedlam beggars were harmless madmen released from their
lunatic asylum, the notorious Hospital of St. Mary's of Bethlehem in
London. Wandering aimlessly about the countryside, with their teeth
chattering from exposure and their bare flesh lacerated by self-torture,
they besought the stranger's alms with their prayers or curses. Edgar
not only dresses the part; he fills it in with apt charms and exorcisms
and brilliant bits of histrionic improvisation. He even seems to have
worked up the names of devils from a current theological pamphlet:
Turleygod, Flibbertigibbet, Frateretto, the last a likely name for a
diabolical brother. Not the least of many ironies is that this innocent
youth must pretend to be the victim of demonic possession, haunted
by the foul fiend in many shapes—albeit these demons, on naturalistic
inspection, are merely vermin.

Dramatic tradition gave Tom of Bedlam a forerunner in the person
of Diccon the Bedlam, the Vice or mischief-maker in the crude old
Cambridge comedy of *Gammer Gurton's Needle*. Edgar, too, will play
the Vice in his later manipulations, when he intervenes on behalf of
Gloucester. Meanwhile he acts as an object-lesson for Lear. The extent
of Lear's reversal may be grasped by contrasting the first scene of

Act I with the last in Act II. In the former the bidding goes up, as Goneril and Regan bid for the kingdom with their large speeches of love. In the latter the haggling goes down, as the daughters cut down the retinue of their father. An hundred, fifty, five-and-twenty knights. 'Ten, or five.' 'What need one?' By that time we are ready to move on with Lear from the court, the world of superfluity, to the heath, the world of necessity—from the heights toward the depths. His retort in farewell is the first of his speeches on need and its opposite, luxury, especially luxurious clothing and the difference it makes between the sophisticated courtier and the basest beggar, between man's life and beast's.

When Lear has exposed himself to the pinch of necessity, when he has felt the storm and first expressed a new insight into the houseless lives of naked wretches, it is then that the ragged Edgar appears as the personification of abject poverty and misery. 'Is man no more than this?' the King demands, striving to emulate Tom by removing his own regal garments. 'Unaccommodated man'—the naked wretch in the state of nature—'is no more but such a poor, bare, forked animal as thou art.' Commentators have told us how richly the prose of this passage is interlarded with primitivistic speculations from Montaigne, whom Shakespeare knew so well through Florio's translation, and who had inspired so much of Hamlet's self-questioning. Lear has his own version of Hamlet's exclamation, 'What a piece of work is a man!' Unaccommodate him, banish him from the commodities of the court, take away the trappings of civilization, complete his exposure to the elements. What is there left to differentiate him from all the other animals, by whose sharpened fangs we feel increasingly surrounded? Will he be naturally good, as Rousseau would argue? Or is he inherently evil, as Hobbes would have it, a wolf to his fellow man?

The Machiavellian bastard, Gloucester's natural son Edmund, dedicates himself to the goddess Nature, as he ruthlessly envisions her; while, through his cruel machinations, Edgar is placed in such a false position that their father calls his legitimate son an 'unnatural villain'. On the other hand, Edgar stands closer to nature; Lear hails him as a natural philosopher, who should be able to answer his questions concerning 'the cause of thunder' and the other mysteries of the cosmos. This affinity, based on the fact that Edgar is Lear's godson, is confirmed by their respective plights, as Edgar keenly realizes: 'He childed as I father'd!' As the pair enter the hovel together, Edgar's snatches of balladry and fairy-tale transform it into a legendary dark tower, where a young squire is undergoing a ritual of knightly initiation while name-less giants objurgate: 'Fie, foh, and fum.' Edgar is more of a spectator than a feature of the spectacle in the ensuing scene, summing it up in the sentencious understatement that 'grief hath mates' or misery loves company.

This is the hallucinatory arraignment, where his own half-hearted pretence meets Lear's actual madness, accompanied by the half-witted folly of the natural fool with his one pathetic joke: the rain rains every day for those who are excluded from the sunshine of royal favour. The only person present who can speak sanely, Kent in his servant guise of Caius, counsels patience. Edgar is so moved at times that his tears inter-fere with his impersonation, 'mar' his 'counterfeiting'. Gloucester, whom Edgar has welcomed as a squinting fiend, re-enters to terminate the scene by ordering that the King be conveyed on a litter to Dover. Thereafter, in his master's absence, he becomes the scapegoat. What follows is the scene of his sacrifice, upon which there is no temptation to dwell, except for pointing out that this reversal—despite its extreme brutality—is humanely mitigated by a recognition. Peripety, according to Aristotle, is most effective when it coincides with such a recognition, *anagnorisis*.

When Cornwall inquires 'Where is thy lustre now?', Gloucester re-sponds, 'All dark and comfortless.' Then, when the malicious Regan apprises him of Edmund's villainy, he suddenly recognizes that Edgar is innocent. Thus, at the very moment of blinding, Gloucester sees how blind he has been all along. 'I stumbled when I saw,' he will live to say. Now, in the absence of eyesight, he will be guided by a kind of ethical illumination. One of the servants, an old man, suggests that the 'roguish madness' of 'the Bedlam' would qualify him to be Glou-cester's guide. Their conjunction is brought about in the first scene of Act IV. Kent has previously consoled himself with the thought that he could fall no lower than the stocks, and that any turn of Fortune's wheel would mean a rise in the world for him. Similarly, Edgar *solus* now views himself as 'The lowest and most dejected thing of fortune,' whose condition any change would improve. But alas, he speaks too soon. The sight of his bleeding father is worse than anything he has met so far.

'The worst is not,' Edgar thereupon reflects, 'so long as we can say, "This is the worst." ' This may be regarded as Shakespeare's variation on the tragic theme of Sophocles, 'Call no man happy until he is dead,' or the cry from the depths when Job curses the light and gropes in the dark. Gloucester, in spite of his infirmity, half-recognizes Edgar as that thing between a madman and a beggar which makes him 'think man a worm', but also made him think of his son. And it is at this significant juncture that Gloucester voices his pessimistic view of the human condition:

> As flies to wanton boys, are we to the gods;
> They kill us for their sport.

The world-view that opens up is as hopeless as Hardy's, governed by nothing more serene or secure than crass casualty and blind chance. It seems proper to Gloucester that a madman should lead a blind man, so long as he knows the way to Dover Cliff. 'From that place,' he declares with grim succinctness, 'I shall no leading need.' In his desperation, faced with what seems to be the pointless hostility of the universe, what can he do but dispatch his own 'nighted life'? That is the last resort of Stoicism; and Shakespeare, in his Roman plays, consistently treats suicide as an honourable mode of death. In his tragedies with a Christian background, his attitude is shaded with disapproval, and he cites God's canon against self-slaughter.

King Lear is supposed to take place in prehistoric Britain, and to be roughly contemporaneous with the ancient Kings of Judea. Shakespeare has taken pains to have his characters invoke 'the gods' in the plural and swear by conspicuously pagan divinities. But Edgar, that Good Samaritan with his faith, humility, and charity, seems to be *anima naturaliter christiana*. Curiously enough, in the original legend, where Lear regains his crown and Cordelia is dethroned again after his death, she ends by committing suicide in prison. It is her ghost which arises to retell the family history and point the moral in the standard Elizabethan collection of poetic case-histories, falls of princes or sad stories of the deaths of kings, the *Mirror for Magistrates*. There the usual reversal, the change of fortune from prosperity to adversity, from the heights to the depths, is presented as a warning to those who are highly placed, lest they be precipitated

> From greatest haps, that worldly wightes atchieue:
> To more distresse then any wretche aliue.

So Cordelia's monologue concludes. Comparably the first play performed before Queen Elizabeth, *Gorboduc*, one of whose collaborators was co-author of the *Mirror for Magistrates*, warned the queenly magistrate against the division of her realm and even foreshadowed *King*

Lear in introducing a dissension between rival Dukes of Cornwall and Albany.

Downfall was the formula for tragedy that Shakespeare inherited and elaborated, not only in plot and characterization but in language and staging as well. The dying fall is its traditional posture. Its vicissitudes, such as the ups and downs of Richard II's reign, lend their thematic pattern to his tragedy, wherein his fall is a come-down literally as well as figuratively. Aloft, on the upper stage, the imagined walls of Flint Castle, Richard compares himself to Phaeton; descending to the lower stage, he condescends to pun about the 'base court'. Descent is even more desperate in *King John*, where Prince Arthur is killed in escaping from the Castle of Angiers. Elevation as the basis of a godlike over-view is dramatized at those moments when Prospero is '*on the top*', apparently looking down from the musicians' gallery. Antony, coming down from his vantage-point after the battle or hoisted up to Cleopatra's Monument in death, acts out the movement of his destiny. The danger of high places, the tragic vertigo, is vividly brought home in Horatio's fear lest Hamlet topple off some dreadful summit, 'That beetles o'er his base into the sea'. And that is all we need to know in order to establish the certainty that Shakespeare never visited Denmark, which is as conspicuous for its summits as Bohemia is for its sea-coasts.

But we must turn back to Dover Cliff. 'Wherefore to Dover?' Three times Gloucester is asked this question by his torturers. Lear was there, of course; and Lear was there because the French Army was there, though the King of France had discreetly withdrawn so that his rescue party would not be mistaken for a foreign invasion. There the gleaming white cliffs, greeting the traveller on his return from the continent, mark a perpetual bourn. 'Within these breakwaters English is spoken,' writes W. H. Auden,

> without
> Is the immense improbable atlas.

Nature in Lear, he has been chastened to learn, 'is on the very verge/ Of her confine'. Just as the tempest in his mind, in the 'little world of man' or microcosm, is a reverberation of the macrocosm, the disturbance of outer nature; so now Gloucester, led by Edgar, has reached the 'extreme verge', the edge of the precipice. It is like the thin line between life and death, between the known and the unknown, that lies before Tolstoy's heroes in *War and Peace*.

Here Edgar, the assumed madman, addresses his charge, the blind man—and remember that we are just as blind as Gloucester. Theatrical convention prescribes that we accept whatever is said on the subject of immediate place as the setting. We may grow slightly suspicious, when Gloucester fails to notice the slant of the ground or the sound of the sea; and we join him in remarking an alteration of tone, since Poor Tom has shifted to blank verse and soon embarks on his topographical passage.

> How fearful
> And dizzy 'tis to cast one's eyes so low!

His downward glance proceeds to the half-way point, where it encounters the samphire-gatherer at his precarious business of picking the herb of Saint-Pierre from the rocks. Thence to the beach, where the fishermen look like mice, the birds like insects, the ships like their boats, and the buoys are invisible. Everything suffers a diminution in scale. 'I'll look no more,' vows Edgar at the end of fifteen lines,

> Lest my brain turn, and the deficient sight

—a relevant phrase, 'deficient sight', which universalizes the blindness of Gloucester while commenting on the trepidation of heights—

> I'll look no more,
> Lest my brain turn, and the deficient sight
> Topple down headlong.

This may strike the average reader or hearer with a distant, dizzying, vertiginous impact; Addison remarked that it could hardly be read without producing giddiness; but Dr. Johnson refused to be impressed. A precipice in the mind, he argued, should be 'one great and dreadful image of irresistible destruction'. Here we were too readily diverted by 'the observation of particulars'. Clearly, Johnson's criterion was the neo-classical grudge against concreteness that prompted him to inveigh against numbering the streaks of the tulip. In Boswell's account, he went even further when he discussed Edgar's speech with Garrick and others: 'It should be all precipice—all vacuum. The crows impede your fall.' It was the same Miltonic taste that emended Macbeth's 'blanket of the dark' to 'blank height'. Yet Lessing finds Shakespeare's description superior to Milton's lines where the angels scan the 'vast immeasurable abyss' of chaos. In *Paradise Lost* the declension is out of scale, Lessing asserted; the distance traversed is too vast to be fathomable in human dimensions. To jump to the beach from a cliff as high as ten masts is breath-taking danger, whereas a limitless precipitation through the void is mere astronomy. That vista may be even less thrilling to-day, as traffic increases in outer space.

The sense of immediacy and the sense of remoteness, the sensation of being up here one moment and down there a few seconds later, together with all the other sensations heightened by the hazards of the plunge, these feelings are concentrated into our identification with Gloucester and our prospective detachment from him. He is presumably standing at the brink as he lets go Edgar's hand, rewarding him and bidding him farewell. Whereupon Edgar, in a cryptic aside, gives us our first hint that the situation is not precisely what Gloucester believes it to be:

> Why I do trifle thus with his despair
> Is done to cure it.

From this announcement, at least, it is clear that Edgar has a strategem for saving Gloucester; but, on a non-representational stage, it would still be difficult to foresee how the rescue might be effected. On a proscenium stage, the whole situation would be impossible; for, depending on realistic scenery, we should be fully aware whether Gloucester was or was not at the top of a hill. The best that nineteenth-century staging could do was to cut the passage heavily, letting Edgar catch Gloucester as he lurches forward into a faint, and quickly shifting to the next phase of the scene with the entrance of Lear. Meanwhile the audience would not be undergoing any throes of suspense, since the scenic arrangements would have indicated that Gloucester was perfectly safe. On occasions, the Dover Cliffs have been painted upon the backdrop; it was to be inferred that Edgar had taken Gloucester directly to the beach, where he should not have had any trouble in hearing the waves.

'He falls,' according to the stage-direction, which editors have embellished but not improved. Most of them add 'forward'; some add 'and swoons'. He falls, at all events, but not far. Not so far as from the upper stage, I should guess, inasmuch as Romeo needed a rope and—lacking one—Prince Arthur lost his life. There may be a single step or a simple platform; or, again, the business may be enough—enough for Edgar to play his trick upon Gloucester and to lay bare the trick that Shakespeare has played upon ourselves, his audience. Gloucester, having gone through the motions of an ineffectual jump, lies on the ground; Edgar, assuming another character, now rushes up to revive him; and both are changed men. In complementary verses, breathless with polysyllabics, Edgar describes how Gloucester has fallen perpendicularly from a vast altitude and somehow survived: 'Thy life's a miracle.' Vainly, but not without irony, he exhorts him: 'Look up a-height.' And in contrast to all the *hybris*, the giddy exaltation of looking down from the heights, we seem to have plunged into the depths and to have touched bottom; we can fall no lower.

This is the nadir; the worst is over; we seem to be looking up; and the situation is framed by larger perspectives. 'As I stood here below methought,' begins Edgar, as if he were recounting a dream, a bad dream which ends with Tom of Bedlam turning into a fiend and flying away. Edgar's portrayal of his departing self is an exorcism, leaving innocence no longer possessed by guilt. Just as Gloucester utters his cry of despair—comparing the gods to boys and ourselves to flies—on his first encounter with mad Tom, so with Tom's departure Edgar voices his answering affirmation:

> Think that the clearest gods, who make them honours
> Of men's impossibilities, have preserv'd thee.

Providence must be at work, after all; and if we discern the workings of cosmic design in our personal destinies, then no man has a right to take his life; he must bear the slings and arrows of fortune, however outrageous they seem. To the Stoic argument for suicide Edgar would oppose the Christian attitude, in words which reverberate from the Gospel of Luke: 'The things which are impossible with men are possible with God.'

Since our eyes have been opened, we are bound to bear witness that Edgar himself has been fully responsible for the stratagem he now attributes to divine intervention. His intentions were kindly, where Edmund's have been malign; but he has deceived their father quite as much with his imaginary fall as Edmund earlier did with his forged letter. 'Let's see,' said Gloucester, snatching at that device, 'come; if it be nothing, I shall not need spectacles.' He saw; he stumbled; and, now that he is sightless, he is rescued by the victim of the letter. Edgar has proved to be as good a stage-manager as Edmund, and in a better cause. Yet, unless his presence in the vicinity is the result of stage-management on the part of the gods—unless it is providential, that is to say, rather than coincidental—we must admit that his miracle is more truly a pious fraud; and we must conclude that the gods help those who help themselves, or else those who are so fortunate as to be helped by their fellow men.

Man stands on his own feet in *King Lear*. There is no supernatural soliciting; there are no ghosts or witches or oracles; and the only demons are those which Edgar imagines while enacting his demonic role. Man takes his questionings directly to nature. Perhaps the ultimate meaning of Gloucester's fall is its symbolic gesture of expiation, re-enacting his own original sin, as well as the fall of man and his consequent progression toward self-knowledge. Other agonists have undergone it under widely differing conditions: Herman Melville narrates it, in his *White-Jacket*, as a fall from the yardarm of a ship at sea. Because he could not bear his great affliction without cursing the gods, Gloucester has attempted to shake it off 'patiently'. But Edmund's moral, which completes the exercise, redefines patience as the ability to bear one's sufferings, to face and endure them in calm of mind: 'Bear free and patient thoughts.'

Patience has been the greatest need of the King. He has resolved to be 'the pattern of all patience'; whereupon he has run the gamut of passions, from rage through hysteria to delirium and finally lunacy. It is as an escaping lunatic, grotesquely decked with weeds, that he is confronted by Edgar and Gloucester at this strategic moment of the play; and it may well be the shock of this reunion that has obscured the significance of their foregoing scene. From the interchange it would appear that, if Lear stands for reason in madness, Gloucester may stand for vision in blindness. When Lear asks if he sees how the world goes, Gloucester replies: 'I see it feelingly.' His groping pun is heavily fraught with shame and remorse for the figure he has earlier cut: 'the superfluous and lust-dieted man . . . that will not see/Because he does not feel.' This parallels the insight that Lear has acquired on the heath: 'to feel what wretches feel'. Gloucester has immediately recognized Lear's voice; Lear rounds out the recognition-scene by naming Gloucester and preaching, 'Thou must be patient.'

Lear is unquestionably the *persona patiens*, as Coleridge insisted; he is the agonizing figure of this passion play where all the characters suffer. Having committed his rash action, he suffers for it on and on, until he is justified in regarding himself as 'a man/More sinn'd against than sinning'. Edmund is the main agent, in Coleridge's estimation; certainly, he is most active in pulling the strings at the outset. 'The younger rises when the old doth fall.' But the defeated opportunist concedes that, with its last revolution, his wheel comes full circle. Edgar, his polar rival, is passive at first; he suffers, then he acts; and it is his suffering that prepares him for action. When Gloucester thanks and blesses him for his anonymous aid, he characterizes himself as

> A most poor man, made tame to fortune's blows;
> Who, by the art of known and feeling sorrows,
> Am pregnant to good pity.

As such, he is the right instrument for conveying a sense of fellow-feeling, both to Lear in the hovel on the heath and to Gloucester at Dover Cliff.

It is a cruel world where the honest Kent must go incognito, and where the once-naïve Edgar has to run through a protean repertory of roles. After the disappearance of Tom of Bedlam, he is more simply a neutral benefactor, the Good Samaritan. But when he protects Gloucester from Oswald's attack and is called 'bold peasant' by the courtier, he adapts himself to that appellation by replying in a rustic dialect. He disposes of Oswald, thereby saving the life that Gloucester would have thrown away. But he cannot disclose his identity before he has made his appearance as a nameless champion; and even this last masquerade is preceded by another one, that of the messenger delivering the challenge. However, the battle must precede the tournament. *Drums afar off* have terminated the Cliff Scene. They grow louder when the French forces, flying Cordelia's colours, march to meet the British. While the engagement is taking place off-stage, we await the outcome with Gloucester under a tree.

Hard upon the heels of retreating soldiers, Edgar reports the defeat and capture of Lear and Cordelia, and Gloucester reverts to his former mood of self-pity. Why should he let himself be led any farther? 'A man may rot even here.' But just as growth yields to decay, so decay fosters growth, in the biological cycle. What is important, fulfilment, is a matter of timing. Man must reconcile himself to the fact that nature will take its course. Edgar, picking up Gloucester's negative image, transposes it into the most positive statement of the play:

> Men must endure
> Their going hence, even as their coming hither;
> Ripeness is all.

Edgar's aphorism can be traced back to Montaigne's essay, 'That to philosophize is to learn how to die'. Such was the end of knowledge for the tragic playwright, as well as for the sceptical philosopher. It is rather more than a coincidence that the same sentiment is expressed, though not imaged, at the same point in *Hamlet*: 'The readiness is all.' The manner of one's death and the moment of it were ultimate concerns to the Elizabethans.

By averting the suicide and nursing his father's miseries, Edgar has saved him from despair. Could he but live to see his son in his touch, Gloucester has feelingly vowed, 'I'd say I had eyes again.' We do not witness the recognition-scene wherein this yearning is fulfilled at last. But in the final scene, when the explanations come out, Edgar relates the circumstances of Gloucester's happy death, 'Twixt two extremes of passion, joy and grief'. These mixed emotions match the smiles and tears with which Cordelia has received the news of her father: 'Sunshine and rain at once.' Edmund, sincerely moved by his brother's report, resolves to do some good; but retrospective narration prolongs the delay, and his one humane impulse is thwarted; the reprieve of Cordelia comes too late. When the brothers fought and were reconciled, Edgar pronounced upon his brother and father in apocryphal terms:

> The gods are just, and of our pleasant vices
> Make instruments to plague us.

Edmund's existence is at once the consequence of, and the retribution for, Gloucester's sin.

> The dark and vicious place where thee he got
> Cost him his eyes.

Where the inequities of this world have made Gloucester and Lear more and more doubtful as to the justice of heaven, Edgar is wholeheartedly its exponent. Albany, too, can point to the death of Cornwall, fatally wounded in the very act of torturing Gloucester, as an indication that the guilty are punished here below. But so are the innocent. So is Cordelia; and this, more than anything else, I suspect, is why critics have flinched at the notion of performing the play. There is a grim sort of poetic justice in the scene where the King refuses to accept her death; and his own demise, just afterwards, is a deliverance for him. But audiences have frequently shared his and Gloucester's unwillingness to bear an unhappy ending patiently; the chronicle-history ended happily; while the adaptation by Nahum Tate, which all but replaced Shakespeare's tragedy for a hundred and fifty years, managed to marry off Cordelia to Edgar, who thanks the King with these concluding lines:

> Thy bright example shall convince the World
> (Whatever Storms of Fortune are decreed)
> That Truth and Vertue shall at last succeed.

Shakespeare's Edgar repeats to the dying Lear his optimistic counsel to Gloucester: 'Look up, my lord.' But he cannot contrive another miracle. The problem of evil is unresolved at the conclusion, though the prevailing catastrophe is accepted. It is, as Kent says, a presentiment of doomsday, 'the promis'd end'. Edgar, rather than Albany, speaks the final speech in the Folio. Well might he proclaim a farewell to dissembling and a renewal of sincerity. It is high time to 'Speak what we feel, not what we ought to say.' And, in his terminal couplet, our deficient sight is contrasted with the insight painfully achieved through old age:

> The oldest hath borne most: we that are young,
> Shall never see so much, nor live so long.

We leave him looking across the straits, listening to the cadence of human misery in the ebb and flow of the tides, and catching that eternal note of sadness which Sophocles heard long ago and which Matthew Arnold caught in his poem, 'Dover Beach'. As with Oedipus, blind and dying at Colonus, so with Gloucester at Dover. In each case, the passion of a patriarch has met with compassion on the part of a filial survivor, be it Edgar or Antigone. But it is Goethe who puts his finger on the archetype in that relationship: '*Ein alter Mann ist stets ein König Lear.*' May I translate freely, in order to keep the rhyme?

> An aged man is always like King Lear.
> Effort and struggle long have passed him by;
> And love and leadership are pledged elsewhere;
> And youth must work out its own destiny.
> Come on, old fellow, come along with me.

7

SHAKESPEARE AND THE DRAMATIC CRITICS

by NORMAN MARSHALL

IN England it has never been disputed that it is the dramatic critics who should be the judges of Shakespeare in the theatre. The professors, the scholars of Shakespeare, have never challenged this right. But in many countries in Europe the university professors have considered it their duty jealously to guard the academic interpretation of the classics against any producer or actor with ideas of his own, and they have had sufficient prestige and authority to demand that when a classic is being performed it is they who should occupy the seats of the dramatic critics. Ernst Stern, in his autobiography, *My Life; My Stage*, describes how Reinhardt, when he sought to interpret Shakespeare's plays afresh, had to battle furiously with the professorial critics who were determined that everything should be done in exactly the same way as it had always been done before. 'The result was that when the classics were performed the audience saw what might be compared with a blackened masterpiece in which all colour and life had been deadened by layer after layer of ancient varnish.' Stern goes on to describe how, when Reinhardt staged his first Shakespearian production, 'the critics howled, "Sacrilege! Reinhardt detracts from the essential! Meretricious superficialities! A debasement of the classical spirit!" And so on. They seem to regard his productions as a personal insult, as an attack on their supreme right to determine what should and what should not be done in the theatre, and they did their best to put him out of business.'

In France Louis Jouvet found himself up against the same sort of opposition when he sought to free the plays of Molière from the weight of tradition which was stifling them on the stage. It was not a genuinely theatrical tradition handed down from the days of Molière. It had been imposed upon the actors by the scholars when they made Molière a 'subject', claimed that he belonged to literature rather than to the theatre, and claimed, too, as their right, that when a Molière play was produced the tickets intended for dramatic critics should be handed over to them. As a result, Jouvet found when he embarked upon his first Molière production that 'the play was choked with opinions, oppressed by explanations, crowded in theories, asphyxiated by controversy, but still green in the sap of the text'.

In England the scholars have never attempted to dictate to the actors and the producers. In fact, until quite recently, in their writings about Shakespeare they so very rarely gave any hint of ever having seen any of the plays on the stage that one felt they were deliberately keeping themselves aloof from the theatre so that their opinions should not be contaminated by seeing the plays in performance. One must admit that there was a good deal of justification for this attitude during the period which lasted for well over two hundred years when the theatre consistently mauled and savaged Shakespeare's texts, ruthlessly cutting them, and extensively rewriting them. Colley Cibber's adaptation of *Richard III*, which was preferred to Shakespeare's for well over a hundred years, was so drastically rewritten that more than half the lines were by Cibber, and a large proportion of those by Shakespeare were taken from his other historical plays. Edward Ravenscroft proudly claimed for his version of *Titus Andronicus* (re-titled *The Rape of Lavinia*) that 'None in all that author's works ever received greater Alterations or Additions.' The prologue to George Granville, Baron Lansdowne's *Jew of Venice*, describes it as 'Shakespeare's play Adorned and Rescued by a Faultless Hand', and goes on to assure the audience that although, 'The first rude sketches Shakespeare's Pencil drew, All the Master-Strokes are new.'

In the later part of the nineteenth century the theatre began to develop a little more respect for Shakespeare's own text and one manager announced, as a great novelty, a Shakespeare play, 'Acted Entirely in Shakespeare's Own Words.' But it was believed that the theatrical public were not really interested in the plays except as a means of providing an exciting star performance and a lavish display of spectacle; drastic surgical operations were therefore performed upon the text to make them fit this theory. Such was Irving's ruthlessness with the texts that Shaw protested in 1898 that 'in a true republic of art Sir Henry Irving would ere this have expiated his acting versions on the scaffold. He does not merely cut plays; he disembowels them.'

In the early days of the present century, as a result of the reforms in Shakespearian acting and production initiated by William Poel and

Granville-Barker, Shakespeare in the theatre began to approximate more nearly to Shakespeare on the printed page: but it took a long time for the scholars to overcome their prejudice against studying Shakespeare on the stage as well as in print. For instance, when Quiller-Couch published his Cambridge lectures under the title of *Shakespeare's Workmanship* he found it necessary to point out that it was 'no disparagement to the erudition and scholarship that have so piously been heaped about Shakespeare to say that we shall sometimes find it salutary to disengage our minds from it all, and recollect that the poet was a playwright'. Nevertheless, in the course of his lecture on *Cymbeline* he casually mentions, without any sort of apology, that he has never seen the play upon the stage, in spite of the fact that during the three years preceding the date when he gave this lecture there were four productions of this rarely produced play given within easy reach of Cambridge.

Today there may be university lecturers prepared to lecture on Shakespearian plays they have never seen upon the stage, but they would certainly do their best to conceal the fact from their audience. Most of those who lecture upon Shakespeare in the universities nowadays have not only frequently seen the plays upon the stage but have often themselves produced Shakespeare for their student dramatic societies. Two eminent Shakespearian scholars, Professor Nevill Coghill and Mr. George Rylands, besides staging many productions at their own universities, also produced Shakespeare professionally in London during Sir John Gielgud's season at the Haymarket Theatre in 1944.

As a result of the scholars becoming practitioners in the theatre the gulf between the academic approach to Shakespeare and that of the dramatic critics has been closed. When I was reading English at Oxford in the 'twenties it was never suggested to me that it might be useful to look up what any of the dramatic critics had to say about Shakespeare's plays; but I would be very surprised to-day if any tutor did not advise his pupils to read such books as Herbert Farjeon's *The Shakespeare Scene*, the selection of James Agate's Shakespearian notices published under the title *Brief Chronicles*, and Ivor Brown's Shakespearian criticisms.

I began this lecture by talking about how the academicians in other countries usurped the critics' function. I sometimes wonder if in England during recent years the reverse has happened, with the result that some of our leading critics have tended to write about Shakespeare as if they were clad in gown and mortar board. Are they perhaps too coolly scholastic and too unemotional in their reviewing of a Shakespearian performance? For instance, James Agate tended to seize upon a single scene and use it as a starting point from which to launch out upon a scholarly analysis of what he personally considered to have been Shakespeare's intentions. His successor on the *Sunday Times*, Mr. Harold Hobson, a critic with an exceptional gift for recalling in detail his past experiences as a theatregoer, is an exponent of the comparative method of Shakespearian dramatic criticism. For instance, writing about that lovely performance of *Much Ado About Nothing* in which Diana Wynyard was the Beatrice and John Gielgud the Benedick he makes, within the space of a single paragraph, comparisons with Henry Ainley's performance in a radio production twenty years previously, then refers to how Renée Asherson and Robert Donat played the parts, and goes on to describe Peggy Ashcroft and Anthony Quayle as Beatrice and Benedick. Personally, I find an enormous amount of pleasure, information and stimulation in this kind of dramatic criticism, but I wonder if it is not too specialized for the sort of theatregoer whom we—and the critics too, I am sure—want to lure into the theatre to see Shakespeare. It is the sort of comparative criticism I often indulge in myself in the course of conversation. Recently, at a small party after an important Shakespearian first night, I was talking about it rather as Mr. Hobson might have written about it (though not nearly so well, I hasten to add), when I sensed that one or two of the people in the room who had not been to the play that night, and had not seen any of the other productions which I had mentioned, were not particularly interested in what Sir John Gielgud did with the part eleven years ago or how Michael Redgrave played it in its last revival. What they were interested in was how the play had gone that night, how the audience had reacted, what the sets and costumes were like, how some of the lesser parts were played, and so on. I suggest that some of our dramatic critics use up too much space in comparative criticism—space which could be more valuably used in exciting the ordinary theatregoer to see the play.

Mr. Kenneth Tynan, the youngest of our leading dramatic critics, is less apt to indulge in comparative criticism, for the simple reason that he has seen far fewer Shakespearian productions than his colleagues. Consequently he is not, to quote Ivor Brown, 'Shakespeare-sodden and inevitably Bard-weary, mainly interested to see what so-and-so will do with such-and-such a passage'. But he too, I think, as a Shakespeare critic has overmuch scholastic zeal. With him it takes the form of wanting to educate and reform Shakespearian audiences. Writing of the Old Vic audience he once said, 'I find them culpable and in need of stricture.' So do I. I have always been in warm agreement with him when he has reproved 'the loud battalions of ingenuous claqueurs'. About any Shakespearian production he writes, as always, penetratingly, wittily and entertainingly, but often he omits to convey the fact that the performance itself was entertaining; sometimes it may not have been so. But even when writing about productions which were, by general consent, memorable, he fails to convey to his readers any real sense of his own enjoyment as a member of the audience. A fine production stimulates him into making a penetrating analysis of some aspects of the play and its performance, but the sum total of his notice is essentially a highly intellectual dissection rather than an account of his own vivid impressions of the performance.

Today the impressionist critic is out of fashion. A. B. Walkley defined the impressionist critic as one who 'takes a pure natural joy in his own sensations, because they are his own, and declines to be "connoisseured out of his senses" '. Walkley believed that 'perhaps the most fundamental of the critics' tasks is to be the ideal spectator'. Our present-day critics have given abundant proof of their ability to fulfil this role. My complaint against them is that they so rarely assume this role when they write about a Shakespearian production. Remember, for instance, the verve and excitement with which they wrote about the first night of *Oklahoma*, how vividly they reported not only their own pleasures but also the delight and enthusiasm of the audience and how that, in turn, stimulated those on the stage to giving a performance of extraordinary warmth and vivacity. I know that many theatregoers who never normally go to musicals found these notices so exciting that they straightway set about booking seats for *Oklahoma*. But how many theatregoers who have never gone to a Shakespearian play of their own free will have been so enthused by a critic's notice of a Shakespearian first night that they felt they must not on any account miss this play?

For instance, I have been re-reading some of the notices of one of the most exciting Shakespearian first nights I have ever attended—that night at the New Theatre in 1944 when Laurence Olivier appeared as *Richard III* in company with Ralph Richardson, Sybil Thorndike and Margaret Leighton. I found these notices made fascinating reading. They were judicial, erudite, finely phrased, but somehow I was often reminded of a dentist probing in a patient's mouth, spending little time over the teeth which are perfect but meticulously examining those which his probing discovers to be unsound. To take but one example, Agate's notice is largely devoted to pointing out why and where Olivier's interpretation was not, in Mr. Agate's opinion, ideal. The performance stirs him to many comparisons—this time not with other actors as Richard but with actors of the past playing parts as varied as Charles II, Robert Macaire, Alfred Jingle, Iago, Iachimo and Mephistofeles. In the end, in spite of all Mr. Agate's reservations, he admits that Olivier 'carried almost complete conviction' but we get hardly any hint in this notice that it was an enthralling night in the theatre. Some months later I heard Agate speak with warming enthusiasm of the occasion, but the nearest he gets in his notice to conveying any enthusiasm is a rather chilly line which describes how he 'sat attentive at this admirable performance'.

It is interesting to compare his notice with that of a much more impressionist critic, J. C. Trewin. 'In Shakespeare's Saturday night melodrama, Laurence Olivier strode across the contentions of York and Lancaster to give the most theatrically overwhelming performance of the period. This was out-and-out acting from the moment that Olivier entered like a baleful raven. It was no strutting, wicked-uncle affair. Olivier, never a mere Crookback gloating among the fanfares of the verse, united intellect and dramatic force, bravura and cold reason: he was the double Gloucester, thinker and doer, mind and mask. Playgoers, generations on, will be told how the actor, pallid, limping, with long black hair and a long, peering nose, moved like a sable cloud into the opening soliloquy. They will hear of the *diablerie*, the crackling, sardonic humours; of the imperious, regal gesture with which he proclaimed his new-born royalty in its very moment of birth; of the Irvingesque figure, crowned and sceptred, that crouched upon the throne like some emanation from a witches' cauldron; of the swoop back to the throne at the line, "Is the chair empty? Is the sword unsway'd?"; of the darkling cry before Bosworth, "There is no creature loves me," of the wistful-despairing, "Not shine today!" as Richard studied the sky; and of the prolonged spasm of the death-agony at Richmond's feet. Here was a figure truly diabolical: a Red King; one raised in blood and one by blood established.'

The value of this sort of notice is not just that it makes one urgently want to see the play; it is immensely valuable to those who many years hence will want to know how Olivier looked and sounded and moved in the part, what sort of excitement his performance generated in an enthusiastic spectator. Mr. Trewin is far more than just a dramatic reporter, but alone among contemporary critics he has much in common with that greatest of all dramatic reporters, Clement Scott. It is unfashionable in these days to admire Clement Scott. If one regards him seriously as a critic one must admit straightaway that his critical sense was, to put it mildly, unreliable. For instance, his opinions of Ibsen's plays were plain silly. He considered that those critics who approved of Ibsen 'were coquetting with the distorted, the tainted, and the poisonous in life', and he ascribed the fact that anyone who could see good in Ibsen to 'the change of tone and thought at our public schools and universities, to our godless method of education, and to the comparative failure of religion as an influence'. I agree with Alan Dent that his work had neither of the two great antiseptics of criticism, wit and style, but I also agree with Dent that Clement Scott 'became in his time, and has remained ever since, immeasurably the most popular and influential dramatic critic who ever lived'. Why? Because no other critic has ever had the same ability to convey the glamour and the excitement and the sense of occasion of a memorable first night. It is impossible to quote him briefly because he had no gift for the incisive, telling phrase. He needed lots of space for his dramatic reporting—and he got it. For instance, his report on the first night of Irving's Hamlet in the *Daily Telegraph* ran to some three thousand, five hundred words. Nowadays Mr. Darlington, the *Telegraph's* present critic, rarely has as much as even five hundred words with which to describe and criticize a notable first night.

Clement Scott begins his notice of Irving's production of *Hamlet* with a description of the atmosphere of excitement in the auditorium as it filled up, of the growing sense of anticipation, until 'with all on the tiptoe of excitement, the curtain rose. All present longed to see Hamlet. Bernardo and Marcellus, the Ghost, the platform, the grim preliminaries, the prologue or introduction to the wonderful story, were, as usual, tolerated—nothing more. Away go the platform, the green lights, the softly-stepping spirit, the musical-voiced Horatio. The scene changes to a dazzling interior, broken in its artistic lines, and rich with architectural beauty; the harps sound, the procession is commenced, the jewels, and crowns, and sceptres, dazzle, and at the end of the train comes Hamlet. Mark him well, though from this instant the eyes will never be removed from his absorbing figure. How is he dressed, and how does he look? No imitation of the portrait of Sir Thomas

Lawrence, no funeral velvet, no elaborate trappings, no Order of the Danish Elephant, no flaxen wig after the model of M. Fechter, no bugles, no stilted conventionality. We see before us a man and a prince, in thick robed silk and a jacket edged with fur; a tall, imposing figure, so well dressed that nothing distracts the eye from the wonderful face; a costume rich and simple and relieved alone by a heavy chain of gold; but, above and beyond all, a troubled, wearied face displaying the first effects of moral poison. The black disordered hair is carelessly tossed about the forehead, but the fixed and rapt attention of the whole house is directed to the eyes of Hamlet: the eyes which denote the trouble—which tell of the distracted mind. Here are "the windy suspiration of forced breath", "the fruitful river in the eye", the "dejected 'haviour of the visage". So subtle is the actor's art, so intense is his application, and so daring his disregard of conventionality, that the first act ends with comparative disappointment. Those who have seen other Hamlets are aghast. Mr. Irving is missing his point, he is neglecting his opportunities.'

Scott continues his reporting even through the interval, recounting the arguments among the audience, the dismay of some of Irving's most ardent admirers, and the spell he had already cast over those who had been watching him carefully and intelligently enough to understand that they were witnessing an entirely new approach to the part. 'The Second Act ends with nearly the same result. There is not an actor living who on attempting Hamlet has not made his points in the speech, "Oh! what a rogue and peasant slave am I!" But Mr. Irving's intention is not to make points, but to give a consistent reading of a Hamlet who "thinks aloud". For one instant he falls "a-cursing like a very drab, a scullion"; but only to relapse into a deeper despair, into more profound thought. He is not acting, he is not splitting the ears of the groundlings; he is an artist concealing his art; he is talking to himself; he is thinking aloud. Hamlet is suffering from moral poison, and the spell woven about the audience is more mysterious and incomprehensible in the second act than the first. In the third act the artist triumphs. No more doubt, no more hesitation, no more discussion. If Hamlet is to be played like a scholar and a gentleman, and not like an actor, this is the Hamlet. The scene with Ophelia turns the scale, and the success is from this instant complete. But we must insist that it was not the triumph of an actor alone; it was the realization of all that the artist has been foreshadowing. . . . Mr. Irving did not make his success by any theatrical *coup*, but by the expression of the pent-up agony of a harassed and disappointed man. According to Mr. Irving, the very sight of Ophelia is the keynote of the outburst of his moral disturbance. He loves this woman; "forty thousand brothers" could not express his overwhelming passion, and think what might have happened if he had been allowed to love her, if his ambition had been realized. The more he looks at Ophelia, the more he curses the irony of fate. He is surrounded, overwhelmed, and crushed by trouble, annoyance, and spies. They are watching him behind the arras. Ophelia is set on to assist their plot. They are driving him mad, though he is only feigning madness. What a position for a harassed creature to endure! They are all against him. Hamlet alone in the world is born to "set it right". He is in the height and delirium of moral anguish. The distraction of the unhinged mind, swinging and banging about like a door; the infinite love and tenderness of the man who longs to be soft and gentle to the woman he adores: the horror and hatred of being trapped, and watched, and spied upon were all expressed with consummate art. Every voice cheered, and the points Mr. Irving had lost as an actor were amply atoned for by his earnestness as an artist. Fortified with this genuine and heart-stirring applause, he rose to the occasion. He had been understood at last. To have broken down here would have been disheartening; but he had triumphed.'

I would like to be able to read you the whole of Scott's notice but that would take too long. You can read it for yourselves in his collected criticisms published under the title of *The Drama of Yesterday and Today* or in James Agate's anthology, *The English Dramatic Critics*. You will find the entire performance vividly described in detail, scene by scene. Let me quote just one more paragraph telling how Irving acted the play scene. 'He acted it with an impulsive energy beyond all praise. Point after point was made in a whirlwind of excitement. He lured, he tempted, he trapped the King, he drove out his wicked uncle conscience-stricken and baffled and with an hysterical yell of triumph he sank down, "the expectancy and rose of the fair state", in the very throne which ought to have been his, and which his rival had just vacated. It is difficult to describe the excitement occasioned by the acting in this scene. When the King had been frighted, the stage was cleared instantaneously. No one in the house knew how the people got off. All eyes were fixed on Hamlet and the King; all were forgetting the real play and the mock play; following up every move of the antagonists, and from constant watching they were almost as exhausted as Hamlet was when he sank a conqueror into the neglected throne. It was all over now. Hamlet had won. He would take the ghost's word for a thousand pounds. The clouds cleared from his brow. He was no longer in doubt or despair. He was the victor after this mental struggle. The effects of the moral poison had passed away.'

We shall never read the like of Clement Scott again—if only because there is no longer room in our newspapers for dramatic reporting on that scale. Today films, television, radio, the ballet and almost nightly concerts compete with the theatre for the space allotted to entertainments in newspapers which are very much smaller than they were in Clement Scott's day, with print which is very much larger, and with headlines in big type which take away still more of the dramatic critics' space. It is getting on for a hundred years since Clement Scott wrote that report of the first night of Irving's Hamlet. A hundred years hence nobody will be able to find comparable reports on the great Hamlets of our day. They will be able to read, in notices which are miracles of incisiveness and compression, highly intelligent and knowledgeable analyses of the Hamlets of Sir John Gielgud, Sir Laurence Olivier, Mr. Michael Redgrave and the rest. They will be able to read occasional descriptions of how these actors took certain lines and certain scenes. But never will they find a criticism which gives a detailed description, act by act, of how the play was performed, besides conveying the theatrical excitement of the occasion in a way which vividly re-creates for us what it must have been like to have been one of the audience on that night.

Please do not misunderstand me, I am not suggesting that Clement Scott's enthusiastic dramatic reporting is preferable to the cool and considered judgments of dramatic critics of today. What would be ideal is if, on the day after an important Shakespearian first night, we could have a vivid, factual account of the performance; then on the following day the dramatic critics' appraisal of its merits and demerits. When a few years ago I took a production of *Hamlet* on a tour of the German theatres there were several occasions when the newspapers adopted this practice. In England, Shakespeare needs dramatic reporting as well as dramatic criticism more than any other author because, let's face it, he is not a popular dramatist. That may seem an odd statement to make in this town where every year the season grows longer and longer and the seats become more and more difficult to obtain. But most of those who come to Stratford see more than one play, and they are drawn from all over the world. Much the same is true at the Old Vic, which presents a considerable number of plays during the course of a season and relies largely on a repeater audience. The total audience for Shakespeare to-day is very small. Clement Scott brought into the theatre to see Shakespeare's plays thousands of people who would not otherwise have thought of doing so. Today the Shakespeare theatre desperately needs more converts. Our dramatic critics have probably done more than the critics of any other age to enhance the pleasure and understanding of the regular Shakespearian playgoer, but I wonder how many converts they have made from among the unbelievers—from those who have never been persuaded that Shakespeare is a genuine part of theatrical entertainment.

Our critics can on occasions write with uninhibited and infectious enthusiasm about every sort of entertainment apart from Shakespeare. Why is it that they can so seldom send their readers scuttling to the box office when they write about a Shakespearian production? I think Ivor Brown has the explanation when he says that a critic attending a Shakespearian performance cannot hope for 'the delight of innocence' with which he watches a new play. Recalling 'the high pleasure' he enjoyed at a particularly good production here in Stratford he remarks that he found it 'strange and distressing' that so many of the next day's notices 'contained so much melancholy evidence of chilly aloofness'.

I suspect that one of the resons for this 'chilly aloofness' has been the influence which James Agate exerted upon many of his colleagues and his successors. He believed that it was the business of the critic attending a Shakespearian play 'not to wonder but to expound'. Writing of Wolfit's Lear, which he considered 'the greatest piece of Shakespearian acting I have ever seen since I was privileged to write for the *Sunday Times*', he describes the audience's 'amazed and sudden surrender to some stroke of passionate genius', but it troubled him that the audience surrendered to it without quite knowing what it was to which they were surrendering. He describes them leaving the theatre 'conscious of having been swept off their feet and not bothering to wonder why'. He makes it clear that in spite of his intense admiration for this performance, *he* had not been swept off his feet, but had remained aloof from the audience, coolly and analytically examining the performance. So he proceeds to tell the audience exactly why, in his opinion, they were so impressed and to explain just exactly what Wolfit did at the peak moments of his performance and how he did it. In fact one is given an analysis of the actor's mental processes but little or no impression of the emotional impact upon the audience, or upon the critic himself.

Perhaps the fundamental trouble about Shakespearian dramatic criticism today is that the critics have had to write about far too many productions of the same play. Inevitably, the more often one sees a play the more detached one becomes as a spectator and nothing but 'the exquisite experience of seeming to see a masterpiece afresh, anew, with its metal as near to new-minted as may be' can prevent the mind from continually comparing what is happening upon the stage with recollections of numerous other performances. As a critic becomes more and more familiar with a Shakespearian play on the stage he finds his attention concentrating more and more on the minutiae of the performance rather than upon the play as a whole. To those who know their Shakespeare well, each notice reveals fresh and undiscovered aspects of the text, but to the ordinary reader, especially if he is youthful, many of the points which a critic deals with may seem finicky and unimportant. The ordinary everyday theatregoer reads a critic's notice mainly to discover the answer to the question: 'Shall I or shall I not go to see this play?' If only editors would give back to the critics just a little more of the space that they used to have, I have no doubt that within the scope of the same notice we could have criticisms which besides being comparative and analytical would also be impressionist, and thus satisfy both the devotees of Shakespeare and the playgoers who want to know 'whether it's worth going to see'.

8

SHAKESPEARE'S MEN AND THEIR MORALS

by J. I. M. STEWART

I

As the industrious years go by, it becomes increasingly difficult not only to add to the criticism of Shakespeare, but even to report adequately upon a single aspect of it. Today, we find a greater variety of opinions about Shakespeare, and a larger body of controversy about his work, than any previous age has known. I shall try, if very briefly, to place this unrest in Shakespeare studies (as one conservative commentator has disapprovingly called it) by relating it to two central works in the history of Shakespeare criticism: Dr. Johnson's *Preface* to his edition of the plays, published in 1765, and A. C. Bradley's *Shakespearean Tragedy*, published in 1904.

It was Johnson's grand contention—as it had been Dryden's, indeed, immediately before him—that Shakespeare gives us Nature: Shakespeare's world is our world in concentration. The heroes of other playwrights are often only phantoms, but Shakespeare's heroes are men. Shakespeare discerns truly and depicts faithfully. His book is thus a map of life, an epitome of human experience. It is true that the plays are not planned moral fables, contrived to edify and instruct, as is Johnson's own tragedy, *Irene*, or as is Johnson's novel, *Rasselas*. Nevertheless Shakespeare affords knowledge immensely valuable to us as moral beings. And he does this all the way through. Even 'the character of Polonius is serious and useful, and the gravediggers themselves may be heard with applause'. It is important to notice that Johnson sees no great difficulty in the fact that these intensely real people of Shakespeare's are involved in some rather unreal fables. Shakespeare's stories are merely the vehicles on which the characters and their moral life are brought to us. It is from the characters, copiously diversified and justly pursued as they are, that our delight and instruction derive. We need not much labour, then, to rationalize the stories.

Again it is important to notice Johnson's strong sense of these so natural characters as yet being fictions. The plays are not *records* of human transactions. They are 'faithful miniatures' of human transactions. They make us free of Nature only by themselves yielding to the rules of Art.

A good many things happen between Johnson and Bradley. First, the characters march out of the plays, led by Falstaff in Maurice Morgann's famous essay. Presently they are being discussed as if they were historical personages, and on this basis a swelling flood of commentary continues throughout the nineteenth century. I think myself that Shakespeare criticism has been enriched in consequence. But the dangers are obvious. There is an invitation to irrelevant reverie, as upon, say, the girlhood of Shakespeare's heroines. We may also come to feel that with a play, as with a historical action, crucial facts are likely to have perished tantalizingly from the record, so that they are recoverable only by ingenious inference. It is incumbent upon us, we may be brought to feel, to reconstruct the truth on the basis of such fragmentary evidence as the play has preserved for us. How many oddities has this persuasion produced!

A second development, unknown to Johnson and associated with the romantic critics (notably Coleridge) has been towards the dogma that Shakespeare never nods, that his judgment is always equal to his genius, and that the several elements in his plays are with a quite exceptional perfection always fused into an artistic unity. This conviction has been reinforced, I imagine, by the rise to the position of a major literary form of realistic and psychological prose fiction. The effect is to make us feel something mildly shocking in any proposal to be merely light-hearted about Shakespeare's plots and situations.

These, then, were the developing trends before Bradley. Correspondingly, we must notice certain aspects of Shakespeare that were no longer much attended to. Any marked feeling for Shakespeare as an Elizabethan, as a man developing and writing within a certain intellectual atmosphere, had died out. So had any strong sense of him as working for a particular theatre and within particular theatrical conventions. Criticism concerned itself, very confidently, with absolute and not with historical judgments.

Bradley came to crown this situation. He brought to it first his genius (for the writer of the best book on Shakespeare must, I think, be allowed that) and secondly a great interest in the philosophy of tragedy. For Bradley, as for Johnson, Shakespeare's heroes are men. But now they are men realized for us, in the two-hours traffic of the stage, in the richest and most delicate psychological detail. They are men moving through actions at once perfectly realistic and supremely poetic—actions subtly contrived in their every implication and affiliation. But, although they belong to works owning the highest degree of artistic unity, they yet have a life that, mysteriously, extends far beyond the limits of their play. Shakespeare's characters have, as it were, a larger personal history which can be reached from the springboard of the play. And they have, too, this as their final greatness: they embody (triumphantly and—we must say—by a mysterious anachronism) a theory of tragedy to the shaping of which Aristotle, Coleridge and Hegel have all contributed the finest essence of their thought.

Perhaps he is a little too good to be true, this serene and timeless Shakespeare, with Aristotle and Hegel in one pocket, the Oxford of 1904 in the other, and the sacred coal ever at his lips. But only perhaps —for who can tell? Is there anything, then, *demonstrably* wrong with Bradley?

Many people now say, Yes. The plays and characters Bradley offers us are his own creation quite as much as Shakespeare's. Really attend to Shakespeare's plain text, disregard the mass of anachronistic subtlety that has long been projected upon it, and you will find no elaborately developed psychological studies and not many genuine human predicaments. You will find—Robert Bridges announced in 1907 in an essay called *The Influence of the Audience on Shakespeare's Drama*—grossly inconsistent characters being bumped and jockeyed through a variety of sensational incidents by a great poet who was constrained by the barbarity of his audience to work in terms of the crudest melodrama. In 1919 Professor Levin Schücking developed this theme in a book shortly afterwards translated as *Character Problems in Shakespeare's Plays*.[1] Schücking maintained that Shakespeare's dramaturgy is essentially popular and primitive. Shakespeare simply moves from scene to scene seeking immediate theatrical effect. Cleopatra is a harlot at the beginning of her play because plays about harlots were a good draw, and is somebody quite different at the end because her creator became belatedly conscious that he must make some contact with the Cleopatra of Plutarch whose story he is following.

But more important than Schücking was Professor Elmer Edgar Stoll, a trenchant, pertinacious and learned American critic who, in a sense, stands Bridges' contention on its head. The psychological in-

[1] Harrap, 1922.

coherence and the ruthless pursuit of a hodge-podge of emotions which Bridges sees as destroying Shakespeare's art Stoll declares to be, in drama, a splendid artistic strength. For, essentially, we go to the theatre to be thrilled—and to be thrilled by 'another world, not a copy of this.' 'Life,' Stoll says, 'must be . . . piled on life, or we have visited the theatre in vain.' Shakespeare, knowing this, chiefly seeks a kind of 'emotional effect, with which psychology or even simple narrative coherence often considerably interferes'.[1]

You see, then, what a confusion of voices the appraisal of Shakespeare's characters can evoke. Take, for example, Othello. For Bradley, Othello is a marvellous study in depth of an extremely noble and at the same time wholly convincing individual. His conflict with Iago— again a complex and perfectly credible figure—fulfils the strictest laws of tragic causality in that the hero's very nobility is his undoing. He is *too* trustful; 'his trust, where he trusts, is absolute'; and so he is helpless before deception. His fate is plausible, convincing, deeply moving, and consonant with a just and elevating philosophical reading of life. Bridges will have nothing of all this. 'The whole thing is impossible,' he cries. There is nothing elevating about it. Shakespeare's aim was merely to scarify a particularly thick-skinned audience. And for Professor Stoll, too, Othello is an impossible figure. Bradley's crucial contention ('his trust, where he trusts, is absolute') is mere cobweb— since, if trustfulness is the key to the character, then surely Othello should trust his wife and friend at least as fully as he trusts a stranger. 'What is to be made of this heap of contradictions?' Stoll exclaims, when he has analysed the hero—and answers, in effect: 'In terms of actual human psychology, nothing; in terms of the emotional artifice that constitutes a good play, a great deal.'

Now, what we may call the negative or destructive side of Stoll's historical realism was much more effective than the obscure aesthetic of sensation that it throws out as a sort of life-line to Shakespeare's reputation. It is almost possible to say that our faith in Shakespeare's characters was shaken; we were at a loss for a reply to the onslaught; and we turned our attention to other things. Textual research very fascinating to keen minds, re-creations of the Elizabethan 'climate of opinion', studies (very valuable indeed, the best of them) in Shakespeare's poetic, explorations of a possible symbolical content, conscious or unconscious, in the plays: there are all these approaches and many more available to the inquirer who hesitates before this perplexed

[1] Stoll: *Art and Artifice in Shakespeare* (Cambridge, 1933).

matter of the characters. But ought we not to face up to the problem? 'Shakespeare's heroes are men.' Is it true, or was Dr. Johnson wrong?

I suspect that we are apt to be a little intimidated, some of us, by the erudition of these 'realists'. We have not read nearly so many plays as they have, and those that we have read we don't seem to remember nearly so well or be anything like so sure about. Indisputable, too, is their claim to know whatever can be discovered about the Elizabethan theatre and audience, about conventional types and roles and situations, about the views of learned and simple Elizabethans regarding the state, and the solar system, and the human soul; about ghosts and witches and devils and angels. And yet I am not quite confident that all this valuable information is really at the heart of the matter. When I ask myself why I have some confidence in Dr. Johnson and am reluctant to scrap him I find that it is because he is known to have been intensely interested not only in Shakespeare's men but in real men as well. Johnson, so to speak, tackled the problem from both ends. And, in the field we have been considering, I should have more confidence in the judgment of one who sat for months on end in what we should now call a police court, just because men interested him, than I should have in one who sat ever so much longer in a carrel in a library, with any distracting view of his fellow mortals ingeniously cut off by worm-eaten oak or by steel shutters. Again, I should listen to a wise man who had worked long in actual theatres for actual audiences more attentively than I should to a man, equally wise, whose frequentation had been all of the ghost of the Globe. I am interested, then, in what men of the theatre think about our problem—and in what is thought about it, too, by certain comparative newcomers to the game, the depth psychologists.

Is it not significant that the late Harley Granville-Barker, a scholar who was at the same time an experienced Shakespearian actor and a brilliant Shakespearian producer, entirely rejected the notion of Shakespeare's primitivism, sensationalism, psychological incoherence and the like; and that he should have given us in his great series of *Prefaces* character-studies almost in the direct line of Bradley, only informed and (we may say) pruned by a closer knowledge of the stage? And is it not significant, too, that Freud vindicated Shakespeare, whose works he had abundantly studied, as a psychologist of genius? As long ago as 1923 a conservative but acute commentator on the cockpit of Shakespeare criticism, the late Professor C. H. Herford, remarked that modern psychology, by its disclosure of such phenomena as those of dual and multiple personality, might unexpectedly illuminate the vexed problem of apparent inconsistency in Shakespeare.

In point of fact, modern psychology has been rather more ambitious than that. Dr. Johnson, you remember, set little store by Shakespeare's stories; it seemed to him of small consequence whether these were probable or unlikely. Freud and his followers have contended that, where the stories are unlikely, they are unlikely much after the fashion of dreams, and for the same reason.

A tragedy is essentially a symbolical representation of wishes and conflicts urgent in us all, but of which a psychic censorship forbids the direct and undisguised expression. Hence the power of tragedy, when imaginatively received either in the theatre or in reading. It affords tremendous relief. It is just the cathartic or purging instrument that Aristotle long ago declared it to be. Hence too all those irrational and puzzling elements evident in tragedy when *not* imaginatively received. For Shakespeare's stories and his people often follow the logic of myth and the unconscious rather than the logic of waking life. This means that they are, in one sense, less 'realistic' than Bradley was inclined to suppose them. But the psychological critics are inclined to maintain, at the same time, that Shakespeare's major characters, taken simply as very actual men and women, become far more explicable in terms of what is now known about the mechanisms and motives of the human mind. Thus when older critics have maintained that the credulity of Othello, the malignity of Iago, the sudden senseless jealousy of Leontes, the equally sudden depravity of Angelo are implausible and theatrical, these newer critics would say: 'No, men are like that, although you find it more comfortable to believe that they are not. People come into our consulting-rooms who are capable of behaving just like Othello, or Iago or Leontes or Angelo. And we can explain how they come to behave as they do.'

I confess to finding all this of great interest. At the same time I am sure that we should be a little chary of feeling, 'Ah—light at last!' Mr. T. S. Eliot has somewhere made fun of criticism that comes forward as 'revealing for the first time the gospel of some dead sage, which no one has understood before; which owing to the backward and confused state of men's minds has lain unknown to this very moment'. And if we trace out the fascinating history of 'Hamlet' criticism (as an American scholar, Dr. Paul Conklin, has begun to do)[1]

---

[1] *A History of Hamlet Criticism*, 1601–1821 (King's Crown Press, New York, 1947).

we shall quickly come upon the chastening fact that Shakespeare's
Prince of Denmark is a veritable chameleon, who has taken on, century
by century and generation by generation, the very form and pressure
of the age. What was Hamlet to the Elizabethan audience? A malcon-
tent, Dr. Conklin assures us; a bitterly eloquent and princely avenger
on the verge of a lunacy from which the players would sometimes
extract a good laugh; but withal a formidable young man and one
much admired for his mouth-filling flood of iambic pentameter. Later,
when England fell under the influence of Scotsmen and went soft, this
young tough went soft too—and softer in the study than on the stage.
In the age of Sterne and Mackenzie, Hamlet becomes a man of sentiment, a man of feeling; Goethe finds him closely related to his own
Werther; Coleridge announces that Hamlet is in fact Coleridge—an
extremely impressive person of vast intellectual powers embarrassed by
an unfortunate weakness of will. Prose fiction takes on a new complexity in its presentation of character: just such a complexity is discovered in the Prince. Scholars distil subtle theories of tragedy out of
philosophies old and new: Hamlet turns out to be the hero who fits
perfectly. Other scholars fall to studying the Elizabethan drama at
large: Hamlet loses his uniqueness and becomes less a character than a
role, a series of stage dodges. The text of Shakespeare is studied with a
new minuteness: it is discovered (as by Dr. Richard Flatter in a most
ingenious book)[1] that the text gives tiny indications which must revo-
lutionize our conceptions of Hamlet's disposition. And finally—finally
for the present—comes Dr. Ernest Jones, with his deeply interesting
psycho-analytic study, *Hamlet and Oedipus*.[2]

What is the lesson of this? The lesson is surely not that all critical
interpretation of Shakespeare's characters is ephemeral modish nonsense. We merely learn that we ought not to let one theory, one reading,
sweep away all the others. These people of Shakespeare's really are
extraordinarily like life, and life is susceptible of many interpretations
which do not necessarily invalidate each other. The danger point
comes when we persuade ourselves that the characters are *only* this or
that: only artifice, only allegory, only theology, only advice to Elizabethan statesmen, only concealed pointers to Sir Francis Bacon or the
Earl of Derby, and so on. And there is perhaps one other danger; that
of forgetting that all these inquiries are for the satisfaction of the intel-

---

[1] *Shakespeare's Producing Hand: A Study of his marks of expression to be found in
the First Folio* (Heinemann, 1948).
[2] Gollancz, 1949.

lect, since Shakespeare has already satisfied the imagination. When our imagination is kindled we do not think to 'interpret' the characters. We know that the characters are interpreting us.

II

So much for the debate on Shakespeare's men; let me now say something about their morals—and about *his* morals, too. And, this time, let our first critic be a lady. It was in 1775 that Mrs. Elizabeth Griffith[1] determined upon 'placing his Ethic merits in a more conspicuous point of view'—and became thereby (I am afraid) one of a good many writers to contrive mainly absurdity in the consideration of this difficult topic. It would appear that Mrs. Griffith proposed (in addition to giving numerous excerpts of an edifying cast from the plays) to offer compendious remarks on the moral intention animating each play in turn. She begins with *The Tempest*—which teaches (she says):

> that the ways, the justice, and the goodness of Providence, are so frequently manifested toward mankind, even in this life, that it should ever encourage an honest and a guiltless mind to form hopes, in the most forlorn situations; and ought also to warn the wicked never to rest assured in the false confidence of wealth or power, against the natural abhorrence of vice, both in God and man.

That is very well, no doubt—but the next play in the Folio is *A Midsummer Night's Dream*. Poor Mrs. Griffith is already stumped. 'I shall not trouble my readers', she says, 'with the Fable of this piece, as I can see no general moral that can be deducted from the argument.' Then comes *The Two Gentlemen of Verona*. 'The Fable', she says, 'of this play has no more moral in it, than the former.' *Measure for Measure* follows and the poor lady becomes desperate: 'I cannot see what moral can be extracted from this Piece.' And with the fifth play, *The Comedy of Errors*, she gives up: 'I shall take no further notice of the want of a moral fable in the rest of these plays.' It is true, indeed, that Mrs. Griffith does not altogether quit the field. In *As You Like It*, for instance, she triumphantly finds 'a very proper hint given . . . to women, not to deviate from the prescribed rules and decorums of their sex'. But on the whole she must be said to discover (what Dr. Johnson could already have told her) that Shakespeare 'is so much more careful to please than to instruct, that he seems to write without any moral purpose'.

[1] *The Morality of Shakespeare's Drama Illustrated.*

Johnson backs up this stricture of Shakespeare by declaring that 'he makes no just distribution of good or evil', thereby ranging himself with those who require of the dramatist the administration of poetical justice. And the conception of poetical justice, indeed, was for a very long time the focal point round which most debate on Shakespeare's morality turned. Eugenius in Dryden's *Essay of Dramatic Poesy* had censured the ancient dramatists for not taking care to punish the wicked; and Dryden's contemporary Thomas Rymer[1] (who seems actually to have coined the phrase *poetical justice*) transferred the censure to Shakespeare. John Dennis[2] argued with great ingenuity for poetical justice. Real people, he said, must face Judgment in a hereafter. But characters in a play have no hereafter; their sole creator is the dramatist; and therefore the dramatist must, so to speak, play deity to them, and reward or punish them while they are yet on the stage and before they escape into nothingness. Dennis in this was partly actuated by his hatred of Addison, in whose *Cato* a virtuous hero is allowed to perish in a just cause. Addison's counter-arguments in *The Spectator* must at first seem very sensible: *good and evil happen alike to all men on this side of the grave*; and poetical justice must entirely vitiate the drama as a mirror of life. Yet Johnson, although working the mirror-of-life idea hard, was unconvinced by Addison, and at least hankered after poetical justice. He could not bear poetry not to vindicate a moral governance of the world; he believed that at the end of plays the evidence should (as it were) be fudged in order to chasten vice and encourage virtue. The dramatist can't go on to show the Last Judgment in operation. He is therefore obliged (if he is to suggest the final and just balance of things) to anticipate, and to show felicity under the figure of prosperity achieved here below. On this ground Johnson preferred Tate's 'happy-ending' *Lear* to Shakespeare's.

The later history of the 'poetical justice' doctrine is more full of curiosity than instruction. Subscribing to it must necessarily lead, in Shakespeare criticism, to one of two conclusions. Either the major tragedies of Shakespeare are extremely faulty performances in which the principle is for the most part flatly contradicted (and this is what Dennis boldly concludes); or the tragedies present a succession of persons only speciously virtuous, who meet a merited doom, intelligible to us if we will only sufficiently reflect. Since the secure establishing of Shakespeare's reputation in the later eighteenth century it is

---

[1] *The Tragedies of the Last Age* (1678).
[2] *The Genius and Writings of Shakespeare* (1712).

only this second supposition that has appeared tenable. Or if this has not been held tenable it has yet frequently been held possible to argue for that (as it were) modified or attenuated form of poetical justice represented by the Aristotelian *hamartia*—the notion that there is *some* relationship or correspondence between conduct and character on the one hand and earthly destiny on the other. Critics consequently find themselves labouring to create for each victim some *hamartia* or other. Thus Rymer would jeeringly find in Desdemona this tragic flaw: that she was careless about her linen—that the play is the tragedy of a handkerchief. Others with more seriousness have averred that Cordelia was blameworthy in failing of a little harmless and tactful prevarication. Even King Duncan has been held gravely at fault in imperilling not only his own life but that of his chamber grooms by rashly disregarding that *hoarser croak* whereby the sagacious raven would have apprised him of the inadvisability of entering Macbeth's castle.

It is apparent to us nowadays (whether rightly or wrongly) that all this represents a false cast in the interpretation of Shakespeare. Yet when Dr. Johnson puts the thing at its most general, and declares 'it is always a writer's duty to make the world better', we are conscious of a proposition which, at least, must be treated more warily. Has Shakespeare any aim to instruct? Poets in his time were certainly *taught* that they had a duty to do so. Even if he had no didactic intention, did he yet take for granted any religious or ethical system, within the affirmations of which he unquestioningly worked? Answering this is very difficult, for the simple and obvious reason that all in Shakespeare is expressed in dramatic or personative form. Thus much has been written of recent years about Shakespeare's adherence to mediaeval notions of order and degree. A speech by Ulysses in *Troilus and Cressida* (I. iii. 75 ff.), another by the Archbishop of Canterbury in *Henry V* (I. ii 183 ff.), a third by Menenius in *Coriolanus* (I. i. 101 ff.) are constantly cited as vindicating this. Yet we may well ask, as Professor Harbage does in *As They Liked It*,[1] perhaps the best book on our subject yet published, if anything of all this is designed as doctrinal. 'It cannot be ignored that each of the three speeches is delivered by an unscrupulous politician meeting an immediate problem—advocating a practical programme of somewhat debatable merit.' Moreover, Professor Harbage shows, this is only one instance of a pervasive ambiguousness in Shakespeare's dealing with ethical issues. It may almost be said to be the rule that when his characters come hard up against a

[1] The Macmillan Company, New York, 1947.

moral problem proper—a moral dilemma or hard choice—the dramatist finds means to let them off. The issue is suspended, dissolved or
dodged; some theatricality, some trick of distraction is brought in.
Even in *Measure for Measure*, the play most commonly cited in arguments here, the dramatist is thoroughly evasive in the end. Then again,
a somewhat similar phenomenon confronts us in the study of Shakespearian character. Swinburne[1] describes Brutus as the 'very noblest
figure of a typical and ideal republican in all the literature of the
world'. But when we look hard at Brutus we see something more
complicated and less edifying. Morally, indeed, it is surely the prime
characteristic of Shakespeare's major characters that they keep us
guessing all the time. Are they, perhaps, constructed to that end?
Here, once more, is Professor Harbage:

> Claudius, Gertrude, and Hamlet require constant evaluation on our part.
> We have to keep weighing them on our scales. Always in Shakespeare we
> perceive that the good might be better and the bad might be worse, and we
> are excited by our perceptions. The virtuous seem to need our counsel, and
> the vicious seem capable of understanding our censure. We are linked to the
> former by sensations of solicitude, and to the latter by moments of sympathy
> and understanding. We are constantly *involved*.

In all this, Shakespeare's characters are at an opposite remove from, say,
Corneille's. They never give the impression of being moral athletes—
a sort of ethical Brains Trust knowing all the answers and existing in
order to give an exhibition of them. They are not, in fact, the creations
of a moralist. They are not even the creations of an artist who is
obliged to pretend at all hard to be a moralist. Rather they are the
elements in an entertainment of which the stuff and substance is, indeed, the moral nature of man, but the end of which is not moralistic.
Shakespeare, in short, sees it as the business of the poet to exhibit, not
to pronounce upon, moral behaviour. In one sense he is dealing with
morals all the time. There is scarcely a speech, scarcely even a song in
all his plays untouched by ethical sentiment. He deals with morals
always; but as a moralist, never. He renders us more aware of ourselves as creatures of good and evil; but he seems to do this rather because such awareness is pleasurable than because it conduces to salvation. He does not work out moral problems for us; yet he leaves us, as
moral beings, more alert than he found us. This may itself be a moral
act, and laudable. But certainly if (as Johnson would have the artist do)

[1] Algernon Charles Swinburne: *A Study of Shakespeare* (1880).

Shakespeare 'makes the world better' it is by exercising our moral interests and perceptions rather than by any deliberate proposal to alter them, to expound patterns of behaviour, or to bend fiction to the support of principle and precept.

It comes down then (I think) to this. Shakespeare is not ambitious to instruct us. He tells us, indeed, in that Epilogue to *The Tempest* which is conceivably his artistic testament, that *his project was to please*. He pleases us as moral beings—in virtue of our being creatures of good and evil, interested in good and evil. But the interest in good and evil for which he caters is the common man's, not the professional's: Shakespeare does not write as a casuist or for casuists. He writes as one good-hearted for the good-hearted. He has perhaps more insight into how human beings do behave than curiosity about how they *ought* to behave.

But to all this it must be added that the plays create for themselves, and exist in, a real and distinguishable moral climate. It is unmistakable! The Victorians were fond of assuring us that Shakespeare, morally, was as sound as a bell; and there can be no doubt that the Victorians were right. Study Shakespeare's silences and avoidances; study the things he dropped as he worked from his sources. The conclusion to which we are bound to come is that he was a thoroughly wholesome person. Some of his plays must strike us as holding shadows dark enough. But the air is clean, the soil sweet, and the plenty (as with Chaucer) distinguishably God's.

9

THE SUCCESS OF 'MUCH ADO ABOUT NOTHING'

by GRAHAM STOREY

MAY I confess that I only added the first words of my title when I was well into preparing this lecture? Do not mistake me: the riches of the play—the sheer exhilaration of the encounters between Benedick and Beatrice and their arabesques of wit; the superb stupidity of Dogberry and Verges and *their* arabesques of misunderstanding; the skilful weaving and disentanglement of the comic imbroglio—all these are a joy to see and hear, and belong to Shakespeare's most assured writing. But it is a commonplace of criticism that a successful play, like any other work of art, must be a unity: what Coleridge called the Imagination's 'esemplastic power' must shape into one its individual forces and beauties. Whether *Much Ado* has this unity was the question that worried me.

It did not worry Shakespeare's contemporaries. The play offered an exciting Italianate melodrama, enlivened by two variegated sets of 'humours': the wit-combats and properly-rewarded over-reachings of Benedick and Beatrice, and the low-life comedy of Dogberry and Verges; and remember that George Chapman and Ben Jonson had just started a run of fashionable 'humour' plays. As in all proper comedies, the story came out all right in the end. 'Strike up, pipers! *Dance.*' The formula ends that other comedy with a similarly riddling title, *As You Like It*; and whatever the differences of tone, the effect does not vary so much from that of the conclusion of *Twelfth Night*, the third of this group of plays written at the turn of the century:

> A great while ago the world begun,
> With hey, ho, the wind and the rain;
> But that's all one, our play is done,
> And we'll strive to please you every day.

The humours were what the contemporary audience remembered the

128

play by. '*Benedicte and Betteris*,' say the Lord Treasurer's accounts for 1613: and *Much Ado* was almost certainly meant. 'Benedick and Beatrice', wrote Charles I in his second Folio, as a second title to the play— exercising a similar Stuart prerogative in renaming *Twelfth Night* 'The Tragedy of Malvolio'. The 'main plot' is clearly being regarded as a kind of serious relief to the much more absorbing comedy. When, with the Restoration, Shakespeare had to face the formidable canons of the neo-Classic critics, this central plot came in for some hard questioning. The criticism was, as we should expect, formal: the *decorum* was at fault. 'The fable is absurd,' writes Charles Gildon, in 1710, in an essay[1] often reprinted during the eighteenth century; 'the charge against Hero is too shocking for tragedy or comedy, and Claudio's conduct is against the nature of love'. He is almost equally concerned that the people of Messina do not act and talk, he says, like natives of a warm country.

But, at the turn of this century, one or two critics began to show a quite new uneasiness about the play. They found, not unity, not the almost unblemished gaiety that they found in *As You Like It* or *Twelfth Night*; but jarring tones, a gratuitous suffering and heartlessness in crisis —the Church Scene—that the rest of the play could not wipe out, and a distressing inconsistency in the characters of Claudio, the Prince and Leonato. The critical approaches were different: but the resultant *uncomfortableness* they generated was much the same. And it has undoubtedly left its mark upon many performances since.

The most frequent cause of uneasiness has been to respond to the play as though the protagonists were psychologically real. It is indeed the most expected response, as the dominant mode of the theatre is still naturalism. But it plays havoc with *Much Ado* as *comedy*. Stopford Brooke, writing in 1913[2] as a Bradleyan, shows what happens. He clearly wants to like the play; yet its very centre, the exposure in church, is, he writes, 'a repulsive scene'. 'In it all the characters will be tried in the fire'; and, as a Victorian clergyman of strong, if sensitive views, he tries them. They emerge—Claudio, Don Pedro and Leonato —shallow, wilful, cruel, inconsistent with what they were before; and the play, its centre contaminated, is virtually handed over to Benedick and Beatrice. That, I am convinced, is not how Shakespeare wrote the play. But the figures of the main plot are bound to appear in this light, if we see them as fully-rounded characters and subject them to the tests

[1] *Remarks on the Plays of Shakespeare:* included in *Shakespeare's Poems*, 1710 (supplementary vol. to Rowe's *Works of Shakespeare*).
[2] *Ten More Plays of Shakespeare*, 1913, p. 21.

of psychological consistency. I see them as something much nearer 'masks': as not quite so far removed from the formalized figures of *Love's Labour's Lost*, where most of the play's life resides in the plot-pattern and the dance of verbal wit, as many critics have suggested. I will return to this suggestion later. Meanwhile, I only want to insist that the opposite approach—that of naturalistic realism—stretches the play much further than a comedy can go, and makes almost impossible demands of the actors for the last two Acts. It can also lead to a quite ludicrous literalism, as where Stopford Brooke, quoting the magnificent, absurd *finale* of Beatrice's outburst against Claudio after the Church Scene—'O God, that I were a man! I would eat his heart in the market-place'—solemnly comments, 'Of course, she would not have done it.'[1]

Others though, besides the 'naturalist' critics, have found *Much Ado* disturbing: and disturbing because they do not discover in it the unity that I have made my main question. Sir Edmund Chambers,[2] writing fifty years ago, was probably the first to note what he called its 'clashing of dramatic planes'. 'Elements,' he wrote, 'of tragedy, comedy, tragi-comedy, and farce are thrust together;' and the result is not unity, but 'an unco-ordinated welter', a dramatic impressionism that sacrifices the whole to the brilliance of individual scenes or passages of dialogue or even individual lines. Other writers have more recently said much the same: the play's elements are incompatible; the plot too harsh for the characters; it is the wrong kind of romantic story to blend with comedy. 'This happy play,' as 'Q.' called it in his Introduction to the *New Cambridge Shakespeare*, 1923, seems, in fact, to be in danger of losing its central place in the canon of Shakespeare's comedies (or it would be, if critics were taken too seriously).

I think that all these critics have seriously underrated the *comic* capacity of both Shakespeare and his audience: the capacity to create, and to respond to, varying and often contradictory experiences simultaneously; to create a pattern of human behaviour from their blendings and juxtapositions; and to obtain a keen enjoyment from seeing that pattern equally true at all levels. I will try to apply this claim to *Much Ado*.

'For man is a giddy thing, and this is my conclusion,' says Benedick

---

[1] Op. cit., p. 27: quoted by T. W. Craik in *Much Ado About Nothing* (*Scrutiny*, October 1953).
[2] Introduction to *Much Ado* (Red Letter Shakespeare, 1904-8). Reprinted in *Shakespeare: A Survey*, 1925.

in the last scene; and this is surely the play's 'cause' or ruling theme. 'Giddy', a favourite Elizabethan word: 'light-headed, frivolous, flighty, inconstant', it meant by 1547; 'whirling or circling round with bewildering rapidity' (1593); mentally intoxicated, 'elated to thought-lessness' (in Dr. Johnson's *Dictionary*). *Much Ado* has all these mean-ings in abundance. And Benedick's dictum, placed where it is, followed by the dance (reminiscent perhaps of the *La Ronde*-like Masked Ball of Act II), suggests eternal recurrence: 'Man is a giddy thing'—and ever more will be so. The impetus to two of the play's three plots is the impetus to all the comedies, the propensity to love-making: one plot begins and ends with it; the other ends with it. And the impetus to the third plot, the antics of the Watch ('the vulgar humours of the play,' said Gildon,[1] 'are remarkably varied and distinguished'), is self-love: the innocent, thoughtless, outrageous love of Dogberry for him-self and his position.

Inconstancy, mental intoxication, elation to thoughtlessness: the accompaniment of all these states is deception, self-deception, miscom-prehension. And deception, the prelude to 'giddiness', operates at every level of *Much Ado*. It is the common denominator of the three plots, and its mechanisms—eavesdroppings, mistakes of identity, disguises and maskings, exploited hearsay—are the major stuff of the play.

In the main plot—the Italian melodrama that Shakespeare took from Matteo Bandello, Bishop of Agen—the deception-theme is, of course, the most harshly obvious. Don John's instrument, Borachio, deceives 'even the very eyes' of Claudio and the Prince; Claudio, the Prince and Leonato are all convinced that Hero has deceived them; Hero is violently deceived in her expectations of marriage, stunned by the slander; the Friar's plan to give her out as dead deceives everyone it is meant to.

The deceptions of Benedick and Beatrice in Leonato's garden-bower serve a function as a comic echo of all this. They are also beautifully-managed examples of a favourite Elizabethan device: the over-reacher over-reached, the 'enginer hoist with his own petar', the marriage-mocker and husband-scorner taken in by—to us—a transparently ob-vious trick. (It is a major part of the play's delight that the audience always knows more than the actors: hints are dropped throughout; a Sophoclean comic irony pervades every incident.) Here, the meta-phors of stalking and fishing are both deliberately overdone; and the effect is to emphasize that each of these eavesdroppings is a piece of play-acting, a mock-ceremonious game:

[1] Op. cit.

DON PEDRO: Come hither, Leonato: what was it you told me of to-day,
that your niece Beatrice was in love with Signior Benedick?
CLAUDIO: O! ay: (Stalk on, stalk on; the fowl sits.) I did never think that
lady would have loved any man.[1]

And in the next scene:

URSULA: The pleasant'st angling is to see the fish
                   Cut with her golden oars the silver stream,
                   And greedily devour the treacherous bait:
                   So angle we for Beatrice. . . .
HERO: No, truly, Ursula, she is too disdainful;
                   I know her spirits are as coy and wild
                   As haggards of the rock.[2]

The contrast between prose and a delicate, artful blank verse
makes sharper the difference of the fantasy each of them is offered.
Benedick is given a superbly ludicrous caricature of a love-sick
Beatrice, which only his own vanity could believe:

CLAUDIO: Then down upon her knees she falls, weeps, sobs, beats her heart,
tears her hair, prays, curses: 'O sweet Benedick! God give me
patience! . . .' Hero thinks surely she will die.[3]

And his own response, a mixture of comically solemn resolutions and
illogical reasoning, is equally exaggerated:

I must not seem proud: happy are they that hear their detractions, and can
put them to mending. . . . No; the world must be peopled.[4]

Beatrice has her feminine vanity played on more delicately, but just
as directly: she is given a not-too-exaggerated picture of herself as Lady
Disdain, spiced with the praises of the man she is missing. And her
response, in formal verse, clinches the success of the manoeuvre:

                   What fire is in mine ears? Can this be true?
                   Stand I condemn'd for pride and scorn so much?
                   Contempt, farewell! and maiden pride, adieu!
                   No glory lives behind the back of such. . . .[5]

'Elated to thoughtlessness' indeed (and particularly after all their
earlier wit): but not only by a trick. Benedick and Beatrice are both, of

[1] II. iii. 98–103.   [2] III. i. 26 ff.   [3] II. iii. 162–5 and 191.
[4] Ibid., 248 ff.   [5] III. i. 107 ff.

course, perfect examples of self-deception: about their own natures, about the vanity their railing hides (and none the less vanity for its charm and wit), about the affection they are capable of—in need of—when the aggression is dropped, about their real relations to each other. This gives the theme of deception in their plot the higher, more permanent status of revelation. Hence much of its delight.

But no one in the play is more mentally intoxicated than Dogberry. He is king of all he surveys: of Verges, his perfect foil; of the Watch; of the peace of Messina at night. Only words—engines of deception—constantly trip him up; though, like Mrs. Malaprop, he sails on magnificently unaware:

> Dost thou not suspect my place? Dost thou not suspect my years? O that he were here to write me down an ass! . . . I am a wise fellow; and, which is more, an officer; and, which is more, a householder; and, which is more, as pretty a piece of flesh as any in Messina. . . .[1]

With Dogberry, the theme of giddiness, of self-deception, of revelling in the appearances that limitless vanity has made true for him, reaches miraculous proportions.

There is, though, the further meaning of 'giddy', also, I suggested, warranted by Benedick's conclusion: 'whirling or circling round'. The structure of *Much Ado*—the melodramatic Italian love-story, enlivened by two humour-plots of Shakespeare's own invention—follows an established Elizabethan comedy-pattern: Chapman was to use it in *The Gentleman Usher* and *Monsieur d'Olive*; *Twelfth Night*—allowing for obvious differences in the tone of the central plot—is the obvious successor. Musically, we could call it a theme and variations. But you have merely to consider the Chapman comedies, where the two plots only arbitrarily meet—or Thomas Middleton, who brought in a collaborator to help him with the 'echoing sub-plot' of his tragedy, *The Changeling* —to see Shakespeare's extraordinary structural skill here. 'Faultless balance, blameless rectitude of design,' said Swinburne: he is right, and it was not what most of his contemporaries recognized in *Much Ado*. But it still does not strongly enough suggest the grasp, the intellectual energy, that holds the play together and makes the kind of suggestions about reality in which the Elizabethan audience delighted. Here, again, Benedick's conclusion says more. Not only the play's wit—a microcosm of its total life—whirls and circles, with often deadly effect ('Thou hast frighted the word out of his right sense, so forcible is thy

[1] iv. 2. 79 ff.

wit,' cries Benedick to Beatrice in the last Act: it suggests that wit—
and wit's author—can destroy or create at will) one of man's main
instruments of living; but, in their vibrations and juxtapositions, the
three plots do much the same.

Twice the plots fuse—once to advance the story, once to deepen it—
and the achievement gives a peculiar exhilaration. Each time it is something of a shock; and then we see that, within the rules of probability
laid down by Aristotle for writers of tragedy (we can validly apply
them to comedy too), it is wonderfully right that it should have
happened like that.

The first occasion is the discovery by the Watch of the plot
against Hero. When they line up to receive their instructions from
Dogberry and Verges—on the principle of peace at all costs—it seems
incredible that they should ever discover anything. But they do:
though, admittedly, Shakespeare has to make Borachio drunk to make
it possible. The Watch and their Officers are now locked firmly into
the main plot, with all their ripples of absurdity; and the final dénouement is theirs. The innocent saved by the innocent, we may say; or,
more likely (and certainly more Elizabethanly), the knaves caught out
by the fools. 'Is our whole dissembly appeared?' asks Dogberry, as he
looks round for the rest of the Court. 'Which be the malefactors?'
asks the Sexton. 'Marry, that am I and my partner,' answers Dogberry,
with pride.

However we look at it, the impact has clearly changed the status of
the villains. 'Ducdame, ducdame, ducdame,' sings Jaques (it is his own
verse) to his banished companions in the Forest of Arden. 'What's that
"*ducdame*"?' asks Amiens. ' 'Tis a Greek invocation to call fools into a
circle.' Here in *Much Ado*, the knaves have been thrust in with the
fools: if it makes the fools feel much more important than they are, it
makes the villains much less villainous; or villainous in a way that
disturbs us less. This is one device by which the interlocking of plots
establishes the play's unity, and, in doing so, creates a new, more inclusive tone.

The entry of the Watch into the centre of the play advances the
story. The entry of Benedick and Beatrice, in that short packed dialogue after the Church Scene, where they declare their belief in Hero
and their love for each other, seems as though it must do so too; but in
fact it does not. Rather, it does not if we see the heart of the play now
as Hero's vindication. That is brought about without help from
Benedick; and, indeed, Benedick's challenge to Claudio, vehemently

undertaken and dramatically presented, is, by the end of the play, treated very casually: only perfunctorily recalled, and easily brushed aside in the general mirth and reconciliation of the ending. Perhaps, then, this scene *removes* the play's centre, puts it squarely in the Benedick and Beatrice plot? That is how many critics have taken it; and what, for example, was in 'Q.'s' mind when he wrote of the scene's climax: ' "Kill Claudio!" These two words nail the play'; and again, '. . . at this point undoubtedly Shakespeare transfers [the play] from *novella* to drama—to a real spiritual conflict'.[1] It is certainly how many producers and actors—with understandable temptation—have interpreted the scene.

Much Ado demands, of course, a continual switching of interest. We focus it in turn on Benedick and Beatrice, on Hero and Claudio, on Don John and Borachio, on Dogberry and Verges, back to Hero and Claudio, and so on. This gives something of the controlled whirl and circling motion I have commented on. It is also true that this scene between Benedick and Beatrice has a new seriousness; that their shared, intuitive belief in Hero's innocence has deepened their relations with each other, and our attitude towards them. But that is not the same as saying that the play has become something different, or that its centre has shifted. That would seriously jeopardize its design; and, although there *are* flaws in the play, I am sure that its design is what Shakespeare intended it to be.

The play's true centre is in fact neither a plot nor a group of characters, but a theme: Benedick's conclusion about man's giddiness, his irresistible propensity to be taken in by appearances. It is a theme that must embody an *attitude*; and it is the attitude here that provides *Much Ado*'s complexity: its disturbingness (where it does disturb); its ambiguities, where the expected response seems far from certain; but its inclusiveness too, where it is assured. For Shakespeare's approach to this theme at the turn of the century (one could call it the major theme of his whole writing-life, probed at endlessly varying levels) was far from simple. The riddling titles of the group of comedies written within these two years, 1598–1600, are deceptive, or at any rate ambiguous. *Much Ado About Nothing, As You Like It, Twelfth Night; or, What You Will*: these can all, as titles, be interpreted lightly, all but cynically, as leaving it to the audience how to take them with a disarming, amused casualness. Or, equally, they can leave room for manœuvre, include several attitudes, without committing themselves to any. This blending or jostling

---

[1] Op. cit., pp. xiii and xv.

K

of sympathies is sufficiently evident in these comedies to have won for itself the status of a convention. Dr. M. C. Bradbrook, who has lovingly pursued all the conventions of the Elizabethan theatre, has called it 'polyphonic music';[1] Mr. S. L. Bethell, more directly concerned with the Elizabethan audience, calls their capacity to respond to difficult aspects of the same situation, simultaneously, but in often contradictory ways, 'multi-consciousness'.[2] *Much Ado* exhibits the one and demands the other in the highest degree.

We must, I think, respond in much the same way as the Elizabethan audience did, if we are to appreciate to the full the scene between Benedick and Beatrice in the church; and that oddly-tempered, but still powerful scene of Leonato's outbursts to Antonio at the beginning of Act V. For both these scenes, however different—the first is set in a half-comic key, the second employs a rhetoric that is nearer the formally 'tragic'—employ deliberate ambiguities of tone and demand a double response.

I will examine the Benedick and Beatrice scene first. Here, Shakespeare clearly means us to sympathize with Beatrice's vehement attacks on Claudio on Hero's behalf, and with the mounting strength of Benedick's allegiance to her. At the same time, he overdoes the vehemence, exposes it to the comedy of his wry appraisal, brings both characters to the edge of delicate caricature. The scene's climax (I have quoted 'Q.'s' remarks on it) has been taken to show the maximum deployment of Shakespeare's sympathy. It also exhibits perfectly his comedy. Benedick and Beatrice have just protested they love each other with all their heart:

> BENEDICK: Come, bid me do anything for thee.
> BEATRICE: Kill Claudio.
> BENEDICK: Ha! not for the wide world.
> BEATRICE: You kill me to deny it. Farewell.[3]

Superbly dramatic: three fresh shocks in three lines, and, with each, a new insight into human nature; but also highly ironical. To demand the killing of Claudio, in the world established by the play, is ridiculous. To refuse it at once, after the avowal to do *anything*, equally so, however right Benedick may be ethically (and the irony demands that he refuse *at once*: I am sure Dr. Bradbrook[4] is wrong in saying that he

---

[1] In *Shakespeare and Elizabethan Poetry*, 1951: the title of Chapter X.
[2] In *Shakespeare and the Popular Dramatic Tradition*, 1948, *passim*.
[3] IV. i. 293–296.
[4] Op. cit., p. 183.

hesitates). And for Beatrice, upon this refusal, to take back her heart, having given it a moment before, completes the picture: passionately generous to her wronged cousin, if we isolate the exchange and treat it as a piece of magnificent impressionism; heroic, absurd and a victim to passion's deception, if we see it—as we surely must—within the context of the whole play.

Mr. T. W. Craik, in an admirably close analysis of *Much Ado* in *Scrutiny*,[1] makes this scene between Benedick and Beatrice a pivot of the play's values. It is, he says, ' "placed" by the scene's beginning [i.e. the earlier events in the church]. Putting the point crudely, it represents the triumph of emotion over reason; the reasonableness of Friar Francis's plan for Claudio and Hero. . . .'[2] I agree with him when he goes on to say that 'emotion's triumph' is laughable in Benedick (though I think he exaggerates its extent). But surely it is an over-simplification to identify Shakespeare's attitude—as he seems to do more explicitly later in his essay[3]—with the Friar's common sense. The Friar is essential to the plot (and much more competent in guiding it than his brother of *Romeo and Juliet*); and his calm sanity admirably 'places' Leonato's hysteria in the Church Scene. But the whole spirit of the play seems to me antagonistic to any *one* attitude's dominating it. And the second scene I want to examine—Leonato and Antonio in v. i.—appears to bear this out.

For here Antonio begins as the repository of the Friar's wisdom, as the Stoic, calming Leonato down. Yet, as experience floods in on him—the memory of wrong in the shape of Don Pedro and Claudio—he too becomes 'flesh and blood', and ends up by out-doing Leonato:

> What, man! I know them, yea,
> And what they weigh, even to the utmost scruple,
> Scrambling, out-facing, fashion-monging boys,
> That lie and cog and flout, deprave and slander,
> Go antickly, show outward hideousness,
> And speak off half a dozen dangerous words,
> How they might hurt their enemies, if they durst;
> And this is all!

LEONATO: But, brother Antony,—[4]

The roles are neatly reversed. But the invective is too exuberantly

[1] October 1953, op. cit.   [3] p. 308.
[3] p. 314.   [4] v. i. 92–9.

Shakespearian to be merely—or even mainly—caricature. Can we say the same of Leonato's outburst that begins the scene?

> I pray thee, cease thy counsel,
> which falls into mine ears as profitless
> As water in a sieve: Give not me counsel; . . .[1]

Considered realistically, it must make us uneasy. Leonato knows (Antonio does not) that Hero is in fact alive: to that extent, most of his emotion is counterfeit. Again, we remember his hysterical self-pity of the Act before, when his attitude to his daughter was very different:

> Do not live, Hero; do not ope thine eyes;
> . . . Griev'd I, I had but one?
> Chid I for that at frugal nature's frame?
> O! one too much by thee. Why had I one?
> Why ever wast thou lovely in mine eyes?[2]

To some extent, he is still dramatizing himself in this scene, still enjoying his grief. But his language is no longer grotesque or self-convicting, as that was. He echoes a theme—'experience against auctoritee', the Middle Ages called it—which in *Romeo and Juliet* had been nearer a set piece:

> FRIAR LAURENCE: Let me dispute with thee of thy estate.
> ROMEO: Thou canst not speak of that thou dost not feel. . . .[3]

but here it has a new authenticity in movement and image:

> for, brother, men
> Can counsel and speak comfort to that grief
> Which they themselves not feel; but, tasting it,
> Their counsel turns to passion, which before
> Would give preceptial medicine to rage,
> Fetter strong madness in a silken thread,
> Charm ache with air and agony with words.[4]

Again, as with Benedick and Beatrice, the whole scene, ending with the challenge of Claudio and the Prince to a duel, presents a mixture of tones: appeal to our sympathy, exaggeration which is on or over the edge of comedy.

Both these scenes, peripheral to the main plot, but of the essence of the play's art, demand, if they are to be fully appreciated, a complex

---

[1] v. i. 3–5.   [2] IV. i. 125, 129–32.   [3] III. iii. 62–3.   [4] v, i. 20–6.

response. What, then, of the crux of *Much Ado*, the shaming of Hero in church? On any realistic view it must, as has been said, be a repulsive scene: an innocent girl slandered and shamed by her betrothed, with apparently deliberate calculation, during her marriage-service, and in front of her father—the city's Governor—and the whole congregation. However we see it, Shakespeare's writing here is sufficiently powerful to give us some wincing moments. No interpretation can take away the shock of Claudio's brutal

> There, Leonato, take her back again:
> Give not this rotten orange to your friend;[1]

or of the Prince's heartless echo:

> What should I speak?
> I stand dishonour'd, that have gone about
> To link my dear friend to a common stale.

The clipped exchange between Leonato and Don John that follows seems to give the lie the ring of finality, to make false true in front of our eyes:

> LEONATO: Are these things spoken, or do I but dream?
> DON JOHN: Sir, they are spoken, and these things are true.

The generalizing assent, helped by the closed-circle form of question and answer, has a claustrophobic effect on both Hero and us (I think of the nightmare world of 'double-think' closing in in Orwell's *Nineteen Eighty-Four*: this is a verbal nightmare too). Momentarily, we have left Messina and might well be in the meaner, darker world of that later play of similarly quibbling title, but much less pleasant implications, *All's Well That Ends Well*. There 'these things' are commented on by a Second French Lord, who knows human nature; knows Parolles and his hollowness: 'Is it possible he should know what he is, and be that he is?'; and Bertram and his meanness: 'As we are ourselves, what things are we!' ('Merely our own traitors,' adds the First Lord, almost redundantly.)

Then, with a jolt, we remember that 'these things' are *not* true. They are not true *in* the play, which is the first thing to remind ourselves of, if we wish to preserve the play's balance as comedy. For in the later and so-called 'Problem Comedies' (tragi-comedies, I prefer to follow A. P. Rossiter in calling them)—*All's Well, Troilus and Cressida*,

[1] IV. i. 31–2.

Measure for Measure—such accusations *are* true, or would be true if those accused of them had had their way—had not been tricked into do-ing something quite different from what they thought they were doing (Cressida comes into the first category; Bertram and Angelo into the second). But here the characters are playing out an act of deception, each of them (except Don John) unaware in fact of what the truth is. To that extent, they are all innocent, Claudio and the Prince as well as Hero: played on by the plot, not (as we sense wherever tragic feeling enters) playing it, willing it. The *situation* is in control.

Secondly, they are not true *outside* the play. To state that at all prob-ably sounds absurd. But genuine tragic feeling in Shakespeare forces its extra-theatrical truth on us: continuously in the tragedies, spasmodically —but still disturbingly—in the tragi-comedies. We know only too well how permanently true are *Hamlet, Othello, Macbeth*. But the exposures of the tragi-comedies (Hero's shaming by no means exhausts the *genre*) inflict on us truths about human nature—we may prefer to call them half-truths. 'But man, proud man,' cries out Isabella (and she has every justification),

> Drest in a little brief authority,
> Most ignorant of what he's most assur'd,
> His glassy essence, like an angry ape,
> Plays such fantastic tricks before high heaven
> As make the angels weep; who, with our spleens,
> Would all themselves laugh mortal.[1]

Here, all the possibilities of human nature are on the stage. We are *in-volved with* the people who are hurt or betrayed or even exposed (Angelo, as he cries out on the 'blood' that has betrayed him, is poten-tially a tragic figure); we are involved too in the language and its searing comments on human frailty or baseness.

But go back to the scene in *Much Ado*, and, after the first shock, we are no longer fully involved. First, because the identities of Hero and Claudio have been kept to an irreducible minimum. That is why I earlier called them 'masks'. They have a part to play in a situation that is the climax to the whole play's theme; but they have not the core of being—or of dramatic being—which suffers or deliberately causes suffering. It would be quite different—ghastly and impossible—to imagine Beatrice in Hero's position.

And, secondly, the whole scene's deliberate *theatricality* lessens our

[1] *Measure for Measure*, II. ii. 117–23.

involvement and distances our emotions. It emphasizes that it is, after all, only a play and intended for our entertainment;[1] we know that the accusation of Hero is false and—as this is a comedy—is bound to be put right by the end. First Claudio, then Leonato, takes the centre of the stage: the effect is to diminish any exclusively tragic concern for Hero, as we appraise the responses of the other two. There can be no doubt about Leonato's: it is highly exaggerated and hovers on the edge of caricature. We recognize the tones from *Romeo and Juliet*. There, vindictive, absurd old Capulet hustles Juliet on to a marriage she abhors; and then, in a stylized, cruelly comic scene, is shown (with his wife and the Nurse) over-lamenting her when she feigns death to avoid it. Shakespeare has little pity for this kind of selfishness. Here, as Leonato inveighs against his daughter—now in a swoon—we have self-pity masking itself as righteous indignation: the repetitions show where his real interest lies:

> But mine, and mine I lov'd, and mine I prais'd,
> And mine that I was proud on, mine so much
> That I myself was to myself not mine,
> Valuing of her . . .[2]

Yet, as he goes on, the tone alters, as so often in this volatile, quick-changing play:

> . . . why, she—O! she is fallen
> Into a pit of ink, that the wide sea
> Hath drops too few to wash her clean again,
> And salt too little which may season give
> To her foul tainted flesh.[3]

That is still over-violent, but the images of Hero's stain and of the sea failing to make her clean introduce a different note. We have heard it in Claudio's accusation:

> Behold! how like a maid she blushes here.
> O! what authority and show of truth
> Can cunning sin cover itself withal. . . .[4]

and in his outburst against seeming: 'Out on thee! Seeming! I will write against it. . . .'

[1] S. L. Bethell makes the same point about the ill-treatment of Malvolio: op. cit., pp. 33–4.
[2] IV. i. 138–41.
[3] Ibid., 141–5.
[4] IV. i. 34–6.

Again, there is more here than his earlier, calculated stage-management of the scene. It is as though the situation has suddenly taken charge, become horribly true for a moment; and as if Shakespeare has injected into it some of the disgust at sexual betrayal we know from the dark Sonnets and from the crises of a host of later plays: *Measure for Measure*, *Troilus and Cressida*, *Hamlet*, *Othello*, *Cymbeline*.

This apparent intrusion of something alien—seemingly personal—into the very centre of the play was what had led me to doubt its success. I was wrong, I think (and it follows that I think other doubters are wrong), for three reasons. First, the intrusion, the cold music, is only a touch; one of several themes that make up the scene. Its language is harsh, but chimes in with nothing else in the play: no deadly vibrations or echoes are set up. Compare Claudio and Leonato with Troilus or Isabella, or, even more, with Hamlet or Othello, in whose words we feel a wrenching, an almost physical dislocation of set attitudes and beliefs: and the outbursts here have something of the isolated, artificial effect of set speeches.

Secondly, the play's central theme—of deception, miscomprehension, man's 'giddiness' at every level—is dominant enough to claim much of our response in *every* scene: including this climax in the church that embodies it most harshly, but most fully. And, in its many-sidedness and 'many-tonedness', this theme is, as I have tried to show, one well within the tradition of Elizabethan comedy.

Thirdly, and lastly, the *tone* of *Much Ado*—animated, brittle, observant, delighting in the ado men make—does not have to stretch itself much to accommodate the moments of questioning in the church. And this tone is ultimately, I think, what we most remember of the play: what gives it its genuine difference from *As You Like It* and *Twelfth Night*. Although two of its most loved figures are Warwickshire yokels (and nothing could change them), the aura of Bandello's Italian plot pervades the rest. The love of sharp wit and the love of melodrama belong there; so do the sophisticated, unsentimental tone, and the ubiquitous, passed-off classical references: to Cupid and Hercules, Leander and Troilus. Gildon was wrong: in essentials, the people of Messina *do* act and talk like natives of a warm country.

The tone I mean is most apparent—most exhilarating and most exacting—in the wit-flytings between Benedick and Beatrice; but it dominates the word-play throughout: and this is one of the most word-conscious and wittiest of all Shakespeare's comedies. If I have said little about the words and the wit, this is because no one was more at home there, and could better communicate his enjoyment of them, than the late A. P. Rossiter: and you can read his lecture[1] on the play from one of the last of his memorable Shakespeare courses at Cambridge. My own debt to him will be very clear to all of you who heard his many lectures here at Stratford.

[1] One of twelve lectures given at Stratford and Cambridge, to be published in 1959 by Longmans.

IO

THE LANGUAGE OF THE LAST PLAYS

by JAMES SUTHERLAND

ALL, or nearly all, the most respected criticism of Shakespeare nowa-days is addressed to the elucidation of particular plays; and when the critic is more particularly concerned with Shakespeare's mode of expression we shall probably find him inquiring into the dominant imagery of the play in question, to the virtual exclusion of all other aspects of Shakespeare's style. Yet imagery, however important, is only part of the total impact of language on a reader or listener; and I hope, too, that it is still a legitimate critical activity to interest oneself in Shakespeare's mode of composition without necessarily relating it closely to its dramatic context. What I wish to discuss is a particular kind of writing that seems to be almost peculiar to the later plays, and that appears in them only sporadically. Such passages, when they occur, do not always seem to have any specially dramatic significance, nor to offer, as the imagery so often does, a clue to the way in which Shakespeare apprehended a total situation: the evidence they provide is rather of the way in which Shakespeare's mind worked, and of how its working varied under different pressures.

If this approach to Shakespeare is at present unfashionable, and may even appear to be misguided, it still seems to me that any light that can be thrown on Shakespeare's mode of composition is worth having. Some years ago, in a notable book called *Shakespeare's Imagination*,[1] Dr. E. A. Armstrong drew our attention to the strange and wayward thoughts that will sometimes slide into Shakespeare's head, and he gave us some valuable clues to understanding how the apparently fortuitous and unpredictable in Shakespeare often follows a recurring pattern of association. But Dr. Armstrong's book, though it was by no means neglected, has not perhaps made the impression that might have been expected; and I can only suppose that his truths are not the ones that

[1] Lindsay Drummond, 1946.

144

the contemporary reader wants to hear. I doubt, therefore, if he will wish to hear mine either; but I have thought it right to warn him at the outset of what I am up to, and to repeat that in what follows I shall be concerned with a mode of composition that appears most frequently in the later plays, that seems to be peculiarly Shakespearian, and that is so odd and idiosyncratic that it asks for some explanation.

If I were to look for examples of this mode of composition in a single play I could find all that I need in *Cymbeline*, and I could begin with the opening lines of that play. Here, as often happens, the dramatist has some necessary information to impart to his audience; but he sets about it in a fashion that must have puzzled nine playgoers out of ten.

1ST GENT: You do not meet a man but frowns; our bloods
No more obey the heavens than our courtiers
Still seem as does the king.

2ND GENT:　　　　　　　　　　But what's the matter?

1ST GENT: His daughter, and the heir of's kingdom, whom
He purpos'd to his wife's sole son—a widow
That late he married,—hath referr'd herself
Unto a poor but worthy gentleman. She's wedded;
Her husband banish'd, she imprison'd: all
Is outward sorrow, though I think the king
Be touch'd at very heart.

2ND GENT:　　　　　　　　　　None but the king?

1ST GENT: He that hath lost her too; so is the queen,
That most desir'd the match; but not a courtier,
Although they wear their faces to the bent
Of the king's looks, hath a heart that is not
Glad at the thing they scowl at.

2ND GENT:　　　　　　　　　　And why so?

1ST GENT: He that hath miss'd the princess is a thing
Too bad for bad report: and he that hath her,—
I mean, that married her,—alack! good man!
And therefore banish'd—is a creature such
As, to seek through the regions of the earth
For one his like, there would be something failing
In him that should compare. I do not think
So fair an outward and such stuff within
Endows a man but he.

2ND GENT:　　　　　　　　　　You speak him fair.

1ST GENT: I do extend him, sir, within himself,
Crush him together rather than unfold
His measure duly.

2ND GENT: What's his name and birth?
    1ST GENT: I cannot delve him to the root: his father
                 Was call'd Sicilius. . . .

Of the first two and a half lines of the play Johnson remarked, 'This
passage is so difficult, that commentators may differ concerning it without animosity or shame'; but as Johnson was struggling with a corrupt
text we should not, perhaps, make too much of his difficulties. It is the
speech of the First Gentleman, 'He that hath miss'd the princess . . .',
that is most characteristic of the kind of writing I have in mind. In the
first place, it is obviously written at speed. It contains a parenthesis
(this in itself becomes a stylistic feature of the last plays): a parenthesis,
too, including the elliptical phrase, 'and therefore banish'd'. But the
lines that follow are still more characteristic of this late style: Shakespeare suddenly changes direction in the middle of a sentence, and then
completes the movement by going off on another foot. After 'and he
that hath her . . . is a creature such as', we expect some such phrase as
'cannot be surpassed' or 'would be hard to parallel'; but the dramatist
wants something much more emphatic than that, and rather than
cancel what he has already written and begin the speech all over again
(he 'never blotted a line') he brushes past the syntactical obstacle, and
the meaning comes through by reason of its force and with the help of
the speech rhythms rather than by any clearness of statement.
    Parenthesis, it is true, helps to give an air of spontaneity to dialogue;
it suggests a man thinking rapidly as he goes along, correcting himself,
modifying his original statement, and so on. It might therefore be
argued that Shakespeare is carefully and artfully inserting parentheses
in the long speeches of his characters in order to give them a natural
turn. I cannot, of course, disprove this, but in the lines I have quoted
Shakespeare cannot be said to be trying very hard to give a naturalistic
turn to his dialogue, and I suspect that the person who is thinking
rapidly, breaking off, making fresh starts, and so on, is not the character,
but Shakespeare himself.
    Parentheses occur again frequently in the long second scene in *The
Tempest* where Prospero is unfolding to Miranda the story of his past
misfortunes (again a passage giving some necessary information to his
audience), and more than once we shall find the same dislocation of the
syntax, when a new idea makes Shakespeare—and therefore Prospero
—swerve from his original intention.

    PROSPERO: The direful spectacle of the wrack, which touch'd

> The very virtue of compassion in thee,
> I have with such provision in mine art
> So safely order'd, that there is no soul—
> No, not so much perdition as an hair,
> Betid to any creature in the vessel
> Which thou heard'st cry, which thou saw'st sink. . . .[1]

There again Shakespeare begins by intending to say something like 'there is no soul lost', and then immediately begins groping his way to something stronger. The idea of 'loss' survives in the word 'perdition' (a much more powerful word), but by that time he has struck out in a new direction and has to finish in a way that leaves 'there is no soul' hanging in the air. Some commentators are so anxious to have Shakespeare writing correctly that they propose to read 'soil' for 'soul'. But the point is that Shakespeare is *not* writing correctly: he is writing at speed. So far is he indeed from slowing up as he grows older that he seems at times in his last plays to be driving himself harder than ever. When Heminge and Condell tell us that 'his mind and hand went together, and what he thought, he uttered with that easiness, that we have scarce received from him a blot in his papers', it may well be that the papers they had in mind were the manuscripts of his *latest* plays, rather than those that had been written twenty or thirty years before the publication of the First Folio. Speed, therefore, an increasing impatience to get the thing down on the paper, with a consequent danger of confusion, and an interesting tendency to be satisfied with a sort of impressionism—those are some of the factors that we have to take into account in the last plays. In the words of Charles Lamb, 'Shakespeare mingles everything, he runs line into line, embarrasses sentences and metaphors: before one idea has burst its shell, another is hatched and clamorous for disclosure.'

To return for the moment to the *Cymbeline* passage: if we are looking for evidence of hurry and impatience in Shakespeare, we may perhaps find it again in the phrase 'so fair an outward and such stuff within', where the dramatist grabs at the comprehensive but undeniably vague words, 'outward' and 'stuff within', to sum up the appearance and character of Posthumus. This has something of the impressionism I have mentioned, but perhaps a better example is to be found in an earlier (though still a comparatively late) play. When the sycophantic Regan and Goneril are expressing their love for their father, Regan seeks to go one better than her sister:

[1] I. ii. 26 ff.

> In my true heart
> I find she names my very deed of love;
> Only she comes too short: that I profess
> Myself an enemy to all other joys
> Which the most precious square of sense possesses. . . . [1]

The commentators have made lame work of 'the most precious square of sense', and one is tempted to suppose that if the matter had been referred to Shakespeare himself he might have given the same answer as Fielding's Shakespeare gave in Elysium when he was questioned about the right reading of a line in *Othello*: 'Faith, gentlemen, it is so long since I wrote the line, I have forgot my meaning.' What Shakespeare seems to be looking for in this passage is something emphatic to put in the mouth of Regan; it would not serve his purpose if Regan merely said 'all other joys that sense possesses', but if she says 'all other joys the square of sense possesses' the statement is considerably heightened, and if she calls it 'the most precious square of sense' it becomes more emphatic still. We have here an example of Burke's distinction between a strong expression and a clear expression. Shakespeare's desire, then, for something emphatic to suit the needs of the context undoubtedly accounts on at least some occasions for the sort of language that I am trying to define. When the First Gentleman in *Cymbeline* says, 'I do extend him, sir, within himself,' that is an odd, and even awkward, way of saying (presumably): 'I do not stretch my commendation further than his character will bear'; and, 'Crush him together,' seems to indicate again an urgent need on Shakespeare's part, rather than the First Gentleman's, for something resoundingly emphatic, although perhaps he is moved to this antithesis ('extend' . . . 'crush') by a feeling that 'I do extend him, sir, within himself' badly needs amplification for the sake of clarification.

I turn now to a later passage in *Cymbeline* from which we get an even stronger impression of hurry and impatience, and of an almost violent forcing of the expression. Guiderius and Arviragus are both strangely attracted by Imogen, who has come among them disguised as a boy. Guiderius expresses his feeling by asserting that he loves this boy 'as I do love my father'. At which Belisarius cries, 'What! how! how!' Whereupon Arviragus, not to be outdone, exclaims:

> If it be sin to say so, sir, I yoke me
> In my good brother's fault: I know not why
> I love this youth; and I have heard you say,

---

[1] *Lear*, I. i. 72 ff.

> Love's reason's without reason: the bier at door,
> And a demand who is't shall die, I'd say
> 'My father, not this youth.'[1]

This is surely an astonishingly and improbable way of saying what has to be said. The rapidity of composition is again noticeable, but there is a new recklessness of expression. Undertakers do not come round to the door like dustmen to demand a corpse—a corpse, too, that is not yet dead when they arrive. What Shakespeare has to express is an avowal of love that will go a stage further than that just made by Guiderius: if Guiderius loves the boy *as much as* he loves his own father, Arviragus is going to go one better and claim that he loves him *more* than he loves his father. Clutching at some means to express this thought powerfully, Shakespeare moves naturally enough to a choice between life and death, a choice involving the (supposed) father of Guiderius on the one hand and the boy on the other. But the simple expression of that idea will not do for Shakespeare, or perhaps it never gets the chance to assert itself. Driven on by some compelling urge for the immediate and the emphatic—perhaps visualizing the death situation in a sudden flash—he never pauses to get it into perspective, but suddenly writes down the elliptical and startling phrase, 'the bier at door', and the rest inevitably follows. It is true that the context, which bears a general resemblance to that in *King Lear* when Regan seeks to outdo her sister in protestations of love, demands an abnormal emphasis of expression. But the question is, how does Shakespeare meet that demand? He meets it—or so it seems to me—by forcing the pace.

It is probably the desire for emphasis again which accounts for the strange speech of Ross to Macbeth,[2] when he is describing Duncan's reactions to the news of Macbeth's victory over the rebels:

> The king hath happily receiv'd, Macbeth,
> The news of thy success; and when he reads
> Thy personal venture in the rebels' fight,
> His wonders and his praises do contend
> Which should be thine or his. . . .

Once more Shakespeare seems to have made a rush at it. When Duncan listens to the news, he is lost in wonder at Macbeth's achievements, and he is moved to praise him. But Shakespeare wants something more compelling than that, and he gets it by suggesting a struggle taking place in the mind of Duncan between two simultaneous emotions: his

[1] IV. ii. 19 ff.   [2] I. iii. 89 ff.

astonishment is contending with his admiration, the astonishment ('wonder') being Duncan's, and the praise which he feels moved to give being Macbeth's ('thine'). Shakespeare has succeeded at once in suggesting a confused and turbulent state of mind, but he has done so, characteristically, by jumping his fences rather than by taking us more normally through the gate.

I have suggested that the man who wrote the passages I have quoted was writing at speed, and I now suggest that this very speed leads to—or, alternatively, perhaps is caused by—some element of intellectual strain. It will not dispose of this suggestion to argue that in those passages the violence or abruptness or obscurity is appropriate to the character or the situation; even if this were so, as it sometimes is, it is not so on every occasion. And even on those occasions which require unusual emphasis, Shakespeare is capable of giving us that with a much quieter and more controlled, and yet completely effective, form of expression. When Imogen cries:

> . . . but if there be
> Yet left in heaven as small a drop of pity
> As a wren's eye . . .[1]

we have an exquisite distillation of the thought into a precise, if still surprising, image. Nothing could be more compelling, and nothing could be more delicately controlled. Nor could anything be less like the violent hyperbole and rough impressionism that we get on other occasions, and that seem to be due to some kind of super-charging in the mind of the dramatist, some conscious effort that causes him to expend more force on the expression than the occasion requires. Near the end of *Cymbeline*, when Iachimo is confessing his crimes, he suddenly exclaims:

> . . . 'twas at a feast—O, would
> Our viands had been poison'd, or at least
> Those which I heav'd to head![2]

The arresting phrase 'heav'd to head' has both the violence and the impressionistic effect to which I have already drawn attention; it gives in words something of the huge and powerful impression of a piece of sculpture by, say, Henry Moore. I will freely admit that Iachimo's emphatic outburst is in character; the man is at last filled with remorse for what he has done, and Shakespeare has to make us feel this. But

[1] IV. ii. 303 ff.   [2] V. v. 156 ff.

again it is the *kind* of emphasis that Shakespeare obtains that is significant, an emphasis which the dramatist seems to have achieved through
the expenditure of a tremendous and consciously-induced intellectual
energy.

The Shakespeare, then, that I am offering for contemplation is a
writer who, in those last plays, sometimes appears to be swept along by
some inner compulsion, and whose mind seems at times to be generat-
ing an immense energy which he is applying, as a man might apply a
pneumatic drill, to the immediate problems of composition. It may
therefore come as a surprise to find Professor W. H. Clemen asserting
that, 'Generally it may be said of the romances that the tempo of the
speech and action has slowed down';[1] and Sir Ifor Evans remarking
of *Cymbeline* that, 'if one looks for highly metaphorical language,
crowded phrase, and bold personification . . . one will suffer inevitable
disappointment'.[2] Are those two distinguished critics right, and am I
therefore wrong? Without trying to discover a face-saving formula,
we may all be said to be right, in the sense that what we say we discover
is in fact there. The last plays are curiously mixed in their style of
composition. (If my title suggests that I am dealing comprehensively
with the language of those plays I must make it clear that I am concerned with only one significant aspect of it.) In all of them there are
passages of apparently leisurely, deliberate, and even artificial writing,
marked by what Granville-Barker called 'a new euphuism of imagination'. There is at times a return to an earlier, formal, decorative or
rhetorical style of writing, and where we have that we often get with it
a pleasing ingenuity of concepts and expressions, without, however,
much pressure of thought behind them. It is obviously this kind of
writing that Clemen and Evans had chiefly in mind; it is certainly
there, and it constitutes an important element in the total impression
made by the romances. If anyone is looking for evidence of a serene
and mellow Shakespeare, with his eyes already fixed on retirement to
Stratford, it is there that he will find it. But it is equally true that there
is frequent evidence of that other and very different mode of thought
and expression—impetuous, violent, straining after the maximum of
intensity. How are we to account fo this variety? Startling divergences
of style within the same play have, of course, been used by textual
critics to demonstrate multiple authorship, or at any rate revision by
the author; it is felt that the man who wrote Act I, Scene 1 couldn't

[1] *The Development of Shakespeare's Imagery* (Methuen, 1951), p. 179.
[2] *The Language of Shakespeare's Plays* (Methuen, 1952), p. 176.

possibly be the same man as the one who wrote Act I, Scene 2. It is certainly difficult to reconcile some parts of *Timon of Athens* or *Henry VIII* with others; but we may be too willing to underestimate Shakespeare's capacity for varying his style within the same play. At all events, there is perhaps a special reason why the variety should be more marked in the later plays.

Some thirty years ago Lytton Strachey published an opinion on the last plays that has had the distinction of provoking almost universal disagreement. 'It is difficult to resist the conclusion,' he observed, 'that [Shakespeare] was getting bored himself. Bored with people, bored with real life, bored with drama; bored in fact with everything except poetry and poetical dreams. He is no longer interested, one often feels, in what happens, or who says what, so long as he can find place for a faultless lyric, or a new, unimagined rhythmical effect, or a grand mystic speech.'[1] In view of the critical wrath that this statement aroused at the time and later, it may seem rash to suggest that Strachey is not so wide of the mark as he has been generally held to be. The word that probably annoyed the critics most was 'bored', and I offer no defence of it. The creator of Imogen and Miranda and Perdita, not to mention Autolycus and Caliban, can hardly be said to have been bored. But if Strachey had said, 'It is difficult to resist the conclusion that Shakespeare was getting tired,' he would have said no more than what may sometimes have been true, and what may well account for at least some of the characteristic features of the passages to which I have drawn attention—passages in which, I have suggested, Shakespeare seems to be driving himself hard and to be consciously using a spur 'to prick the sides of his intent'. In the last plays he appears to be writing much more by fits and starts. Sometimes, for a whole scene, the ideas will be flowing in upon his mind as naturally as ever, and finding the old apparently spontaneous expression. But then, perhaps, the inspiration fades; the play goes dead on his hands, the dramatist who has written so many plays, such an infinitive number of speeches for his characters, is beginning to tire. The tiredness, however, is still the tiredness of Shakespeare. He responds to it, not by a collapse into mediocrity, but by putting forth a conscious effort, sometimes a gigantic effort, by seeking (as I have said) to force the pace. What once came almost unsought can still be found by an effort of will, but what is found in that way will carry unmistakable marks of its origin. I do not know of any other explanation which will account so satisfactorily

[1] 'Shakespeare's Final Period', *Books and Characters* (Chatto, 1924), p. 52.

for those sudden transitions from natural, easy, and unforced expression to difficult and even tortured writing. We might indeed apply to those two different modes of expression the words of Hermione to Leontes:

> You may ride's
> With one soft kiss a thousand furlongs ere
> With spur we heat an acre.[1]

In the early plays and the plays of his maturity, it seems usually to have been the curb rather than the spur that Shakespeare found most necessary.

Our problem, however, is complicated by the fact that even in the earlier plays we may come upon passages in which Shakespeare is already forcing the pace; and though we can still look for an explanation in the habitual rapidity of his writing, we can hardly postulate fatigue. An interesting early example of Shakespeare's helter-skelter, hit-or-miss mode of expression occurs in *Love's Labour's Lost*:

> The extreme part of time extremely forms
> All causes to the purpose of his speed,
> And often, at his very loose, decides
> That which long process could not arbitrate.[2]

Here, as usual, the meaning comes through; but in the first two lines it has to some extent been *pushed* through by the vigour and determination of the writer. When we meet with such writing in the plays before the last period, it will often be found at the very beginning of the play. On such occasions the dramatist sometimes appears to be 'revving up the engine' before it has warmed to its work, and the effect is very similar to that which I have been trying to isolate and define in the last plays—a conscious expenditure of intellectual effort, with a resulting impression of labour and strain. No doubt the bombastic speech of the bleeding sergeant at the beginning of *Macbeth* may be accounted for in various ways, but his flamboyant and orgulous utterance may be partly due to the fact that Shakespeare has not yet got going, and is having to put too much conscious will-power into the writing. In a different fashion the opening speeches of *The Merchant of Venice* have an air of being thought up for the occasion; the mind of the dramatist is not yet fully engaged by his theme, but is still circling over it. To return to a later play, we may hear again the characteristic sound of Shakespeare putting forth a mighty effort in the opening

[1] *The Winter's Tale*. I, ii. 94–6.   [2] v. ii. 748 ff.

scene of *Henry VIII*. The Duke of Buckingham tells the company that he has been ill, and consequently unable to attend the meeting between Henry and the King of France. The Duke of Norfolk then proceeds to describe the pageantry.

DUKE OF BUCKINGHAM: All the whole time
   I was my chamber's prisoner.
DUKE OF NORFOLK: Then you lost
   The view of earthly glory: men might say,
   Till this time, pomp was single, but now married
   To one above itself. Each following day
   Became the next day's master, till the last
   Made former wonders its. . . .
          The madams, too,
   Not us'd to toil, did almost sweat to bear
   The pride upon them, that their very labour
   Was to them as a painting. Now this masque
   Was cried incomparable; and the ensuing night
   Made it a fool, and beggar. The two kings,
   Equal in lustre, were now best, now worst,
   As presence did present them; him in eye,
   Still him in praise; and, being present both,
   'Twas said they saw but one; and no discerner
   Durst wag his tongue in censure. . . .[1]

Shakespeare has braced himself here for a magnificent effort, but it *is* an effort. The old eagle is soaring with his mighty spread of wings, but he is toiling upwards where once he sailed along the wind.

  There is a passage in *Cymbeline* where, I fancy, we can see Shakespeare casting back over his manuscript when the inspiration has flagged. The Queen is trying to get rid of the faithful Pisanio by giving him a box containing poison, which she tells him is a sovereign remedy against disease. The whole episode is rather ineffective, and Shakespeare may well have grown tired of it—even, I will dare to say, bored. The speech that he has been writing for the Queen is certainly rather flat; and then suddenly she refers to Posthumus in a rather surprising metaphor. 'What shalt thou expect,' she asks Pisanio,

   To be depender on a thing that leans,
   Who cannot be new built, nor has no friends,
   So much as but to prop him.[2]

Posthumus, the man whose fortunes are tottering, is seen as 'a thing

    [1] I. i. 12 ff.   [2] I. v. 57.

that leans', a building that is leaning over. I have never had the courage to put into print what I am now going to say; but my guess is that Shakespeare had come to a full stop in the middle of the Queen's speech, and, as he was wondering what should follow, his eye wandered idly over his manuscript, and he saw the words that he had written for Pisanio's entrance—'Enter *Pisa.*'—and the leaning tower came into his head.

If anyone is inclined to resist my thesis that Shakespeare was growing tired I will not press it too far. In any case, as an explanation of what was happening in the last plays it is apt to break down at any moment; for Shakespeare, beginning perhaps with a conscious effort, is always apt to pass on to something more spontaneous, as the wheels (in Coleridge's phrase) take fire from the mere rapidity of their motion. Something, too, must be allowed (and this would tell against my general thesis) for Shakespeare's tendency to use an exaggerated and strained language in those contexts where a character is speaking insincerely or craftily (e.g. the protestation of Goneril and Regan in *Lear*, I. i. or Iachimo's, 'It cannot be i' the eye,' *Cymbeline*, I. vi. 39, quoted below). Still more relevant to our problem is Shakespeare's tendency to put forth the sort of effort that we have been considering when he is writing a piece of retrospective narrative. The bleeding sergeant in *Macbeth* is describing events that have occurred off stage, and his words are a sort of substitute for action. As such, they do suggest with a rough effectiveness a violent and bloody struggle on the battlefield. It will have been noticed that most of my quotations come from passages of narrative. It may be that Shakespeare was afraid on such occasions that the attention of the audience might begin to wander, and therefore consciously wrote up his narrative passages to prevent any danger of flatness. On the other hand he was quite capable of writing a long narrative passage, such as Hotspur's speech beginning, 'My liege, I did deny no prisoners,' (I *Henry IV*, I. iii. 29 ff.), in which the language is so natural and so vivid that the blank verse melts into the rhythms of colloquial speech.

It would be reasonable, again, to account for at least some of the recklessness of Shakespeare's later style by saying that he had now reached that point of assured mastery in his profession where he felt that he could let himself do whatever he liked. Expression is always a compromise between how one would put it if one were perfectly free, or if one were sure of having a perfectly sympathetic listener who could be trusted to get one's meaning from half hints and broken phrases, and, on the other hand, how it is normally put. Even in the earlier plays there are fairly frequent signs of Shakespeare being willing to take short cuts, to indulge his idiosyncrasies, to coin words, to rely on the sound helping to carry the sense to the audience; but there is also a corresponding centripetal force that keeps him from flying out too far from the normal. In the last plays he seems to be much less concerned to remain within the bounds of the normal and the expected—less concerned with communication, less careful to make his characters speak *as you like it*, and more ready to make them speak *as he likes it*. This Shakespeare would not be the bored elderly playwright, bored because he had played all the old tricks over and over again, but the acknowledged master of the theatre, who knew, as Dickens came to know, that his public would take anything that he cared to give them. He did not have to trouble about being *easily* intelligible; he could afford to take chances, and he took them. He had reached the point where he could say with Ben Jonson, 'By God! 'tis good, and if you like't, you may.'

There is one other alternative to the diagnosis I have offered. In the last plays we constantly meet with natural human thoughts and feelings which seem somehow to have been rethought, so that they emerge in the most tortured and unlikely expression. When Imogen is told that Cloten has drawn his sword upon her husband, and that Posthumus, who could have killed him with ease, was content merely to parry his thrusts, she exclaims:

> To draw upon an exile! O brave sir!
> I would they were in Afric both together,
> Myself by with a needle, that I might prick
> The goer-back.[1]

How that needle came into Shakespeare's head it would be hard to say. The context, of course, implies sharp pointed swords, and from them Shakespeare's vision may have narrowed to a needle-point. Or the needle may give us a clue to Shakespeare's conception of Imogen: gentle, womanly, the housewife.[2] But either way, the idea of Imogen

---

[1] I. i. 166 ff.

[2] Imogen mentions her needle again in I. iii. 17ff, when she has been listening to Pisanio's account of how he watched the ship that carried Posthumus from Britain:

> I would have broke mine eye-strings, crack'd them, but
> To look upon him, till the diminution
> Of space had pointed him sharp as my needle. . . .

dancing round the angry swordsmen pricking with her needle the buttocks of the retreating Cloten is a highly recondite one.

Again, when Iachimo is making his diabolical suggestions that Posthumus has forgotten his wife, and is amusing himself at Rome with whores, Shakespeare conveys this to us in at least one quite extraordinary image. 'What makes your admiration?' Imogen asks. What Iachimo has to say in reply is that it passes all comprehension how Posthumus, with such a lovely wife, could even look at other women. His eye and his judgment must tell him that Imogen is infinitely more desirable; and even if Posthumus were moved by mere lust, the memory of Imogen's 'neat excellence' would surely make those other women seem nauseating. But how oddly Shakespeare says it:

> It cannot be i' the eye; for apes and monkeys
> 'Twixt two such shes would chatter this way and
> Contemn with mows the other; nor i' the judgment,
> For idiots in this case of favour would
> Be wisely definite; nor i' the appetite;
> Sluttery to such neat excellence oppos'd
> Should make desire vomit emptiness,
> Not so allur'd to feed.[1]

This kind of writing, with its remote and far-fetched ideas, is what we normally associate with metaphysical poetry. Was Shakespeare, then, turning into a metaphysical poet in his middle age, and if so, why? When this sort of question is asked there are always two possible ways of answering it. You can either say that Shakespeare was following a fashion, or you can say that this development in his style was due to some change in himself. As for following a fashion, it has been suggested that the tragi-comical romances which he wrote at the close of his career—with their tyrannical and unpredictable characters like Leontes, their unexpected and fantastic events, and much else—were influenced by the early work of Beaumont and Fletcher. But even if the plays could be dated precisely enough to make this suggestion plausible, the writing of Beaumont and Fletcher is in general so diffuse that Shakespeare could never have learnt to write like a metaphysical poet by imitating them. Nor is it easy to point to any other contemporary who could have influenced him in that way.

Was there, then, a change in Shakespeare himself? That he had come round to writing at times in the manner of a metaphysical poet would not be—to me—incompatible with my thesis that in the last plays there are signs of mental fatigue. Without wishing to revive the notion of the Romantics that there is a poetry which is conceived in the wits and another kind of poetry which is conceived in the soul, I would still hold that metaphysical poetry is, to an unusual degree, the product of cerebration. *Good* metaphysical poetry is, no doubt, the result of a predominantly unconscious cerebration; yet there is always about it a suggestion of the poet putting his mind to work, chasing his thoughts, pursuing them into all sorts of remote and unlikely places. In that sense, in the sense that he is often going out of his way in the last plays to *look for* his ideas, Shakespeare may be said to be writing in the manner of a metaphysical poet. The process had not gone very far when he stopped writing plays altogether. I doubt if he could have continued to write plays for successful performance on the stage if he had carried it much further.

In what I have written I have been more concerned to draw attention to a mode of writing in Shakespeare than to account for it. I have, it is true, tried to explain it in various ways, but if none of my explanations should commend themselves to the reader, the phenomenon itself still remains—awaiting explanation.

I I

THE MIND OF SHAKESPEARE

by JOHN WAIN

My title, I realize, might be felt to need a word of explanation. It so happened, a few weeks before I gave my Stratford lecture, that one of our young literary lions had described Shakespeare as having a 'second-rate mind'. Challenged to say more precisely what he meant, he obliged in a letter to *The Times Literary Supplement*. Shakespeare (he explained) had a great sensibility; he was a great poet; but as a speculative instrument, able to *do* things, his mind was second-rate compared with that of a philosopher (Kant, I remember, was the example given). This being in the air at the moment, it seemed reasonable to lecture on the mind of Shakespeare, one's object being to show that this postulated 'great poet' with a 'second-rate mind' was a mere contradiction in terms; that such an idea can only spring from a misunderstanding of the nature of great poetry and also a too *naïf* view of the psychology of literary creation; and that Shakespeare's work, attentively read, offers abundant proof of all this. Concluding, perhaps, with Coleridge's prayer, 'From a popular philosophy and a philosophic populace, Good Sense deliver us!'

Coleridge comes in well here, because he spoke of the 'esemplastic' power of the imagination, meaning its power of creating new organic wholes out of disparate elements. This is something that no one has ever failed to notice who has looked at the nature of the imagination at all closely; it is part of all the definitions that try to say what the imaginative writer is really doing, from Johnson's description of wit as 'the unexpected copulation of ideas', to Shelley's 'metaphorical language . . . marks the before unapprehended relations of things'. If we want to see this power demonstrated at its highest pitch, we turn to Shakespeare before any other great writer; because he, more than anyone, made it the governing principle of his work. He had the kind of mind that seeks always to reduce multiplicity to unity, to take the widest possible spread of material and weld it together into a whole. The resultant whole is often of a rather sophisticated kind, not at all apparent to the casual glance; Shakespeare's original audience were at an advantage in this respect, because their civilization had more of a gift for making unity out of diversity than ours has; certainly no one in his own time seems to have considered him primitive, even rustic, a native genius working entirely by intuition, as the criticism of the eighteenth and nineteenth centuries would have it. We have not quite got rid of this bad tradition of criticism yet; the new Shakespearian criticism, that takes it for granted that he was as intelligent as we can possibly be, and works by means of perceiving structures, counting images, and what not, is firmly entrenched in the universities, but there is still (in the theatre, for instance) a tendency to think of Shakespeare's work as so much raw material, deposited by some kind of process in nature, and lying about in heaps asking to be worked on. Actually the only 'working' that is necessary, or indeed permissible, is the effort to see the relationships that are already there in the plays, to perceive them as wholes bearing on a single focus: to accept, in short, what Shakespeare gives us, rather than in trying to make his work interesting in some other idiom—as nineteenth-century criticism tries to make them sound like novels, and the modern stage turns them into vaudeville.

To Shakespeare's contemporaries, as I say, the impulse to make unity out of complexity was nothing strange. In the pre-scientific world, unity was prized just as particularity is prized in our world. Our civilization proceeds on the assumption that if we want to know the *truth* about a thing, we take it into a laboratory, break it down into its constituent parts, and then proceed to weigh and measure these parts, and to observe their properties. And this procedure, carried out literally in the physical sciences, is carried out figuratively—the same *method* is applied, though naturally with different techniques—in other departments of life. In fact it is a mark of this same mind that the phrase 'departments of life', comes so naturally to my pen. In the pre-scientific world, life was not divided this way. Everything bore on everything else. Hence the encyclopœdic tradition of medieval and renaissance learning was not so quaint as it seems to the modern novice. It really was not impossible to take, say, a chapter of Scripture and proceed to build round it an elaborate commentary which said, quite literally, everything worth saying. After all, the Bible contained the word of God, and it was surely not straining one's piety, or one's ingenuity, to try to bring everything into a direct relevance to that word. Knowledge had to hang together, or they had no use for it.

For us, of course, the pendulum has swung far enough, and we are already aware of a gathering swing back. Everywhere, people are tired of the old compartmented, cut-into-strips thinking. The characteristic modern prophet—D. H. Lawrence, for example—always begins by insisting on the basic unity of life. And that insistence ripples out, having its effect on everything. Literary criticism, for instance, is slowly getting over the withering effect of an attitude that could separate scholarship—the acquisition of facts *about* literature—from aesthetic 'appreciation', and then go further and cut that same appreciation off from its roots in day-to-day living; so that the critic, as well as the artist, was left in the echoing cul-de-sac of 'art for art's sake'. To-day, even quite minor critics, men who have no claim to originality but merely implement the policies handed down from above, show an impressive willingness to allow literature its full set of ramifications. And Shakespeare is bound to be seen more clearly by such a criticism, just as the music of Byrd and the theology of Hooker will also lose their quaintness and appear more natural to us than our fathers would have thought possible.

To labour the point a little more—for, if I do not make this clear, I make nothing clear—let us imagine ourselves explaining to a Victorian audience (in, say, the period of early H. G. Wells) that Elizabethan medical science could seriously discuss such a question as: what is the relationship between the number of planets in the sky and the number of diseases to which the human body is subject? Our audience would have smiled, confident that their frock-coats, the railway shares in their pockets, the whole rational and institutional life they were building up, put them far above such superstitious fancies. To them, a disease was a disease, which could be isolated, studied, and attacked with drugs or surgery. But to us—though a disease is still all these things—the notion of a correspondence is one that wins far more respect. There may well be no relation between the diseases and the planets, for that notion depends on a doctrine of 'influences' which did not survive the Middle Ages. But a relation between the diseases and *something* there certainly is; if a man falls ill, he does so because of some disturbance which may have no local cause, but a cause it has; and this cause can be philosophical, metaphysical, moral. The individual is at the centre of a web of contacts with life; let something get tangled in the most distant part of that web, and there is a tremor at the centre.

Yeats knew this instinctively, when he turned from the dismembering scientific rationalism of his day to crystal-gazing and secret brother-hoods; the subject-matter was absurd, but the attitudes which informed them were valuable. He knew, with a poet's intuition, that life cannot be separated into its individual grains, even for the purpose of examina-tion. For, if we do so, what we are examining is not life.

What this means in terms of our appreciation of Shakespeare is, clearly, nothing less than a revolution. It means that at last we can heed what Shakespeare is telling us. Instead of concentrating our entire energy on irrelevances (from character-study to source-hunting) we can, for the first time since the Civil War closed the theatres, hush our wearisome clatter and let Shakespeare speak to us; simply, naturally, and quite clearly.

Clearly? A strange word to use of Shakespeare, surely—Shakespeare who is known for his riddling, his multiple significances, his compli-cated superimposition of plot on plot. 'The style of Shakespeare is itself perplexed, ungrammatical and obscure.' And Johnson was right; it is all those things. But it is clear too. Even the most flagrantly ungram-matical and illogical sentence-constructions, such as:

> like one,
> Who having, into truth, by telling of it,
> Made such a sinner of his memory,
> To credit his own lie—he did believe
> He was himself the duke

even a sentence like that is not, in fact, difficult to understand; it is put together in a way that would be obscure in a prose writer, but then one of the things Shakespeare so magnificently exemplifies is that the verse-writer can get away with a much looser syntax, provided he is able to use his verse to hold up the sagging edges of what he has to say. The verse-rhythms will present the words in their most effective order, and they will enter the hearer's mind clearly; it will not puzzle him to construe the sentence until he gets it down on paper and begins to look for the grammar.

Shakespeare's mind, then, lends itself to clarity; all the famous ridd-ling and quibbling, the density of construction, is in the interests of richness, but it is not against those of clarity. If we are interested in knowing what he has to say, rather than merely appreciating him for incidental beauties, we shall understand fast enough.

Not, of course, that Shakespeare is preaching. His fundamental attitude, which the plays very strongly convey, is not so much a doctrine, to be taught, as an opinion which, since he held it naturally, formed a natural base for his imaginative work. That opinion can be stated baldly as follows: there is a natural order, or *pietas*, which must not be violated; certain emotions, certain observances and attitudes, are right and necessary; to reject them is unnatural, rather like trying to make crops grow in the snow, and equally futile; it will result in failure, and, if done on a large enough scale, it will unleash 'chaos', the state in which:

> Strength should be lord of imbecility,
> And the rude son should strike his father dead;
>
> Force should be right; or rather, right and wrong,
> Between whose endless jar justice resides,
> Should lose their names, and so should justice too.
> Then everything includes itself in power. . . .

This is, of course, an attitude Shakespeare shared with most people at that time; Elizabethan minds naturally pivoted on the metaphors of music, on the one hand, and chaos on the other. Shakespeare's characters nearly always begin to talk about music as soon as a state of peace and happiness is attained or glimpsed—as they do, for instance in the fifth act of *The Merchant of Venice*, when the disruptive element, Shylock, has been expelled, leaving the young people to get on with their natural business of loving each other.

This is no idiosyncrasy of Shakespeare's; Milton, only a few years later, cannot write a poem about music without bringing in the idea:

> That we on Earth with undiscording voice
> May rightly answer that melodious noise;
> As once we did, till disproportion'd sin
> Jarr'd against nature's chime, and with harsh din
> Broke the fair music that all creatures made
> To their great Lord, whose love their motion sway'd
> In perfect Diapason, whilst they stood
> In first obedience, and their state of good.

For an illustration of the companion metaphor, 'chaos', we might turn to Hooker (*Ecclesiastical Polity*, Book I):

His commanding those things to be which are, and to be in such sort as they are; to keep that tenure and course which they do, importeth the establishment of nature's law. This world's first creation, and the preservation since of things created, what is it but only so far forth a manifestation by execution, what the eternal law of God is concerning things natural? And as it cometh to pass in a kingdom rightly ordered, that after a law is once published, it presently takes effect far and wide, all states framing themselves thereunto; even so let us think it fareth in the natural course of the world: since the time that God did first proclaim the edicts of his law upon it, heaven and earth have hearkened unto his voice, and their labour hath been to do his will: He 'made a law for the rain'; He gave his 'decree unto the sea, that the waters should not pass his commandment'. Now if nature should intermit her course, and leave altogether though it were but for a while the observation of her own laws; if those principal and mother elements of the world, whereof all things in this lower world are made, should lose the qualities which now they have; if the frame of that heavenly arch erected over our heads should loosen and dissolve itself; if celestial spheres should forget their wonted motions, and by irregular volubility turn themselves any way as it might happen; if the prince of the lights of heaven, which now as a giant doth run his unwearied course, should as it were through a languishing faintness begin to stand and to rest himself; if the moon should wander from her beaten way, the times and seasons of the year blend themselves by disordered and confused mixture, the winds breathe out their last gasp, the clouds yield no rain, the earth be defeated of heavenly influence, the fruits of the earth pine away as children at the withered breasts of their mother no longer able to yield them relief: what would become of man himself, whom these things now do all serve? See we not plainly that obedience of creatures unto the law of nature is the stay of the whole world?

The polarity was in everyone's mind, and no one doubted that a wholesome unity was what we had to preserve. (It was this attitude that made Pride a deadly sin, since Pride will brook no one higher than himself.) And Shakespeare would have been astonished to have any originality claimed on his behalf, for holding such an attitude. What he understood best was how to give this concept the strength and concreteness of great art; in that, he unquestionably led the way; as an artist, there can be no doubt, he would be perfectly well aware of the extent of his own originality.

The more closely one looks at Shakespeare, the more one finds that the key to his work lies in this combination of a world-view that called for unity and correspondence with a natural turn of mind that sought always to resolve discord into harmony and multiplicity into singleness. Certainly a criticism that puts anything else at the centre is bound to find itself with some awkward explaining to do. If—for instance—*Macbeth* is primarily a character-study, what pitiful mumbo-jumbo are the two prodigies that come in at the *dénouement*, the 'Birnam Wood coming to Dunsinane' business and the appearance of an adversary owing his birth to a Caesarian operation. What can such things have to do with character, or the drawing of a political moral? But as soon as we see that the main thread of the play is the description of *pietas*, causing a widening circle of further disruptions, it becomes plain that such an open defiance of Nature is bound to involve prodigies—horses that turn cannibal, a hawk killed by an owl, a woman who cries out to be unsexed, and a man who wishes it would go dark in the day-time. Of course the character-portrayal is there; the establishment of Macbeth's character in so few lines at the beginning is a model of economy that any novelist might ponder; but the important thing about him is that as long as he is loyally fighting for his king, he can be described by an admiring fellow-soldier as:

> Nothing afeard of what thyself didst make,
> Strange images of death.

The corpses of enemies legitimately slain in battle do not inspire nervous dread, but the body of one old man who is murdered in the face of 'double trust' turns out to contain a horrifying amount of blood. An Oxford tutor of my acquaintance was once told by an undergraduate that *Macbeth* 'contained nothing to interest a mature mind'. Ludicrous enough; but one can hardly blame the youth if he had always had the play offered to him as a story of blood-and-thunder on a remote Scotch moor.

King Lear is a particularly clear example, as it not only contains the fullest possible statement of the *pietas* theme, but is virtually unintelligible on any other basis. The aged despot, proud and opinionated ('He hath ever but slenderly known himself.'), endangers the stability of the social order by wanting to divide England into three parts, and, not content with that, utters a formal renunciation of the bonds that unite him to his daughter:

> Let it be so; thy truth then be thy dower:
> For, by the sacred radiance of the sun,
> The mysteries of Hecate and the night,
> By all the operation of the orbs
> From whom we do exist and cease to be,
> Here I disclaim all my paternal care,
> Propinquity and property of blood,
> And as a stranger to my heart and me

> Hold thee from this for ever. The barbarous Scythian,
> Or he that makes his generation messes
> To gorge his appetite, shall to my bosom
> Be as well neighbour'd, pitied, and reliev'd,
> As thou my sometime daughter.

After that, the pelican daughters and the symbolic thunderstorms not only may but *must* go into operation, until the natural order has shuddered itself into calm once more—the Shakespearian version of that calm which always returns at the end of a great tragedy.

Once that theme is grasped, the play—like *Macbeth*, like all Shakespeare—seems more logical, less full of frills and inconsistencies: in a word, better art. The repetition of the theme from plot to sub-plot, which once seemed justifiable mainly as a decoration (so that Watts-Dunton, for instance, could say, 'Perhaps from a merely theatrical point of view it complicates the action to excess, though it does not really divide the interest; but the practical effect is enhanced, as that of a thunderstorm by reverberations among the mountains'), is seen as structurally essential: there have to be two suffering parents, who have flouted *pietas* in contrasting ways, and, while one has to go mad in order to understand, the other has to be blinded in order to see.

However, there is no point in spinning out these routine examples; to demonstrate the working of this great principle throughout all Shakespeare's plays is easily done, and, though not criticism, it is an essential preliminary to criticism; one must hope that in the appropriate places—sixth forms, university extension classes, popular handbooks—the work will go quietly forward. For, as I remarked earlier, the elementary business of getting Shakespeare's major concerns into focus is, as yet, by no means complete.

This, unfortunately, applies to detail as much as to outline. If the broad lines of Shakespeare's designs are still not clear to so many of those who love him, neither are the concrete details of his procedure. His use of language, for example, both as regards the individual word (the unit of meaning, the versification, the elaborated structure of such units) is still in need of elementary explanation. One gathers this need, not so much from the remarks one sees or reads made about Shakespeare himself, as from literary generalizations at large. Joyce's puns, for example, would never have seemed as miraculous as they evidently do, had his admirers grasped the simple fact that Shakespeare had anticipated the entire method, though without proffering it so obtrusively. This side of Shakespeare's mind earned him the disapproval of the Age of Reason ('a quibble is to him the fatal Cleopatra', &c.); but, since that disapproval died down, it seems to have been quietly forgotten that Shakespeare used puns on a scale not attempted again till the twentieth century, and for the most impeccably *avant-garde* motives. It looks as if the pioneering work done by Mr. Empson and others, plus the admirable presentation for the general reader in such a book as Miss Mahood's *Shakespeare's Word-Play*, is still not enough. This is a pity, for there is a good deal in the literature of his own time that encourages the modern playgoer to enjoy and appreciate Shakespeare's habit of throwing in a pun whenever the dramatic tension mounts more than ordinarily high.

> I'll gild the faces of the grooms withal;
> For it must seem their guilt.

The meeting of double, or multiple, significance in one word seems to attract Shakespeare as the means of tying a knot round the bundle of themes and statements he is handling. Here, as elsewhere, his effort is to unite, to fuse, to present with lightning simultaneity.

I believe that whatever other movements may be traced on the chart of Shakespeare's development, this one remains steady. All his life, he voyaged towards a greater and greater inclusiveness. His early work, like that of many artists, is compartmented; he seems concerned, for the first ten years of his career, with showing how many already existing *genres* he can successfully tackle. When, in these early days, he writes a tragedy, it is an unrelieved storm of blood and tears; when he writes comedy, it is a pretty straight exercise in one or other of the standard comic modes. This is all very sympathetic; he is learning his trade; faced with two traditions of comic writing, he sets himself to produce specimens, and concocts the *Comedy of Errors* out of the materials of Latin comedy, *The Two Gentlemen of Verona* from those of romantic comedy as written by, say, Peele, and (for already the impulse to *fuse* is at work) *Love's Labour's Lost* as an example of how to blend material from either source. But if we let our minds range from one end of Shakespeare's working life to the other, we find him still engaged, though now with far greater placidity and strength, in the task of making a new whole out of already proven components; taking the new fashion for loosely-constructed 'romances' as practised by Beaumont and Fletcher, he turns them into something new in English literature: structures of meaning that we cannot help calling 'symbolic',

M

though the symbols are not reducible; works in which we feel the pressure of a shadowy allegory, as we feel it in Conrad's novels, deepening and thickening our sense of the 'meaning' that is coming over to us, without being able, except in extremely cumbrous ways, to expound it.

Inclusiveness in argument, inclusiveness in symbolic structure, inclusiveness within the individual word: this was the quest of which Shakespeare never tired. The later plays, even when they were passing through a period of incomprehension and neglect, were at any rate recognized as miracles of versification. (*Cymbeline* was Tennyson's favourite play, and it is obvious that the technical fascination for the Laureate must have been immense.) Not that one would sacrifice the lyrical, uncomplicated movement of the early verse; *Richard II* alone would be enough to establish Shakespeare as a great poet if he had written nothing else: those springing, unclogged lines, full of open syllables, which balance so delicately that they can at any moment veer towards the weighty or the staccato—it is for Shakespeare a necessary starting-point, but for any other poet it might well be the crown of a lifetime's effort.

> Now mark me how I will undo myself:
> I give this heavy weight from off my head,
> And this unwieldy sceptre from my hand,
> The pride of kingly sway from out my heart;
> With mine own tears I wash away my balm,
> With mine own hands I give away my crown,
> With mine own tongue deny my sacred state,
> With mine own breath release all duteous rites:
> All pomp and majesty I do forswear;
> My manors, rents, revenues, I forego;
> My acts, decrees, and statutes I deny:
> God pardon all oaths that are broke to me!
> God keep all vows unbroke are made to thee!
> Make me, that nothing have, with nothing griev'd,
> And thou with all pleas'd, that hast all achiev'd!

As Shakespeare went on, he integrated his poetry more and more closely with drama, running the rhythms of naturalistic speech contrapuntally across those of decasyllabic verse; but that, the familiar formulation, is only half the story. The complicating, contrapuntally involving process was done as much in the interests of beauty as of dramatic realism; the aim was not merely to get the verse to sound

'lifelike', but to endow it with a more supple life of its own, a more
fastidious lyrical movement:

> With fairest flowers
> While summer lasts and I live here, Fidele,
> I'll sweeten thy sad grave; thou shalt not lack
> The flower that's like thy face, pale primrose, nor
> The azur'd hare-bell, like thy veins, no, nor
> The leaf of eglantine, whom not to slander,
> Out-sweeten'd not thy breath: the ruddock would,
> With charitable bill, —O bill! sore-shaming
> Those rich-left heirs, that let their fathers lie
> Without a monument,—bring thee all this;
> Yea, and furr'd moss besides, when flowers are none,
> To winter-ground thy corse.

A comparison is in order here. Not many years separate *Julius Caesar*
from *Coriolanus*, but in the intervening period Shakespeare's stylistic
preoccupations had shifted considerably. Here are two speeches devoted
to unsympathetic description of a triumphal progress; in each case, the
speaker is a tribune.

> Wherefore rejoice? What conquest brings he home?
> What tributaries follow him to Rome
> To grace in captive bonds his chariot wheels?
> You blocks, you stones, you worse than senseless things!
> O you hard hearts, you cruel men of Rome,
> Knew you not Pompey? Many a time and oft
> Have you climb'd up to walls and battlements,
> To towers and windows, yea, to chimney-tops,
> Your infants in your arms, and there have sat
> The livelong day, with patient expectation,
> To see great Pompey pass the streets of Rome:
> And when you saw his chariot but appear,
> Have you not made a universal shout,
> That Tiber trembled underneath her banks,
> To hear the replication of your sounds
> Made in her concave shores?
> And do you now put on your best attire?
> And do you now cull out a holiday?
> And do you now strew flowers in his way,
> That comes in triumph over Pompey's blood?

All tongues speak of him, and the bleared sights
Are spectacled to see him: your prattling nurse
Into a rapture lets her baby cry
While she chats him: the kitchen malkin pins
Her richest lockram 'bout her reechy neck,
Clambering the walls to eye him: stalls, bulks, windows,
Are smother'd up, leads fill'd, and ridges hors'd
With variable complexions, all agreeing
In earnestness to see him: seld-shown flamens
Do press among the popular throngs, and puff
To win a vulgar station: our veil'd dames
Commit the war of white and damask in
Their nicely-gawded cheeks to the wanton spoil
Of Phoebus' burning kisses: such a pother
As if that whatsoever god who leads him
Were slily crept into his human powers,
And gave him graceful posture.

The increase in dramatic immediacy and concreteness is immediately
apparent in the second passage. Admittedly the comparison is not quite
a straight one; in the first extract, Marullus is rebuking the gaping
crowd, and he does so in dignified and lofty rhetorical accents; in the
second, Brutus is hissing and spitting his rage and disappointment to
his fellow-official. Naturally his accents have more of the actual tang,
the taste and texture, of bitterness and contempt than would be proper
in the mouth of Marullus.

> the kitchen malkin pins
> Her richest lockram 'bout her reechy neck . . .
> . . . press among the popular throngs, and puff . . .

The lines are made up of sounds that would convey angry contempt to
a hearer who knew no English. Nevertheless, the difference is a real one;
Shakespeare has, in the intervening period, moved into his mature
manner of kinesthetic unification. The wonderful word 'horsed' contains within itself the dense, physical sensation of overcrowding, as well
as the implied judgment of the incensed observer (the people are
carrying on like animals); one remembers the agonized disgust of
Leontes:

> Is whispering nothing?
> Is leaning cheek to cheek? is meeting noses?
> Kissing with inside lip? stopping the career
> Of laughter with a sigh?—a note infallible
> Of breaking honesty,—horsing foot on foot?

And if 'horsed' carries a strong suggestion of the non-human, there is a similar force in the way various parts of the human body are picked out to stand for the whole, in Marullus's contemptuous description of the crowd. The Romans who jostle so eagerly for a chance to look at Coriolanus, their hero and nine days' wonder, are people; but to Marullus, in his present mood, they are simply so many gaping eyes, prattling tongues, and pushing limbs. The suggestion is reinforced by what might otherwise seem extraneous detail—the 'reechy neck' of the unwashed servant-girl, the cheeks of the 'veil'd dames'; the way the normally aloof 'flamens' (i.e. priests) 'puff' to get a point of vantage; all these isolated physical activities rob their performers of humanity. The speech makes an interesting contrast to Menenius's fable of the belly and the members in the opening scene; where Menenius was adjuring the crowd to remember their status as men (i.e. as co-ordinating and co-operating animals), Marullus is implicitly denying them this status.

This essay will have to break off, rather than end. The theme is one that could be documented through volume after volume, and it is a job that could be done by anybody, Elizabethan scholar or novice, who had read Shakespeare attentively. All that is necessary is to have one's attention focused in the right places. The mountains of misplaced ingenuity which humanity has heaped up round Shakespeare's work is, very obviously, a tribute to his genius; but it seems to have curiously little to *do* with him. (Masterpiece though it is, who can avoid the impression that Bradley's *Shakespearean Tragedy* is not really 'about' Shakespeare at all?) Perhaps a more rational criticism will, in time, put an end to the state of affairs in which it is felt legitimate to remark that Shakespeare, though very well in his way, was not as clever as Kant; and will help to make it clear that one of Shakespeare's achievements was to demonstrate just how strong, how wide-ranging, how subtly adjusted, the intelligence of a great poet has to be.

12

MEDICINE AND SURGERY IN THE 1955 SEASON'S PLAYS

by HENRY YELLOWLEES

WHEN I was occupied with the preparation of this lecture some weeks ago, a friend rather startled me by asking what the object of the lecture really was. I realized, on thinking the matter over, that it certainly was not to attempt to teach you anything about medicine or surgery. That would be an absurd and impossible task and I should not use Shakespeare as a vehicle even if I were making the attempt.

The real object of this lecture and, I suppose, of all the lectures in the course, is simply to look together at the art of Shakespeare—each speaker from his particular angle—so that we may have the pleasure of discovering various beauties and points of interest, great or small, which had not occurred to us before, or which we had not fully appreciated or understood.

Apart from the intellectual pleasure that this gives, it is also of the greatest practical benefit to those whose business it is to introduce others, particularly boys and girls, to the study of Shakespeare.

Yes, but who am I to have an angle at all—let alone one from which anything new or interesting might be seen? Last year I readily admitted to you that I am very far indeed from being a profound, expert, or scholarly student of Shakespeare, and I strongly suspect that the professional critics would be justified in calling me a 'Philistine'. My equipment for lecturing about Shakespeare is slight indeed compared with that of my distinguished fellow-lecturers. I read Shakespeare (omitting all 'explanatory' notes!) for the sheer joy it gives me, I possess a distinctly adhesive verbal memory, and I have a long practical experience of psychological medicine. That's all there is to it.

Fortunately, for me at least, I think that, even with such a limited equipment, a speaker can occasionally shed new light on some word or phrase in a play, not because he is cleverer than his hearers but because his particular occupation or experiences enable him to appreciate the meaning of some reference or some point of detail more fully than his neighbour. That is where my special training and experience in psychological medicine comes in, and that is why I am going to begin this talk with a short discussion of the wonderful psychological process known as Projection, which is at the very root of both appreciation and censure—indeed, of all criticism, apart from the passing of purely intellectual judgments.

We can only see what is in us to see. You cannot understand conduct which is completely foreign to your own nature, and you are therefore little concerned either to praise or blame it. King Arthur's heart, you may remember, was 'too wholly true to dream untruth' in Guinevere. Sexual infidelity being, as we are told, completely alien to his nature, he was incapable of even suspecting it in others.

I once knew a small but highly intelligent boy who one morning had just mastered the first seven letters of the alphabet. Later that day, on seeing the word BANK in large gilt capitals over its door, he shouted out: 'Look! Stupid! It should be A—B.' The letters N and K meant nothing to him, nor had he any idea that letters could be combined and arranged in various ways and, indeed, existed for that purpose. But he did know that B comes after A and not before it, and he was quick to criticize and resent any tampering with the scheme of things on which he had become an authority.

A young child will greet a picture of some bearded personage such as King Lear or the Prophet Elijah with a gleeful shout of 'Daddy!', should his father be similarly afflicted, and will completely ignore a multitude of striking dissimilarities. A similar result can be achieved if such vanities as a kilt or a top hat can be made the basis of the experiment.

You cannot criticize a piece of music unless you have, as we say, music in you. You cannot appreciate a picture unless you are at heart, although not necessarily in performance, an artist.

This ability to see only what is in us to see is but one of the varieties of projection. Instances of it in all its forms abound, of course, in Shakespeare, and I have made this little excursion into psychology at the very start because we shall be coming across examples of it before the lecture is over.

The approach to Shakespeare from the viewpoint of medical psychology is one of truly fascinating interest. Last year I discussed some general psychiatric disorders and psychological principles, and illustrated them from the behaviour of many of his characters. My more modest aim today is merely to mention and discuss quite simply, but not, I hope, too superficially, a few of the points in this season's plays which, because of their medico-psychological interest appeal particularly to me as a psychiatrist.

I inserted the word 'Surgery' in the title of this address because, without it, I should not have been able to refer to that remarkable, blood-stained melodrama *Titus Andronicus*. As I insisted last year, I am the very reverse of an authority on theatrical or dramatic art, but I do understand just a little about poetry and psychology. I can find no trace of either in *Titus Andronicus*, although I notice with interest that Masefield says it contains three lines of poetry and, of course, there is plenty of psychology, of a sort, behind wholesale and indiscriminate lust, murder, mutilation, rape, premature burial, poisoning, torture and so forth.

I am told that the piece makes good theatre, and I wish I could have seen it before giving this talk. I hope to do so to-morrow, and feel that if my ignorant private views on the play can ever be changed, it will be by the great artists who will appear in it. I will confess to you that I am eager to see how even they can escape getting a laugh of the wrong sort in the very last two lines of the play. About half the original cast have died violent deaths, and a distinct majority of the dwindling band of survivors should, on the most lenient view, be serving life-sentences in prison. Undeterred, however, by this, they order further torture, fling another corpse to the wild beasts, and then move off . . . 'to order well the state'—as they naïvely remark. The wildest performances of our 'planners' are milk and water compared with the blood and iron policy of this criminal gang.[1]

The 'surgery' of the play is, of course, nothing but butchery, and very rough and ready butchery at that. To suggest that Lavinia could conceivably have recovered from amputation of the tongue and both hands, performed in Roman times, without anaesthetics, by the amateur surgeons who had just finished raping their patient after murdering her husband, is the crowning medical absurdity of this fantastic and disgusting business. Throughout the play, the characters make a positive hobby of cutting off each other's heads and hands, and sending them to and fro by messenger.

[1] The lines in question were 'cut' at the performance I witnessed.

There is also, I am almost sure, someone who cut off his own hand for some obscure purpose, but I lost the place and couldn't bring myself to go through the play again in search of him. But if anyone really imagines that it is possible to cut off one's own hand with a sword, in hot blood or cold, let him come to me after the lecture and I shall gladly supervise his efforts. Bring your own swords.

Now that we are done with that highly spiced *hors-d'œuvre*, let us deal with the other one of the five plays which, although it does contain a medical practitioner, is of no great medical interest, namely *The Merry Wives*. Dr. Caius is no doubt duly qualified but, clearly, he is a graduate of a French university and thus as 'a damned foreigner' starts off on the wrong foot in the mind of every true Englishman. From a medical point of view he is not one of Shakespeare's happiest creations. I can find no mention in the play of his undertaking any medical activity whatever, and his professional repute rests entirely on the testimonial to his prowess given in rather crude and outspoken terms by mine host of The Garter Inn.

The testimonial is not altogether free from the suspicion of being in the nature of a *quid pro quo*. Dr. Caius had—or professed to have—an excellent practice in Windsor, presumably at the Court, as we learn from him that his patients included, 'Earls, Knights, Lords and Gentlemen'. In return for mine host's help to him in the matter of Anne Page, plus, no doubt, flattering references to his skill as opportunity offered, the doctor undertook to recommend the Garter Inn to his exalted patients and their relatives. The medical ethics of this proceeding are questionable, to say the least.

Dr. Caius shouts his way through the play in a state of noisy, querulous bad temper, for which it is often hard to find any reason. Nobody likes him very much, really. Page calls him 'the renowned French physician' but says in a delightful phrase that he is at odds with his own gravity and patience. Shallow says that he never heard of a man 'so wide of his own respect', while the good but choleric Sir Hugh Evans first disparages his medical knowledge and then calls him a cowardly knave.

And so to the medical aspect of that—to me—singularly unpleasant and bitter comedy, *All's Well That Ends Well*. In my salad days I accepted the view that Bertram was a loathsome mixture of snob and cad, whose treatment of the fair and virtuous Helena was truly contemptible. I hold it still, but I have come to realize that he was in some

ways sinned against as much as sinning, and that Helena, in spite of the
many beautiful and pathetic things she says, is really an obnoxious
young woman who merits, if ever woman did, the classical title of
'designing minx'.

For years I have mistrusted her, but it was only when rereading the
play with this lecture in mind that I realized how thoroughly she is 'on
the make' from start to finish, and how very well able she is to look
after her own interests. She is the centre and focus of all the medical
interest of the play; she is the perfectly drawn representative of the un-
qualified practitioner, the Quack. And yet it is all so quietly and gently
done that Coleridge, for example, spoke of Helena as 'Shakespeare's
loveliest creation'.

Well, it's a matter for the experts. I may be quite wrong but I don't
think Shakespeare's truly loveliest creation would have opened a discussion on the keeping and losing of virginity with such a half-bred bit
of riff-raff as Parolles. But I must mind my own business and discuss
Helena as Queen of Quacks.

The story is quite typical in every single detail. To begin with,
Helena uses every means in her power to thrust herself on the king's
notice. Perhaps she might be forgiven for that, but she admits very
frankly that her chief motive in getting permission to treat the king is
to use him to entrap Bertram into marrying her. All this is perilously
near what would be regarded, even in these degenerate days, as
'infamous conduct in a professional respect'.

The medicine is, of course, a secret remedy, kept in the family. She
cashes in, so to speak, on her father's reputation. Further, the remedy
appears to be a cure-all. The king is suffering from fistula—a disease
which cannot be radically and permanently cured by medicine alone—
but that does not disconcert Helena. Falling back, like all quacks, on a
process of suggestion—to which fistula is not amenable—she guaran-
tees a complete cure in forty-eight hours, and offers to stake her reputation and her life on the success of her treatment. Needless to say, the
case is one which 'has baffled all the doctors'. The king holds out for
quite a time. He will not catch at straws when all the doctors have
given him up and when, as he puts it, 'the congregated college have
concluded' that he hasn't a hope. But he agrees in the end, reasoning
that a harmless and painless forty-eight-hour treatment on which a
prepossessing young woman bets her life is perhaps worth trying.

Nowadays the quacks don't bet their life: they say 'money back if
not satisfied'. Helena puts the thing in more melodramatic fashion: 'If

my magic doesn't work, kill me!' but in essence it's the very same thing; the central principle of quackery: no cure no pay. The king yields, and Helena turns to the business side of the contract with almost indecent haste:

> HELENA: . . . Not helping, death's my fee;
>   But, if I help, what do you promise me?
> KING: Make thy demand.
> HELENA: But will you make it even?
> KING: Ay, by my sceptre, and my hopes of heaven.

Then comes her absurd request, cunningly phrased in general terms, although Bertram alone is in her mind from the start. Bertram, the aristocrat, who has addressed her once only in the play so far, with an off-hand formula of farewell and a patronizing instruction to attend to her duties as his mother's lady's maid. I've often thought, by the way, that Helena must have been an ancestress, in the direct line, of Uriah Heep.

The king, now up to the neck in it, keeps his bargain after the two-day cure. I don't know what his legal authority may have been in relation to the young lordlings about the Court, but I know that his dealings with Bertram in this matter are as devoid of moral right as they are of common sense.

The Mikado, you will remember, punished the advertising quack by decreeing that all his teeth should be extracted by terrified amateurs. But Shakespeare devised a much worse fate for his advertising quack, Helena; he married her to Bertram.

And now for the medicine and surgery in *Twelfth Night*, that loveliest and sunniest of plays, of which Masefield has written: 'It will stand as an example of perfect art till a greater than Shakespeare set a better example further on.'

No doctor appears in *Twelfth Night*. There is but one solitary reference to a member of my profession, one Dick Surgeon, who, I imagine, was probably only the local barber. On one occasion, at least, his services were urgently required: 'For the love of God, a surgeon! Send one presently to Sir Toby,' and the only thing we are told about him then is that he was reported as having been dead drunk since before eight o'clock in the morning. On hearing this news, Sir Toby, of all people, says: 'I hate a drunken rogue.'

We have all laughed many a time at this classical example of Satan reproving sin, but I wonder to how many of us it has occurred that in all probability Sir Toby was speaking in complete sincerity without any attempt at humbug or humour, and that he seriously believed that he was expressing his real feelings.

We are back at projection, in one of its most important and interesting forms. We can only see what is in us to see, and if what is in us is too painful or humiliating for us to realize and accept, we ignore it, turn away from it, and see and criticize it as it is reflected in the conduct of others. We cannot deny its existence, but we hurl it away into our environment.

But the environment acts like the wall against which we throw a tennis ball, and we may expect difficulty in dealing with the rebound. 'A bad workman blames his tools.' Of course he does. He cannot accept the fact of his own incompetence, so fastens the accusation on his tools.

It is the muddle-headed man who complains that none of his colleagues is capable of presenting a clear statement; it is the man whose own level of conduct and degree of adjustment are questionable, who talks most incessantly about cads and snobs and bounders and people who don't know how to behave. It is the man who dare not face the fact of his own dishonesty, who casts the truth away from him, and receives back the suspicion that others are conspiring to deceive and swindle him.

Projection, you will notice, offers to the individual the fascinating occupation of condemning his own unacknowledged faults and tendencies as they appear in other people, thus becoming more royalist than the king, instead of saying: 'There, but for the grace of God, go I.' It is difficult to realize that a man can force himself to be blissfully unconscious of what is painfully obvious to everyone else, but so it is, and this type of projection, as it happens, is particularly well seen in alcoholic patients. I myself have had at least four or five alcoholic patients who assured me in all sincerity that their wretched and ruined homes were entirely due to the alcoholic habits of their wives! You will realize how interestingly this practice of projecting unrecognized aspects of ourselves into our judgments is related to such occupations as those of the professional dramatic critic. I cannot help adding that, though it is far from a complete analogy, the legend of Perseus and Medusa has features which inevitably suggest themselves in this connection. The originator of the fable that Perseus cut off the head of Medusa with averted eyes while he looked at its reflection in the mirror of Athene's shield, must have been a natural psychologist of no mean order.

But to return to *Twelfth Night*. Although my profession does not appear to advantage in it, we have as compensation the antics of a band of amateurs, whose enthusiasm and *joie de vivre* would adorn any medical students' rag.

They are engaged in organizing an elaborate practical joke which results in the wrongful detention of an alleged lunatic. 'Wrongful detention' is, of course, a trumpet call which rouses all true Britons to write to the papers or their M.P., but they don't worry much about it in the cloud-cuckoo land of Illyria. The practical jokers are well up in the kind of psychiatric treatment in vogue at the time, and let fall much interesting information concerning it, but they do not regard Malvolio as insane and are merely concerned to bring him into a notable contempt, so we need not regard their methods as altogether typical of contemporary medical thought.

One of the suggested aids to diagnosis is urine-analysis: a well-known and common procedure even then, and one to which Shakespeare often refers. 'Carry his water to the wise-woman,' says Sir Toby. I don't know how she conducted her analysis or what were her qualifications for the job, but her title reminds me of a young man much interested in clairvoyance and the occult, and with a totally inadequate knowledge of the French language, whom I met in France in the 1914–18 war. He came upon a very solid and respectable little house in the village, with a neat brass plate on the door bearing the word *sagefemme*. Concluding that this must be the abode of some elderly giver of sage counsel—a soothsayer of no mean order—he knocked and entered, in happy ignorance that *sagefemme* is the French for midwife!

Malvolio was not mad: he has, indeed, been called, I think with justice, the one wise man in the play, but he was much nearer insanity than his persecutors imagined, or than any Shakespearian critics have, to my knowledge, suggested.

Malvolio suffered from that mysterious disorder of personality technically known as the paranoid temperament, the result of his over-staying his leave in a dream world of his own in which all enemies are routed, all difficulties overcome, and all goals attained, without any effort on the part of the dreamer. This, of course, involves a divorce from reality and a turning of the day-dreamer's attention inwards upon his own fancies, instead of outwards upon healthy human contacts. He thus becomes, as Malvolio did, 'sick of self-love', and 'contemplation' —of his own excellences—'makes a rare turkey-cock of him'.

We must remember, of course, that Malvolio was in this condition long before the incident of the faked letter. He was in it, for that matter, long before the beginning of the play, and I don't suppose he became really insane till long after its close. Perhaps he never became insane at all. It all depends on whether the trick played on him made his hatred of, and contempt for, his fellow men more implacable than ever, or whether, by some happy chance, it jerked him back out of dreamland by bringing him to a realization of the virtues of forgiveness and goodwill, and restoring his sense of humour.

I cannot help fearing that he went from bad to worse. He shut himself off from reality and human intercourse by a fence of his own construction, and to break that fence down again is an almost impossibly hard task as a rule. You cannot read the play without realizing that Malvolio is aloof from everyone else in it. From beginning to end he is separated from all the others by an invisible barrier, of which we are almost painfully conscious, which he does all in his power to strengthen by word and action. 'I am not of your element.' And, of course, his sense of humour, if it ever existed, is completely dead. Not a laugh from him in the entire play. Not one single bit of 'off the record' informality or friendliness. Smiles, yes, to order and by request, and what a pitiable performance his smiling was! His facial contortions were such that Maria could 'hardly keep from throwing things at him', and there was no more humour or humanity in his smile than there was blood in Sir Andrew's liver.

I have always thought that Barrie's John Shand in *What Every Woman Knows* has a good deal in common with Malvolio. He, too, is a man of much ability, but, like Malvolio, he takes himself so seriously that he can never be really human; he, too, is unable to forget his own importance and his ambitions, to relax and to be at ease. You may remember that, happier than Malvolio, Shand finds psychological salvation at the very end of Barrie's play, by achieving for the first time a laugh—at himself.

There are two classical methods of avoiding painful reality. We can avoid the presence of an unwelcome intruder either by throwing him out or by running away ourselves.

The first method corresponds, psychologically, to Projection, which I have briefly outlined and illustrated, while the second is the retreat into Fantasy of which Malvolio is a perfect example.

It is the simpler, pleasanter, and less harmful of the two methods, and most of us are prone to take occasional holidays in the land where dreams come true, with good rather than bad results, provided always that we have been careful to arrange for the return journey to the workaday world. The penalty for overstaying one's leave is a severe one: the dream world becomes more real than the real world, and the dreamer, like Malvolio, becomes completely cut off from effective contact with human life. But most of us have the sense to take a return ticket for a limited period, and we pay the price—temporary divorce from reality—with a smile. After all, one cannot expect to get into fairyland for nothing. Some of us find it easier than others; children in arms, I believe, are admitted free, and those under twelve pay half-price.

Now we come to *Macbeth*, which is fuller by far of medical interest than the other four plays at which we have been glancing together. The play takes us into my native country, and the medicine in it takes us into the very heart of my own specialty.

Two doctors appear in the *dramatis personae* of *Macbeth*. They are referred to as 'an English doctor' and 'a Scotch doctor' and, of the two, I am glad to inform you that the latter is by a long way the more efficient, interesting and hard-working. I don't know if such a thing has ever happened in real life, or if Shakespeare just invented it as a compliment to King James I. Anyhow, the English doctor has such a small part that he has completely vanished from this season's production! 'Enter a doctor' says the stage direction, clearly to relieve the tension after the long interview between Malcolm and Macduff. The doctor is asked if the king is going to put in an appearance. He replies in a speech of thirty-four words about the old practice of touching for the king's evil. Malcolm says politely, 'I thank you, Doctor.' Exit doctor, and we hear no more of him.

The Scotch doctor appears to be a man of much more robust fibre. He is seen in two remarkable interviews: one with the nurse in charge of his patient, and one with his patient's husband.

The patient is Lady Macbeth, who is having a series of what are known as hysterical fugues. The psychological principle involved, put as simply as possible, is this. Some people, when they undergo an emotional experience which is completely unendurable, can obtain relief from it—at a price—by turning away from it and banishing it entirely from their conscious mind. Its memory sinks into their unconscious mind and the price they pay for this respite is that the buried memory constantly seeks elbow-room and opportunity to express itself in consciousness in one of many roundabout, disguised forms; disguised so that consciousness will not recognize it for what it is and be faced with the intolerable idea once again. That is what is called psychological repression.

The intolerable idea may manifest itself as an obsession or an hysterical symptom such as paralysis of a limb or loss of voice, by dreams or, as in this case, by a sleep-walking fugue, in which the conscious mind is in abeyance, while the unconscious takes the stage and relives the intolerable scene. Probably it would not have been relived in this case so accurately without medical help, but Shakespeare certainly got the principle of the thing perfectly.

The medical science of his day, however, had not taken the one step further which might have saved Lady Macbeth. Nowadays she could have been made to relive that terrible scene in complete detail by a competent psychiatrist with the assistance of certain drugs or, possibly, hypnotism. If, thereafter, the physician had gone over the material with her in her waking state, and thus broken the repression, there would have been a terrible emotional reaction but Lady Macbeth would have recovered. Perhaps, therefore, it is just as well that this form of treatment, which is called abreaction, was unknown in her time.

But let us get back to the Scotch doctor who, I should say, is dignified by the title of 'a doctor of physic'. His scene with the 'waiting gentlewoman' whom we should nowadays call the night nurse, is a medical delight. The doctor begins by casting doubt on the nurse's powers of observation, but when she gives him a detailed account of her patient's behaviour he accepts it, summarizes it intelligently and asks for further details. These the nurse promptly refuses to give, a proceeding which would be frowned upon by any hospital matron that I have ever had anything to do with. The doctor is quite nice about it and tells her that it is the proper thing to do to confide in him, but again she refuses because she has no witnesses and quite obviously fears that she will be disbelieved. As the doctor had begun by telling her that he could perceive no truth in her report, I don't know that I blame her very much. Anyhow, a painful professional bickering is avoided by the entrance of Lady Macbeth.

The best thing the doctor does at this stage is to produce his notebook and make a written record of the case. Apart from that he almost plays second fiddle to the nurse and, finally, he is so staggered by what he hears that he confesses frankly 'this disease is beyond my practice'. I can't remember when I heard a doctor saying that last. Then comes the line 'more needs she the divine than the physician', a phrase which I take to be not a reference to pastoral psychotherapy, of which we hear so much nowadays, but to the moral aspect of the crime the patient has committed. She needs forgiveness rather than psychotherapy, he says, though in those days psychotherapy, as we understand it, was only guessed at. I should say that she needed forgiveness *as well as* psychotherapy. They are two quite distinct things and it is a sad pity that many of the public are so prone to slovenly thinking and to seeking for magic that they fail to realize the fact.

The doctor pulls himself together at the end of the scene and orders continuous observation, the only safe rule if you are dealing with a suicidal patient. He then leaves, confessing frankly that the whole thing has been too much for him and that he dare not say what he thinks. I wish every modern psychiatrist had to learn the whole scene by heart before being allowed to practise.

It is a commonplace in psychiatry that patients' relatives are infinitely more trouble than the patients themselves. I feel sure that the doctor must have been looking forward with but little relish to his interview with Macbeth. For my own part I would rather interview a dozen night nurses, however touchy and austere, than the angry husband of an acutely neurotic patient. I speak from long practical experience of such patients, and such nurses.

By the time the doctor comes to make his report, Macbeth is in such a state of mind that anything the doctor said would have been the trigger to set off an outburst of rage. It would have made no difference if the doctor had merely told him that Mary had a little lamb; he would have flown into a fury just the same.

I must digress for a moment to tell you that I have just come across an extremely interesting essay which, no doubt, many of you know. It was written by a Thomas Whately, who was an Under-Secretary of State and died in 1772. In his essay, which is well worthy of study, he compares and contrasts with great skill and insight, Macbeth and Richard III, pointing out that there are no two characters in Shakespeare who are placed in such parallel circumstances and who yet differ so much in disposition.

They are both kings by usurpation and murder: they both lose their thrones by death in battle, and there are very many parallel situations

N

in the two plays but, through them all Macbeth is the introspective, self-tortured, reluctant villain, while Richard is the clear-headed, whole-hearted, cynical, extraverted one. His cool, crisp, practical orders before the battle of Bosworth are a wonderful contrast to Macbeth's excited outpourings, eloquent indeed, but increasingly disjointed and frenzied, till they merge into the courage of despair.

The unfortunate doctor finds himself standing by, during a fierce and confused conference between Macbeth and his attendants. His report is suddenly demanded, and his non-committal reply, suggesting very tactfully that the patient is really a mental case, prompts the famous speech about ministering to a mind diseased. This speech is a wonderful forecast of modern psychological treatment, written 300 years before Freud, but all I have to say about it just now is simply that the 'mind diseased' about which he is talking is not his wife's, but his own. There is nothing more common among patients' relatives than the attempt, under cover of inquiries about the patient, to obtain information and advice for themselves. The doctor realizes this and very neatly keeps the matter on the general level, saying: 'Therein the patient must minister to himself.' He was too honest to say 'herself' when he knew perfectly well that it was not his wife Macbeth had in mind, and he had too much regard for his own expectation of life to say: 'Therein *you* must minister to *yourself*.'

Next we have the typical laugh-it-off reaction of the man who is terrified in his heart. How often have I observed it in patients' relatives, and with what amazing accuracy and insight has Shakespeare depicted it! First, physic is to go to the dogs. Then, with a strained facetiousness, Macbeth invites the doctor to treat the sick country. Note the reference here, as in *Twelfth Night*, to urine-analysis. Rambling on again in forced, unnatural jocularity, he suggests some good strong purgative to get rid of the English invaders. Finally he asks, with sudden suspicion, how much the doctor knows, makes a last arrogant boast to keep up his courage, and storms out. Who can blame the doctor for his quiet aside with which the scene ends? He does not pretend to be a hero, but his frank acknowledgment that if he could only get out of this he wouldn't come back for any money, at least does some credit to both his profession and his nationality.

Well, there it is. I have run over several scenes and passages in these plays, and I have sandwiched in among them three or four little excursions in everyday language into elementary medical psychology. Whether you have regarded these as the interesting middle bit of the sandwich or as the unpleasant powder with jam round it, I cannot say.

I have tried to avoid reference to the more obvious and hackneyed psychological questions which arise in these plays, and to confine myself to smaller points which are, perhaps, less well-known. I assure you, however, than even from these few plays, I could have selected at least half-a-dozen characters, in addition to those I have discussed, any one of whom would have made an adequate text for a full and interesting medico-psychological lecture: Sir Toby, the chronic alcoholic; Parolles, the spiv; Sir Andrew, the high-grade defective; Olivia, the frustrated, maladjusted spinster; about half the cast of *Titus Andronicus* as sadistic psychopaths; Shallow, the senile, and many others.

Shakespeare's characters—especially his minor ones—are what one might call lightning sketches, drawn from life, rather than profound psychological studies, because he is writing a play, not preparing an essay.

He gives them just a few words—the merest touch here and there. But these touches are so wonderfully and inevitably just right that the characters leap into life and we cannot help filling in the picture for ourselves.

So comes about Shakespeare's greatest miracle: that we regard people who never existed outside his imagination as real and living acquaintances of our own, whom we should know at once, if we met them on leaving this hall.

As I have been speaking, that miracle has once more been at work, on me, at least. I can see Sir Toby at the door of 'The Dirty Duck', hoping to find someone who will stand him a drink. Dogberry and Juliet's nurse are inside it, exchanging verbose reminiscence and pointless anecdote. In the garden, there, Benedick and Mercutio are keeping a party of ladies in fits of laughter—I can see Beatrice, Viola and Rosalind among them—and there, coming down the street, is dear old Peter Quince with a worried look on his face, carrying an enormous basket of stage properties.

If we have got far enough away from the professional critics today to share these feelings and fancies together, I am very glad.

INDEX